Award
inal Bö
duo. Their unique ability to con
the brutal reality of criminal life with searing social criti-
cism in complex, intelligent plots has put them at the
forefront of modern Scandinavian crime writing.

Praise for Roslund and Hellström

' ell-written and powerful' *The Times*

'ipping, intelligent' *Guardian*

'rnalist Roslund and ex-criminal Hellström are among
eden's most popular thriller writers with a reputation
r down-and-dirty detail and an eye for political intrigue
 police corruption . . . extraordinarily compelling'
 Mail

' is crime writing at its most ambitious and morally
plex' *Financial Times*

' Ewert Grens] the authors have created an eccentric,
aated, socially inept hero worthy of comparison with
Sdish mystery master Henning Mankell's Inspector
 t Wallander' *Wall Street Journal*

' Swedish team of Roslund and Hellström is writing
cplosive crime novels as good, if not better, than those of
Sg Larsson' *USA Today*

'oslund / Hellström are among the very best crime nov-
elists around. They write with courage and intensity about
the important issues of our time' Maj Sjöwall

ROSLUND & HELLSTRÖM

BOX 21

Translated from the Swedish
by Elizabeth Clark Wessel

riverrun

First published in Sweden in 2005 by Piratforlaget under the title *Box 21*
First published in Great Britain in May 2005 by
Little, Brown under the title *The Vault*

This translation published in Great Britain in 2016 by

riverrun
an imprint of
Quercus Editions Ltd
Carmelite House
50 Victoria Embankment
London EC4Y 0DZ

An Hachette UK company

Published by agreement with the Salomonsson Agency

A CIP catalogue record for this book is available
from the British Library

ISBN 978 0 85738 479 9
EBOOK ISBN 978 1 78429 152 5

10 9 8 7 6 5 4 3 2 1

Typeset by Jouve (UK), Milton Keynes

Printed and bound in Great Britain by Clays Ltd, St Ives plc

Extract from an accident & emergency primary assessment Söder Hospital, Stockholm

'. . . UNCONSCIOUS FEMALE, IDENTITY UNKNOWN, arrived by ambulance at 9:05 a.m., found in an apartment at 3 Völund Street, neighbour alerted police.

[Gen:] Unresponsive, not reactive to pain. Pale and cold. Decimetre-long fresh lacerations across her back, multiple bruises, and minor abrasions on the face. Severe swelling on the upper part of her left humerus.
    Circ: Shallow breathing with increased frequency.
    Cor: Regular, but weak/thready pulse; 110.
    BP: 95/60
    Abd: Tense, rigid.

Prel. impression: Female in her 20s, appears to have suffered from multiple external acts of violence (whipped?). Shows signs of shock. Suspect intra-abdominal bleeding, possible injury to the spleen and fractured humerus. Transferred to ICU for further care . . .'

Eleven Years Earlier

SHE HELD ON TO her mother's hand tightly.

She'd done that many times in the last year, squeezed her mother's soft hand hard and received a strong squeeze back.

She didn't want to go there.

Her name was Lydia Grajauskas, and her stomach had been hurting ever since they climbed onto the bus at the ugly bus station in Klaipeda, and the further away they travelled, the worse it got.

She'd never been to Vilnius before, she'd fantasised about it, seen pictures and heard stories, but now, she absolutely didn't want to, it wasn't her place, she didn't belong there.

It was more than a year since she'd seen him last.

She had been about to turn nine back then, and she'd considered a hand grenade a really good gift.

Dad hadn't seen her, of course, he'd been sitting with his back turned to them in a crappy room, busy with the others, the ones who drank and screamed and who hated Russians. She'd been lying head to foot with Vladi on the sofa, a big smelly piece of furniture covered with worn brown corduroy. They sometimes lay there when school was off, and Dad was working. They'd been listening. They could hear something about guns and boxes of gunpowder and the loud voices of the men fascinated them, which made them lie here more often than might be good for them. Dad's cheeks had been so red, which was rare, only now and then at home when he drank straight from the bottle and crept over to Mum and pressed himself against her back. They didn't think that she noticed, of course, and she didn't show them that she had. He always drank a little more then, and now Mum would take a swig straight from the bottle, and then they'd go into their little bedroom, shooing everyone else out, and close the door behind them.

Lydia liked it when he had red cheeks. Both at home and there among the men who were cleaning the guns in front of them. It was as if he seemed a little more alive then, not as old as he usually did, my God, he was almost twenty-nine years old.

She peeked cautiously out through the bus window.

Her stomach hurt more as the bus started speeding along roads covered with potholes, and every time the front wheels banged against the asphalt, her seat shook, and she felt a stabbing pain just under her ribcage.

So this was what it looked like for real. The unexplored world, that whole long stretch between Klaipeda and Vilnius. She had never gone with Mum before. She hadn't been allowed to: it was expensive, and it was more important that Mum went. Mum had been going there every Sunday for almost a year, taking food and whatever money she could get her hands on. Lydia thought it was hard to know how Dad was doing, what he would say, and it was probably Mum he missed the most.

That day with the hand grenades, he hadn't even seen her.

She'd been lying on the sofa and leaned forward and dug through the boxes of plastic explosives and grenades and put her finger to her mouth to tell Vladi to be quiet – the fathers didn't want to be disturbed. But she'd known how all of it worked. The explosives and the hand grenades and the small guns. She had always watched them as they practised, and she knew as much about their weapons as some of the men.

Now she was staring through the dirty window of the bus.

It was raining heavily, so the windows should be getting cleaner, but instead of washing away the dirt the heavy drops drove up the brown mud, obscuring the landscape outside even more. At least the road was better now, no potholes, no jerking, no stab of pain under her ribs.

BOX 21

She'd been holding a hand grenade in her hand when police broke down the door and rushed into the big room.

Dad and the other men had shouted to each other, but they'd been too slow, and in just a few minutes they were all pressed up against a wall, handcuffed, getting blow after blow. She didn't remember how many came into that room, maybe ten, maybe twenty. She only remembered them screaming *zatknis* again and again, while carrying guns like the ones Dad sold. They'd won before it even began.

Their screaming joined the rattle of guns and smashing of bottles.

All those sounds rang in her ears, and then stopped suddenly. A strange silence fell as Dad and the other men were pushed down on the ground.

That was what she remembered the most. The silence that came after.

Mum's hand, she squeezed it again. She pulled it closer, on to the seat between them, held it until the skin turned white, and she couldn't squeeze any harder. Just as she'd done when they sat outside the courtroom in Klaipeda during Dad's trial. She and Mum had sat there and held each other's hands, and Mum had cried for a long time when the guard in the grey suit came out to tell them that all the men had been sentenced to twenty-one years in prison, every single one.

She hadn't seen him in a year. He probably wouldn't recognise her.

Lydia clutched the cotton bag that Mum had brought with her. It was filled to the brim with food. Mum had told her about what they ate, the gruel they got, pretty much only gruel every day. Mum told her about vitamins, that a person gets sick without them, that everyone there needed them, and got extra food from those who came to visit them.

The bus was driving pretty fast now. A wider road with more

traffic and the buildings outside their muddy window got bigger the closer they got to Vilnius. The buildings she'd seen back when the roads were full of potholes had been run-down. Now she saw huge apartment buildings with grey walls and metal roofs, much more modern than the ones before. Soon came even more expensive-looking buildings, then petrol stations standing close together. She smiled and pointed, because she'd never seen so many petrol stations before.

It had almost stopped raining, which made her happy. She didn't want to get her hair wet, not today.

———

Lukiškės prison lay just a few hundred metres from the bus stop. It was huge, covering a whole city block, and surrounded on all sides by high walls. It was originally a Russian church, but had been rebuilt and had new buildings added to it, and now it was home to more than a thousand prisoners.

There was already a line out of the heavy, grey, iron door that stood in the middle of the concrete wall. Other mothers and other children. One family at a time was allowed to go in, armed guards in uniform waited in a dark room inside. They had to answer questions. Present their IDs. Show what they brought. One of the guards smiled at her, but she didn't dare to smile back.

'If one of them coughs you run away immediately. You leave the room.'

Mum turned towards her as she said it. She looked so stern, as she always did when she was being serious. Lydia wanted to ask why, but didn't. It was clear Mum didn't want to talk any more about it.

They were led down a path from the main building, barbed wire at the top of the fence, and white dogs barking and throwing themselves against it. In a window behind bars, she saw two faces watching them. They waved and shouted at her.

BOX 21

'Hey, little girl, look over here, cutie pie.'

She just kept walking straight ahead, staring straight ahead. It wasn't much further to the next building.

Mum was carrying the bag in her arms, and Lydia searched for her hand in vain. There was that stab of pain in her stomach again. Just like in the bus when the wheels bounced off the asphalt. They entered a stairwell with sterile green walls. The colour shone so brightly that she had to look at Mum's back instead, keeping her hand there as they climbed up. They stopped on the third floor, where a guard pointed them towards a long dark corridor that somehow smelt both stale and like detergent at the same time. Outside every door they passed stood barrels with the letters TB on them. She peeked down into one that was a little open and saw bloodstained tissues inside.

All the prisoners had shaved heads and looked pale and tired.

Some were lying down, some sat with a sheet wrapped around them, some stood by the window talking. Eight beds stood in a row along the wall, in what they called the infirmary. Dad was sitting on the one furthest away.

Lydia looked at him furtively, thinking that he'd shrunk somehow.

He didn't see her. Not yet. She waited for a long time.

Mum went over to him first. They said something to each other, discussing something, but she couldn't hear what. Lydia was still watching him, and after a while she realised that she wasn't ashamed, not any more. She thought about the past year. The scorn of her classmates no longer hurt her, not when she was here, standing so close. It was as if that thing in her stomach, that stabbing pain, had disappeared.

When she hugged him, he coughed, but she didn't leave the room as she'd promised Mum. She held him tightly and didn't let go.

She hated him. He should be going home with them.

8

Now

Part One

Monday, 3 June

THE APARTMENT WAS SILENT.

It had been a long time since she'd thought about him, or anything else from her past. Now she sat here doing just that. She was thinking about that last hug, there in the Lukiškės prison, when she'd been ten years old, and he'd seemed so small, coughing with his whole body, and Mum had handed him a tissue, and he'd filled it with clumps of blood, then crumpled it up and threw it away in one of the large barrels in the hall.

She hadn't understood that it was the last time. She still couldn't understand that.

Lydia took a deep breath.

She shook off her uneasiness, smiled at the large mirror in the hall. It was still early morning.

————

There was a knock on the door. She was still holding the hairbrush in her hand. How long had she been standing here? She looked in the mirror again. Her head cocked a little to the side. She smiled again, trying to be pretty. She was wearing a black dress, dark fabric against pale skin. Her body, she looked at it. It was still the body of a young woman. She hadn't changed much since she got here, not on the outside.

She waited.

There was another knock, harder now. She should open the door. She put the brush on a shelf next to the mirror and started walking. Her name was Lydia Grajauskas, and she usually sang it. She sang it now to a nursery rhyme melody she remembered from school in

Klaipeda. The chorus had three lines, and she sang Lydia Grajauskas on each one. She'd always done that when she was nervous.

Lydia Grajauskas.
Lydia Grajauskas.
Lydia Grajauskas.

She stopped singing when she got to the door. He was on the
other side. If she put her ear close to it, she could hear him breathing. She recognised the rhythm – it was him. They'd met a few
times now, eight, maybe nine? He smelt different. She already
knew his smell, like the men her father worked with in that shitty
room with the corduroy sofa, almost the same, cigar and some
type of cologne and sweat under the tight fabric of this jacket.

He knocked. This was the third time.

The door opened. He stood there. Dark suit, light blue shirt,
gold tie clip. His fair hair was short. He was tanned. It had been
raining since the middle of May, but he still had a deep tan, he
always did. She smiled, like she'd just done to the mirror. She
knew he liked it.

They didn't touch each other. Not yet.

He left the stairwell, stepped over the threshold into the
apartment. She glanced at the hat rack, towards the hangers
there, I'd be happy to hang up your jacket for you? He shook his
head. He was probably ten years older than her, around thirty,
she guessed, but she did not really know.

She wanted to sing again.

Lydia Grajauskas. Lydia Grajauskas. Lydia Grajauskas.

He raised his hand, as he always did, put his fingers gently
against her black dress, slowly running them along the shoulder
straps, her chest, staying on the outside of the fabric.

BOX 21

She stood motionless.

He made a wide circle with his hand around one breast, then moved on to the other. She didn't breathe, her chest still, had to keep smiling, had to stay perfectly still and keep smiling.

She even kept smiling when he spat.

They were standing close to each other. It was more like he was releasing saliva than spitting, and it rarely landed in her face, it usually landed at her feet near the black shoes with high heels.

He thought she was dawdling. He pointed.

His finger straight down.

Lydia bent down, still smiling at him. She knew he liked that, and sometimes he smiled back. There was a slight click from her knees as she pressed her legs together, got down on all fours with her face bent forward. She begged for forgiveness. That's what he wanted her to do. He'd learned how to say it in Russian. He wanted to be sure that she was saying the right words. She sank down to the ground, her nose almost touching the floor, her tongue against the cold as she took his spit into her mouth and swallowed it.

She stood up again then. That's what he wanted. She closed her eyes, trying to guess which cheek.

Right, it would probably be the right.

Left.

He slapped her, his palm covering her entire cheek. It didn't particularly hurt. It left a red mark. He'd used the full force of his arm, but it only stung. Because it only stings if that's what you really want.

He pointed again.

Lydia knew what she was supposed to do, so the pointing was unnecessary, but he did it anyway every single time, waved his finger in her direction, wanting her to go into the room, to stand in front of the red bedspread. She walked ahead of him.

She was supposed to walk slowly and absently stroke her butt. He wanted her to breathe heavily, and she could feel him looking at her back, almost as if his eyes were inflicting pain as they moved across her body.

She stopped at the bed.

She unbuttoned three buttons on the back of her dress, lowered it down over her hips to the floor.

Her bra and panties were black lace, as he'd requested. He'd given them to her, and she'd promised to use them only with him.

He lay down on top of her, and she ceased to have a body.

That's what she did. That's what she always did.

She thought about home and about what had been and what she missed and had missed every day since she got here.

Here, here and now she didn't exist. Here she was just a face without a body. She had no neck, no breasts, no womb, no legs.

So when he pressed hard against something, when he penetrated something, when an anus started bleeding, it had nothing to do with her. She was somewhere else and all that was left of her was a face singing *Lydia Grajauskas* to a melody she'd learned a long time ago.

IT WAS RAINING as he pulled into the empty parking spot.

It was the kind of summer where people woke up, crept over to the bedroom window, held their breath hoping that today would be the day the sun finally streamed in from behind the blinds. It was the kind of summer where the rain fell freely, and every morning tired eyes looked defeated as they saw the grey liquid hammering against the glass.

Ewert Grens sighed. He parked the car, turned off the engine,

13

BOX 21

and sat in the driver's seat until it was impossible to see out any longer, the raindrops turning into a river that obscured his view. He was too tired to move. He didn't want to. His uneasiness took whatever was left to take. Another week had passed, and he had almost forgotten her.

He breathed heavily.

He would never forget.

He lived still with her, every day, almost every hour. Twenty-five years hadn't changed a thing.

The rain subsided a little. He caught a glimpse of the house through the front window. A large, red-brick house built in the seventies with a beautiful garden on the verge of being over-elaborate. He liked best the six apple trees that had just lost their white flowers.

He hated the house.

He loosened his tight grip on the steering wheel, opened the door and stepped out. Large puddles stood on the uneven asphalt. He zigzagged between them, and his shoes got soaked before he was even halfway there. He continued forward, trying to rid himself of the feeling that his life was closer to being over with every step that took him towards the front door.

It smelt like old people. He came here every Monday morning, but still wasn't used to the smell. The people who lived here, in wheelchairs and behind walkers, weren't even especially old, so he couldn't understand where the smell came from.

'She's inside. In her room.'

'Thanks.'

'She's expecting you.'

She had no idea he was coming.

But he nodded to the young nurse's assistant who had started to recognise him, because she was just trying to be friendly, and had no idea how much that statement hurt him.

He passed by a smiling man around his own age who usually sat in the armchair in the hall waving happily to everyone. Then he saw Margareta, the one who started screaming if you didn't look at her and ask her how she was feeling. Every Monday morning, they were always there, like props for a photograph he didn't need to take. He wondered if he would miss them if they ever left, or if he would be relieved to skip this particular ritual.

He waited quietly for a moment outside her room.

He sometimes woke up in the middle of the night covered in sweat to the sound of her loud *welcome* as he arrived, to the feeling of how she took his hand and held it, happy to grab on to someone who loved her. He thought about this recurring dream, and worked up the courage to open her door as he always did, to enter into her life, fourteen square metres, a window overlooking the parking lot.

'Hello.'

She was sitting in the middle of the room. Her wheelchair was facing the door. She looked at him. But there was nothing in her eyes that resembled recognition, she hadn't even heard him say hello. He walked over to her, put a hand against her cold cheek, and spoke to her again.

'Hello, Anni. It's me. Ewert.'

She laughed. An ill-timed, too-loud laugh, a child's laugh, like always.

'Do you recognise me today?'

She laughed again, suddenly and too loud. He grabbed the seat next to the desk she never used and sat down. He took her hand, held it, put it in his own.

They'd made her look nice.

Combed her blonde hair, put it up with pins, one on each side. Put her in a blue dress he hadn't seen for a long time that smelt newly laundered.

BOX 21

He marvelled at how little her appearance had changed. Twenty-five years in a wheelchair, barely conscious of her surroundings, and she didn't seem to have aged much. He'd put on twenty kilos since then, lost his hair, could feel the many lines on his face. She was so unspoiled. As if the reward for being unable to participate in the real world was a carelessness that kept you young.

She tried to say something. It was babbling, but she turned to him, and he got the feeling that she was really trying to say something. He pressed her hand, tried to swallow the lump in his throat.

'He'll be released tomorrow.'

She babbled and she drooled. He took his handkerchief from his pocket, wiped the saliva from her chin.

'Do you understand, Anni? He's getting out of prison tomorrow. He's free. He'll be making our streets filthier again.'

Her room looked the same as it had when she moved in. He himself had chosen the furniture she brought from home, and he had arranged it. He was the one who knew how important it was to her to sleep with her head towards the window.

She'd looked so safe on the very first night.

He'd carried her to the bed and laid her down, tucked the bedspread around her slender body. He'd been sitting next to her until the dark subsided, she'd slept deeply, and he'd left her in the morning when she woke up. He'd left his car there and walked all the way to the police station on Kungsholmen. It was late morning by the time he arrived.

'I'll get him this time.'

She looked at him as if she was listening. He knew she wasn't, but because it looked that way, he sometimes pretended they were having a conversation, just like before.

Her eyes might be expectant or might just be empty.

If only I'd had time to stop.

16

If only that bastard hadn't pulled you out. If only your head hadn't been softer than the wheel.

Ewert Grens leaned towards her, his forehead against hers, kissed her cheek.

'I miss you.'

THE MAN IN the dark suit with the gold tie clip, who spat on the floor in front of her, had just left. It hadn't helped this time, thinking of Klaipeda and turning off the rest of her body, becoming just a face. She'd felt him inside her. That happened sometimes, she'd feel the pain as someone penetrated her, while screaming at her to move.

Lydia wondered if it was his smell.

A smell she recognised from the men who spent their time with her father in that dirty weapons room. She wondered if it might be good that she recognised it, wondered if that meant that she still belonged to that time in some way, that time she missed so much. Or had something inside her broken down even more, maybe what could have been, what was far in the past now, was rubbing even deeper into her.

He hadn't said much afterwards. He'd looked at her and pointed one last time, nothing more. He hadn't even turned around when he left.

Lydia laughed.

If she had had a womb, she would have been sorry that his body fluids were in it. Then she would have felt his body even more. Now that wasn't the case. She was just a face.

She laughed and rubbed white soap all over her body, her skin turning a blotchy red as she pressed hard, soap on her neck, shoulders, her breasts, vagina, thighs, feet.

Suffocating the shame.

She rinsed it off. His hands, his breath, his smell. The water was so hot it almost hurt, the shame was an ugly film that wouldn't let go.

She sat down on the shower floor and sang her refrain, the children's song from Klaipeda.

Lydia Grajauskas.
Lydia Grajauskas.
Lydia Grajauskas.

She loved that song. It had been theirs, hers and Vladi's, they'd sung it loudly every morning as they walked through their neighbourhood on the way to school, one syllable with each step, her name out loud again and again.

'Stop singing!'

Dimitri screamed from the hall with his mouth against the bathroom door, but she continued. He pounded on the wall, screamed again, she was supposed to get out of there, right now! She continued sitting on the wet shower floor, but stopped singing, her voice barely made it to the door.

'Who's coming now?'

'You're in debt, you fucking whore.'

'I want to know who's coming.'

'Wash your pussy! You have a new client.'

Lydia heard the anger in his voice, got up, wiped off her wet body, then stood in front of the mirror that hung above the sink, painting her lips red, layer upon layer. She got dressed, put on the creamy white underwear, some kind of thin velvet, that a man had sent ahead, and which Dimitri had given her this morning.

Four Rohypnol and one Valium. She swallowed, smiled at the mirror, washed down the pills with half a glass of vodka.

She left the bathroom and went out into the hall. Her next

BOX 21

customer, the second one today and a new one that she'd never seen before, was already waiting in the stairwell. Dimitri sat in the kitchen and glared at her as she passed. The final steps.

She let him knock one more time. Then she opened the door.

HILDING OLDÉUS dug at the sore on his nose.

There was a chronic infection on his right nostril from his habit of scratching at it after he took heroin. The deep sore had been there for years. It was as if it burned, and he had to dig at it with his finger, poking under the skin.

He looked around.

It was an ugly fucking welfare office, and he hated it, but he always came back. As soon as he got out of prison, he came here, ready to smile for more money. A week had passed. He'd bowed to the guards at Aspsås prison, hastily paid his respects to Jochum Lang, whose arse Hilding had been kissing for the last few months. Hilding had needed someone to hide behind, and big Jochum worked well enough, not one bastard would ever consider messing with him when he was in Jochum's shadow. Jochum had had one lousy week left at the time – Christ, Hilding suddenly realised, he'd be out tomorrow – and they would probably never see each other outside prison walls. Jochum had been his protector for a while, but he wasn't a junkie, they were different kinds of criminals, moving in different circles.

There weren't many people in the waiting room now.

Some Gypsy bitches and a Finnish bastard and two fucking old people. What the hell did they need?

Hilding dug at his sore again, they took their time, a whole shitload of people were in line in front of him. It was that kind of day. When he felt. He didn't want to feel, didn't allow himself to, and then a day like this came and he felt felt felt. He

21

BOX 21

needed a fix, had to get rid of this shit, needed some junk, and all those goddamn people were sitting in his way in this ugly fucking welfare waiting room. It was his turn now, for chrissakes, his turn.

'Yes. Next?'

She'd opened the door again. That big, fat social worker.

He hurried over. The skinny body was carried by a jerky gait, and it was plain that this young man, not yet thirty, with his childish features and junkie skin, was headed somewhere, but not towards life.

He scratched at his nose again, knew he was sweating. It was June and rainy as hell, and he walked around wearing a long raincoat. It didn't breathe, and he probably should have taken it off. He'd considered it, but didn't bother to. He sat down on the visitor's chair in front of a bare desk and some empty bookshelves and looked nervously around the room. No one else was there, no other fucking welfare ladies, they usually came in twos.

Klara Stenung left the doorway, sat down on the other side of the desk. She was twenty-eight years old, just like the drug addict in front of her. She'd met him before and knew who he was, and where he was headed. There were some like that. She'd worked as a social worker in the suburbs for a couple of years, then in the Katarina-Sofia Social Services office in the centre of the city for three more. Skinny, stressed, loud, and just out of jail, they'd disappear for ten months at a time, but they always came back.

She stood up, stretched her arm across the table. He looked at her hand, considered spitting on it, but shook it in the end, held it loosely.

'I need cash.'

She met his eyes silently, waiting for more. She had his file in front of her. She knew everything about him. Hilding Oldéus was just like the others. No father. Not much of a mother. A couple of older sisters who were doing the best they could. Quite talented, quite confused, quite abandoned. Alcohol at thirteen, cannabis at fifteen. Things had gone fast after that. Smoking heroin, injecting heroin, his first prison sentence at seventeen. Now, at twenty-eight, he'd been in prison ten times in eleven years. Mostly for theft, a few times for handling stolen goods. A small-time crook. The kind that would run into a 7-Eleven with a bread knife in his hand and grab whatever was in the cash register and buy smack from a dealer right outside the store, go to the first stairwell he could find and shoot up, at which point he would cease to be aware of anything, not of the people in the store pointing the police in his direction, and not of the fact that he was sitting in the back of a police car on his way back to jail.

'You know the answer. There is not going to be any money.'

He moved restlessly on the chair, rocking on it, almost to the point of losing his balance.

'Jesus Christ! I just got out of prison!'

She looked at him, he screamed, tearing at the sore on his nose. It started bleeding again.

'I'm sorry. You're not in the system. Not on unemployment. And not in any retraining programme.'

Then he stood up.

'Listen to me, fat bitch! I'm completely fucking destitute! I'm hungry, for chrissake!'

'I understand you need money for food. But you're not in our system. So I can't give you any.'

Blood from his sore dripped onto the floor, running so fast it was turning the yellow linoleum red. He screamed, and hurled threats, but nothing ever came of it. He was bleeding, but he wouldn't attack. He wasn't the type, and she knew it. She didn't even bother to call in any reinforcements.

BOX 21

He slapped his hand hard against the bookshelf.

'I don't give a fuck about your goddamn rules!'

'You can do what you want. You're not getting any money. But I can give you food stamps for two days' worth of food.'

Outside the window a truck drove past, the sound bouncing back and forth between the buildings on either side of the narrow street. Hilding didn't hear it. He didn't hear anything at all. The bitch in front of him was talking about giving him food stamps. And how the hell was he gonna be able to buy smack with food stamps? He stared at the fat woman sitting across the desk from him, at her big fucking tits and her fucking necklace with its fucking round wooden balls. He laughed and screamed, turned over the chair he'd just been sitting on and kicked it against the wall.

'I don't want your fucking food stamps! Guess I'll have to find the fucking cash myself! Fucking bureaucrat bitch!'

He almost ran out of the door, saw the Finn and the Gypsy hags and the old people in the ugly waiting room. They all looked up at him but said nothing, continued sitting silently, almost squatting. He screamed *fucking welfare cases* at them as he passed, and then something else that was impossible to catch, his shrill voice cracked and mingled with the blood running from his nose. He left a trail down the stairs and out of the front door and all down Östgöta Street towards Skanstull.

NOT MUCH OF a summer.

Windy, rarely above seventy degrees, now and then a morning or afternoon of sunshine, otherwise rain on the rooftops and the garden barbecues.

Ewert Grens had held her hand as long as she let him, then she started getting anxious, as she usually did when she stopped laughing and the saliva ran down her chin. So he hugged her, kissed her forehead, and told her he'd be back next week, always next week.

If only you could have held on a little longer.

Now he was in a car headed over Lidingö Bridge, on his way to Bengt Nordwall's house in Eriksberg, south of the city. He was driving way too fast, and suddenly he was sitting behind another wheel.

In the SWAT team van he'd commanded twenty-five years ago.

He could see Lang outside the van, knew he was a wanted man, and he did exactly what they'd done so many times before. He drove alongside the running man while Bengt opened the bus's side door, and Anni, who was sitting closest to the door, grabbed hold of Lang and screamed that he was under arrest, just as she was supposed to.

She was the one was sitting in that place.
That's why Jochum Lang was able to pull her out.

25

BOX 21

Ewert Grens blinked and swung off the road temporarily, leaving the line of stressed-out morning commuters. He switched off the engine and sat there until the images ceased. Every time he'd visited her in recent years the same thing happened. Memories pounded around in his head, making it hard to breathe. He stayed there for a moment, didn't care about the idiots honking, waited until he was done.

In fifteen minutes he was there.

He and Bengt greeted each other on the narrow street of small houses and stood in the rain together, staring at the sky.

Neither of them smiled very often, maybe because of their age or maybe it had always been that way. But the dense grey wind and rain pouring down forced them to smile, what else was there to do?

'What do you say?'

'What do I say? I'm too tired to care any more.'

They shrugged their shoulders, sat down on the soaked cushions of the garden sofa.

They'd known each other for thirty-two years. They'd been young then, burning through their lives, which were more than half over now.

Ewert Grens looked silently at his friend.

The only person he actually talked to outside work, who he could actually stand.

Still slim, still with a full head of hair, they were the same age, but Bengt looked much younger. That's how it was when you had small children. They brought out your youth.

Ewert didn't have children, or hair, and his body was heavy. His steps were limping and Bengt's were feather-light. They shared a past and a profession, both were policemen in central Stockholm, but they'd both been given a limited amount of time, and it seemed like Ewert had burnt through his faster.

Bengt sighed in resignation.

'This rain. I can't even get the kids outside any more.'

Ewert wasn't sure if he was invited to his oldest friend's house because they expected to enjoy his company. Or if it was out of duty, because they felt sorry for him, so lonely, so naked outside the corridors of police headquarters. He came every time they invited him, never regretted it, but couldn't help wondering about it.

'She was feeling good today. She said hello. I'm sure of it.'

'And you, Ewert? How are you?'

'What do you mean?'

'I don't know what I mean. But it's like . . . you're more weighed down nowadays. Especially when you're talking about Anni.'

Ewert heard what he said, but didn't answer. He looked around with disinterest at the suburban life, which he didn't understand. They had a nice little house, of course. One of those small ordinary brick ones with a bit of a lawn, manicured shrubs, and sun-bleached plastic toys scattered across the garden. If it hadn't been for the rain, the two kids would have been running around playing something that kids their age play. Bengt had them late. He'd been almost fifty, and Lena was twenty years younger. It was as if he'd been given a second chance. Ewert didn't understand what a young, talented, beautiful woman saw in a middle-aged policeman; he didn't begrudge Bengt, but he'd never understand it.

Their clothes were wet, heavy material hanging off their bodies. They didn't feel it any more, had forgotten the rain for a moment. Ewert leaned forward, looked at his friend.

'Bengt?'

'Yeah?'

'Jochum Lang is being released today.'

Bengt shook his head.

'You have to let go of that at some point.'

BOX 21

'That's easy for you to say. You weren't driving.'

'And I wasn't the one who loved her. But it doesn't matter. You need to let it go. It was twenty-five years ago, Ewert.'

He'd turned around, towards the back seat.
He'd seen her grab onto the body that was fleeing.

Ewert Grens was breathing heavily, ran his hand over his rain-soaked head, felt the rage that lingered there.

Jochum Lang had felt her hand and started to turn around.
He'd grabbed hold of her, jerked hard, and Bengt, who was sitting next to her, didn't have time to catch her harness.

Ewert sighed. Hand on his wet scalp again.

At that very moment, when she fell out of the bus, and one of the rear wheels ran over her head, he'd realised that the rest of their life together was over.
Lang had laughed as he ran away, and laughed again when he was later sentenced to a few shitty months for bodily harm.

Ewert Grens hated him.

Bengt undid a button on his wet shirt, tried to make eye contact with his friend.

'Ewert?'

'Yeah?'

'You seem like you're someplace else.'

Ewert Grens looked out over the rain-drenched lawn, at the tulips crouching in the well-tended flowerbed. He felt tired.

'I'll get the bastard.'

Bengt put his arm around his shoulder. Grens winced. He wasn't used to it.

'Leave him now, Ewert.'

He'd just been holding her hand. She'd laughed like a child, and it had been cold, limp and absent. He remembered the other one, could still feel it, hot, firm, present.

'He'll be walking the streets starting today. Do you understand that? Lang is walking around shitting on us.'

'Ewert, was it Lang's fault? Are you sure? Or was it my fault? I was the one who couldn't hold on. Maybe it's me you should hate. Maybe it's me that you should take down.'

The wind came back, carrying the rain with it and lashing it against their faces. Behind them the door to the patio opened. A woman came out with an umbrella in her hand. She was young, around thirty, her long hair in a ponytail, and she smiled.

'You're not very smart.'

They turned around.

Bengt smiled back.

'Once you're soaked, it doesn't make much difference.'

'I want you to come in. Breakfast is ready.'

'Now?'

'Now, Bengt. The kids are hungry.'

They stood up. The fabric of their pants and jackets glued to their bodies.

Ewert Grens looked up at the sky again. It was just as grey.

IT WAS STILL MORNING. She could hear the birds outside, singing to each other, as they always did around this time. Lydia sat on the edge of the bed listening. It was beautiful. They were singing just like they used to among the ugly concrete buildings of Klaipeda. She didn't know why, but she'd woken up several times during the night from dreams about her visit with her mother to Vilnius and the Lukiškės prison many years ago. She'd dreamed of her father as he stood waving goodbye to her. As she'd left him in the dark hallway outside the TB section, passing by fifteen other prisoners slowly rotting away in what they called the HIV-room, she saw him collapse in the distance. She had immediately stopped, stood completely still for a moment. When he didn't stand up again, she rushed back along the stone floor. She'd pulled at him until he stood up again and coughed and rid himself of the blood and mucus that needed to come up. In the dream it had been exactly the same, her mother arrived and cried and screamed until somebody in the infirmary came and took him away. The same dream continued every time she'd fallen back asleep – she'd never dreamed about it before.

Lydia sighed deeply, moved a bit away on the edge of the bed and spread her thighs, slowly, just like the man in front of her wanted.

He was sitting a few metres away.

A middle-aged man, she guessed forty, just as her father would have been.

She'd been meeting him once a week for almost a year, every

Monday morning, he was usually punctual. He was the third customer of the day and always knocked on the front door as the church bell rang nine times through the closed window.

He didn't spit. He didn't penetrate her. She didn't have to touch his dick. She didn't even recognise his smell.

He was the kind who wanted to give her a hug when she opened the door and then didn't touch her any more, just held on hard to his own dick with one hand and used the other to show her how he wanted her to undress.

He wanted her to move her genitals back and forth, and he squeezed his dick harder. He wanted her to whine like a dog he once had and his dick turned a pale red as he squeezed it. He leaned back in the black leather chair as his cum ran down its sleek surface.

He was finished by nine twenty and out of the apartment before the church clock struck half past nine. Lydia was still sitting on the edge of the bed as he went, the birds were chirping, she could hear them again.

THE SORE ON his right nostril bled all along the pavements of Östgöta Street. Hilding was almost running – not because he was just out of prison and in good shape, because he wasn't the type to spend his time in the prison gym working out to dissipate his hate or trying to win respect – he was almost running from the panic and anger he felt after meeting that fucking social worker bitch, and towards his longing for dope, and he was panting by the time he made it to the ring road and the Skanstull subway station.

I don't want your fucking food stamps. I'll just have to get the dough myself.

'Hey you.'

Hilding poked the shoulder of one of the children standing in front of him on the platform. He guessed twelve, maybe thirteen years old. She didn't answer, and he poked again. She turned purposely away in the direction that the train would soon be arriving from.

'Hey you. I'm talking to you.'

He'd seen her mobile phone. He reached for it, took a step forward, snatched it from her hand and dialled a number while ignoring her protests, waiting for the signal to go through.

Hilding cleared his throat.

'Sis? It's me.'

She hesitated, so he continued.

'Sis, damn it, I need a loan.'

He heard her sigh before answering.

'You're not getting any money from me.'

'Sis, it's for food. And clothes. Nothing else.'

'You'll have to go to social services.'

He stared angrily at the device in his hand, breathed deeply and then shouted with his mouth close to what he thought was the microphone.

'Fuck you! I guess I'm on my own! And it's your fault!'

She replied in the exact same way she had last time.

'That's your choice. Your problem. Don't make it mine.'

Hilding Oldéus screamed into the electronic silence after she hung up and threw the bloody phone onto the concrete of the platform. The kid was standing there crying as he boarded the train.

He stood in front of the subway doors and tore deeper at the dripping red sore. Bloody and sweaty, his thin face lacked life, and he smelt of it.

He got off at the Central Station and took the escalator up from underground. It was hardly raining, but he looked around and continued sweating in his buttoned up raincoat, his back totally soaked, then crossed over Klaraberg Street to the pavement on the other side. He hurried between the houses next to the Nils Ferlin statue and went through the gate to the St Clara Cemetery.

Empty, just as empty as he'd hoped.

A drunk bum in the grass some distance away, but otherwise deserted.

He walked past the big Bellman gravestone and over to the park bench that stood behind it, under a tree that he thought might be an elm.

He stretched out his legs, humming something. One hand in the right pocket of his raincoat. He could feel the detergent, let his fingers slowly slip through it. Put his other hand into his left pocket and took out and opened a package of twenty-five postage stamp plastic bags, mixed the detergent with some amphetamines that barely covered the bottom of each one.

He needed cash, and he'd soon get some.

IT WAS EVENING. She was done for the day. No one else would be coming.

Lydia walked slowly through the apartment, pleasantly dark, just a few lights shining. It was fairly big, probably the biggest she'd been in since she got here, four rooms.

She stopped in the hall.

She didn't know why, but she started searching through the pattern on the wallpaper, along the narrow lines that filled the empty space between floor and ceiling. She often did that, stood there, forgetting everything else. She knew it was because the pattern resembled something she'd seen before on another wall in another room long ago.

Lydia remembered that wall, that room, so clearly.

The military police rushed in and pushed her father and the other men up against the wall, screaming *zatknis zatknis* and then that strange silence afterwards.

She'd known even then that her father had already been in prison once before. He'd put a Lithuanian flag up on his wall at home and been sentenced to five years in prison in Kaunas. She'd been so small then, only a few years old, but a flag, she shook her head, she still couldn't understand it. Of course, he was never allowed back in the armed forces again, and he'd asked out loud once, she remembered it clearly, when the vodka was finished and his cheeks red, surrounded by that wallpaper and stolen weapons that would soon be sold, he'd asked out loud what else he was supposed to do? His kids were screaming for food and the state refused to pay, what the hell was he supposed to do?

Lydia liked the silence, the evening darkness that slowly wrapped her up and rocked her to sleep. The narrow lines on the wall went far up, she followed them and had to bend her neck backwards. The ceilings were high in this old building. She thought about the few times she'd worked alone in significantly smaller apartments, but usually they were always two, and the men who stood in the stairwell and knocked on the door could choose which of them to touch.

At least twelve of them came to her every day.

Sometimes more, never less. If so, Dimitri beat her, or he screwed her as many times as she had left, in the anus.

She had her ritual. Every evening.

She showered, and the far-too-hot water scoured away their hands. She took her pills: four Rohypnol and a Valium washed down by some vodka. She dressed in bulky clothes that hung off her body so she had no outlines, no one could see her, no one could take anything.

But despite that, sometimes her genitals hurt more than usual.

She could feel them aching. She knew why. A few of them had been new, and the new ones were always too rough. But she rarely said anything – she'd learned how important it was to make them want to come back.

Lydia tired of the narrow lines on the wall and instead turned her face to the front door. It had been a long time since she'd stepped outside it. How long? She didn't know for sure, four months, that's what she guessed. She'd thought about smashing the window in the kitchen a few times, it didn't open, just like the others. She'd thought about smashing the glass and jumping, but she was too much of a coward. They were on the sixth

BOX 21

floor, and she didn't know what it would feel like to jump and hit the ground. She went to the door, grey metal, touched its cold, hard surface. She stopped and closed her eyes, held her hand towards the red lamp. She breathed slowly and cursed that she didn't understand how both electronic locks worked. She'd tried to see what Dimitri did, but had never succeeded. He always stood in the way. He knew she was there behind him, watching.

She left the hall, walked through a room without furniture that for some reason they called the living room, then past her own room. She looked at the big bed that she hated, but had to sleep in anyway.

She continued, to the end of the apartment, to Alena's room.

Her door was closed, but Lydia knew she'd finished working, that she'd showered and was alone in there.

She knocked.

'Yeah?'

'It's just me.'

'I'm trying to sleep.'

'I know. But can I come in?'

A few seconds. Lydia waited. While Alena decided.

'Sure. Come in.'

Alena was lying naked on the unmade bed. Her body was darker than Lydia's, her long hair still wet – she'd have a hard time getting a brush through it in the morning. She often lay there like that after everyone had gone, staring at the ceiling, thinking how she never told him that she was going, and now it had been years, and she still could feel the last time they held each other. It was supposed to be just a few months, then she was going to return to him, to Janoz, and they were going to get married.

Lydia stood still. She looked Alena's nudity and thought of her own body, which she hid in baggy clothes. She knew that's what she was doing, hiding. She saw, and she wondered how Alena could lie in that bed with no clothes on. She realised that she was looking at her opposite; some let things linger, don't hide from them, almost hold on to them.

Alena pointed to an empty corner of the bed.

'Sit down.'

Lydia walked into a room just like her own, same bed, same shelf, nothing else. She sat down on the unmade bed. Where someone else had just been lying. Stared a while at the red wall-paper, the small billowing velvet flowers. She searched for Alena's hand, took it, squeezed it while almost whispering.

'How are you?'

'Oh, you know.'

'Same as usual?'

'The same.'

They'd known each other for more than three years. They'd met on the boat. They'd laughed together then. They'd been on their way somewhere. Down below them the boat split the white foamy water in half. Neither of them had ever been on the sea before.

Lydia pulled her friend's hand close to her, squeezed hard, stroked the top of it for a moment, braiding it with her own.

'I know. I know.'

Alena lay still, her eyes closed.

Her body had no bruises on it, not like Lydia's, not in the same way.

Lydia lay down beside her. They were silent. Alena was with Janoz, whom she'd left, who hadn't known about her plans. Lydia was in the Lukiškės prison, among the men with shaved heads coughing in the dusty infirmary.

Then Alena suddenly sat up, put a pillow behind her back and leaned against the wall.

She pointed towards the floor, to a newspaper lying there.

BOX 21

'Get that.'

Lydia let go of Alena's hand, leaned forward, picked up the newspaper.

She didn't ask Alena how she got hold of it, she knew it was from someone who'd visited her today, someone who brought things with him because he wanted extra and got it. Lydia didn't have many who brought things. She wanted money. She wanted to fool Dimitri with the only thing he was interested in. If someone wanted extra from her they had to pay a hundred more.

'Open it. Page seven.'

She had told Alena – clients paid five hundred kronor per visit. Lydia knew what five hundred kronor times twelve a day was. But Dimitri took almost everything. They were allowed to keep two hundred and fifty kronor for each full day. The rest supposedly went to room and board and paying off their debt. She'd asked for more in the beginning, and Dimitri responded by raping her, in the arse, again and again, until she promised not to ask for more. So she decided she'd take an extra hundred now and then. In her own way. More to fool Dimitri Pimp-Fucker than for money.

She got beaten. She took a beating.

She let them beat her, and it cost a hundred kronor extra. Most didn't hit hard, they just wanted to get started like that, before screwing. She took six hundred, Dimitri got his five hundred, and he had no idea she kept a hundred for herself. She'd been doing it for quite a while now. She'd saved quite a bit, and that Dimitri Pimp-Fucker didn't know a thing.

Lydia didn't speak Swedish. And she read even less. She didn't understand the headline of the article, nor the bold introduction, nor the body of the text. But she saw the picture. Alena held the newspaper so that Lydia could see it. Lydia stopped looking at the picture and screamed, wept and cried and ran out of the room and back again. Her hate streamed towards the newspaper Alena was holding.

'That bastard!'

She threw herself onto the bed, lay down beside Alena's naked body again, sobbing more now than she screamed.

'That goddamn fucking bastard!'

Alena waited a while, it was useless to say anything yet. Lydia had to finish weeping, just as she herself had just finished weeping.

She held her friend.

'I can read it for you.'

Alena spoke Swedish. Lydia had no idea how she'd managed to learn it.

They had been in this country for the same amount of time, met the same number of people, it wasn't that.

Lydia had just decided to shut down. To never listen. Never to learn the language she was raped in.

'Do you want me to?'

Lydia didn't want that. She didn't want it. She didn't want it.

'Yes.'

She crept closer to the naked skin, borrowing her warmth. Alena was always warm, whereas she was always freezing.

The picture was rather uninteresting, just a middle-aged man leaning against a building. He looked pleased with himself, like somebody who'd been praised. He looked fit, had a moustache, light, newly combed hair. Alena pointed at him, the caption above. She read it first in Swedish then translated it to Russian. Lydia lay still, listening, not daring to move. The text was clumsily written in haste, about a drama that had taken place early this morning, just an hour before they went to press. The man leaning against the building, a policeman, had convinced a panic-stricken petty criminal who suddenly took five people hostage behind the closed door of a bank vault to first start

BOX 21

talking, then retreat, then give up. It wasn't remarkable. A policeman, something ordinary on page seven; tomorrow he'd be replaced by another cop, something else ordinary.

But he smiled.

The policeman in the picture smiled, and Lydia wept with hatred again.

SERGEL'S SQUARE WAS full of them. Speed freaks. All high and wanting to stay that way.

Hilding climbed a few steps up the stairs that led to Drottning Street. That was his usual spot. They needed to be able to see him. He didn't give a shit about the cops running around with their binoculars.

She was waiting by the entrance to the subway. The tiniest immigrant bitch he knew. Barely one metre fifty tall. She was young, not yet twenty, but she was ugly as hell with big hair and an oversized sweater and on her third or fourth day of a speed trip. She was cocky and horny and wanted to shoot up and fuck and shoot up and fuck. He knew her name was Mirja, and that she had an accent so thick it was hard to know what she was saying, and when she was speeding it got even worse, as if her mouth wouldn't work.

'Got something?'

He smirked.

'What do you mean something?'

'You have something?'

'If I have something? What the hell do you want?'

'A g.'

Fucking woman. Speed and fucking. Hilding stretched before he continued, looking out over Sergel's Square – the cops didn't care.

'Meth or the usual?'

'Usual, three hundred.'

She leaned forward, rooting around in one shoe, near the

BOX 21

laces. She pulled out a few crumpled bills and gave him three of them.

'Just the usual.'

Mirja had been speeding for almost a week.

She hadn't eaten, just needed more more more to avoid the high-voltage lines in her head, the manias that buzzed and pulled at her brain, that hurt like high-voltage lines through your head would.

She walked as fast as she could away from Hilding, up the stairs and over Drottning Street, towards the statue in front of the church and into the cemetery.

She could hear the people she passed by talking about her. Their loud voices knew everything, knew her secrets, and they talked talked talked, but that would soon disappear, at least for a few minutes.

Mirja sat on the bench that was closest to the entrance. She was in a hurry, dropped the bag from her shoulder, took out a Coca-Cola bottle half filled with water, held it in one hand and a syringe in the other. She pulled up the water with the tip of the syringe, and dropped it in the plastic bag.

She wanted it so bad. She'd been going for so long, so she didn't notice when the contents of the bag started to foam.

She smiled and put in the needle, held it still for a moment. She'd done this many times before. She steadied her arm, searching for a vein, pulled hard, and shot up.

The pain was immediate.

She stood up quickly, her voice barely audible, she tried to pull back what she'd shot up.

The vein had hardened, a centimetre-thick mound from wrist to elbow. The pain stopped as the skin suddenly turned black, as the detergent broke down the walls of her veins.

Tuesday, 4 June

JOCHUM LANG couldn't sleep. The last night was always the worst.

It was the smell. When the key was turned in the door one last time, he felt it again. These small cells always smelt the same, same shit no matter what joint you were in, even at the detention centres the walls and beds and cupboards and tables and white-painted ceilings smelt the same.

He sat on the edge of the bed. Lit a cigarette. Even the air pressure was the same. It was so fucking stupid that he'd never tell this to anyone, but that's just how it was, every cell in every prison and every jail had the same air pressure, like no other rooms anywhere else.

He flagged down a guard, just as he always flagged down a guard on the final night. He went over to the metal plate on the wall and pushed in the red button.

The guard took his time.

'You want something, Lang?'

The red light was lit and the central guard station responded. Jochum leaned forward and pressed his mouth against the worthless microphone.

'I want to wash this fucking smell off me.'

'You can forget that. You're still just as locked up as everyone else.'

Jochum hated them. He'd done his time, but those little shits had to chastise him to the very end.

He remained in bed, looking around the cell. He'd give it ten minutes. Then he'd flag them again. They usually gave in. After three or four times they usually stepped aside. They knew he wouldn't be so stupid as to threaten them when there was only one night left, but they also understood that they could meet each other on the street as early as tomorrow, and sometimes it was smart to just leave the slate clean.

He stood up. Took a few steps over to the barred window, then a few steps over to the metal door.

He packed two books and four packs of cigarettes, plus some soap, a toothbrush, a radio, a pile of letters and an unopened packet of tobacco, he put two years and eleven months into a plastic bag, and he did it as slowly as he could, then he put it on the table.

He buzzed them again, hissed in annoyance with his mouth pressed against the microphone and the metal that surrounded it, the surface fogged up by his breath. The bastards dawdled again.

'I want my clothes.'

'At seven o'clock.'

'I'll wake the whole damn section.'

'Do what you want.'

Jochum banged on the door. Someone on the other side of the corridor banged back. Then another one. They heard it. The guards were faster this time.

'You'll wake everybody up!'

'Told you so.'

The guard sighed.

'Fine. Here's what we're gonna do. We'll go down to baggage. And to storage. You can try something on. Then up again. But you're not leaving until seven.'

The hallway was empty.

No one was in a hurry. The other men sitting behind those doors had several more years to wait, why would they want to be up at dawn? He walked through the section, sixteen cells,

BOX 21

eight on each side, past the kitchen, past the pool table, past the TV corner. He walked right behind the guard, staring at his back, a thin bastard, he could have taken him in an instant, ten minutes after serving his sentence, he'd done it before.

They walked out through the locked door of the section, through one of the long underground corridors he'd walked down so many times, towards the central guard station. The storage room was right next it, on the other side of the wall from the video monitors. It was as if this was the real moment they released you from prison – when you were taken to those musty burlap sacks, picked one out of the hundreds, opened it, and tried on the clothes stuffed inside. They were almost always too small. He'd gained seven kilos this time, had been lifting weights like mad, and was as big as he'd ever been. He looked around. No mirror. He saw the labelled boxes that belonged to the lifers with no homes on the outside. That's all they had, just a few cardboard boxes in a storage room at Aspsås prison.

He fished out a bottle with Karl Lagerfeld on the label – the guard either didn't see or didn't care. Jochum Lang hadn't smelt it since they'd confiscated his belongings on the first day, nothing containing alcohol was allowed in the section. Now he stripped naked, unscrewed the cap, and held the bottle over his shaved head. He shook it, and emptied its contents, which ran down his head to his shoulders and all along his upper body, dripped down to his feet and the floor, the stink of perfume rinsed off the layers of prison.

Ten to seven.

The guard was an arsehole, but he was punctual. The door was wide open, and Jochum picked up the plastic bag, spat on the floor of his cell, and walked out. All he had to do was walk through the corridor, change into those too-small clothes, get his fucking three hundred kronor and train ticket, and tell the guard to go to hell, while the gate slowly opened up.

Then he was going to walk out with his bag in his hand and flip off the surveillance cameras and continue on to the closest prison wall, unzip his trousers, and piss on the concrete.

It was windy outside.

AT THE FAR end of the police station's lower section, the dawn arrived accompanied by the singing of Siw Malmkvist. It had always been that way. Ewert Grens had spent thirty-one years as a police officer, and for thirty of them he'd had his own office. That was exactly how long he'd had this old cassette player as well, the kind with mono speakers and tape recorder in one. It had been a present for his thirtieth birthday, and he carried it gently in his arms every time he'd changed offices over the years. He only played Siw Malmkvist. He had a collection of mix tapes, all with the same content: her entire repertoire, her classics recorded in various sequences on different cassettes.

This morning it was 'Tunna skivor' (1960), originally 'Everybody's Somebody's Fool'. He always got to work first and played it as loud as he wanted to, eventually somebody would complain about the volume, but as long as he was surly as hell, they left him alone. With his door closed and Siw cranked all the way up, he could hide inside his investigations, avoiding life.

He was still reliving yesterday. Anni had looked so nice when he arrived, hair combed and dress ironed. She'd looked at him more than usual, it was as if they made contact, as if for a moment he'd been more than a stranger holding her hand. Then Bengt's tidy house had been so full of life. Breakfast surrounded by scampering children and well-meaning glances. He'd been grateful as he always was and nodded cheerfully as he always did and had been treated like a family member by Bengt and Lena and the kids in the same way as usual, but still he'd felt lonelier than ever before. He was living inside it, that terrible feeling, and he raised the volume to force it away.

He left his office chair, walked slowly back and forth across the shabby linoleum. He needed to think about something else. Anything else. No doubts, not today, not again. He had given all that up, for work, for the life of a police officer – for this. That's how it had turned out. First one day, then another day, then another, then thirty-one years, and no woman and no children and no real friends, just long and faithful service that in less than ten years would be over, and he'd be over then.

Ewert Grens looked around. His office was only his for as long as he put in his hours, and then it would be someone else's. He continued to pace with his limping gait, his big, clumsy body going back and forth between window and bookcase. He wasn't handsome, he knew that, but he had been powerful and present and dangerous, now he was mostly angry. He ran his hand over what had once been hair, just a few short grey wisps left. He was listening

The tears I cried for you could fill an ocean
But you don't care how many tears I cry

and he could forget. For a moment, it was just a morning and he had piles of investigations on his desk that had to be read and taken care of if it was the last thing he did.

There was a knock on the door. Too early. He ignored it. Someone opened it and peered inside. Sven.

'Ewert?'

Ewert Grens didn't say anything. He pointed to the visitor's chair. Sven Sundkvist stepped into the office, a generation younger than his colleague, short blond hair, slender, straight back. Sven was clever, the only person in the building besides Bengt Nordwall that Ewert didn't despise. Sven sat down, but didn't say anything. He'd learned long ago that for Ewert Siw

BOX 21

meant another time, a happier time, memories that Sven knew nothing about, but realised were important.

They sat in silence, just the music.

Until they heard the noise of the cassette coming to an end, the quick pop that an old cassette makes when the play button is released again.

Two and a half minutes.

Ewert was still standing up. He cleared his throat – this would be the first thing he'd said today.

'Yeah?'

'Good morning.'

'Yes?'

'Good morning.'

'Good morning.'

Ewert walked towards his desk and chair. He sat down and looked at Sven.

'Did you want something? Besides saying good morning?'

'You know that Lang was released today?'

Ewert admonished him with his hand.

'I know that.'

'That was all. I'm on my way to an interrogation. A heroin addict who was selling detergent.'

A few seconds. Then Ewert Grens slammed his hands full force onto the piles of paper in front of him. They flew off his desk and scattered all over the floor.

'Twenty-five years.'

He slammed them down again onto the empty place where his investigations had just been. Fists against wood.

'Twenty-five years, Sven.'

She'd been lying under the car.

He'd stopped, run over to her still body. Blood was gushing from her head.

Piles of paper now covered most of the floor. Sven Sundkvist could see that Ewert was deep in a thought and not about to share. He bent down and picked up a few random documents to read aloud.

'A student teacher naked in Rålambshov Park. One lower leg removed. Two broken thumbs. *No crime is proven.*'

He moved his index finger to the next paper.

'An insurance salesmen in Eriksdalslunden. Stabbed four times in the chest. Nine witnesses. No one saw anything. *No crime is proven.*'

Ewert was enraged. The feeling radiated from his gut, making his whole body ache, and it needed to come out. He waved his hand at Sven, urging him to take a few steps back, to get out of the way. Sven moved, he knew. Ewert took a deep breath, and kicked the waste-paper bin across the room. The contents scattered all over the floor like a gentle rain. Quiet, almost mechanically, Sven bent down again, picked up the empty cans of snus and the empty coffee cups. He stood up and continued reading.

'Suspicion of aggravated assault. *No crime is proven.* Suspicion of attempted manslaughter. *No crime is proven.* Suspicion of murder. *No crime is proven.*'

Sven had interrogated Jochum Lang more times than he could remember. He'd used every interrogation technique in the book and out of it. Sven got close a few years ago, almost gaining Lang's confidence by taking any kind of shit Lang threw at him, that if Lang wanted to open up Sven Sundkvist would be there to listen. Lang had understood that, but he backed down at the last minute. Instead, he just asked for a cigarette and stared out the window and went back to denying everything, even denying that he ever went to the toilet.

Sven turned towards his boss.

'Ewert, this stack of paper you just scattered all over the floor, well I could go on like this for ever.'

BOX 21

'That's enough.'

'*Witness intimidation, aggravated kidnapping* . . . at least twenty cases of probable cause for suspicion.'

'That's enough, I said.'

'Convicted just three times and short sentences. The first time . . . here . . . *causing serious injury.*'

'Now you need to shut your mouth!'

Sven Sundkvist winced. He didn't recognise the face that was screaming at him. He'd seen Ewert Grens yell at many people, but never at him, never, that's how it had always been. Now Ewert turned his back on Sven and walked over to the tape recorder, put the same cassette in the ancient machine, loud enough to drown out Sven reading out loud.

'cause everybody's somebody's fool,
everybody's somebody's plaything

Grens listened, her voice replacing his rage. I can't take any more, he thought. Perhaps this is the moment where it ends, right now, right here. Jochum Lang was exactly the type that had been fuelling his thirty-one years of professional work, the type that kept him working no matter what, never stopping until the verdict had been handed down, and if he couldn't handle scum like that then maybe it was time to go home, try to live some other life. He'd been thinking this way with increasing frequency over the past year, and when he pushed those thoughts away they came back even more clearly and more often.

Sven sat down in front of him, tapped his chin, ran his fingers through his light hair.

'Ewert.'

Grens raised his hand.

'Shhh. One more minute.'

Yet darlin' I'd be twice as blue without you.

Sven waited. Siw fell silent. Ewert looked up.

'Yes?'

'I don't know. Just a thought. Aspsås prison. I'm thinking about Hilding Oldéus. That skinny little junkie I'm about to go interrogate.'

Ewert nodded – he knew who Hilding Oldéus was. Sven continued.

'We know he served his time with Lang. We even know that they were good friends, or as good a friend as you could be with a guy like Jochum Lang. Hilding ingratiated himself early on by giving him prison wine they'd hidden in a fire extinguisher. They were disciplined once when a guard found them wasted.'

'Hilding traded mash for protection.'

'Yes.'

'You had a thought?'

'After we interrogate him about the detergent, we'll talk to him about Lang. Make Oldéus help us get him.'

The music had stopped. Ewert let Siw wait. He looked around the room again. It wasn't that big, and not a bit personal. Aside from his stereo it was like any other institutional room, a room furnished with standard office furniture made of light birch, a room that just as easily could have been at the Swedish Tax Agency on Göt Street or at Social Services in Gustavsberg. But he spent more time here than at home. He came at dawn, went home late, if at all. He often slept on the little couch by the window, much smaller than his big body, but still somehow he slept better there than in his own apartment. He was spared the

BOX 21

long sleepless nights, those slow painful hours spent searching for a peace that never came. He didn't know why.

He just knew that what used to be a night here and there had turned into weeks of not going home.

'Oldéus and Lang. Hardly. They live in two different worlds. Oldéus is a junkie, all he wants or needs are the drugs. Lang is a criminal, not an addict. He's tested positive for weed now and then at Aspsås, but nothing more serious. They have nothing in common. Not out here.'

Sven changed his position, leaning back in the visitor's chair. He sighed. He suddenly seemed tired.

Ewert looked at him for a long time.

He recognised it. Resignation.

He thought about Oldéus, about how tired he was of wasting his time on junkies who scratched holes into their noses. His day was too short and the list of idiots too long.

'Well Christ. Let's do it. One fool more or less. We'll set him on Lang.'

THE CAR THAT was slowly rolling up to the big prison gate was brand new. The kind of car that smelt like leather seats and an untouched dashboard.

Jochum Lang saw it immediately when he passed by the central guard station and into the courtyard. He hadn't spoken to them, and he hadn't asked for this, but they'd understood nonetheless. They were supposed to stand there outside, that was part of it as well.

He nodded curtly to the man sitting in the driver's seat, and the man nodded back.

The engine idled while Jochum flipped off the surveillance camera, his urine still running down the concrete. You don't rush a ritual. The car would wait, and he slowly raised his finger again until he stopped pissing, then pulled down his trousers and flashed his arse at the slowly closing gate. He knew it was meaningless and childish, but he was free now, and he had the urge to prove there was no bastard he would bow to. They could bow to him. He had waited for two years and eleven months, and it seemed like his sentence was truly over at the moment he flashed his arse at the guards.

He walked over to the car, opened the door to the passenger seat, and climbed in.

They scrutinised each other in silence, measuring each other without knowing why.

Slobodan had aged. He wasn't older than thirty-five, but his long Yugoslavian hair had turned grey at the temples, his eyes

BOX 21

had new wrinkles, and he'd grown a thin moustache, also tinged with grey.

After a moment, Jochum tapped the windscreen.

'You've traded up.'

Slobodan nodded, looking pleased.

'What do you think?'

'Too Yugoslavian for my taste.'

'It's not mine. It's Mio's.'

'Last time I saw you, you were driving something you'd pinched with a screwdriver for a key. That suited you better.'

The car was slowly moving again, a tap on the accelerator. Jochum Lang took the train ticket out of his back pocket, tore it into small pieces, and held the pieces outside the open window. He screamed loudly in a broad Uppsala accent that the prison's parting gift wasn't even good enough to wipe your arse with, and then released the pieces of paper into the wind. Slobodan answered his mobile phone, while speeding up. They left the gate and the high grey walls behind them. After a few hundred metres, the rain began to fall, the wipers started out slow, but soon beat rapidly.

'I'm not picking you up because I want to. Mio asked me.'

'He ordered you.'

'He wants to see you as soon as possible.'

Jochum Lang was tall, with broad shoulders, a shaved head, a big scar from his left ear down to his mouth – some poor wretch had tried to defend himself with a razor. He took up a lot of room in the front seat of the car. He spoke with his hands, waving in the air in front of him, demanding even more space now that he was upset.

'The last time I did something for him, I ended up on this fucking vacation.'

They left the narrow road from the prison, entered a wider one now, some traffic, commuters on the way to work.

'You did time. But we took care of you and your family. Right?'

Slobodan Dragovic smiled as he turned towards Jochum, flashing his bad teeth, and then answered the phone when it rang again. Jochum said nothing. He stared straight ahead as the wipers spread water all over the windscreen. He knew that was true. A pick-up had gone to hell and a fucking witness, who really should have known better, talked to the police. Jochum watched the raindrops beating against the window, thinking how he knew all that, knew shit happens, knew Mio had always been close, watching with borrowed eyes and ears from the first morning he'd woken up in his cell, taking care of him, taking care, and they did that.

The shiny new car drove faster and faster, making its way through the landscape, which slowly shifted from rural to urban, from the northern suburbs to central Stockholm.

THE INTERROGATION ROOM was on the floor below the detention cells.

There wasn't much to it.

Dirty walls that had once been white, one window with thick bars on it, a table in the middle, like a kitchen table of beaten-up pine, four simple chairs that looked like they might have come from a school cafeteria.

INTERVIEW LEADER SVEN SUNDKVIST (IL): I want you to sit down.

HILDING OLDÉUS (HO): What the hell do you want with an innocent guy?

IL: You mixed amphetamines with detergent, do you call that innocent?

HO: I don't know shit about that.

IL: You were selling dirty speed. So far we have three people with corroded veins. They all gave us your name.

HO: What the fuck are you talking about?

IL: You had that dirty speed on you.

HO: That wasn't mine.

IL: We had the National Forensic Laboratory check the bags of powder you had in your possession at the time of your arrest. All six of them.

HO: Those aren't mine, for chrissake.

IL: Twenty per cent amphetamines. Twenty-two per cent caffeine pills. Fifty-eight per cent detergent. Sit down right now, Oldéus.

Ewert Grens entered the room. During his walk here from his office, he'd passed through eight locked doors, but wasn't aware of any of them. His mind was still on the investigations. He could still hear Sven reading aloud, repeating inside his head, *bodily harm*, how a SWAT car stopped too late, how he held her in his arms until the paramedics lifted her onto a stretcher and took her away.

He fought against that voice, stared up for a moment at the harsh light of the lamp, then at the lean face opposite Sven, at a man who was tearing anxiously at the sore on his nose, drops of blood flowing towards his mouth, chin.

IL: Detective Superintendent Ewert Grens has entered the room at nine twenty-two.
HO: (inaudible)
IL: What did you say, Hilding?
HO: Wasn't mine.
IL: Hilding, listen to me now. We know you were selling dirty speed at Sergel's Square.
HO: Fuck what you know.
IL: We arrested you there. With the bags. And the detergent.
HO: It wasn't mine! I got them from a guy when I got there. Fuck that dude. Selling dirty speed to me. I'm gonna kick his ass when I get out of here.
EWERT GRENS (EG): You're not getting out of here.
HO: What are you talking about, pig?
IL: There are a lot of people who'd like to get their hands on you. And if we receive a complaint from somebody who bought your shit, we consider that attempted murder. Between six months and eight years.

This thin body, screaming for heroin, which consumed and vomited it up, which was falling apart in front of them, stood up

BOX 21

and walked jerkily around the cramped room, struck out one arm, took it back again, walked a few steps, stopped and babbled incoherently, jerking his head, throwing it back and forth. Ewert looked at Sven. They'd seen this before. He might sit down in front of them and tell them everything they wanted to know. Or, just as likely, he might lie down on the floor in the fetal position and shake himself into unconsciousness.

EG: Between six months and eight years. But we're in a damn good mood today. Your confiscated dirty speed could just disappear.
HO: What do you mean disappear?
EG: We're a curious about a guy named Lang. Jochum Lang. You know him.
HO: I've never heard of him.

His face started twitching sharply. He grimaced, raised his eyes to the ceiling, turned his head back and forth several times. He tore at his sore. Jochum's name had a powerful effect on Hilding. He was scared. He wanted nothing to do with this, not here. He was about to protest when there was a knock on the door. A female colleague with a southern accent, Ewert didn't remember her name, who was here to fill a short vacancy over the summer.

'Excuse me. Superintendent Grens, I think this is important.'
Ewert waved her in.

'It doesn't matter. We're not getting anywhere. This little junkie is in a hurry to get out of here so he can go and die.'

A brief glance at Sven, who nodded, and she entered the cramped room behind Hilding, who stood up, pointed at her, and made a feeble attempt at a lewd gesture with his crotch.

'Damn, Grens, some new cop pussy!'
She slapped Hilding hard across the cheek.
He lost his balance, stumbled a bit. He leaned forward,

holding both of his hands against his cheek, a large red welt was slowly forming.

'You fucking Nazi!'

She looked at him.

'That's Sergeant Hermansson to you. You can go now, Hilding.'

Hilding was still holding one hand over the welt as he swore his way out of the room. Sven was just behind Hilding, a firm grip on his arm, pushing him in front of him.

Ewert looked at Sven in surprise, then turned to his young colleague.

'Hermansson, was it?'

'Hermansson.'

She was young, maybe twenty-five years old, her eyes had no hesitation in them. They revealed nothing. Neither surprise nor anger. Nothing of her reaction to Hilding's comment about cop pussy, or the violent slap she'd given to his face.

'It was important, you said.'

'From the command centre. They want you to go to 3 Völunds Street. An address in the Atlas neighbourhood.'

Ewert listened, searched his memory, he'd been there before, not long ago.

'Down towards the railroad? By St Eriksplan?'

'Yes, there. I checked the map.'

'What's this about?'

She was holding something in her hand, a notepad, she glanced at it quickly, didn't want to be wrong, not in front of Grens.

'Some colleagues have broken in a door after a violent assault in an apartment on the sixth floor.'

'Yes?'

'This is urgent.'

'Yes?'

'There's a problem.'

IT WAS AN older building in a beautiful neighbourhood.

The historical façade of each building had been carefully restored, and the little lawn in front of each entrance door perfectly maintained, red and yellow strips of narrow flowerbeds, a few small trees that didn't quite fit.

Ewert Grens opened the car door, scanning the building's rows of windows. A turn-of-the-century apartment building, the kind of place where you could hear your neighbours when their steps were heavy in the kitchen, when they turned up the volume on the news at half past seven, when they walked half a floor down to put their rubbish in the chute. The windows he was looking at had expensive curtains. Floor after floor, people living their lives inside, being born and dying, all these worlds taking place just a few breaths away from each other without ever meeting, no one knew a thing about the person who lived next door.

Sven Sundkvist had parked the car, muttering as he stood beside Grens.

'Three Völund Street. Looks expensive. Who can afford to live here?'

Sixth floor. Eighth window. One of those. Ewert Grens compared them, stopped at each one. They all looked alike to him, same damn curtains, the same damn house plants, just different colours and patterns, but still alike.

He took a deep breath and snorted at the tidy façade.

'I don't like cruelty. Not inside those fancy walls. And yet that's always where you find it.'

He looked around. An ambulance, two police cars, both with cold blue lights. Nosy neighbours, maybe a dozen or so, stood by their cars, keeping their distance out of respect, which wasn't always the case. Ewert and Sven walked down the stone path towards the door, which stood open, the door handle tied to a bicycle rack with a piece of rope. They went in, Ewert nodded contentedly to himself, it *was* turn of the century, 1901 written in large iron numbers on the wall inside the doorway. He turned towards the board next to the door, a list of tenants, floor by floor. The sixth floor, four surnames: Palm, Nygren, Johansson, Löfgren.

Swedish names through and through. It was that kind of building.

'Do you see anything familiar, Sven?'

'No.'

'They're not exactly advertising themselves.'

'How about you?'

'Not a clue.'

There wasn't much to the lift. Narrow, with a black metal lattice door that could be pushed aside: no more than three people or 225 kilos. A police officer in uniform was standing in front of it, an older colleague who Ewert hadn't seen in a long time.

I forget what fools there are in this profession, he thought. I'd completely forgotten about that one, for example. When you don't see any idiots for a while you forget they exist.

Ewert Grens smiled, studied the man in front of him.

The kind of guy who always stood with his legs wide apart like police officers do on TV when they're guarding something important while the music is all dangerous strings, the kind of guy who clicked his heels together when he answered a question, the kind who spelled out loud when he wrote reports, the kind of guy who would never be good at much more than guarding a lift.

BOX 21

The idiot did not smile back, he'd felt Grens's contempt, and therefore turned markedly towards Sundkvist when he began his presentation.

'We got the alarm an hour ago. Some drunk pimp. And a really bruised whore.'

'Yes?'

'A few neighbours called. He'd managed to beat her up good. She's unconscious. She needs medical attention. And there's another one in there. Also seems to be a whore.'

'Beaten?'

'Don't think so. He didn't have time.'

Ewert Grens had stood silently while Sven talked to the idiot guarding the lift. Now he was done.

'One hour! So what are you standing here waiting for still?'

'We can't go in. To the apartment. Something about Lithu-anian territory.'

'What the hell are you talking about? If there's been an assault you just go in!'

Ewert Grens was having a hard time breathing. Each step was a struggle, and it was six floors up. He should of course have taken the lift, but had hurried past the fool standing in front of it in a rage. Now he could hear voices above him, louder the closer he came. On the fifth floor he passed a doctor and two EMTs. He nodded towards them and received quick nods back, then he went up the last steps.

He was panting now, saw Sven approaching with light steps from the corner of his eye. He couldn't give up now, forcing his unwilling and no longer familiar legs.

On the top floor of the building there were four apartment doors. One of them had a big hole in it. Outside the door stood three uniformed police officers Grens couldn't remember having seen before, but there was one familiar face: Bengt Nordwall, in civilian clothes just like Ewert Grens and Sven Sundkvist. It had been just over a day since they'd seen each other, that shitty rainy morning in their happy family garden. Ewert had eaten breakfast there, been welcomed and cared for. Nowadays they met infrequently at work, so he looked at his friend disconcertedly.

'What are you doing here?'

They greeted each other with a brief handshake, as they always did.

'Russian. The guy inside doesn't speak anything else.'

Bengt Nordwall was one of the few Russian speakers in the Stockholm police.

He gave him a short update.

'Pimp beats the crap out of a whore. When the police get here she yells loudly, and they break down the door. Then we encounter this.'

Bengt Nordwall pointed to the man standing inside the door, who seemed to be guarding the large hole, short in stature and flabby, forties, wearing a shiny grey suit that seemed expensive, but it didn't suit him, hung more than it fitted.

Bengt continued.

'So he waves his diplomatic passport. Screaming that this is Lithuanian territory and that the Swedish police have no right to enter. He refuses to release the girl. He refuses to even let our doctors in. If anyone is allowed in it will only be the Lithuanian embassy doctors. The abused girl is unreachable, but the other one in there has screamed a few times. She's called him *Dimitri Lydi*, in Russian, of course. She makes him furious, but he can't do more than shout back as long as we're here.'

Sven Sundkvist had stopped a few steps further down beside the garbage chute on the landing between floors five and six with a mobile in his hand. He was now trying to get Grens's attention, gesturing excitedly with one hand, getting ready to end the call. He flipped the phone shut, walked the last steps up to the sixth floor.

BOX 21

'I just called the Stockholm Housing Authority. The apartment is owned by a Hans Johansson. It's not leased to anyone. That corresponds to the board in the entrance as well.'

Ewert Grens looked silently for a moment at the man standing in the doorway wearing a shiny grey suit, claiming he had the right to beat women up because he was an embassy official, then looked at the uniformed police officers behind Bengt, stretched his hand towards one of them, asked for his baton.

'Well then. Dimitri Pimp-Fucker can wave whatever diplomatic passport he wants to.'

He walked towards the door. The man in the grey shiny suit established immediately that he was going to block Grens, took a few steps back and stretched out his hands on either side. Grens continued walking, and when he got close he drove the baton hard into the gap of his unbuttoned coat. The body in front of him doubled over. The man who'd just been carrying on about Lithuanian territory clutched his stomach and hissed something in Russian. Ewert Grens walked past him, shouted to the EMTs and the doctor waiting downstairs, gestured to the other police officers to go in, and then hurried through a long hall and an empty living room.

He couldn't make sense at first of what he was seeing.

The bed had a red bedspread and the woman lying on top of it was naked, her back to him. It was difficult to determine at first where the fabric stopped and the body began, as if the reds flowed together.

It had been a long time since he'd seen someone so badly beaten.

The light was always the same in the emergency room at Söder Hospital.

Morning, noon, evening, night – the same light shone.

A young doctor with tired eyes and a long lean body was staring at one of those lights in the ceiling of the corridor, trying to collect himself, walking beside a stretcher, listening to a nurse. Maybe he could go home after this patient, out into the light that sometimes changed.

'Unconscious female, probably beaten, head injuries, broken arm, evidence of internal bleeding. She has difficulty breathing without assistance. I alerted the trauma unit.'

The young doctor looked silently at the nurse. He didn't want to hear any more today. He didn't want to know any more about all the ways human beings destroyed each other.

'She has to be intubated.'

He nodded in confirmation, stood for a moment by the woman on the stretcher. A few seconds that were just his. It had been a long day. He'd treated more young people than usual, his own age or younger, patched and mended their broken bodies as best he could, and he knew none of them would continue living as they had before. He knew that they would always bear this day with them. It would be visible on some of them, and for others it would be inside, never let out.

He studied her face. She wasn't Swedish, not from here but not from far away, she was blonde and probably beautiful. She reminded him of someone, but he couldn't remember who. He took the paper out of the plastic folder, the one given to him by the paramedics. He read the short sentences. He knew now that her name was Lydia Grajauskas, information that came from another woman who had been in the apartment where the assault had taken place.

He observed her. All these women.

How had she looked when he hit her? What did she say?

People dressed in white and green hurried through the corridors. They were waiting for the doctor with the tired black eyes, they tried to meet those eyes to show him they were ready.

BOX 21

They took over the stretcher, rolled it into the trauma room, lifted her gently from it and put her on an operating table. They checked her pulse, ECG, blood pressure. They opened her mouth and sucked up the contents of her stomach. She became less of a body and less of a human, became statistics and graphs, it was easier that way, easier to deal with it that way.

Did she say anything at all?

Maybe she screamed, what do you scream when someone thinks they have the right to strike you?

The doctor with the tired eyes couldn't leave yet. He wanted to see. He didn't know what he wanted to see.

One of his colleagues, who was now in charge, stood a few metres in front of him and gently lifted the woman, turned her light body on its side, saw her broken skin mixed with blood and shouted in dismay.

'I need help here!'

The doctor with the tired eyes hurried over. He saw what the doctor next to him was looking at.

He counted them.

He stopped at thirty. The stripes were red, swollen.

He had to suppress the urge to cry. He had to struggle to remain professional. She should be just statistics and graphs. He tried to think that way, I don't know her, I don't know her, I don't know her, but it didn't work, not today, there had been too much meaningless suffering, and he couldn't understand it.

That red destruction. He had to say it out loud, as if to hear how it sounded, or to inform the others, he didn't know.

'She's been whipped!'

He said it again. More slowly, quietly.

'She's been whipped. From her neck to her buttocks. Someone flayed her.'

It was a beautiful apartment with polished wooden floors, a fireplace in every room, high ceilings, a home like that should be filled with peace. Ewert Grens was sitting at the kitchen table on one of the four plastic folding chairs. He, together with Sven Sundkvist and two technicians, had tried to find some kind of information in the rooms of this apartment: who was this woman who according to her roommate was named Lydia Grajauskas, who was the woman who called herself Alena Sljusareva, who was Dimitri Pimp-Fucker who had been waving around a diplomatic passport and claiming this was Lithuanian territory?

The two women, the beaten-up Grajauskas and her friend Sljusareva, who had managed to disappear after the stretcher had been carried out, were both prostitutes from the Baltic. That much he knew. He'd seen that before. Always the same story. Young, poor girls from the Baltic region were cultivated by a man who went to their villages with gifts and with the promise of work and a good life. He gave them false passports, and the moment they accepted the passport they were transformed in his eyes from hopeful teenage girls to fake horny women. The false passport was expensive, with it came a debt, a debt that had to be worked off. The few who dared to refuse learned the hard way what force was. They were raped by their tour guide until their wombs were bleeding, with a gun to the head and again: spread your thighs, work off your debt and your trip across the Baltic Sea, fuck or I'll drive this up your arse again! Then the man who had persuaded, beaten, raped them, and put a gun to their temple, sold them, three thousand euros for every teenage girl who was transferred from east to west and who had the ability to groan when someone penetrated her.

Ewert Grens sighed, looked at Sven Sundkvist, who came into the kitchen to report on a storage room they'd missed on their first time through.

BOX 21

'Not a thing in there either. No personal belongings at all.'

Several pairs of shoes, a few dresses, a lot of underwear, of course, perfume bottles, plastic bags with assorted make-up, a box of condoms, dildos and handcuffs. Nothing else. They hadn't found anything in the apartment that they hadn't expected, nothing of who these women really were.

'These faceless children.'

The girls didn't even officially exist. They lacked work permits, identities, lives. They breathed carefully in an apartment with electronic locks on the sixth floor of a city quite different from the village they'd left.

'Ewert, how many do we have in this town anyway?'

'As many as the market demands.'

Ewert Grens sighed again, leaned forward, fingering the wallpaper. It was in here that the fucking pimp had whipped her. He felt the blood that had solidified on the flowery wall, saw how it had been splashed over large areas, a great portion of the ceiling. He was pissed off and tired, wanted to shout, but ended up whispering.

'She's here illegally. She has to have a guard.'

'She's being operated on now.'

'In the ward. Afterwards.'

'A couple of hours left, according to the hospital. Then she'll be done.'

'Can you arrange that, Sven? A guard. I don't want her to disappear.'

It was empty and silent outside the house with the beautiful façade.

Ewert Grens was looking in the windows on the other side of the street, also empty, also with identical curtains and houseplants.

He felt uneasiness creep into him.

The battered woman and the pimp with his shiny suit, and Bengt and his colleagues waiting outside for an hour while she was unconscious and bleeding.

He tried to shake it off, he froze. How can you shake off what you don't even know yet?

IT WAS TEN THIRTY and Jochum Lang was eating from the breakfast buffet at Ulriksdals Castle. The Yugoslavians liked to do that – invite you someplace classy and expensive and then talk work. They'd been driving through the northern suburbs, heading for the conversation they were just about to have. Just a bit more omelette, a cup of coffee, and a couple of mint-flavoured toothpicks.

Lang looked away towards the dining room's interior. White tablecloths and real silverware and conference people. Women who had red cheeks and smoked cigarettes, men who sat as close as they could, drinking a second cup. He smiled at their meetings and expectations, he didn't participate in that kind of thing, never had, hadn't understood the point of such a predictable game.

'You had something.'

They hadn't spoken to each other at all, not since Slobodan had met him at Aspsås prison's gate in a shiny new car, and Jochum had thrown his train ticket through the window as they drove away.

Now they were watching each other across a beautiful table at an expensive restaurant ten minutes from central Stockholm.

'It's Mio.'

Jochum stayed stubbornly silent. With his big shaved head, tanning bed tan, the scar from his mouth to the top of his cheek like a muzzle, he still took up room.

Slobodan leaned forward.

'He wants you to have a little talk with a guy who's selling our dope mixed with detergent.'

Jochum Lang was still waiting. Not a word. Not until the mobile phone on the table started ringing, he reached out and grabbed Slobodan's wrist.

'You're talking to *me*. You can take care of your fucking business later.'

His eyes were defiant for a moment.

Slobodan pulled back his hand just as the phone stopped ringing.

'He's selling shit, like I said. He even sold some to Mio's niece.'

Jochum lifted a salt shaker off the starched tablecloth and laid it on its side, pushed it and watched as it rolled over to the edge of the table and fell down onto the floor, then rolled on towards the window.

'Mirja?'

Slobodan nodded.

'Yes.'

'Mio never gave a shit about crack-whores before.'

Lift music came from the speakers on the wall. The women with red cheeks laughed and lit new cigarettes, the men unbuttoned the top buttons on their shirts and tried to hide the rings on their fingers as best they could.

'I think you know the guy.'

'Get to the point.'

'It's mixed with detergent. And it's ours. Do you understand that?'

He was starting to get loud.

'I don't like it! Mio doesn't like it! Fucking dirty speed!'

Jochum leaned back, said nothing. Slobodan's face was turning red.

'Credibility goes quick. Detergent in a few veins and that's that.'

Jochum was getting tired of the smoke from the conference

BOX 21

women, the smell of fried sausages and the too-polite waitress. He wanted to get out of here, out into the day, another day. He thought that Aspsås should have fed his desire for this kind of thing, but the exact opposite was true. Always after he'd served a few years, it got so much harder to stand any pretending.

'Just tell me what the hell it is you want me to do.'

Slobodan could see that he was impatient.

'No fucker should be selling laundry detergent in our name. A few broken fingers. An arm. But not more.'

They looked at each other. Jochum nodded.

The lift music kept playing, a piano destroying an already tired pop song. He stood up, walked towards the car.

STOCKHOLM'S CENTRAL STATION was still yawning drowsily despite the fact that it was long past morning. Always somebody on their way, always somebody's temporary bedroom, always room for one more lonely soul. It had been raining since midnight, so the roofless had flocked to the enormous doors and found their way to benches in the middle of a hall the size of a football field. They changed positions regularly, before any security guards noticed and drove them away, hid themselves among stressed-out travellers, among those with a suitcase in one hand and a latte in the other.

Hilding Oldéus had just woken up. Two hours of sleep in the middle of the day. He looked around.

His body ached, the bench had been hard, and some fucking security guard kept poking at him all the time.

He hadn't eaten since one of the cops offered him a few crackers at his fake interrogation this morning.

But he wasn't hungry. He wasn't horny. He wasn't anything at all.

He laughed out loud, a couple of bitches stared at him, and he gave them the finger. He was nothing, and he needed more dope, because if he got more dope he could continue being nothing, continue turning off, continue not feeling.

He stood up. He smelt strongly of urine, his hair was straggling and uncombed, and the blood from the wound on his nose had just solidified again. He was skinny and dirty and twenty-eight years old, closer to the other side than ever before.

He walked slowly towards an escalator, held on tight to the

BOX 21

black rubber strip, stopped a few times when it swayed too much.

The storage lockers lay a bit further into the concrete hall, opposite the toilet where a man sat in the entrance charging you five kronor to take a piss. Might as well piss in the fucking subway passages instead.

You could always find Olsson near the boxes in the back, somewhere between number one hundred and twenty and one hundred and fifty. The fucker was asleep. One of his feet was bare, no shoe or sock, but the bastard had cash, so who the hell cares about a fucking shoe.

He was snoring. Hilding tugged at his arm, shook him as best he could.

'I want cash.'

Olsson looked at him, unsure if he was still sleeping.

'D'you hear me! I need cash. You should have paid up last week.'

'Tomorrow.'

They called him Olsson. Hilding knew he wasn't named Olsson, they'd been in treatment together in Skåne, and he still had no idea why they called him that.

'Olsson. A thousand kronor, for fuck's sake! Now! Or did you inject the dope yourself, you fucker!'

Olsson sat up now. He yawned, threw out his arms.

'Damn, Hilding, I don't have any money.'

Hilding Oldéus ripped at his sore. The fucker had no cash. Just like that bitch at social services. Just like his sister. He'd called her again, begged profusely just like he'd done from the subway platform a few days earlier, and she'd said the exact same thing, *It's your choice, your problem, don't make it mine.* He continued to dig at the wound, the scab fell away, and it started bleeding profusely.

'I need cash. Don't you get that?'

'Don't have any. But I have information that might be worth a grand.'

'What kind of fucking information?'

'Jochum Lang's looking for you.'

Hilding tore at the wound, he was panting, he tried not to show that he was gulping.

'I don't give a shit about that.'

'What does he want, Hilding?'

'We served time together. At Aspsås. Probably just wants to chat.'

Olsson tensed his cheek towards his eye again and again, like winking, just one of his junkie ticks.

'Worth a thousand?'

'I want my cash.'

'Don't have any.'

Olsson patted one pocket of his windbreaker.

'But I've got a little smack.'

He took out a plastic bag he'd hidden in the fabric, held it forward so that Hilding could see.

'A g. You can have it. A g then we're even.'

Hilding stopped tearing at the sore.

'A g?'

'Good shit.'

Hilding showed his hands, he waved them around, pushed Olsson lightly.

'Let's see then.'

'Horse. Strong stuff.'

'A fourth. I'll only take a fourth. Happy now?'

The train to Malmö and Copenhagen was delayed, the speaker on the ceiling shouted through the hall, fifteen more minutes, sit down on the benches and keep waiting. The café was

BOX 21

rumbling and bubbling not far away, the smell of freshly brewed coffee and pastries filled the hall. They didn't notice it. They didn't notice anything at all, not the big hall around them filled with hurrying commuters and backpackers with flags on their huge backpacks, not the families travelling at odd times on the cheap tickets that company representatives disdained. They didn't notice any of it. They walked jerkily over to a photo booth standing by a pillar near the entrance. Olsson stood guard outside, making sure no one tried to get in, and that Hilding didn't overdose. Hilding sat on the low chair. He was shaking.

He drew the curtains, his legs were visible, and Olsson moved over a little to obscure them.

The spoon was in the pocket of his raincoat.

He filled it with white heroin and a few drops of citric acid, held it over a lighter flame until the contents melted, mixed it with water and sucked up the liquid into the syringe.

He had lost a lot of weight, his belt loop was usually buckled on the third or fourth hole, but now he could pull it back to the seventh. He did, pulled hard until it was long enough to go another lap around the forearm, the leather cut deeply into the skin.

He bowed his head, held the belt fast and taut by biting it, slapped hard but still saw no veins in the crook of his arm. He kept searching with the needle, pressing it against the chewed up cartilage and into the large cavities formed in his arm where injection after injection over many years had eaten away a piece of his body.

He rooted around a few times, trying again and again, and suddenly felt the needle pierce its way through the wall of a vein.

He pulled hard and smiled, it wasn't usually this easy. Last time he'd been forced to inject it into his neck.

He saw a streak of blood floating in the clear liquid inside the plastic syringe. At first it held together, then it dissolved, like the petals of a red flower as it blooms, it was beautiful.

He lost consciousness after just a few seconds.

He lay face down over the photo booth chair, clearly visible under the drawn curtain. He had stopped breathing.

Wednesday, 5 June

SHE HAD JUST WOKEN UP.

Lydia tried to turn around, to her right side, trying to relieve the burning on her back a little. She was alone in a large room. She had been unconscious for half a day, at least according to the one nurse who spoke Russian.

Her left arm had been broken. She didn't remember it. She didn't know what he'd done to it. She must have already lost consciousness by that time. It was in a cast, it would be there for a few weeks.

He'd kicked her several times in the stomach. That she remembered. He had screamed that she was a *whore, that whores fuck like they're told to.* After he stopped kicking her, he'd forced himself into her anus, first with his cock, and then with his fingers.

She'd heard Alena trying to stop him, screaming and beating on his back, until he locked her into her room and told her to undress. It was her turn next.

Lydia remembered what happened up until the whip. Everything before that she remembered.

First he whipped her lightly across her butt, *I'm not going to destroy your arse, but your back doesn't do any fucking, does it, so there's not much to be afraid of there.*

She had counted to eleven. That was as much as she remembered. He'd kept going. The nurse had told her that. There were more than eleven. You could see the stripes clearly.

'Good morning.'

The nurse was dark-haired, named Irena, and from Poland,

you could hear it in her Russian. She'd lived in Sweden for almost twenty years. She was married and had three children. She liked it here, she said. She liked Sweden.

'Good morning.'

'Sleep well?'

'Sometimes.'

Irena washed her wounds, as she'd done the day before. First her face, then her back. Her legs were just bruised. Those would go away on their own.

She winced as hands touched her back.

'Does it sting?'

'Yes.'

'I'll be as careful as I can.'

There was a guard outside her room.

He was wearing a green uniform like the ones she'd seen on guards at the Scandinavian train stations they hurried through every time Dimitri got scared and forced her and Alena to hurriedly pack up and change cities. Five cities in three years. The apartments had all been alike, always the top floor, always red bedspreads, always electronic locks.

Her back burned as the sterile liquid poured into her open wounds. She didn't know why, but she thought of a funeral somewhere on the road between Klaipeda and Kaunas, where her grandparents lay, where her father also lay. She realised she no longer missed the man who'd looked so small in Lukiškės prison's corridor. He didn't exist any more. He had disappeared while she stood next to her mother, weeping in a cemetery. He hadn't existed for her since then.

Lydia moved restlessly, stifled a scream, her wounds burning again.

She stared straight ahead at the guard in green uniform. If she concentrated on him, maybe it would hurt less.

She didn't know why he was there. Didn't know if Dimitri

BOX 21

Pimp-Fucker was going to come back. Or maybe they thought she would run away.

Irena spoke to her while washing her back, asked her about the notebook lying on the bedside table, asked what she thought of the food. They both knew these were pointless questions, meant to get Lydia to relax, to think of something else for the moment and forget the pain coming from her destroyed back. She replied that it was just a notebook where she wrote down some of her thoughts about the future, that she thought the food didn't taste like much, it was hard to chew, and her cheeks ached.

'Oh, sweetie.'

Irena looked at her, shook her head.

'Sweetie, I can't understand what you've been through.'

Lydia didn't respond. She knew. She knew what she'd endured. Her body, the one she usually didn't feel, she knew what it looked like now. She knew what she'd written in the notebook lying on the table.

She knew that this would never happen again.

'We're done now. I'll do it again later today, this afternoon. It'll sting less every time. You are such a good patient.'

Irena squeezed her shoulder, smiled at her, and started to leave the room. At the door she met a doctor, who had four people with him, three men and a woman. He first spoke to the guard and then to the nurse. She turned around and went back into the room.

'Lydia.'

Irena was standing by her bed again, pointing to the doctor and the other four in white coats.

'This is the doctor. You've met him before. He examined you when you first came up here. He has four medical students with him who are training here at the hospital. The doctor wants to show you to them. Your wounds. Will you allow that?'

Lydia looked at their faces. She didn't recognise them. She felt too tired to be examined, people kept looking again and again. She was in pain. She didn't want them to see.

'They can look.'

Irena translated, the doctor waited, he looked at Lydia and nodded a thank you.

He asked Irena to stay, asked her to continue translating, to make sure that Lydia understood. He turned to the four medical students, talked about how it worked when a person came into Casualty, about Lydia's journey through the corridors of the hospital, from the ambulance to the surgical department. He then pulled a laser pointer out of his pocket, pointed at her bare back, the red dot crawling slowly across her wounds.

'Severe redness and swelling. Do you see?'

'She's received powerful lashes. A whip. Do you see?'

'We believe that it was a bullwhip. Three to four metres in length. Do you see?'

He turned to Lydia again, searching her eyes. Irena translated. Lydia nodded in confirmation. The four students were silent. They'd never seen the lashes of a whip on a person's back before. The doctor waited for them to absorb what he said, then continued.

'A bullwhip is a tool used to drive animals. She has received thirty-five lashes.'

He talked for a while longer, but Lydia couldn't listen any more.

Then they disappeared, she hardly noticed when.

She looked at her notebook.

She knew.

She knew what she'd endured.

She knew that it would never happen again.

ONE FLOOR BELOW.

There were three people lying there, in Ward Two of Söder Hospital's intensive care unit.

They didn't know anything about the woman one floor above with lashes on her back.

She knew nothing about them.

Lydia Grajauskas's floor was their ceiling, nothing more than that.

Lisa Öhrström had been standing in the middle of Ward Two looking at her three patients for a while. She was thirty-five years old and tired, after several years in the job she was exhausted, like the other doctors her age that she knew. They often talked about it. No matter how hard she worked it was never enough – it was that feeling more than the long days that she took home with her at night – never enough time to talk to someone, just rattling off a diagnosis and prescription and then hurrying to the next bed, the next room, forced to make crucial decisions, but never allowed to see them through.

She looked at all three again, one at a time.

The older man at the window was awake and sitting up in bed. He was in pain, clutching his stomach, searching for the call button on his rolling table, which also had his untouched food on it.

The younger man next to him, really more a boy than a man, eighteen or nineteen years old, had been in and out of the hospital for almost five years. His body had been strong, but suddenly he fell ill. He had refused to die, had wept and swore and clung to each slow breath. He had long ago lost his hair and his looks and most of his weight, but he lay there anyway, staring into the wall, making sure he'd woken up to one more morning.

The third one had just arrived.

Lisa Öhrström took a deep breath. He was probably the one who made her feel so tired, that made her stand in silence while patients buzzed furiously from the corridor.

He was in the furthest corner, next to the older man. He had come in the night before. It was so unfair – she probably had no right to think that way but she did anyway – he, and he alone of the three, would survive, would leave this building with a beating heart.

And he was the only one who had tried to make it stop. He took her time, her energy, and he didn't understand. It didn't matter that he'd just been more dead than alive. He didn't even understand that, or maybe he did. He would surely do it again and again and again, and she or one of her colleagues would stand there in the middle of the room, apathetic and furious again.

She hated him for it.

She went to his bed. She had to.

'You're awake again.'

'Fuck. What the hell happened?'

'You overdosed. We were barely able to save you this time.'

He tore away the bandage wrapped around his head – he'd fallen to the ground and smashed his face. He pulled at it with one hand and began to tear open the wound on his nose with the other, the sore he'd had for a long time, that she used to try to get him to stop picking at, back when she still cared about him. She looked through his file. She knew it all already.

BOX 21

Hilding Oldéus, twenty-eight years old. She counted the dates, she knew them by heart, this was the twelfth time he lay here, the twelfth time he occupied a bed here because of a heroin overdose. She'd been terrified and cried at the first five or six. Nowadays, she felt indifferent.

She had to save her energy, make sure she had enough for everyone. She couldn't help it.

She no longer cared much about his future.

'You were lucky. The person who called this in, a friend of yours I guess, gave you artificial respiration and a heart massage on site. At a photo booth at the Central Station apparently.'

'Olsson.'

'You wouldn't have made it otherwise. Not this time.'

He tore his sore. She was about to stop him, like she usually did, but she knew his hand would be back there immediately. He was welcome to tear up his entire face if that was what he wanted.

'I don't want to see you here again.'

'Sis, fucking hell.'

'Never again.'

Hilding tried to get up, but fell back immediately. He was dizzy, put his hand over his forehead.

'You see. This is what happens when you don't loan me any money. I take whatever I can get my hands on. Don't you see that?'

'Excuse me?'

'You can't trust any motherfuckers.'

Lisa Öhrström sighed.

'Hilding, it wasn't me who dissolved the heroin in citric acid. It wasn't me who drew it up into the syringe. It wasn't me who injected it. That was you, Hilding.'

'What the hell are you talking about?'

'I don't know. I really don't know what I'm talking about.'

She couldn't. Not today. He was alive. That was enough. She thought of how his addiction had slowly become her addiction. She'd held every syringe, lived in every treatment centre, every overdose had made her stop breathing. She'd been to Nar-Anon meetings, taken all those self-help courses. She'd learned what co-dependency was, and she finally understood why her own feelings had never been important to her for very long. She had barely existed, it was Hilding's abuse and only that, and that's what had ruled their family and that's what had ruled her.

She'd barely left his bed and gone out into the corridor before he started shouting for her. She decided not to turn back, to keep moving on to her patients, but he continued to yell, louder each time. She could only stand it for a minute, weeping with rage as she ran into the room again.

'What do you want?'

'Sis, fucking hell.'

'Tell me what you want!'

'Should I just lie here? I overdosed.'

Lisa Öhrström could feel the gaze of the old man and the boy who refused to die, they were looking at her, and she wanted to give them strength and courage, but couldn't, not right now.

'Sis, I need a sedative.'

'We are *not* going to give you any dope in here. Go ahead and take that up with the doctor who's responsible for you. He'll give you the same answer.'

'Diazepam.'

She swallowed, tears running down her cheeks – he always managed to get to her.

'We have put up with this shit for years. Mum and me and Ylva. We have lived with this fucking anxiety. So don't whine to me.'

Hilding didn't hear what she said. He didn't like it when her voice sounded like that.

BOX 21

'Or Rohypnol.'

'We've been happy every time you've gone to prison. Like now at Aspsås. Don't you get that? Then we at least knew where you were.'

'Valium?'

'Next time. Next time you'll do it for real. So when you decide to overdose, be sure to take enough to kill yourself.'

Lisa Öhrström leaned forward, clutching her stomach, she cried and turned away, he shouldn't see. She didn't say any more, just left his bed and walked over to the old man, the one pushing the call button, which sounded from the alarms in the hall. He sat up, holding a hand over his chest, he needed more painkillers – the cancer was having its way. She greeted him, took his hand, but turned immediately back to Hilding.

'By the way.'

Her brother didn't answer.

'You have a visitor. I promised to tell you as soon as you woke up.'

She went to the door, had to get out of this ward again, disappear into the blue-green corridor.

Hilding watched her go. He didn't understand. How could anyone know he was here?

He hardly knew that himself.

Jochum Lang left the car parked outside the entrance to Söder Hospital. In just a few hours he'd come to hate the smell of those black leather seats as much as the smell of his prison cell after two years and eleven months. Another smell, but it meant the same thing. Something had enclosed you, the smell of power and control. He'd been doing this so long that he'd finally realised there was no real difference between being locked up taking orders from a guard, or free and taking orders from Mio.

He passed by people standing outside hospital doors wishing for home, walked down a corridor full of people on their way somewhere else, stepped into a glistening lift with a recorded voice kindly telling you which floor you were on.

He has only himself to blame.
It's his own fault.

Jochum Lang had his mantra. The same process every time, how he'd always done it, and he knew it worked.

He has only himself to blame.

He knew where he was. Intensive care. Sixth floor. Ward Two.

He hurried inside. He had a mission, and he wanted to get it over with.

It was too quiet in the room. The old man opposite him and a guy that looked more dead than alive were both about to fall asleep. Hilding didn't like the silence. He'd never liked it. He looked around anxiously, glancing at the door, waiting.

Hilding saw him as soon as he opened the door. His clothes wet, it must be raining outside.

'Jochum?'

His heart started pounding. He tore deeply at his sore. He didn't want to feel the fear that was ripping him apart.

'What the hell are you doing here?'

Jochum Lang looked exactly the same as always. He was just as big, just as bald. Hilding could feel. He couldn't avoid it now. He didn't want to feel. He didn't want to. He wanted Valium. Or Rohypnol.

BOX 21

'Sit up.'

Jochum was impatient, his voice wasn't loud, but it was clear.

'Sit up.'

Jochum grabbed the wheelchair next to the old man's bed. He bent down, took off the brake, pushed it across the room, put it next to Hilding, and waited until Hilding was sitting on the edge of the mattress.

He pointed from the bed to the wheelchair.

'You're gonna sit here.'

'What do you want?'

'Not here. Out by the lifts.'

'What do you want?'

'Sit the fuck down.'

Jochum pointed at the wheelchair again, one hand near Hilding's face. *He has only himself to blame.* Hilding closed his eyes, his lean body was weak, just a few hours ago he'd fallen on his face in a photo booth. *It's his own fault.* He moved slowly from the edge of the bed to the wheelchair, stopped to tear at the wound on his nose, blood ran down his chin.

'I didn't say anything.'

Jochum stood behind him, pushed the chair through the room, past the old man and the young boy asleep in their beds.

'Jochum, dammit. I didn't say anything. You hear me? The fucking pigs asked about you when they interrogated me, but I didn't say anything.'

The hallway was empty. The blue-green floor, white walls, all of it was cold.

'I believe you. You're too much of a coward to talk.'

They met two nurses, both nodded towards the wheelchair, said hello. Hilding wept. He hadn't wept since he was a child, since the first time he took dope.

'But you're dealing dirty speed. To the wrong people.'

They left the ward and went out to the hall with the lifts. The corridor was wider, a different colour, grey floors and yellow walls. Hilding's body trembled, he didn't know fear could hurt this much.

'The wrong people?'

'Mirja?'

'Mirja? That fucking cow.'

'She's Mio's niece. And you were fucking stupid enough to sell her speed mixed with detergent.'

Hilding tried to force away the tears, he couldn't feel this. This wasn't happening to him.

'I don't understand.'

They stopped in front of the lifts, four of them, two on their way here.

'I don't understand!'

'You will understand. I'm gonna make you understand. We're just gonna have a little chat.'

'Jochum, dammit!'

The lift doors. If he stretched out his arms, he could reach them, grab them, hold on.

He just didn't know where all these fucking tears were coming from.

ALENA SLJUSAREVA RAN along the edge of the docks of Värta-hamnen. She stared down into the dark water. It was raining and had been raining all morning. Water that would have been blue in the sun was black now, the waves lashing against the concrete wall. It felt more like autumn than summer.

She was crying and had been crying for almost a day. First from fear, then anger, then longing, and now hopelessness.

She'd lived three years in one long day. She relived the years that had passed since she and Lydia had boarded a Lithuanian ferry. Two men had led them, had politely opened doors for them, had smiled and told them how beautiful they were, one Swede who spoke good Russian had given them fake passports, their keys to the a new life. Their cabin had been as big as a bedroom for four in Klaipeda. Alena had laughed so much, she'd been happy, they were on their way to another time.

She'd been a virgin.

The boat had just left the port.

She could still feel the blood running down the inside of her thighs.

Three years. Stockholm, Gothenburg, Oslo, Copenhagen, Stockholm again. Never fewer than twelve. Every day. She tried to see some of them in front of her, their faces, the men who lay on top of her, the men who just wanted to watch.

She couldn't remember a single one. They were nobody.

Like Lydia and her body, only in reverse. For Lydia, her body didn't exist. Alena had never understood it. She had a body. She knew that it was being violated. She counted how many times every night. She would lie naked and count, multiply twelve times a day for three years.

She had a body, no matter how hard they tried to take it from her. It was their faces that didn't exist, not for her.

She had tried to warn Lydia. Calm her. But it hadn't worked. It was as if she'd transformed as soon as Alena showed her that newspaper article. Her powerful reaction, her eyes filled with hatred, she'd seen Lydia angry and humiliated, but she'd never seen her so filled with hate. Alena regretted it now. She should have hidden it, thrown it away as she'd first planned to.

Lydia stood straight-backed in front of Dimitri. She said from now on she was keeping the money. She was the one they fucked, so she'd earned it. He'd struck her in the face first. She'd counted on that, it's what he usually did, but she didn't back down. She said she wouldn't accept any men for a few days, that no one would be allowed to lie on top of her, that she was tired, and she didn't want any more.

Lydia had never protested before. Not out loud, not to Dimitri, she'd been afraid of the blows and the pain and the gun he sometimes pointed at their heads.

Alena sat down on the edge of the dock, her legs dangling freely above the water. Three years. She missed Janoz so much, her longing tore at her again, why had she left, why hadn't she told him that she was leaving?

She'd been a child. Now she was someone else.

She had been ever since the Swedish man had grabbed her in that cabin, spat twice in her face and forced himself inside her body. And she became even more so every time someone took from her.

She stood in her room watching as he took up his whip and held it in front of Lydia's face, that's when Alena had rushed

BOX 21

out, threw herself at him. He'd never used his whip before, just showed it to them to scare them. Now he was going to use it, and she tried to take it from him, but he kicked her in the stomach and locked her in her room, said she was next.

She looked down into the water.

She was going to go back. To Klaipeda. To Janoz, if he was still there. But not yet. Not until she'd heard from Lydia. Not until then.

She counted the strokes. One at a time. The police arrived when Dimitri got to thirty-six. She'd heard it all through the closed door, first how he lifted the whip, then how he lashed it against Lydia's bare skin.

If she stretched her legs she could almost touch the dark water with her feet. She could jump in. She could stand up and board the ferry.

Not yet.

They'd seen each other being raped. She had to wait.

Someone unlocked her room, they were searching the apartment, and Dimitri lay on the floor in the hall holding his stomach. She'd stood there alone for a few seconds, then recognised the policeman, panicked and ran the few steps to the front door with a big hole in it. Then she stopped, turned around, kicked the prone Dimitri Pimp-Fucker in the scrotum as hard as she could with the heel of her shoe, then ran six floors down an empty stone staircase.

It was in the bag that hung from her shoulder. She heard it ringing.

She knew who it was.

'Yes?'

'Alena?'

'It's me.'

Lydia was in pain – Alena could hear it. It was difficult for her to speak, but it felt so good to hear her voice.

'Where are you?'

'At the harbour.'

'You're on your way home.'

'I was waiting for you. I knew you'd call. Later. Then I was going to go.'

She'd got the phone as a gift from one of the faces she didn't remember. Lydia usually took a hundred extra. Alena didn't want money, she wanted things, and got things for doing extra. She got clothes, two necklaces, earrings sometimes. Dimitri didn't have a clue. Not about the phone either. It was fairly new, the face she didn't remember got extra from both of them at the same time in exchange. It was Lydia's idea. She wanted them to have it just in case.

'What are you going to do?'

'When?'

'When you get home.'

'I don't know.'

'Do you miss it?'

Alena held her breath, she saw Klaipeda as it had been then, dark and messy. And not especially beautiful.

'Yes. I want to see them again. How they look. How we would have looked.'

She told Lydia about how she'd fled down the stairs without ever looking back, fled the apartment she hated and the building she hated, how she'd spent twenty-four hours walking the city, and now all she wanted was to sleep, just sleep for a moment. Lydia didn't say much. A little about the hospital that they'd both been in a couple of times before. A little about the

BOX 21

bed, the food, the nurse who was from Poland and spoke Russian.

Nothing about the lashes on her back.

'Alena?'

'Yes?'

'I want you to help me.'

Alena looked down at the surface of the water, which was still at the moment, and saw a blurred image of herself, of her legs dangling, and her hand holding the phone against her head.

'I'll help you. Whatever you want.'

Lydia breathed slowly into the phone. She was searching for the right words.

'Do you remember the basement storage room?'

Alena remembered. The hard floor, the solid darkness, the humid air. Dimitri had locked them in there for two days when someone was visiting. Someone who wanted to borrow their beds. He'd never said who it was.

'Yes. I do.'

'I want you to go there.'

On the surface of the water her image was disappearing, small waves from a passing motorboat.

'I'm being hunted. Maybe I'm wanted. I can't move freely.'

'I want you to do it.'

'Why?'

Lydia was silent.

'Why, Lydia?'

'Why? So this will never happen again. What happened will never happen again. That's why.'

Alena stood up. She walked along the dock, back and forth between two iron poles.

'What do you want me to do?'

'In the storage room there's a bucket with a towel in it. Under the towel there's a gun. A revolver. Next to the Semtex.'

'Semtex?'

'Plastic explosives. And some detonators. Together in a plastic bag.'

'How do you know that?'

'I saw it.'

'How do you know what Semtex is?'

'I just know.'

Alena Sljusareva listened. She listened, but she couldn't really understand. She shushed Lydia. When Lydia didn't stop talking she shushed her again, and more loudly. She hissed into the phone until Lydia stopped talking.

'I'm hanging up now. You can call back in two minutes. Two minutes is enough.'

One boat left at lunchtime. About two and a half hours. She could take it. She had the money. She had everything she needed in her bag. She wanted to go home. To what she called her home. She wanted to close her eyes and forget that those three years had passed. She was still beautiful, still happy, still seventeen years old, and had never left Klaipeda, never even seen Vilnius.

But that wasn't how things were. That was another time. She was someone else. The phone rang again.

'I'll help you.'

'Thank you. I love you, Alena.'

Alena continued pacing restlessly between the iron posts on the edge of the dock, back and forth while holding the phone up to her ear.

'Number forty-six. They're small numbers, pretty high up on the door. There's a small padlock, not fancy at all. The bucket is standing just inside the door, immediately to the right when you enter. The gun and ammunition are in a small bag. The explosives are right next to it. You take it with you and go to the Central Station. To our locker.'

'I was there yesterday.'

BOX 21

'Is it all there?'

Alena hesitated. A square box in a stone wall in one of the waiting rooms. Their whole lives were in there. In box 21.

'It's all there.'

'Then I want you to take our videotape with you from there.'

The cassette. Alena had almost forgotten it. The faceless man who always demanded to be filmed. Who had once asked her to make love to Lydia. She'd said no, but Lydia had caressed her cheek while he watched, said that they would touch each other and he could film it, if afterwards they were allowed to record something on his cassette.

'Now?'

'Yes. It's time. We're going to use it.'

'Are you sure?'

'Completely sure.'

Lydia cleared her throat, took a breath before she explained.

'I've been lying here going through everything. My arm aches, my back burns. It hurts too much to sleep. I've written it all down. Read it, crossed it out, written it again. Alena, yes, I'm completely sure. Someone has to know. This can never happen again.'

Alena stopped, looked at the big blue ferry waiting just a few hundred metres away. She wasn't going to make it. Not today. Tomorrow. It set sail at the same time tomorrow. She just needed to disappear for one more night, that wouldn't be a problem.

'And then?'

'Then you come here. To Söder Hospital. I'm being guarded, so we can't talk to each other. I'll be sitting in the common area watching TV. I won't be alone. There are usually a few other patients there. There's a toilet right next door. If I'm sitting on the sofa, I'll see you as you walk by. Go into the bathroom and put what you have in the trash, throw a few paper towels over it. Leave it in a plastic bag, because it could get wet. The gun, ammunition, explosive, videotape. And some twine. I want some twine too, can you get that?'

'So I should pass by you without even saying hello?'

'Yes.'

Alena Sljusareva turned around, her back to the water, and walked away. The wind was blowing a bit by the time she reached the road, the one that cut through the harbour area, passing by warehouses, leading towards the centre of the city.

———————

There were a lot of people on the streets, tourists shopping desperately because of the rain. She was grateful for that. The more people there were, the more there were to hide behind.

She took the subway, first to Stockholm Central Station and to their box there, took the videotape, stuffed it in her bag. She stood for a long time in front of the open door, staring into the darkness, two shelves full of their shared belongings. Their lives. The only life they recognised. All that was left of those three years.

She had only been here twice before, yesterday and when she got it the first time.

They'd changed trains, almost two years ago, Dimitri Pimp-Fucker had explained that in a couple of weeks they'd move from the apartment in Stockholm to another apartment in Copenhagen, not far from the harbour and the Ströget, mostly drunken Swedes who took the boat from Malmö, showed up smelling like Toblerone and beer and often paid for two goes in advance. They got drunk the first night and then came back and slapped them around or jerked off or fucked them the next day before going home.

She said she needed to go to the toilet, while they were waiting for the train to Copenhagen, that it was an emergency. Dimitri had been alone with both of them and warned her that

BOX 21

if she didn't come back with plenty of time to spare before their departure, he'd kill Lydia. She'd been sure he was serious, and she never intended to leave her friend, never ever.

She wanted a box, a home.

One of her regular customers, a man with a plumbing company in Strängnäs who drove over an hour from there to Stockholm and to her, told her about the boxes you could rent for two weeks at a time, intended for guests to the capital, but mostly used by the homeless.

Instead of going to the bathroom, she'd used her fifteen minutes to get one of them. She made it back, stressed but pleased, with a key in each of her shoes, in time for departure.

The loyal customer with the plumbing company had copied the keys and extended the rental each time it expired, it had been his way of paying her for doing extra. She'd always bled heavily afterwards, but it had been worth it.

She understood that now that she stood in front of the open door.

It had been worth every single blow to know there was a place that was only theirs, a place Dimitri Pimp-Fucker could never reach, no matter how much he threatened.

She knew she would never be back. She took everything that belonged to her – necklaces, earrings, dresses – she left Lydia's box and money. They both had a key, when she was healthy, she could go get it.

She locked it and walked away.

Subway again, green line. She stood up. She left the crowded car at St Eriksplan, walked up the stairs to the wet pavements, searching for the Vietnamese restaurant that was her landmark. She'd pass by that and make her way to a beautiful building with big stone angels anchoring its railings. She followed it down to Völunds Street.

She saw the police car as soon as she left the last stair. There were two men in it, both in uniform. She bent down, took off one shoe, pretended to empty it. She needed time and had to think fast.

She couldn't.

She watched two children, each with a bike as they went past the police car. They barely looked up.

She couldn't think.

What would be would be. It was always what would be would be.

She put on her shoe, walked calmly by as if she didn't care about the rain falling around her, straight to the door. She thought about the men who used to lie on top of her, their faces, she couldn't remember those faces, she thought of them and walked straight ahead, stared straight ahead.

They didn't move. They sat in the front seat and watched her pass. She walked to the door, waiting.

Nothing.

They just sat there. She counted to sixty. One minute. In one minute she would continue downstairs.

She had been prepared to hear footsteps behind her, a voice, an order to turn around and walk slowly back towards the car.

But nothing happened.

She shrugged off her close call and instead started walking down the stone stairs. Two floors. She wasn't particularly fast, didn't want to start panting, wanted to stay silent, thinking about the door on the sixth floor.

The gaping hole, a kind of freedom.

She closed her eyes, could still hear the blows of an axe as someone in uniform broke through wood, and Dimitri released Lydia's body to the floor and ran towards the man who was about to enter.

She stopped short, suppressing her panicked breaths.

For almost one of those three years she'd been waiting inside. She couldn't understand it.

BOX 21

She'd only been free for a day, and it was as if that were long enough to make one whole year feel foreign. She had never been there. If she decided that, then it was so, she had never been inside that apartment with its two large beds, had never stood in the hall staring at the electronic locks.

She continued down to the last landing, the basement. She turned around, glanced up in the direction of the door with the hole. She raised her middle finger in the air – to all the men who rang that bell.

The door to the basement was made of cold, grey steel. She wasn't strong, but she was still able to break it open with a crowbar. She'd done that once long ago in Klaipeda. She'd considered it a hellish night back then, but now when she thought back it seemed like a happy memory, from another time.

She lifted the bag off her shoulder, put it on the stone floor. Dresses, plastic boxes of necklaces and earrings, she put to the side and laid the videotape and the roll of twine next to it.

It was near the bottom of the bag. He'd laughed at the hardware store, *a crowbar and twine, is this for a burglary, you don't look like a burglar*. She'd laughed, too. *I live in an old house*, she'd said, *you know, I just need a strong man and some tools*. She'd looked at him like she'd looked at the men who lay on top of her, the way she knew they wanted her to look. He'd given her the roll of string free, and he'd wished her luck with the old house and with the strong man.

It was a light crowbar. The smallest one they had. She lifted it, shoved the two teeth into the lock and put her full weight behind it. She prised once, twice, three times. Nothing happened.

She was afraid somebody would hear and didn't dare to push any harder than that.

But she had no choice.

She aimed the iron teeth at the lock again, rocked them

lightly against the doorframe, testing it, then put her full weight behind, and with all her strength pushed forward.

There was a dull bang as the lock gave way, the sound bounced through the stairwell, anyone at home could have heard it.

She lay down on the floor. As if somehow that would make her harder to see. She waited. She counted to sixty, again.

Her wrist ached, she'd pressed harder than her body wanted to.

Then sixty, one more time.

It was still quiet. No apartment doors opened, no steps were on their way to check. She got up, gathered her things, put them back in the bag.

She pushed lightly on the door, and it opened wide.

A long corridor with white concrete walls pressing against her. At the far end was a new door. She knew that on the other side stood four aisles of basement storage rooms. That was where she was headed.

She squeezed the crowbar tight and was just about to use the same strength as before when she noticed that the door was unlocked.

Someone was inside. Someone had unlocked it, someone who would soon be coming back to lock it again, and leave here.

She opened the door.

It smelt stuffy, like basement storage and damp carpets.

It took a moment for her eyes to adjust to the darkness. There was another smell too.

Cologne. Sweat. Dimitri's smell. Or like some of the men used to smell. She stood still. Her chest ached. It was difficult to breathe, no air came in, no matter how hard she tried.

There was someone here.

Alena thought about the ferry she'd purchased a ticket to, the water she'd sat looking down into.

BOX 21

She could hear someone walking.

Someone's feet against the rough brick floor.

She started to weep. She wept and moved cautiously along the wall of the closest corridor, sat down next to a storage room that stuck out a little, closed her eyes again, she was going to keep them closed until this was over.

She had no idea how long she sat there. Someone walked around opening and closing doors, lifting heavy stuff up and put it down. The sounds cut their way into her until she couldn't hear them any more.

The silence afterwards was almost worse.

She was hyperventilating, crying, shaking. Until she finally let herself understand that she was alone.

She stood up, her legs weak, her head aching. She didn't turn on the light. She didn't need to see the number on the storage room.

She knew where it was.

She'd sat in the dank air of that room for two days and two nights.

The storage room was in one of the middle aisles. Wooden walls painted brown and a narrow opening at the top. Too narrow for her. Just for ventilation. The lock, she weighed it in her hand, was only a small simple padlock.

She took a deep breath.

She wedged the crowbar in between the golden rectangle and the metal arch. She stood close to the door, braced the tool against the wood that the padlock was hanging on, put her whole weight behind it, like she had before.

She looked in surprise at the lock ring and the padlock swaying freely in the air.

She went inside.

IT WAS STILL morning, Wednesday, 5 June, and the rain that had been falling since dawn was still dancing just as powerfully down the streets. The sky was so dark it could have been a sleepy evening in November. Ewert Grens opened the door to the civilian police car and sat down in the passenger seat. He wanted Sven to drive. He wanted that more and more often these days. He got tired of concentrating on the road, couldn't stand the lights, which made his eyes water. Suddenly he was old, and he hated it. Not his body's outer decay, that didn't matter to him any more – he'd given up on that years ago. There was nobody to look good for. It was the strength. He used to be able to do anything. He used to have an engine driving him, forcing him to chase away his restlessness. Fifty-four years old and alone. What good is your past to you then?

Sven was driving fast, on their way from the airport to central Stockholm. They were late, it had been a strange morning. What should have taken only a few minutes had turned into a few hours at Terminal Five. They'd wanted to make sure that a man sometimes known as Dimitri Pimp-Fucker boarded a blue and white plane to Vilnius. They wanted to see for themselves that he left, to be done with him after this afternoon's report.

Ewert stared at the two-lane road in front of him, didn't notice the irritation in Sven's voice.

'We're in a hurry.'

'What?'

'I need to drive faster. Any of our colleagues out there?'

'Not that I know of.'

BOX 21

The exit from the airport was nearly deserted. Sven drove at a much higher speed than was legal. He felt homesick, and he had decided he was going to make it home in time.

They had finished with Dimitri Pimp-Fucker just as they'd hoped.

He'd walked down the departures hall with two burly guards next to him and was preparing to enter his gate. Ewert and Sven had stood some distance away in front of the ticket counter. They'd watched the nervous movements of his head, his too-short steps that never seemed to carry him forward, to the annoyance of his escorts. He was searching for his boarding pass in every pocket of his jacket when a short, heavy man in his sixties wearing a suit had arrived and started screaming at him, slapping him on the cheek. For a few minutes the man attracted everyone's attention by screaming and waving his hands in the air, while Dimitri Pimp-Fucker slowly crouched down, almost to a squat. The older man had given him one more slap, then pushed him in the back in the direction of the metal detectors and the X-ray camera.

Ewert and Sven watched and waited. There were security guards there to intervene if necessary. The two of them were only there to satisfy themselves that they wouldn't ever need to see this man who abused young women again, nothing else.

The old man finally finished screaming, turned his back on Dimitri Pimp-Fucker, and then headed straight for Ewert and Sven. He hadn't hesitated and seemed to have always been aware that they were watching. He had approached with a surprisingly light step, a briefcase in one hand and an umbrella in the other. He stopped in front of them, took off his hat, shook both of their hands.

Now the car left the on-ramp, they were driving down the E4 on their way south to Stockholm. The rain made it hard to see, the windscreen wipers were at the highest setting, but Sven still refused to slow down.

Ewert sighed loudly and turned on the car radio.

He had forgotten the name of the elderly man with his hat in his hand as soon as he heard it. The man stood in front of them while frazzled travellers shoved and swore their way past him. He started to talk to them just as Dimitri Pimp-Fucker disappeared onto his plane. He had explained that he was the Lithuanian embassy security chief in Sweden, and that he wanted to buy them a drink. Ewert had declined, he was tired and thirsty and wouldn't have minded an early drink, but with Sven next to him there was no way. A cup of coffee then, the diplomat had insisted, a cup of coffee at the bar on the second floor where the escalator ended.

They had hesitated a moment too long, and he pointed to a table next to a glass wall overlooking the runway. He went to the counter and brought three cups of coffee and just as many pastries, served them, and then sat down on the vacant chair, facing them, waiting quietly and drinking from his cup.

He spoke good English with a strong accent. It was significantly better English than either Ewert's or Sven's. He'd asked their forgiveness for his behaviour, he was generally opposed to violence and shouting, but sometimes it was necessary. This had been one of those times.

Then he began a long, convoluted speech thanking them on behalf of the people of Lithuania.

He watched them for a long time before explaining how appalled he was by the revelations concerning his embassy coworker Dimitri Simait – apparently the pimp's name – and told them how embarrassing it was for his country as it slowly tried to recover from decades of oppression. He'd fished around for their consent to keep the whole thing quiet. They could see for

BOX 21

themselves that Dimitri Pimp-Fucker was leaving the country and let that be enough.

Ewert Grens and Sven Sundkvist had politely thanked him for the coffee and greasy pastries, got ready to get up and go, and tartly explained that an investigation couldn't be hushed up, not by them in any case, human trafficking rarely could.

The music on the car radio – Ewert had long since grown tired of it. To him it all sounded the same. He held one of his cassettes in his hand.

'Sven?'

'Yes?'

'You listening?'

'Yes.'

'Not much to it, is there?'

'I want to hear about the traffic, we're getting close to the city.'

'I'm gonna change it now. To this.'

Grens turned off the announcer talking about crashes on Radio Stockholm, put in one of his Siw Malmkvist mix tapes. Her voice – he closed his eyes and was able to think again.

The cheeks of the Lithuanian embassy official had turned red when they stood up from the table. He'd begged them to sit for a little longer, to at least hear him out. He'd sounded so tired when he said it. Ewert and Sven looked at each other and sat down again. Thin hair hung down on his forehead, he was sweating profusely, and it shone under the fluorescent light. He grabbed their hands, put his own chubby, sticky fingers on top of them and left them there.

Several hundred thousand young women, he said. All from Eastern Europe. Several hundred thousand lives! Involved in the illegal sex trade with the West. The number was rising as they sat here talking. Our girls. Our girls!

He had squeezed their hands, his voice desperate.

There is high unemployment, he continued. It's not difficult to persuade a girl. What do you think? They're young, they're looking for work, money, a future. These men are so skilled, these men who promise them the world. They promise and threaten and they sell them, and keep them in rooms with electronic locks, like those two girls on Völunds Street. That was their address, right? Once it's done, once the men who promise and threaten get their thousands, they disappear – no responsibility, no investment, no risk. Money. Take the money and run!

The embassy official suddenly lifted their hands. Ewert had stared angrily at Sven and thought about protesting, but decided to let it go – the little man had brought their hands to his cheeks, and kept them pressed there, hard.

Do you understand, he'd said, do you?

In my Lithuania it is a serious crime to deal in, say, narcotics. Lots of sentences, harsh sentences, long sentences. But to deal in young women is treated as completely harmless. In Lithuania a pimp is barely punished. No sentences, no punishment.

I see what's happening to our children. I weep for them. But I can't do anything. Do you really understand?

Now they were approaching the northern edge of the inner city.

Ewert slowly let go of the image of the desperate little man appealing to them for understanding with his hat and his brief-case. He focused instead on what was in front of him – long queues of rain-soaked cars. The red light swallowed ten vehicles at a time, a quick estimate, and he noted that at least one hundred cars were standing in front of them. So they would be waiting here for at least ten more minutes. Sven swore irritably, he didn't do that often, they were late, and were going to be even later.

BOX 21

Ewert leaned back in the passenger seat, turned up the volume, her voice

today's teardrops are tomorrow's rainbows
and tomorrow's rainbows we will share

drowned out Sven's profanity and those honking idiots. Ewert was resting, far far inside was a time that was long long ago, when everything was simple, a photo in black and white, when he had more life in him, ahead of him. He looked at the empty plastic envelope in his hand, 'För sent skall syndaren vakna', 1964, the original 'Today's Teardrops', at the picture of Siw he himself had taken at an outdoor concert, she was smiling straight into the camera. That night they'd said hello to each other, and she'd waved at him and left. He looked at the list of songs, each one his choice, recorded by him, written down.

He was listening to Siw, but couldn't stop thinking about the short diplomat and his despair. When the coffee ran out, Ewert and Sven had managed to loosen their hands from his. They'd thanked him for the chat and were about to leave the café when he shouted after them. He had begged them to stop, to wait for him.

He'd then walked between them down the stairs, telling them that he knew all about Lydia Grajauskas and her father. That he was at the airport not just to make sure that Dimitri Simait got onto the plane, but also out of respect and sorrow for Lydia, the story of her father was miserable and seemed never-ending.

He'd stayed silent until they reached the entrance hall, then told them about a man who'd been imprisoned and separated from his family because he refused to be a hypocrite and proudly displayed the Lithuanian flag, then after serving his sentence he'd been fired from the military, and a few years later sentenced to prison again for crimes against the state. He – along with three former colleagues who were still in the military at that point – was caught smuggling weapons to a foreign power.

The diplomat had suddenly ended this story by lamenting the young girl's tragic fate, shook their hands one last time, and walked off towards a line of suitcases near the check-in counters. He seemed to have done what he had come to do, told a story that affected him for some reason to two Swedish police officers, perhaps trying to lighten his own load by sharing it.

Ewert Grens looked away from the tape deck for a moment, and out along a line of cars that was still just as long. Sven was squirming restlessly in the driver's seat, tapping the accelerator now and then, revving the engine.

'Ewert, we're not going to make it.'

'Not now. I'm listening to Siw.'

'I promised. I promised this time, too.'

Sven Sundkvist was turning forty-one years old. He'd left Anita and Jonas sleeping this morning, they were supposed to celebrate his birthday today. He was supposed to be home for lunch at their townhouse in Gustavsberg. He'd taken the afternoon off. At least on his birthday he wanted to hold the woman he had loved since high school, on this day he wanted sit close to Jonas, squeeze his hand until he protested.

The child they'd waited almost fifteen years for.

They'd decided early on that they wanted to have a family together. They'd never succeeded. Anita had fallen pregnant three times, given birth to the first baby – stillborn in the seventh month. They'd induced labour in a hospital bed, straining and in pain, and she'd cried in his arms with their dead little girl next to them. Then two late miscarriages, little hearts that suddenly stopped beating.

He felt that longing again, for so many years it had muddied everything they did, stolen everything they had together, came

BOX 21

close to stifling their love. Until nearly eight years ago, they'd travelled to a town two hundred kilometres west of Phnom Penh. The official at the adoption agency had met them at the airport and guided them through a country they'd never been to before. He was there in a small crib at the local orphanage. He had arms and legs and hair, and even then his name was Jonas.

'I should be on the Värmdö bus by now.'

'You have time.'

'I should at least be at the bus stop at Slussen.'

'You'll soon be there.'

He'd promised. This time too.

He remembered a year ago today, turning forty. There was a heatwave, and he left his cake in the car. On that day a five-year-old girl's genitals had been ripped apart and her body dumped in a forest outside Strängnäs. He had been on his way home when that happened. Jonas had been waiting at the dinner table, and it had been difficult on the phone to explain that someone had cut up a child and that was why he couldn't come home yet.

He missed them terribly.

'I'm turning on the blue lights. I don't give a shit. I'm going home.'

Sven looked at Ewert, who shrugged. Sven put the plastic bubble on top of the car and waited for the sound to come. He broke away from the traffic jam, crossed two solid lines, zigzagging between cars trying to find an escape that didn't exist. A few minutes and they were past the jam, past three red lights, and on their way to the centre of the city.

The alarm sounded at that very moment.

They didn't hear it at first – the siren and Siw Malmkvist almost drowned it out.

A female doctor had found Hilding Oldéus.

Dead in a staircase, just outside the department where he was being treated for a drug overdose.

Oldéus had been severely disfigured, difficult to recognise. The doctor had told them in weak voice that he'd just had a visitor. She herself had let him in, and her description was why the call had gone to Grens and Sundkvist. A big man, shaved head, fake tan, a scar from mouth to temple.

Ewert stared straight ahead, it looked like he was smiling.

'One day, Sven. It took one day.'

Sven looked at him.

He thought about Anita and Jonas waiting for him at home, but said nothing. He changed lanes, drove towards Väster Bridge and Söder Hospital.

SHE SAT IN the very back of the bus. Virtually alone other than an elderly woman a few seats ahead of her and a woman with a stroller taking up most of the aisle. No one else. Alena Sljusareva had hoped there would be more. More people meant it was easier to disappear, but everyone got off two stops earlier, most wearing the same team's jersey on their way to some sporting event.

They left the ring road and drove past the Söder Hospital Casualty department, where she and Dimitri went a few years ago when a man who wanted extra went too far, did things she hadn't agreed to. There was a small hill up and then a semi-circular drive, the bus stop was just in front of the main entrance. She didn't even need to press, this was the last stop.

She looked around. If someone was watching her, they were so discreet she couldn't see them.

She raised the umbrella, making sure that it obscured her face. She left the pouring rain and entered the main entrance, searching walls covered with metal works of art, glancing at the hard benches where visitors sat drinking coffee out of paper cups, then glanced hastily down the corridors that led off the main room.

No one turned around. No one seemed to care about her. Everyone was busy trying to heal their own lives, their own bodies.

She took a few steps to the right, towards the newspaper kiosk and the flower shop. She bought a box of chocolates, a weekly newspaper and a bouquet wrapped in cellophane. She paid and made sure what she was carrying was visible. People would think she was on her way to visit a patient, just one of the many who had time for a visit over the lunch hour.

The lift to the surgical department was at the far end of the hall. The long hall led into what seemed like an infinite building. She passed by the recently admitted patients on their way to do tests, patients who were slowly fading away, and patients who didn't know where they were and never would. The halls connected from right and left, all were similar to the one she was walking down. She didn't like them.

The lift was open and waiting for her. The seventh storey, she wanted to go to the top. She was alone in the cramped space, and the person in the mirror looked twenty years old, in a too-big raincoat. All she wanted was to go home, just that, to go home.

A box of chocolates and a bouquet, she held on more tightly as the doors opened, like a shield in front of her. A doctor passed by her in a hurry, disappeared into a room with a closed door halfway down the hall. Two patients came from the opposite direction, wearing simple hospital clothing and plastic bracelets around their wrists. She glanced at them, wondering if they had been here a long time, if they would ever leave.

The TV room was on the left side. She could hear the loud sounds of a newscast as she approached, its serious-sounding transition music. She saw the guard standing next to the door. Green uniform, baton, a sheath for handcuffs, his arms crossed. His head was pointed at the sofa and the person sitting there. Two young boys, both in their own clothes, and a woman next to them. Her face was scratched up, one arm was in a cast, her eyes seemed elsewhere. She was staring straight ahead towards the man on TV, but she didn't seem to see him. Alena wanted to catch those eyes, if only for a moment, but she didn't move, staying completely still as if nothing else existed.

BOX 21

A few more steps and she passed by the guard and the three people in the sofa. In front of her the corridor ended with a disabled toilet. She opened the door, went inside and locked it behind her.

She was shaking. She dropped what she was carrying and leaned forward, both hands against the wall, supported by legs she wasn't quite in control of.

She saw that person in the mirror again. The one who wanted to go home.

Wanted to go home.

She put down the duffel bag that was hanging over her shoulder onto the toilet seat. The plastic bag inside it was tied up tight. She had tried to make it as small as possible. She took it out of the bag, weighed it in her hand for a few seconds, then put it in the rubbish bin under the sink. She turned on the tap, she should have done that from the beginning, she should have let the water run, she chided herself for her stupidity and flushed the toilet just to be safe, sounds that needed to be here so that no one would notice them. She was looking for paper towels in the almost empty container on the wall. She crumpled them up and put them in the rubbish on top of the almost invisible plastic bag.

———

Lydia was in pain.

Her body punished her for her every move, and she had just asked the Polish nurse for two more morphine pills to suppress the pain.

She was sitting on the sofa next to two boys, who'd been there since this the morning. She'd smiled at them, but hadn't spoken. She didn't even want to try. She didn't want to know anything about them. In front of her a newscast that she wasn't paying attention to played, on the other side of her stood the guard who was always watching her.

From the corner of her eye, she'd seen a woman walk past with a box of chocolates and a bouquet of flowers in her hands.

Since then she'd been having a hard time breathing.

She waited for the door to open again, for the sound of the woman's steps to reappear. She wanted to close her eyes, to lie down on her stomach on the sofa, to go to sleep and wake up when this was all over.

It didn't take long. Or if it did she didn't know. The woman opened the toilet door. Lydia heard it clearly.

She tuned out the sound coming from the TV, heard only the sounds in the hallway. The woman's steps were approaching, without turning her head she could sense her passing by, caught a glimpse of someone disappearing in the same direction she'd come from.

Lydia glanced at the man in the green uniform.

He noted the visitor who passed by, but nothing more than that, he didn't follow her. She ceased to exist for him the same moment she left the ward.

Lydia asked the two boys to stand up, she wanted to leave the sofa, walk past. She looked at the guard, nodded to him, pointed to her crotch and to the toilet. He nodded back, she could go, and he stayed where he was.

She locked the door. She sat down on the toilet seat lid. She took deep breaths.

It would never happen again.

She stood up, limping slightly, Dimitri Pimp-Fucker had kicked her hip hard. She turned on the tap, let it flow. She flushed the toilet twice. She walked over to the trash, used her good arm to push away the crumpled paper towels lying on top.

Lydia saw it. Just a normal grocery store plastic bag.

BOX 21

She picked it up, opened it. Everything was inside – the gun, explosives, videotape, roll of twine. She didn't know how, but Alena had done what she'd asked her to, gone to box 21 in the Central Station, visited 3 Völund Street, got past the guards who were presumably still there. She had even made it down to the basement and through two locked doors.

She'd done her part. Now it was Lydia's turn.

The clothes that almost all patients wore were white and the opposite of form-fitting. Lydia's dressing gown had been too big from the beginning, but she'd asked for an even bigger one. It now hung around her as if her body didn't exist. She took the white medical tape she had in one pocket, wound it around her chest twice to keep the gun in place, two more laps to keep the explosives on her left side, the videotape and the roll of twine she kept in the plastic bag and stuffed underneath her robe, she pulled up her underwear and adjusted it until the bag was sitting partially inside.

She looked in the mirror one last time.

Her face was battered. She gently put her fingers on several large bruises around both eyes. Her neck was in a brace. Her left arm hung stiffly, encased in plaster.

It would never happen again.

Lydia opened the bathroom door, limping slightly. A few steps into the corridor, the guard turned to her, she signed with her fingers that she wasn't going back to the sofa. She was going to her room and her bed again. He understood, nodded curtly. She walked slowly, used her fingers to communicate that she wanted him to accompany her into the room. He didn't understand, and threw out his arms. She showed him again. She pointed at him and at her room for him to go in there and help her. He raised his hand, he understood now – she didn't need to explain again. He mumbled an OK, she smiled a *thank you* and curtsied as deeply as she could, then entered before him.

She waited until she was sure that he was inside the room. When she heard him breathing behind her.

Then everything happened fast.

Still standing with her back to him, she pulled the gun out of the tape, turned around, showed the guard her weapon, and cocked it.

'On knee!'

She pointed the gun at the floor, her English was clumsy, her accent very thick.

'On knee! On knee!'

He stood in front of her. He hesitated. He saw a woman who just the day before had arrived at Casualty unconscious. She limped, one arm was in a cast, her face was bruised. She looked like a scared bird in those big clothes. But now she was pointing a gun at him.

Lydia saw his hesitation. She raised her arm and waited.

She had only been nine years old.

She remembered that she had thought about death before, but not in that way. She'd been alive for just nine measly years and a man in uniform, like the man in front of her now, put a gun to her head and screamed *zatknis zatknis* while his saliva hit her face. Her father had trembled and wept and screamed that if what they wanted was his submission, they could have it, if only they stopped pointing a gun at his daughter's head.

Now *she* was threatening someone with a gun. She was holding it against someone's head, just like someone had held it to hers. Lydia knew how it felt. She knew how fear started to break you down inside. A single tap of the finger, and your life was over in an instant. She knew he was thinking about how he would never smell, taste, see, hear, feel again. His life would end, but everything else around him would continue, only he would be gone.

She thought about Dimitri and his gun, which he'd pointed

BOX 21

at her head countless times. She thought about his smile, which had been just like the smile of the military policeman when she was nine years old. It was the same smile on the faces of all the men who lay on top of her, stole from her, penetrated her.

Lydia hated them.

She looked at the guard standing in front of her, holding the gun steady, and stared at him in silence.

He sank down to his knees.

He clasped his hands behind his neck.

Lydia pointed the gun again, gesturing to him to turn his back to her.

'Around! Around!'

He didn't hesitate any more. He turned around on his knees and faced the door. She turned her weapon, holding the handle against his neck, then hit him in the back of the head as hard as she could.

He lost consciousness before he hit the floor.

She picked up the plastic bag again, holding it in her hand now like a regular bag, and hurried across the room into the hallway and towards the lifts. It took a minute for it to arrive. A few people passed by, but they barely looked in her direction. They kept walking, preoccupied with their own journeys.

She entered the lift and pressed the button on the bottom of the row of lights.

She didn't think much as she stood there. She knew what she was going to do.

She rode the lift all the way down and when it stopped she stepped out and walked down the brightly lit corridor towards the morgue.

JOCHUM LANG WAS sitting on a bench in Söder Hospital's large waiting room when Alena Sljusareva passed by him. He didn't see her, because he didn't know who she was. She didn't see him, because she didn't know who he was.

He sat on the bench, trying to shake off his uneasiness.

It had been a long time since he'd beaten up someone he knew.

He has only himself to blame. It's his own fault.

He needed a few minutes, needed to sit for a while, gather his thoughts, figure out where this tension was coming from.

Hilding had held onto the lift doors desperately. He had wept and pleaded and called him by his first name.

Jochum knew that Hilding was a fucking drug addict. That he was a junkie. That he would be a junkie until his lean body couldn't take it any more. He needed his injections, and he'd fuck over anybody to get them. But there was no particular evil, no hatred, no bad intentions, just blood mixing with a chemical substance in order to turn off all the things he didn't want to feel.

Jochum sighed.

It hadn't been like this before. Back then it wouldn't have mattered that it was somebody he knew. If they wept and begged for their lives.

It never had before.

It's his own fault.

123

BOX 21

The entrance hall to a hospital was a strange place. Jochum looked around. People were in constant motion. Someone unlucky on his way in, someone relieved on her way out. Nobody laughed here. This was a place for something else. He'd never liked hospitals. He felt vulnerable here, without any power, naked and unable to control other people's lives.

He stood up, walked towards the doors, which opened automatically when he approached them. It was still raining, the concrete covered with puddles, water that had nowhere else to go.

Slobodan was still sitting in the car a few metres behind the bus stop, in a taxi zone, with two wheels up on the pavement. He didn't turn when Jochum opened the door to the passenger seat. Slobodan had seen him when he came outside.

'You took your fucking time.'

Slobodan stared straight ahead, turned the key, pushed on the pedal. Jochum grabbed his wrist.

'Don't drive.'

Slobodan switched off the engine, turned for the first time towards Jochum.

'What the fuck . . .'

'Five fingers. A kneecap. According to the rates.'

'That's what it costs to mix our dope with laundry detergent.'

Slobodan was acting like the little boss. He'd started to form some bad habits. Such as sighing loudly and raising his hands to show how fucking unimpressed he was.

'And?'

Jochum had run around with this little shit since before he'd even had a driving licence. He didn't like these little-boss tendencies and was maybe going to have to have a talk about this.

Then, he'd set things straight.

'He put up a hell of a fight, and I never got him into the lift, stopped outside. Suddenly, he got hold of one of the wheels and jerked a few times and disappeared down the stairs. Into the wall.'

Slobodan shrugged, turned the key again, stepped on the accelerator, put on the windscreen wipers. Jochum could feel the anger eat at him. He grabbed Slobodan's arm, forced it away from the steering wheel, then pulled out the key and put it in his pocket. He moved his hand to Slobodan's face, pressed his cheeks hard, turned his head until they were looking at each so Slobodan had to listen.

'Someone saw me.'

Sven Sundkvist drove straight up to Casualty at Söder Hospital. He usually did that, that's where most of their errands were. People recognised them around here, and they had plenty of space to park the car. They didn't say anything to each other. They'd been silent since they'd got the alarm, and Sven changed lanes and headed for the hospital, away from the birthday lunch he'd promised to be on time for. Ewert knew that was important to Sven, even if he didn't know why, he'd chosen to give up those kinds of things or they'd given up on him, so he had a hard time figuring out what to say, something comforting. He tried several variations in his head, but they all sounded as flat as he feared, what the hell did he know about how it felt to miss your wife and child?

Everything.

He knew everything about it.

They hurried up the loading dock and into Casualty, walked side by side to the lift, pushed the button for the intensive care unit on the sixth floor.

A female doctor was waiting for them when they exited the lift. Rather tall, young and good-looking. Ewert looked at her

BOX 21

slightly too long, holding her hand slightly too long when he shook it. She felt it, glanced at him, and he felt ashamed.

'I was the one who let in the visitor. But I never saw them leave together.'

The doctor who was named Lisa Öhrström pointed to the entrance to the stairs next to the lift. Oldéus was lying on the first landing, his face pressed against the concrete, blood had solidified at his mouth and had spread in a large red pool around his body.

He was finally still. No more tearing at the wound on his nose, no more avoiding your gaze, no more waving his arms around. He possessed a kind of peace that they'd never seen on him before, as if the terrible anxiety and fear had finally flowed out of his body, along with his blood. They took the twelve steps down to the landing. Ewert bent down on his knees and examined the dead man. He'd hoped to find something, anything, but knew he wasn't going to. If this was Lang, then there would have been gloves and caution and absolutely no evidence. They were waiting for Ludwig Errfors. Ewert had called him as soon as the alarm came in. He'd already decided. If this was Lang, they were going to do everything the right way. And Errfors was the best. He didn't make mistakes.

A few minutes passed. Ewert sat down on the steps, took his time looking at the dead man in front of him. He wondered if Hilding Oldéus had been the kind to think much about death. Had he known what he was rushing towards with the help of those drugs? Had he been afraid? Or maybe that was what he wanted. Fucking idiot. The kind of life he led, surely he knew things would end like this, just a corpse in the way on an ugly staircase, before he even hit thirty. Ewert sighed, snorted at the dead man who couldn't hear him. I'd like to know where they'll find me, he thought, then stood up and walked over to Hilding Oldéus again. I wonder if I'll be in the way. I wonder who'll snort at me. There's always some bastard who snorts.

Ludwig Errfors was a tall, dark man in his fifties. He was wearing civilian clothes – jeans and jacket – just like when they'd met with him before in his workroom at the Forensic Centre in Solna. He greeted them both, then pointed to the body that was Hilding Oldéus not that long ago.

'I'm in a bit of a hurry. Can we start right away?'

Ewert shrugged.

'We're here.'

Errfors got down on his knees and examined the body. He started to speak, his face still turned towards the floor.

'Who is this?'

'A petty thief. Heroin addict. Hilding Oldéus was his name.'

'In that case, what am I doing here?'

'We're searching for the butcher who killed him. Have been for a while. We need a proper post-mortem.'

Errfors pulled open the black bag he was carrying with him. He took out a pair of plastic gloves. He passed by them, waving his white hands in annoyance – he wanted Ewert to move up at least a step or two.

He searched for a pulse that was no longer there.

He listened to a heart that was no longer beating.

He shone a small flashlight in both eyes, measured the body temperature with a rectal thermometer, pressed both hands repeatedly on the belly.

He didn't take that long. Ten, maybe fifteen minutes. Only later would he open up the body, lift out the organs, and do the real work.

Sven Sundkvist had long since gone to the top of the stairs and was sitting with his face turned towards the never-ending

BOX 21

blue corridor that ran from the lifts into the intensive care unit. He remembered the last time he'd seen Errfors at work, Sven had left the room in tears, and it was just as difficult now. He couldn't handle death, not like this, not at all really. Errfors changed position. He looked up towards Ewert Grens, who was waiting on the lowest step, and Sven, who was waiting on the top. He turned to Ewert, almost whispered.

'He doesn't have the stomach for this. It was the same thing last time.'

Ewert turned around, looked at his younger colleague.

'Sven?'

'Yeah?'

'Our witnesses. I want you to take care of that now.'

'We only have Öhrström.'

'Good.'

'We've already talked to her.'

'Do it again.'

Sven Sundkvist cursed his own inability to face death, but was grateful that Ewert understood. He got up, left the stairs, walked towards the end of the corridor and opened the door to the ward that Hilding Oldéus left in fear not long ago.

Ludwig Errfors watched him disappear, then turned to the corpse that lay at his feet. A man had lost his life, transformed to nothing, now he was an object to make note of for the sake of protocol. He cleared his throat, he had a tape recorder in hand, brought it to his mouth.

'External examination of a dead male.'

One sentence at a time.

'Pupils dilated.'

Then a pause.

'Four fingers broken on right hand. Haematomas around fractures suggest they occurred prior to death.'

A few breaths.

'Left knee exhibits extensive damage with effusions that suggest it occurred prior to death.'

He was meticulous. Weighed each word. Ewert Grens had wanted an examination that was watertight, and he was going to get one.

'The abdomen presents multiple bruises and is distended and ripples on palpation. Suggests blood accumulation and probable intra-abdominal haemorrhaging.

'Injection marks of various ages, some of which are infected, the probable cause is drug abuse.

'Death thirty, no longer than forty minutes ago based on inspection and witness statements.'

He continued speaking into the tape recorder for another minute. He would open him up later, at the Forensic Centre, but knew what he was saying now wouldn't be much different from what he'd say then. He'd seen this kind of thing before.

———

Jochum took his hand off Slobodan's face. The red marks on his cheeks moved as he spoke.

'Are you sure? Somebody saw you?'

Slobodan ran his fingers over the red, hot skin on his cheeks. He sighed.

'That's not good. If there are witnesses we need to talk to them.'

'Not witnesses. Witness. Just one. A doctor.'

The endless rain made it hard to see through the windows, and their combined body heat and breath and aggressiveness fogged up the glass from the inside, destroying whatever visibility they might have had. Slobodan pointed to the glass surface and the bonnet of the car, and Jochum nodded and took out the key he'd snatched and put in his pocket, gave it to Slobodan to start the car and blow away some of the moisture running down.

BOX 21

'I can't go back. Not now. The doctor is still there. The cops are probably already there.'

Slobodan waited quietly while the water was slowly driven away from the windscreen. Let the bastard squirm a little. Power was going to be split between the two of them, and every time Slobodan took a little more, Jochum had to give up the same amount.

When the windscreen was half clear, he turned to Jochum.

'I'll take care of it.'

Jochum hated having to be grateful. But that's just how it was now.

'Lisa Öhrström. Probably thirty to thirty-five. One metre seventy-five. Slender, almost skinny. Dark medium-long hair. She has glasses in her breast pocket, small glasses with black frames.'

He'd spoken to her. He knew how she sounded.

'Some kind of northern accent. High voice. Bit of a lisp.'

Jochum Lang stayed where he was, stretched out his legs, turned off the fan. He looked in the rear-view mirror as Slobodan disappeared through the automatic doors into the entrance hall of the hospital.

SHE WAS SINGING. Just like she always sang when she was worried.

Lydia Grajauskas.
Lydia Grajauskas.
Lydia Grajauskas.

She did it quietly, almost murmuring, didn't want to risk being discovered.

She wondered how long it would take for the security guard she'd just beaten unconscious to wake up again. It had been a heavy blow to the back of his head, but he was a burly guy and could probably take quite a bit. Maybe he'd already raised the alarm.

Lydia left the lift and walked into the brightly lit hallway in the basement of Söder Hospital. She couldn't shake the feeling of holding a gun to somebody's head, pushing it hard against his temple while he hesitated. She was there again, still nine years old, her father on his knees and the military police bashing his head and screaming that smugglers were going to die.

She stopped and opened her notebook.

She had carefully studied the information brochure – which she'd borrowed from the Russian-speaking nurse – showing all of the hospital's various floors. Now she looked at it again, or at the shaky copy with Lithuanian text she attempted to make while lying in her hospital bed with a security guard right next door.

BOX 21

It matched. This was the way to the morgue.

Lydia started walking quickly, carrying her grocery sack in her unbroken right hand. She was going as fast as she could, but her hip ached. She was limping and frightened by the sound it made every time she stepped with her good leg. It seemed to echo along the corridor's walls, so she walked slowly, not wanting to be heard.

She knew exactly what she was going to do.

No Dimitri Pimp-Fucker would ever again tell her to undress or that some stranger had bought the right to touch her body.

The people she passed seemed not to see her. She felt their eyes, thought they saw who she really was, until she realised that she was invisible to them. She looked like any other patient in hospital clothes in a hospital corridor.

That was why she wasn't really prepared. She had started to relax a little. She shouldn't have lowered her guard. By the time she saw him, it was too late.

It was his way of moving, that's what she noticed first. He was tall, his stride long, his arms reaching everywhere. Then came his voice. He was walking beside someone, another man, talking loudly, and she heard his voice, high and nasal. She'd heard that voice up close.

He was one of the men who touched her. One of the men who liked to hit. Now he had a white lab coat on. They were going to pass each other in a few moments. He walked straight ahead, and she walked straight ahead, and the corridor that existed between them was straight and had no doors.

She tried to walk slowly, looking down, keeping one hand inside the huge hospital gown, on the gun that lay there.

She almost bumped into him as he passed. He smelt just like he had when he'd bought her. Only a moment, not more, then he was gone.

He hadn't seen her. The woman he'd paid to fuck every other

week for the last year usually wore a black dress and underwear that he picked out. She usually had her hair down, and her lips red. The woman he'd just walked past, he'd never seen her before – smashed-up face, arm in a cast, white slippers with the hospital logo on them. He didn't see her now either.

Afterwards, what she felt wasn't fear, or panic, but surprise that turned to anger. He walked around here just like everyone else, and nothing was visible on the outside.

One last stretch of hospital corridor.

Lydia stopped in front of the door she'd soon open.

She'd never been in a morgue before. She had an image of what it should look like from American movies she'd seen before she left Lithuania, but that was all she had, and it was the basis of her planning. She knew from the notebook sketch how big it was and how many rooms there were. Now she was going inside, and she had to stay calm if she was going to handle the living as well as the dead.

She hoped that there were people in there. Preferably more than one.

She opened the door. It was heavy, as if a current of air were pressing against it, even though the rooms lacked windows. She heard voices. Muffled ones in the next room. She stood still. There was life in there, and now it was up to her. She had the gun and the explosives that Alena had managed to pick up and deliver, and she'd taken down the guard and found her way to the morgue, and now, the voices. She was lucky – there were people in there.

Lydia took a deep breath.

She was going to follow through on what she'd decided.

She was going to make sure this would never happen again.

There were at least three different people speaking. She didn't understand what they were saying. A word here and there, but no context, her Swedish was non-existent, and she cursed that.

BOX 21

For a second time, she lifted the gun out of the tape, and carried the weapon in her good arm. She walked slowly through the first room, which was empty and oblong like a hallway in an apartment.

Lydia saw them now.

She stood in the dark, oblong room and watched them. They were preoccupied. Their attention was directed at something in front of them that she couldn't really see.

There were five of them, and she recognised them all. She'd seen them early this morning.

They had stood around her bed. One of them, a little older with grey hair and big glasses, was the doctor who examined her when she first entered that department, the doctor who came back just a few hours later to show her to his four medical students. He had pointed at her body, at the lashes on the back. He had talked about diameters and the healing process and bullwhips, while the four young people wondered silently how many different body defects they'd need to study in order to know how to treat them.

Now they were standing some distance away from her looking at a trolley. Lydia saw it now. The trolley was placed in the centre of the room under two bright lights that hung from the ceiling. There was a body on it. From her vantage point in the doorway, she guessed it was a dead man, his pale colour, his still chest. The grey-haired man with the big glasses pointed to the body. He used the same laser instrument he'd pointed at her and the four medical students were just as silent, just as grim in front of this dead man as they'd been when faced with a battered woman.

Lydia lingered in a dark part of the room. They didn't see her.

She was able to take eight steps closer before they discovered her. She was two, maybe three metres away from them.

They saw her, and yet didn't.

They recognised her as the woman with the lashes on her back, who lay with a sad absent smile in a bed covered by hospital sheets. She stood in front of them now, looking the same and yet somehow completely different. She wanted something. Her eyes demanded attention. She lifted a gun, aimed it at them, and took another step forward. The glow from the bright overhead light fell across her face, it was scratched up and bruised, but she didn't seem to be in pain. She was both intense and calm. The grey-haired doctor had just been interrupted, and he tried to start talking again about the corpse in front of them, but broke off before he could even finish that sentence.

The woman in front of him had cocked her gun.

She raised it a few centimetres more, pointing it at his face, at everyone's faces, moving from one person's eyes to another. She held it on each one long enough for them to feel that cramp in their stomachs, the same one she'd felt every time Dimitri Pimp-Fucker pointed death at her temple.

Nobody said anything. They were waiting for her to speak. Lydia motioned the gun towards the floor.

'On knee! On knee!'

They all got down on their knees, forming a ring on the floor around the trolley and what was once a person. She searched their eyes to see if they were afraid, but they wouldn't meet her gaze, not a single one of them. Two kept their eyes closed, one woman and one man, another just stared straight ahead, past her, through her. They weren't strong enough to look at her, not even the grey-haired one, not even him.

She was nine years old again. In that room again. The military police put the gun to her head and her father was forced to his knees. He was supposed to lie down on the floor with his hands tied behind his back, and she remembered how he fell forward, the thud of his face on the hard floor, a free fall and then blood flowing from both nostrils.

BOX 21

Now she stood here. And she was holding the gun. Lydia took one last step forward.

She stumbled, losing her balance. She knew she had to be careful. It wasn't just Dimitri's kicks that had left her limping, her sense of balance had been worse in the last two years. A john had wanted extra, doubling her fee, and she had said yes, had let him hit her across the left ear, the pain had been unbearable, and afterwards she'd permanently lost part of her hearing and something inside her ear that controlled balance had been injured. She never knew quite what, but apparently the hit was more than it could take.

Now she managed to catch herself mid-step. She stumbled, but didn't fall, regained her balance, and still aimed the gun at the five people crouching in front of her.

She was careful to keep her distance from them, a few metres, no more, no less. She checked to see if they all had their knees firmly on the floor, and when she was sure, she rapidly put her good hand under her hospital gown, took the plastic bag out of the waistband of her underpants, and dropped it at her feet. She put her foot into the plastic bag, rooted out the roll of twine and kicked it in the direction of the trolley.

She pointed to the female medical student, shouted at her. 'Lock! Lock!!'

She stared at the frightened woman who was trying to make herself as small as possible. They were quite similar, really. They both had semi-long strawberry-blonde hair. They were about the same height, the same age. Not long ago Lydia had been lying down, and the medical student had stood above her looking down at her face.

Lydia almost smiled.

Now the tables are turned, she thought.

Now she's down there. Now I'm standing here looking at her from above.

'Lock!'

The young woman stared straight forward. She could see that someone was holding a gun to her head. She could also see that whoever was holding the gun was shouting something. But she couldn't hear, didn't know what it meant. She couldn't think straight. Words didn't mean anything. Not now. Not with a gun to her head.

'Last time! Lock!'

The older grey-haired doctor understood what was happening. He turned carefully towards the female medical student, searched her eyes, spoke softly to her.

'She wants you to tie us up.'

The woman looked at him, but didn't move.

'She wants you to tie us up with the twine.'

His voice was calm. She seemed to listen and met his gaze, then looked in fear at Lydia.

'I don't think she'll shoot. Do you understand what I'm saying? If you tie us up she won't shoot.'

The woman nodded. Slowly she moved her chin up and down. She also nodded to Lydia, trying to show that she'd understood. She moved cautiously towards the roll of twine. She grabbed it and got up from her kneeling position, searched the trolley and the dead man. She found the knife that had just been used to cut open the dead man's belly. She lifted it, unwound some string, and cut. She then went to the older doctor, squatted behind him, brought his hands together, wrapped the twine around them.

'Hard! Very hard! You lock hard!'

Lydia took a step forward and waved the gun at the woman. Lydia stood there until she was sure the rope was tight, cutting deep into the man's skin.

'Lock!'

The woman moved on from the older doctor to each of her

BOX 21

fellow students, cut off pieces of twine and wrapped them around their wrists, and didn't stop tightening until the twine drew blood. When she was finished, and panting, she sought out Lydia's eyes, waiting for eye contact.

Lydia pointed with her weapon for the woman to turn around, get down on her knees with her back to her. She then walked forward, took the roll and cut off the last piece with the support of her plastered arm, tied the hands of the woman who'd tied up all the others.

It had taken six, maybe seven minutes. Lydia had been in this room a little longer than she'd intended. She'd never thought that there would be five. One, maybe two. Not five.

Someone must have found the guard by now. Someone knew she was gone. Someone had alerted the police.

She was in a hurry.

She quickly searched through five white medical coats. The outer pockets, the inner. Then their trousers. She put what she found in a pile on the floor. Some key rings, a couple of wallets, loose coins, IDs, plastic gloves, half-filled packages of throat lozenges. In the older grey-haired doctor's pocket, she also found a mobile phone. She examined it, tried it, saw it had plenty of battery life left.

Five people were on their knees before her, tied up, hiding from the gun she held in her hand. Beside them lay a half-open dead man on a trolley under bright light.

She had taken hostages.

And when you take hostages, you make demands.

SHE WEPT.

It had been a long time since he'd managed to make her do that. She hated him for it. Lisa Öhrström hated her brother.

That damn call from the subway platform a few days earlier, she replayed it inside her head, him begging for more money like he always did and her saying no, just like she'd learned to do at her Nar-Anon meetings.

Tears and a lump in her throat, her body shook. She'd picked him up so many times when he was lying somewhere, and every time he promised it was the last. He would look at her as only he could, and slowly he'd sapped her energy and her worry and without knowing it, he'd taken years of her life away.

Now he lay there.

In a staircase just a few metres from where she worked.

Now was really the last time, and for a moment she almost felt relieved, until she realised he no longer existed, until she knew that was the only thing she couldn't stand.

INTERVIEW LEADER SVEN SUNDKVIST (IL): I know Hilding Oldéus was more than just a patient. But I still need you to answer my questions.

LISA ÖHRSTRÖM (LÖ): I was just about to call my sister.

IL: I understand that this is difficult. But you were the only one who was here. You're our only witness.

LÖ: I need to talk to my nieces and nephews. They idolised their uncle. He was always newly released when he was with

BOX 21

them. Always whole and clean. Colour on his cheeks. They've never seen the man who's lying down there.

IL: I need to know how close the other person was. The visitor.

LÖ: I was going to call right now. Aren't you listening? I'm trying to explain it to you!

IL: How close?

They were sitting on hard wooden chairs behind the glass walls of the nurses' station, in the middle of Söder Hospital's sixth-floor corridor.

Lisa Öhrström continued to cry, her dignity deserting her. She was trying hard to hang on, but could feel her fingers slipping as she tried to maintain some grip on life.

This was her brother.

But she just couldn't take it any more.

She refused to help him those last times, and all the tears in the world couldn't make up for that.

Sven Sundkvist observed her in silence. Her white lab coat had started to wrinkle. He waited while she closed her eyes and blew her nose and ran her hands through her long hair. He'd met her before. Well not her, but her type. He had interrogated women like her so many times before. Women who stood in the background supporting others, who felt constantly guilty and singled out. He usually thought of them as guilt addicts, and they had a tendency to create problems for him. Their ability to blame themselves for everything made it difficult for even the most experienced interrogators. They behaved as if they were guilty of everything, and no matter what he said they took it as an indictment. Their whole lives were just one long accusation, and they somehow managed to stand in the way of an investigation without being the least bit guilty.

LÖ: Was it?

IL: What?

LÖ: My fault?

IL: I understand that you might have feelings of guilt. But that's just a feeling – there's nothing I can do about that.

Lisa Öhrström looked at him, at the police officer in front of her, sitting with his legs crossed, wanting something from her. She didn't like him.

He was softer than the older one, but she still didn't like him. There was something authoritarian about officers, and this didn't feel like just an interrogation, it felt like a confrontation, like the beginning of a quarrel she was too tired to have.

IL: The man who was here. The one who probably killed your brother. How close were you standing to him?

LÖ: As close as you are to me now.

IL: Close enough for you to see him clearly?

LÖ: So close that I could feel his breath.

She turned and peered out through the glass wall. She didn't like sitting here. People walking by could see in, and their curious gazes invaded her privacy. She found it hard to concentrate and asked to move her chair so her back was to the window.

IL: Could you give me a physical description?

LÖ: He was the kind of man you fear.

IL: How tall?

LÖ: Much taller than me. And I'm quite tall, one seventy-five. As tall as your colleague. Maybe ten centimetres taller.

Lisa Öhrström nodded towards the end of the corridor, towards the stairwell where Ewert Grens was standing with

141

BOX 21

Ludwig Errfors next to a dead man's body. Sven turned instinctively in the same direction, measuring Ewert from memory.

IL: His face?
LÖ: Powerful as well. Strong nose, chin, forehead.
IL: His hair?
LÖ: He didn't have any.

There was a knock on the door. Lisa Öhrström was sitting with her back to it, so she hadn't noticed someone approaching and the knock startled her. A police officer in uniform opened the door and stepped inside. He handed Sven an envelope then left again.

IL: I have a few pictures here. Various individuals. I want you to take a look at them.

She stood up. No more. Not now. She didn't care about the brown envelope lying on the table.

IL: Sit down.
LÖ: I have to work.
IL: Lisa, look at me. It wasn't your fault.

Sven Sundkvist took a step forward, held the woman who was carrying grief and guilt on her shoulders, gently pushed her down in the chair again. He pushed aside two binders of medical records, making the empty space on the table bigger, then opened the brown envelope and poured out the contents.

IL: I want you to try to identify the visitor. The man who got close enough you could feel his breath.

LÖ: It seems like you know who I'm describing.

IL: Please look at the pictures.

She held up the photographs one at a time. She looked at them and took plenty of time. She put them one by one in a pile face down. She'd gone through over thirty pictures of men standing against white walls when she felt a pull in her chest, as if she were a child again and afraid of the dark, she'd described it back then as a dance inside her body, as if the fear were light and lifting her.

LÖ: It was him.

IL: Are you sure?

LÖ: Completely sure.

IL: For the record, the witness is pointing to the man in photograph number thirty-two.

Sven Sundkvist was unsure of what he felt. He knew how grief eats at people, and the woman in front of him was suffocating from it, and yet he forced her to swallow and keep it together. He understood that she could break down at any moment, and it was his duty to ignore that.

And now.

Now she'd pointed out the person they'd wanted her to.

He hoped that she was strong.

IL: You have identified a man who is considered very dangerous. We know from experience that a person who identifies him is always subject to threats.

LÖ: What does that mean?

IL: That we are going to assign you a police detail.

She didn't want to hear that. She'd wanted everything to be over. She wanted to go home, go to bed, wait for the alarm

BOX 21

clock, wake up to it ringing, eat breakfast, get dressed, go to Söder Hospital.

But that wasn't how things were. That's never how they were. The past wasn't over, no matter how much she wanted it to be.

She sat on the hard chair and tried to cry, to squeeze out what was eating her from inside. But it was impossible. She no longer had them in her, those awful sobs. Sometimes you just don't.

She was just about to get up and go somewhere else, anywhere else, when the door to the nurses' station opened again.

Someone stepped inside without knocking.

It was the older policeman, the one who'd held her hand too long. Now his face was red, his voice loud.

'Dammit, Sven!'

Sven Sundkvist rarely got annoyed with his boss. Unlike everyone else. Most of their colleagues disliked Grens, some even hated him. But Sven had decided to accept Grens, to take the bad with the good. He could either put up with it or avoid it altogether, and he'd decided to do the former.

With one exception.

'For the record. Detective Superintendent Ewert Grens has interrupted my questioning of the witness Lisa Öhrström.'

'Sorry, Sven. But this is an emergency.'

Sven leaned over the tape recorder, switched it off. He gestured to Ewert to speak.

'The woman we found unconscious in the apartment in the Atlas neighbourhood.'

'The one who'd been whipped?'

'She's disappeared.'

'Disappeared?'

Ewert nodded.

'She was a patient here at the hospital, in one of the critical care units. Until just now. I got a call from command central.

144

She's not there any more. And she's armed. She knocked out the guard we placed on her room. She's probably still in the building, with a gun.'

'Why would she do that?'

'I've told you everything I know.'

Lisa Öhrström laid photograph number thirty-two back down on the table. She then looked at the two police officers, one at a time, pointed to the ceiling of the glass box.

'Up there.'

'What?'

'That's where the critical care unit is.'

Grens looked up at the white ceiling and was about to leave the room when Sven took him by the arm.

'Ewert, wait. We have just received one hundred per cent identification of Jochum Lang.'

The burly, clumsy man paused in the doorway. He turned, nodded towards Lisa Öhrström, smiled at Sven.

'Now, Anni.'

'What did you say?'

'Nothing.'

Sven looked at Ewert without understanding, then turned to Lisa Öhrström, put his hand lightly on the doctor's shoulder.

'She's going to need protection.'

It was just after lunch on Wednesday, 5 June.

Ewert Grens and Sven Sundkvist hurried up one of Söder Hospital's many stairwells, from the sixth floor to the seventh.

This had been a very strange morning.

ALL FIVE OF THEM had been squirming for the last few minutes – gently twisting a leg, slowly tilting a head towards one shoulder. As if their bodies ached there on the floor, as if they didn't dare to remind her of their existence, and for that very reason couldn't keep still.

Lydia could feel their anxiety and let them be. She knew how hard it was to breathe when you were looking up at someone who'd taken away your right to your own body. She remembered the *Stena Baltica* and how a death threat silences any obvious cry for help.

Suddenly one of them fell forward.

One of the young men lost his balance and fell out of the ring of people kneeling around a trolley bearing a dead man.

Lydia quickly pointed her gun at him.

He was bent forward, his knees still on the floor, his face just above, his hands tied tightly behind his back. His body trembled, he couldn't stay upright. He was weeping from fear. He'd never thought about dying before, his life moved forward, he was young, and the future felt like for ever. Now he realised it could stop at this moment. He was only twenty-three years old – his body shook – he wanted to live so much longer.

'On knee!'

Lydia walked over to him, pressed the gun against his neck. 'On knee!'

He slowly raised his upper body, sat up straight again. He couldn't stop shaking, tears ran down his cheeks.

'Name.'

He looked at her in silence.

'Name!'

It was difficult for him to speak. The words wouldn't come.

'Johan.'

'Name!'

'Johan Larsen.'

She leaned towards him, pressing the gun hard against his forehead. Just like the men on the *Stena Baltica*. She held it there while she was talking.

'You on knee! If again. Boom!'

He sat up straight. He wasn't breathing. He was incapable of making his body quit shaking, not even when urine ran down his leg. He'd wet his trousers and didn't even realise it.

Lydia looked at them one at a time. They still weren't able to meet her eyes, didn't dare. She lifted the grocery bag from the floor, took out the plastic explosives and detonators. She walked over to a small table made of stainless steel that stood next to the trolley, put the mass on it, worked it by hand, making it sufficiently soft and pliable, easy to fasten around the door she'd just sneaked through. She held the gun in her healthy hand while pressing with it at the same time, kneading half of the dough onto the doorframe in a thin straight, unbroken line. She then put the remaining half of the plastic explosives onto the five people down on their knees in front of her. They sat in a circle around a naked, newly autopsied man, and they had death draped around their shoulders, a pale beige membrane of dough around their necks.

She had been in there for almost twenty minutes. It had taken her another ten to move from the surgical department on the seventh floor down to the morgue in the far end of the basement.

She knew her escape would have long ago been discovered. She realised that the police had been alerted and were searching for her.

BOX 21

Lydia walked over to the female medical student, the one who looked like her with the strawberry-blonde hair and a thin body, the one who had bound the others' hands.

'Police!'

Lydia showed her the phone she'd taken out of a coat pocket, held it in front of the woman's face. She then put her hand on the plastic explosives that lay on the medical students' shoulders, wanting to remind the woman to obey before gently loosening the rope around her wrists.

'Police! Call police!'

The medical student hesitated. She was afraid to misunderstand. She looked around anxiously, searching for the eyes of the older, grey-haired doctor.

He did as before, talked to her, managed to keep his voice calm, hiding his anxiety.

'She wants you to call the police.'

The medical student understood and nodded in confirmation. The older doctor forced his voice to remain steady for a few more sentences.

'Do it. Do what she wants.'

Her hand trembled, and she dropped the phone on the floor, picked it up again, pushed the first digit of the emergency number wrong, glanced at Lydia and apologised, then pushed the right one. Lydia heard the dial tone, which satisfied her, then showed the medical student how she should lie down on her stomach. She took the phone from her, took it over to the older doctor, and pressed it against his ear.

'Talk!'

The older doctor nodded. He waited. His forehead glistened with sweat.

The room was completely silent. One minute.

Then a voice answered.

He spoke with his mouth close to the microphone.

'Please connect me to the police.'

He sat quietly, waiting. Lydia was next to him holding the phone. The others closed their eyes or stared down at the floor in front of them, away, far away.

A new voice.

The grey-haired doctor spoke again.

'My name is Gustaf Ejder. I am a chief physician at Söder Hospital. I'm currently in the hospital's morgue in the basement. I, along with four others, have been taken hostage by a young woman in patient's clothing. She's armed, and she has pointed her gun at our heads and cocked it. She has also placed what I think might be some kind of explosive on our bodies.'

Johan Larsen, who just moments earlier had been unable to sit upright, who had fallen prostrate on the floor while his body shook, yelled towards the phone now.

'Semtex plastic explosives! That's what it's called. She's used half a kilo. There'll be a huge fucking explosion if she detonates it!'

Lydia pointed the gun at the screaming man, then relaxed.

She'd heard the word Semtex and his voice had sounded wild, the message had been conveyed, the ones who were listening would understand.

She took up the pages she'd torn from her notebook again. She held the phone to the older doctor's ear and put the papers in front of him on the floor, the top sheet was empty except for a single line. She indicated that she wanted him to continue talking.

He did.

'Are you there?'

The voice confirmed that it was.

'The woman wants me to read a name off a piece of paper, probably torn from a notebook. It reads *Bengt Nordwall*. Only that.'

BOX 21

The voice on the phone asked him to repeat that.

'*Bengt Nordwall.* Nothing else. What she's written is difficult to decipher, but I'm sure I'm reading it correctly. The English she uses is also very difficult to understand. I would guess she's Russian. Or maybe from the Baltic region.'

Lydia took the mobile phone from his ear. She gestured that she wanted him to sit upright again.

She'd heard him pronounce the name she wrote. She'd also heard him say Baltic.

She was pleased.

BENGT NORDWALL STARED up at the sky. It was unrelentingly grey. Rain had followed their every step this summer. He sighed aloud. It was time for him to gather his strength, try to relax for a while, so that he'd be able to handle what was coming later. It was going to be one of those autumns again, where people went into hiding in mid-October, weary of everything but themselves.

It was quiet. Nothing but the raindrops pattering against the fabric of the parasol.

Lena was sitting next to him reading a book, just like always. He wondered if she remembered the stories she read beyond the next day and the next book, but it was her way of escaping. She curled up in a chair with her legs under her and a pillow behind her back and forgot about what was around her.

He'd been sitting here the other morning too, two days ago, in the same persistent rain. Ewert had been beside him on the garden sofa, their clothes getting soaked by the rain, but their conversation had been more important than the wet. They had a closeness sometimes, one that only comes from the passage of time.

He hadn't expected to see him the next day, there outside the Baltic whores' apartment.

Bengt could see her in front of him.

The skin on her back torn apart by the lashes. He felt uneasy, not her, not the whip again, not now.

Their garden wasn't big, but he was proud of it. The kind a kid could run around in. He'd worked part-time for the last

BOX 21

two years, and would never have young people growing up around him again. This was his only chance, and he was going to take as much he could from it. They were bigger now, could do pretty well on their own most of the time, but he wanted to be here anyway. He watched them and took part in their games vicariously. This summer they'd finally grown tired of being outdoors. The rain-soaked lawn was empty, no footballs in the flowerbeds, none hiding in the lilac hedge, and nobody playing hide and seek with their eyes closed counting to a hundred. Now they sat in their rooms, in front of their computers in electronic worlds he didn't understand.

Bengt looked at Lena again. He smiled. She was so beautiful. The long blonde hair, the calm in her face, a stillness he'd never had. He thought of Vilnius and the Swedish embassy, where he'd worked as a security officer for a few years. One day she was just sitting there, a young, curious civil servant. He didn't understand why she'd chosen him. Which was exactly what she'd done, *chosen* him, and somehow he, who had already been discarded once, had been lifted back into the realms of the eligible people who married and settled down.

A washed-up cop, twenty years older than she was.

He was still terrified that she'd wake up one morning, look into his eyes, and realise she'd made a mistake.

'Lena.'

She didn't hear him. He leaned forward and kissed her lightly on the cheek.

'Lena?'

'Yes?'

'Shall we go in?'

She shook her head.

'Not yet. Soon. Three more pages.'

He didn't think the rain could get worse, but somehow it had, and it seemed like it might soak right through the fabric above their heads. The lawn around them was slowly becoming a swamp.

Bengt looked at his wife. She was holding the book in both her hands, her face hidden behind a chapter that had three pages left.

Suddenly the other woman demanded his attention again.

Lena sat in front of him, but he didn't see her, he saw that whipped back – stiff blood and oozing skin. He tried to push it away but the image of that fucking whore took up space. He closed his eyes, and she became even clearer, the stretcher they carried her out on when she was unconscious. He opened his eyes, there she was, silent, on her way past the broken-down door, and he was overcome by discomfort that was turning into fear. He tried his best not to feel.

'What is it?'

Lena put the book on the armrest and looked at him. He was quiet at first, then shrugged his shoulders.

'Nothing.'

'I can see it is something. What are you thinking about?'

He shrugged again as casually he could.

'Nothing.'

She knew him too well. She knew it was anything but nothing.

'It's been a long time since I've see you look like that. Afraid.'

One riven by deep lashes, the other screaming, both of their bodies young and shattered. The images haunted him. Maybe he should tell her. Lena had a right to know. He hadn't been prepared to meet them.

'Your phone is ringing.'

He looked at her, at her finger pointing to his jacket pocket. He rooted around in the fabric.

It was stressful. The phone would ring four times, then it wouldn't ring any more.

BOX 21

'This is Nordwall.'

Bengt Nordwall held the phone tight against his ear as he listened. A few minutes and the call was over. He looked at his wife.

'Something's happened. They need an interpreter. I have to go.'

'Where?'

'Söder Hospital.'

He kissed Lena on the cheek, bowed his head as he stepped out from under the parasol and into the rain that was pouring down.

Söder Hospital. The whore. The morgue. He felt it again – fear.

THE GUARD IN the green uniform was sitting on the room's only bed, a bandage wrapped around the top of his head. He'd been bleeding heavily – the white fabric had turned bright red. A nurse with a Polish name sewn onto her breast pocket stood beside him, two brown tablets in one hand that Grens assumed were painkillers.

He didn't have much to tell.

She'd been watching television in the common room. Two boys who were housed in room four were also sitting there. The lunch-hour newscast was playing, he couldn't recall which channel. She had wanted to go to the bathroom. He'd seen no reason to deny her. She was thin and weak, one arm in a cast, an injured hip that made her limp – he'd concluded she was harmless. Besides, was he really supposed to follow her into the toilet?

Ewert Grens smiled. Of course you should. You were supposed to guard her. When she slept, when she took a shit.

The guard was in pain. He put his head in his hands. His neck had received a powerful blow. She'd flushed the toilet, he'd heard it twice. Twice she'd flushed water through the toilet. She came out and signed to him that she wanted to go back to her room and her bed. She wanted him to follow her. He hadn't seen anything strange about that. He had followed her into room twelve, into the room they were sitting in now. He had, as usual, closed the door behind him.

That was when she suddenly had a gun in her hand. He had no idea how. All he knew was that she had known how to turn

BOX 21

the safety off, and she'd pointed it at his head, and that after a moment he realised that she was serious.

————————

The room was basic and bare.

The guard had left with a sigh, holding his neck. Grens was still sitting in the visitor's chair, looking around.

A metal bed. A bedside table next to it. Near the window, a small table and the chair he was sitting on. Only that. As big as a living room, designed for four patients, but cleared out and adapted for the needs of a severely beaten woman.

He sat in silence, his thoughts bouncing off the bare white walls.

He waited, preparing himself. He needed strength, more than he'd realised when he first got the alarm on his way back from the airport. What started out as the murder of a junkie and the chance to finally make something stick to the man who'd taken his life with Anni away, had suddenly turned into a hostage situation with enough Semtex to blow a large portion of a densely populated building to kingdom come.

Ewert Grens was a detective superintendent. He investigated murders after they'd been committed, and he did it better than anyone else. But it had been a long time since he'd been part of a big operation from the moment it started, mobilising in the midst of chaos. So here he stood with a fresh lead on Lang just one floor below the room where a prostitute knocked down a guard and escaped, and only seven floors above the morgue where she'd taken five people hostage and hung a strip of death around their necks.

So he had a patrol car pick up the police uniform he had hanging in a closet in his office at Kronoberg.

He would soon be appointed head of operations. These were both his tragedies now.

————————

156

Slobodan turned and looked back towards the car and Jochum Lang, before going through the doors to Söder Hospital. He could see the top of Lang's shaved, tanned head and his wide neck through the rain-soaked windows. He really was kind of fond of that fucking bald head. Lang had been like a big brother to him. The kind you looked up to, but were a little scared of. But this was about respect. Slobodan was thirty-five now, and he had to demand respect, even from people who weren't expecting it. And this time it was Jochum who had fucked everything up, talking to that little detergent-dealing junkie and leaving a witness. This time it was Slobodan who had to clean things up.

Lisa Öhrström. Northern accent. Between thirty and thirty-five. One seventy-five. Dark hair. Glasses in her breast pocket, small with black frames.

Slobodan took the lift up to the sixth floor. He walked slowly into the intensive care unit and into a deserted corridor. He stopped near a glass box with a woman inside.

She stood with her back to him. He tapped on the window until she turned around. It wasn't her. This one was at least twenty years older.

'I'm looking for Dr Lisa Öhrström.'

'She's not here.'

He smiled.

'I see that.'

She didn't answer his smile.

'She's busy. What's this concerning?'

The woman, head nurse, he could see the title on her breast, was tense, her face anxious.

'We had the police here just now. They spoke with her. With Dr Öhrström. Is that what this is about?'

'You might say that. Where did you say she was?'

'I didn't say.'

BOX 21

'Where?'

'She has patients. And more waiting. Things have been busy here today, we're a bit behind.'

He took a step back, pulled over a chair that was standing along the corridor wall and sat down. He showed her that he had no intention of going anywhere.

'I want you to go and get her.'

Ewert was sitting at a small table by the window in the former hospital room of a battered woman, a woman who had gone from victim to perpetrator, a room that had gone from home to crime scene. He made calls until his mobile phone ran out of battery, and he had to change to a new phone.

Ewert had ordered every available police car to head immediately to the Söder Hospital Casualty department, a site he judged to be at a safe distance from any possible explosion. He announced his decision to block off all non-essential traffic from the road outside the hospital, and the driveway to the hospital was now closed. He'd contacted the hospital administration and ordered them to vacate the portion of the building connected to the morgue, everyone had to go, there was a woman with explosives and guns, and people needed to be evacuated, now!

He looked briefly at Sven Sundkvist, who was entering the room, pointed at the door. They walked in silence out into the corridor. It had been an intense few minutes.

'I need an explosives expert, too.'

'Yes.'

'Can you take care of that?'

'I'll take care of it.'

They had arrived at the lifts. Sven walked towards the one that was opening now.

'Shall we take this? Or the stairs?'

Grens held a hand in the air.

'Not yet.'

He held an envelope in his hand and gave it to his colleague.

'I found this at her bedside. The only personal item in the room.'

Sven Sundkvist took the envelope, looked at it, handed it back. He went into the next room, searching for a while until he found what he sought. A pile of plastic gloves lay on a shelf above the sink. He took a pair, put them on.

'Now. Can you hand me that again?'

He opened it. A notebook with a blue cover. Nothing else. He flipped through it. A couple of the pages had been torn out. On four of the other pages stood densely written text in a Slavic language, that much he could make out.

'Hers?'

'I would suppose so.'

'I don't understand a word.'

'I want to get it translated, Sven. Can you arrange that?'

He held out his hand, waited while Sven put the blue notebook back in the envelope and handed it back. Grens pointed past the lift.

'Stairs.'

'Now?'

'We don't want to get stuck if something should happen.'

They headed down the steep concrete stairs. They passed the large red stain that had once been Hilding Oldéus. The only thing left of him, now that the orderlies had carried his body away. Ewert shrugged his shoulders as they walked past.

'We'll have to take care of that later.'

A few more steps, then Sven stopped and turned back towards the bloodstain.

BOX 21

'Wait a minute, Ewert.'

He stared at it, following its outer edges, the blood that was spattered far up onto the wall.

'What is it that drives humanity? You see, Ewert? This is what remains of someone who was alive just this morning.'

'We don't have time for this.'

'I don't understand. I know exactly how it works, what it is, what drives us, but still I don't *understand* it.'

Sven Sundkvist squatted down, swaying gently, and almost lost his balance as he stood up again.

'We know who he was. He had things going for him. Hilding Oldéus was smart. We know that. But he was weighed down by his shame, just like every other fool in this world. Where does it come from?'

'We're in a fucking hurry.'

'You're not listening, Ewert. Shame eats at you. Shame drives them all. We shouldn't chase criminals. We should hunt the shame that drives criminals.'

'I don't have time for this right now, Sven. Let's go now.'

Sven Sundkvist remained where he was. He knew Ewert was annoyed, but ignored it.

'Hilding Oldéus thought he knew who he was, deep down, and didn't want to have anything to do with that person at any price. He didn't want to know him, he was ashamed of him. Why?'

Ewert Grens sighed.

'I don't know.'

'Probably he didn't know either. He just knew that heroin turned it off. That much he knew. It turned off the shame.'

Sven Sundkvist looked at Ewert Grens. He hadn't been listening. He was already on his way down the stairs.

'We have a hooker holding people at gunpoint down there. You'll have to excuse me, Sven. We can discuss this later.'

One floor down.

Sven caught up, and Ewert turned to him, speaking as they continued to walk.

'Sven?'

'Yes?'

'I need a hostage negotiator as well.'

'He's already on the way.'

'On the way?'

'That was her one demand.'

Ewert stopped mid-step.

'What the hell are you talking about?'

'I found out just now. When I called in your request for re-inforcements. She'd asked one of the hostages to speak. A chief physician. Apparently he was the one describing the situation in there, on her orders. She doesn't speak Swedish. Hardly any English either.'

'And?'

'When he was finished, she asked him to read a name she'd written down on a piece of paper. Bengt Nordwall.'

'Bengt?'

'Yes.'

'Why?'

'It wasn't clear. Command couldn't interpret it any other way than that she was demanding to get him here. I would probably have made the same assessment.'

Ewert hadn't met Bengt in the line of duty for a long time. Not until yesterday, outside a broken-in door. Now they were going to meet again after just a day. He preferred to see him privately, breakfasts in the rain, his only relationship outside the uniform.

They hurried through the ground floor. A few hundred metres down a straight corridor, then to the Casualty department. They nodded to the doctors and nurses they passed by,

BOX 21

hoping to avoid any questions, no time to explain, not yet. They walked out of the front door, out onto the loading dock where ambulances usually arrived at all hours of the day to unload injured people on heavy stretchers.

This was where they'd ordered all available cars. Sven counted fourteen vehicles already in the large parking lot, fifteen if you added the one driving in through the large automatic gate, its blue lights still flashing.

Ewert Grens waited another five minutes. Eighteen marked police cars stood side by side. He unfurled a map of Stockholm and put it on the roof of the closest vehicle.

Everyone was gathered behind him, saying little, waiting for the detective superintendent who was large and noisy with thin grey hair, limping slightly, his neck still stiff from the time he'd been caught in a noose, a sullen bastard that they'd all heard of, but none had ever worked with or even seen. They knew he sat in his office listening to Siw Malmkvist, alone with his investigations. There weren't many who were admitted behind that door, and it was a door not many had any desire to knock on.

'We have a female perp. Just a few days ago we found her unconscious in her pimp's apartment. She was being cared for at the hospital. That much is simple. That we've all seen before.'

Grens looked around. They stood in silence, listening. They're so young, he thought. They were a good-looking crew and strong, but he doubted they'd ever seen anything like this before.

'But for some reason, for some goddamn reason, around lunchtime today something we've *never* seen before happened. The woman got her hands on a small weapon, God knows how. She can barely walk, but somehow she knocks out her guard with a gun. She walks down to the basement and into the morgue. She locks the door behind her and takes the five people inside hostage. She drapes their bodies with plastic explosives. And then she calls us.'

Ewert Grens was speaking calmly to colleagues he'd never seen before, who had probably never seen him.

He knew what to do, what was expected.

He decided to evacuate an even bigger portion of the hospital than he'd previously wanted to. She had half a kilo of plastic explosives underneath this building, with detonators. That was just what they knew about. But she could have placed, or hidden, much more. She'd passed through a large portion of the building on her way to the morgue, that shit could be almost anywhere.

He cordoned off a wider area outside, fenced off the entire street outside the hospital for several blocks in each direction, a main thoroughfare in this part of Stockholm that would otherwise be packed with commuters. He requested via the city chief of police that the national response team be ready for a possible assault within sixty minutes. He personally called one of the response team leaders, John Edvardson, an experienced, Russian-speaking man that Grens had met several times before, and went over the situation with him. With Bengt already in place, he now had two people who could communicate in the language they'd be negotiating for lives in.

Sven Sundkvist was standing a few metres away, watching his colleagues near the Casualty entrance listening to Ewert's orders.

They were here. They were really here.

Present, concentrated, in the moment and nothing else. He wasn't.

Deep down he didn't give a shit about a woman who had her weapon aimed at five people in white coats who just happened

BOX 21

to be in the wrong morgue at the wrong time, and he didn't care that just a few floors up Jochum Lang had been identified as the person who killed Hilding Oldéus.

He had no objection to his work. None at all. He even liked it. It was still easy for him to go to work. He'd played around with the idea of doing something completely different, something that didn't require facing the consequences of violence, something a bit lighter, but he'd always pushed those thoughts away. They were just dreams. He was a cop. He liked being a cop. He had no desire to start over with something else.

But at this moment, he wasn't here.

He wanted to go home. Just for today. He belonged with Anita and they belonged with Jonas, and he had promised. This morning he'd kissed their sleeping cheeks and whispered that he'd be home just after lunch. They could start over again then at being a family.

He took another few steps away, partially obscured behind a parked ambulance, and called home. Jonas picked up. Answered with his first and last name. That's how he always did it. *Hello, this is Jonas Sundkvist.* Sven explained, and felt ashamed. Jonas started crying because Sven had *promised*, and Sven felt even more ashamed. Jonas screamed that he hated him because he and Mum had made such a nice cake and put on candles. Sven couldn't take it. He stood silently for a moment with his phone held in front of him and glanced over at Ewert, who was just finishing up his orders. Sven watched as his colleagues dispersed in every direction. He took a deep breath and collected himself, then lifted the telephone and whispered *sorry* into the silence left by someone who has already hung up.

It was June, news was slow, and when a large hospital in central Stockholm was evacuated and the roads closed for blocks in all directions, then every camera, every microphone, every pen shouted with joy. It smelt like blood and chaos and something to sell papers with. The media followed the eighteen police cars with flashing blue lights here and now they flocked side by side with curious onlookers in front of the two narrow exits that uniformed policemen were guarding as medical professionals were evacuated. Ewert Grens had asked the press officers for both the police and the hospital to arrange a press conference as far away from here as possible and say as little as possible. He wanted peace and quiet in the Casualty-cum-temporary-command-centre and in the basement corridors around the morgue. He remembered with horror a hostage situation a few years ago on the west coast when kidnappers, violent and well-known to the police, while in a private home with high-calibre guns pointed at their hostages, were contacted for an interview by a journalist, who'd managed to track down their mobile numbers in the middle of negotiations.

He knew it wouldn't help. He could send them as far away as he wanted to.

An abused Baltic prostitute taking hostages at the hospital where she was being cared for was too good a story.

They'd be standing there until this was over.

The command centre was actually an operating theatre. There were two other operating theatres in the Casualty area, and this one was the least used. With the help of the staff, they'd pushed aside whatever could be pushed aside, formerly sterile surfaces now served as makeshift desks and chairs. Police officers came and went, but there were always at least three members of Grens's command team stationed in a place they'd already made their own.

Ewert Grens had hurled threat after threat until a marketing

BOX 21

manager at the telecommunications company finally gave him the number to the mobile phone that had called the police from the morgue at twelve thirty-one p.m. today. An unlisted number registered to a Söder Hospital chief physician, Gustaf Ejder. He wrote the number down on a piece of coloured paper and hung it on the wall between two stainless steel cabinets, right next to another taped up number, the morgue's landline.

He sat down in the corner next to the operating table, the seat that had become his.

He'd been waiting almost an hour. He drank coffee from hospital cups and felt impatient.

'She's testing us.'

Nobody heard. But he continued, as if to get it out of himself, or just to say it out loud.

'Maybe she knows exactly what she's doing. Knows silence is stressful. Or she packed up, realised this was bound to end up bad.'

He drained the cup, crumpled it up in his hand, and started pacing restlessly around the room. He looked over at Sven, sitting in another corner of the room, using a stretcher as a desk, a phone to his ear, he'd been talking to someone for a long time and hung up now.

'That was Ågestam. He'd just come from a meeting with Errfors about the post-mortem. Apparently he wants to open up Hilding Oldéus this afternoon. He was also curious, wanted to know what we're up to here, he'd heard about the alarm and evacuation and figured this was going to be a big deal.'

Ewert stopped in the middle of the room, threw the crumpled plastic cup forcefully against the wall.

'That little prosecutor prig! He smells something big, all right, and it smells like his career so he comes crawling to us. But when we ask him to hold on to Lang, he's not so interested, mafia hitmen who beat up junkies don't lead to any juicy interviews.'

Ewert Grens didn't like Lars Ågestam.

He didn't like it when young prosecutors with expensive haircuts and shiny shoes, whose only life experience came from universities, told him what constituted reasonable suspicion or sufficient cause for action. They had met and fought and hated each other for the first time a year ago, when Ågestam was appointed the lead prosecutor on a manhunt for a sex offender. Ågestam had sought out the limelight during the trials, and Ewert Grens told him repeatedly to go to hell. Since then, the Big-Time Prosecutor wannabe had stood in their way on more than one occasion, and they'd continued to yell at each other. He swallowed his anger now. It had already occurred to him an hour ago on his way from Lydia Grajauskas's empty bed in room twelve that Ågestam was going to realise this situation meant more media attention, and he'd bow and fawn and get naked if need be in order to be named prosecutor this time as well.

He continued to pace around the brightly lit room, intrusive fluorescent lights on the ceiling, powerful enough to use during emergency surgery, but just annoying now, he waved at them as if that would help.

'It's the same thing for Grajauskas.'

Sven Sundkvist sat in the far corner of the room, hands on the trolley. He pretended not to notice that Ewert was swatting at the overhead lights.

'Do you understand that, Ewert? It's really the exact same thing happening now. It's shame that drives her and her actions. Just like Oldéus.'

'Sven, not again. Not now.'

'Do you remember Völunds Street? You remember the vodka and Rohypnol in the bathroom? What do you think that was for? She did the same thing. She turned off. She was ashamed. She couldn't stand to feel.'

BOX 21

Ewert Grens turned, asked his question with his back to Sven.
'How long has she been down there now?'

'Do you understand what I'm talking about? They assaulted
her again and again. She hated what they were doing to her, but
had to continue. Maybe it almost felt like she was allowing
them to do it to her. As if she were a participant every time.
She's tried to live with that shame. But it seems apparent that it
was impossible for her. Ewert?'

Ewert Grens slapped his hand hard against the wall in front
of him and screamed.

'I asked how long, Sven? How long has that woman been
threatening to kill five people who just happened to cross her
path? I want an answer!'

Sven Sundkvist took a few deep breaths then looked away,
away from the man who was screaming at him. He took a few
more deep breaths, then looked at the clock that stood beside
the phone.

'Fifty-three minutes since we received her call.'

'And how long down there?'

'We're estimating an hour and twenty minutes. The guard
had a pretty good sense of what time it was, the lunchtime news
was on when she went to the bathroom, so a few minutes there
and a few more before she knocked him out. Then we measured
how long the route down to the morgue took. I think an hour
and twenty minutes is a fairly accurate assessment.'

Grens looked down at his own wristwatch.

'An hour and twenty minutes. In a closed room, with hostages and still no demands. She asked for Bengt in order to
speak Russian. Nothing more. Just a long, arduous silence. She
knows she's testing us. Now we're going to test her.'

Ewert Grens had Sven Sundkvist at his side when he'd set up
this command centre. He'd called in John Edvardson, one of

four SWAT team leaders at the National Task Force. He'd also contacted the violent crimes division, and invited the young officer Hermansson to join. He'd made a note before that she was careful and methodical, and now he knew that she was strong. She hadn't shown any hesitation when Hilding Oldéus had provoked her at his interrogation by humping and shouting obscenities, and had slapped the bastard hard on the cheek.

He now had the core of his command team.

He looked over at Hermansson, who shared Sven's provisional desk, her papers on the other end of the trolley.

'I want you to call the phone company. I made it clear to the suits in the marketing department that they're going to have to accommodate us. You tell him to block that hooker's bloody mobile. But only outgoing calls. Nothing else. Then call the hospital and ask them to do the same thing with the morgue's landline.'

She nodded to him, she understood. The armed Russian woman would no longer be able to choose when to communicate. Only they'd do the communication, and on their terms.

Ewert Grens walked over to the electric kettle that someone had placed on a high stool. He filled it up using the pitcher of water standing next to it and turned on the machine. He then took a plastic cup from a stack on the floor and dumped in three heaped teaspoons of instant coffee.

'Then *we* are the ones who decide when to talk. It's *us* testing her. *We* make *her* wait.'

He didn't wait for any reply.

'And Bengt. Where is he?'

Bengt held on to her. His hands wrapped around her harness and then he wasn't able to hold on any more. She'd been pulled out of the van while it was still rolling.

BOX 21

Twenty-five years. Soon. He was close. When the situation in the morgue was over.

There was a witness up there. And the punishment Lang should have faced long ago.

Punishment for Anni.

Sven pointed out through the door.

'Nordwall is sitting outside. In the waiting room. On a sofa with the few remaining patients in Casualty.'

Ewert looked quietly in the direction Sven was pointing. He paused, then spoke.

'I want him in here. It's time. In half an hour we'll have our task force in place outside the morgue. That's when he'll make first contact.'

The electric kettle snorted angrily. He turned it off, filled the mug with water and stirred it with a teaspoon. He blew on the brown liquid and was just about to take a sip when the telephone sitting on a cabinet in the middle of the room, there for a single purpose, started to ring.

Hermansson hadn't yet had time to contact the telephone company and get them to turn the morgue's phone off for outgoing calls.

The emergency call centre recognised the number and according to their instructions forwarded it to this phone.

Ewert Grens picked up the ringing phone. He held it in his hand, saw the numbers illuminated on the caller ID. She'd been faster than them.

He stood where he was, letting it ring. He counted to fourteen rings. He smiled when it stopped.

LYDIA GRAJAUSKAS glanced at the clock hanging above one of the doors. She'd just phoned again, like before, the female medical student dialled and pressed the phone to the ear of the older grey-haired doctor.

She'd let it ring fourteen times. She'd waited, heard the muffled tones, one at a time, fourteen times. No answer. She was unsure if they'd been connected, or if the policemen who were supposed to answer had simply not done so.

She sat on a chair about three metres in front of them.

It was a good distance, she was in complete control without risking getting too close. They sat in silence, no one had said a word since the first phone call. They kept their eyes closed mostly – their fear ruled them.

She looked around.

The morgue actually consisted of several rooms.

First, the hall-like entrance she'd come in through, where she'd paused for a moment before taking her gun out and approaching the five white coats standing around a corpse on a trolley.

There was an even larger room waiting behind the wall where those five now crouched on their knees. A storage area of some sort, filing cabinets and trolleys and switched-off electronic equipment.

She knew all that before she arrived. She had carefully studied the information brochure she'd borrowed from the Polish nurse. She'd sketched it into her notebook and then torn out the pages she needed.

BOX 21

She also knew that there was one more room.

She hadn't been in there yet. She'd been guarding her hostages and teaching them to respect her, but she knew that it lay behind her, behind a big grey metal door.

The largest room. The morgue. Where the dead bodies were stored.

Suddenly one of the three male medical students, the one who had wept uncontrollably and slowly kneeled up again when she pressed the gun against his forehead, started breathing heavily – breathing that quickly turned into hyperventilating.

She stayed where she was, lowered the gun, watched him fall forward with his hands tied behind his back.

He started to shake violently with his face pressed against the floor.

'Help him!'

The older doctor who spoke on the phone earlier was hoarse, he shouted at her, but couldn't move, stared at her with his neck and cheeks flushed.

'Help! Help him!'

Lydia hesitated. She saw the man lying on the floor shaking. She raised the gun again, a few short steps and she was in front of him. She kept her eyes on the other hostages, wanted to make sure they stayed seated with their backs pressed against the wall.

That was why she didn't see it.

His hands were free.

He lay trembling on the floor in front of her, his face to the floor and his hands loose against one hip. She bent down, her plastered arm near his neck when he threw himself at her. She fell backwards, he was on top of her, punching a hand at her head while he tried to pull the gun out of her clenched fingers with the other.

He was much stronger than her. He was like the others. The ones who lay on top of her, beat her, raped her, the men she hated who would never be allowed to hurt her again.

That's probably why she was able to resist.

At least that was what she thought afterwards.

He had his hand on the gun, but she was able to hold on long enough to put her finger around the trigger. The shot screamed out into the room, and her abuser let go, fell to his side, made a thud when he hit the floor. He grimaced when he realised that the pain was coming from his legs.

She had hit him just below the knee, he wouldn't walk for a long time.

The first members of the SWAT team had started to gather in the downstairs corridor when they heard a voice coming from the vicinity of the morgue's door. It was weak and difficult to understand, even as they slowly approached, it remained impossible to make out anything other than short moans. Then they saw him lying prostrate across the hall near the morgue's front door. He was bleeding from his legs and his head. He'd lost enough blood for them to know he needed immediate care.

They prepared carefully, but nothing happened when they finally reached him and lifted his injured body onto a simple stretcher. This elite group didn't hurry, they moved deliberately step by step, just as they planned – never faster, never slower. They knew this injured man might be bait, but they had to bite.

When they carried the stretcher into the provisional head-quarters in Casualty twelve minutes later, Ewert Grens was waiting impatiently. He'd been told by radio that the injured man was a medical student named Johan Larsen, one of the five people held hostage, and that the woman holding them captive had just shot him with a high-calibre weapon straight through

BOX 21

both his kneecaps and then repeatedly beat his head with the butt of her gun. Grens stood up as soon as the stretcher came into the room and tried to establish contact, but was unceremoniously pushed away by one of the doctors, he would have to wait a little longer, the patient needed immediate treatment.

Grens had so many questions. He needed so many answers.

Lydia Grajauskas was sitting on the chair again in front of the four remaining hostages. She was tired – it had been a terrible few minutes.

As soon as she shot him, she knew it wasn't enough. She had tried to show them from the beginning that she was serious, that she needed their respect. But it hadn't worked. When he was lying on top of her, just like other men, she knew what she had to do.

Push them down again and again, because she had to be in power, and they had to feel fear.

She didn't want any more trouble, next time they might succeed. She had been lying on the floor with the gun still in her hand, the medical student next to her, he'd screamed in pain and grabbed his right knee. She had stood up, looked at the four who sat pressed against the wall, looked at the man who attacked her.

She had shown them her weapon, pointed to it.

'Not again. If again. Boom.'

She had then taken a step towards him, stood above him with her legs on either side of him. She'd shown them the weapon for a second time, said *boom* and fired a shot at the kneecap on his left leg. He had screamed again and she leaned forward, looked at the four, said *boom boom* and pushed the barrel into his mouth. She'd kept it there until he was silent, then pulled it out and flipped the gun around and beat him with the butt until he lost consciousness. She'd beaten him like the men had beaten her. She then removed the plastic explosive from his shoulders, pointed to the female medical student and the grey-haired doctor, temporarily loosened their hands and showed them how they should pull the unconscious body towards the entrance, then open the front door and put him in the empty corridor.

She sat still, holding the gun, pointing it at them.

By now the people outside would have seen the man she shot, maybe they'd even picked him up and got him talking.

That was good.

He would tell them that she's wasn't going to give up, she was serious, and for as long as this lasted she would demand their respect.

She wanted to talk to them. The people out there.

She wasn't going to wait any longer.

She was going to tell them what she wanted.

She gestured in the air with the gun. She wanted the woman to take the mobile and dial the number. This was the third time she'd called. First the call to announce that she had taken hostages. Then those fourteen rings without a response. Now the young female medical student dialled the number again, pressed the receiver to the older man's ear.

He waited, then shook his head.

'Dead.'

She heard what he said, but wasn't sure she understood. She waved the gun.

'Again!'

'Dead. No dial tone.'

The female student drew her hand across her throat, like in an American movie when someone was going to be executed, and said *dead* twice.

Lydia understood. She stood up, kept the gun pointed at

BOX 21

them. She went to the desktop phone that hung on the wall above their heads.

She picked up the receiver and heard silence.

Two phones. Her contact to the outside world. They had cut them off. She shouted at the four hostages in Russian they didn't understand. She screamed and pointed towards the door to the room next door, the one filled with filing cabinets and electronic devices. They stood up, legs and backs sore after hours on the floor, and walked over and sat down at a new wall. She knew they would obey her now, but still she pointed the gun at them and said *if again, boom*, before closing the door behind her. She hurried through the room, past the trolley and the dead body, and walked towards the blue steel door on the other side.

She opened it, walked in there alone, into the huge room that constituted the actual morgue.

JOHN EDVARDSON WAS only thirty-four years old when he was appointed chief of operations at the National Task Force. The Swedish Military Interpreters School, university studies in Russian and political science, the police academy, and a few years on the force had pushed him to the head of the queue of candidates for the job. There'd been a lot of grumbling at the time, as there usually was when egos get bruised, but he'd been just as good at his job as the police leadership had hoped: wise, well-liked, the kind of man you don't push around, and the kind who doesn't have to raise his voice to prove that.

Ewert Grens had met him several times. There was no friendship, Grens had no interest in that, but he'd spent enough time with the man to get a good sense of who he was and to see how good he was at his job. He was glad to have him here in this provisional command centre among the trolleys and scalpels.

Edvardson walked over to Ewert, took him by the arm, led him away from the medical student with a bullet in each knee.

'You don't need to interrogate him. Not yet. I asked one of my guys to talk to him on the way up from the morgue.'

Ewert listened, then looked towards the doctor who was examining both knee joints.

'I need to know everything.'

'You're not going to be able to get everything yet. You can later. But we know now that the shooting victim, Larsen, is sure about the Semtex. He won't say how he knows, but he seems confident. His description matches the substance. She's rigged

BOX 21

the hostages and every door. She has detonators and he has no doubt that she'll use them if she needs to.'

'He should know.'

'And you know what that means?'

'I suppose so.'

'We can't go in there. It's impossible. We're risking the hostages if we go in.'

Ewert Grens slammed his hand in irritation on a stainless steel rolling table. The sound it made was loud and made even louder by the vibrating metal surface.

'I don't understand anything. Since when did little hookers start arming themselves and taking hostages!'

'He said she was in control. Her level of self-control was terrifying. She was well prepared, she had string to tie them up, enough ammunition to last her a while, and enough plastic explosives to keep us out.'

'Self-control.'

'That's what he said. Self-control and courage. He repeated that several times.'

'I don't give a shit about her self-control. I want you to get your men in place. Use your best judgement. And I want snipers. If we need to, we'll shoot her.'

Edvardson started to leave the room, but Grens asked him to stay. The envelope lay on one of the trolleys they'd temporarily pushed aside, Ewert Grens grabbed it, asked Edvardson to put on some plastic gloves, then took the blue notebook.

'This belonged to Grajauskas. Can you read it?'

John Edvardson carefully turned the pages. He shook his head.

'No. Unfortunately not. That's Lithuanian. I don't know it.'

'Sven, how's it going with that damn interpreter?'

Just as Ewert Grens turned to the corner where Sven Sundkvist sat, the doctor in the adjoining room who was examining

Johan Larsen's gunshot wounds waved his hand, trying to get Grens's attention.

'Grens?'

'Yes?'

Ewert started walking over to the trolley in order to quickly question the medical student. But the doctor raised his hand to stop him.

'No. Not yet.'

'I need more answers.'

'Not yet. He's in no shape to answer.'

'It's just a couple of fucking knees! There are more people down there!'

'This isn't about the knees. You can see that for yourself. The shock has set in. If we aren't careful, you'll never get any answers.'

Ewert Grens looked at Larsen, whose face was chalk-white, saliva running down his chin. Grens clenched his hand around the handkerchief in his pocket, the one he usually used to wipe Anni's face. He closed his eyes, then looked at Larsen's open mouth and considered hitting the metal table again.

'She takes hostages. She makes sure we find out. She rigs the whole fucking morgue with explosives. *And still she makes no demands!*'

He let his hand fall, and the sound of vibrating metal bounced off the walls.

'Sven!'

'Yes?'

'Call her! Call her. It's time to have a chat.'

She'd never been in a real morgue before. She stopped walking and looked around when the grey metal door slammed behind her. It was bigger than expected, a bright yellow hall with sterile

BOX 21

lighting, white tile where the autopsies were performed, as big as the two dance halls she and Vladi used to go to as teenagers in Klaipeda. The row of refrigerators covered almost the whole of one wall, steel-grey doors that were fifty by seventy-five centimetres, stacked three by three on top of each other.

Lydia counted fifteen rows. Forty-five freezers. And there were people inside them. Cold bodies at rest. She couldn't understand it and didn't want to.

She thought of Vladi – she did that sometimes. She missed him. They'd grown up together, gone to school together. She used to like to hold his hand. They took long walks, talking about how they'd get out of Klaipeda. Sometimes they walked all the way to the city limits, stopped there and turned around, looked out over the whole city, really seeing it, and longed to be somewhere else. That's what they did together, longed for something else.

She thought of him as hers. *He* thought of *her* as *his*.

Lydia walked slowly over the hard, grey-tile floor. She hadn't seen him in over three years. She wondered where he was, what he was doing, if he ever thought about her.

She thought of her parents. Her father and Lukiškės prison. Her mother and the apartment in Klaipeda. They probably did the best they could. There hadn't been much love, but no hatred or violence either. They'd enough on their plate as it was. She wondered if they'd ever been filled with longing, if they'd ever gone to the city limits and looked around, searching for something else.

She was glad her mother didn't know where she was now – a broken-down whore in a morgue with a gun aimed at other people. She was glad Vladi didn't know. She wondered if he would have understood. She thought so. He would have understood. There comes a time when you have suffered enough, and you have to make them suffer instead. That's just how it was. At a certain point you just can't take more. It's that simple.

It took her a few seconds to realise the phone was ringing. The landline hanging on the wall in the middle room, a few steps from the dead man on the trolley. She hurried past the fridges, opened the grey metal door. She guessed it rang at least four, maybe five times.

She picked it up, waited silently. She was in pain. The morphine was slowly wearing off. It was starting to be difficult to move around, and she realised it would only get worse.

It took a moment – and she wasn't prepared for that male voice speaking Russian with a Scandinavian accent. She didn't realise until he said his name.

'Bengt Nordwall. I'm with the police.'

She swallowed. She hadn't truly believed it. She'd hoped, but hadn't believed it.

'You asked for me.'

'Yes.'

'Lydia? Is that right? I'll listen as long as—'

She interrupted him abruptly, tapping her finger on the phone and speaking loudly.

'Why have you turned off my telephones?'

'We—'

She knocked hard on the phone's mouthpiece again.

'You can call me. But I can't call you. I want to know why.'

He hesitated, and she realised he must be looking at the colleagues around him for some kind of support, gesturing with his hands.

'I don't know what you mean. We haven't turned off any phones. We evacuated large parts of the hospital because you've taken hostages. But we haven't turned off any phones.'

'You're going to need a better explanation than that.'

BOX 21

'Lydia, we also evacuated the hospital switchboard. I'm guessing that's why your phone doesn't work.'

'Phones! Not one, two! Do you think I'm an idiot? Some stupid Eastern European whore? I know how phones work. And you know now that I won't hesitate to hurt someone. So no more bullshit! Five minutes. In exactly five minutes from now you will have those phones back on again. Or I'll shoot one of the hostages. And not in the legs this time.'

'Lydia, we—'

'And don't even try getting in here. I'll blow up both hostages and the hospital.'

He hesitated again. He was looking at his colleagues again. He cleared his throat.

'If we turn on the phones what do we get in return?'

'What do you get? You get no dead hostage. That's what you get. You now have four minutes and fifteen seconds left.'

Ewert Grens listened to the whole conversation simultaneously translated by Edvardson. He took off his headphones, put them on the table between Sven Sundkvist and Hermansson. He picked up his plastic cup and drank the rest of what was now cold coffee.

'What do you think?'

He looked at Sven, at Hermansson, at Edvardson, at Bengt Nordwall.

'What do you think? Is she bluffing?'

John Edvardson was wearing the same uniform as the officers he'd just placed in the hospital corridors. Black leather boots, camouflage pants with large square pockets on the thighs, two jackets in grey: first an equipment vest with spare ammunition for the rifle he'd left on a trolley, and under it a vest lined with metal plates sturdy enough to withstand most types of ammunition. The too-crowded room was hot, and he was sweating. His forehead was shiny, and he had large dark patches under his armpits.

'She's already proved she's not afraid to hurt hostages.'

'But is she bluffing?'

'She doesn't need to. She has the advantage.'

'And why would she give up that advantage?'

'That's not what she's doing. If she shoots one, she still has three left.'

Grens looked at Edvardson and shook his head.

'Why the hell did she take hostages in a morgue? No windows, no exits. Even if she shot them all, we'd get her in the end. We'd take her as soon as she tried to leave. Either that, or one of our snipers would get her. She must know that. She must have known that when she went in. I don't get it.'

Hermansson was sitting quietly in the middle of the room, at her seat by a trolley. Ewert had noticed she hadn't said much since she got here. Maybe she just didn't talk much, or maybe she was finding it difficult to express herself surrounded by male colleagues with experience and no fear of taking up a lot of room. Now she stood up, looked at him.

'There is another possibility.'

Grens liked her thick southern accent. It inspired confidence, he felt compelled to listen to her.

'What do you mean?'

She hesitated, even considered dropping the idea, but she was sure she was right. Still she felt some level of uncertainty, which she despised but couldn't completely abandon. It felt like they were looking at her condescendingly, as if she were a little girl, and even if that weren't the case, she couldn't quite shake the feeling.

'She's badly hurt. She's in pain. She can't keep this up much longer. But I don't think she thinks like you. She's already crossed the line, committed acts she probably didn't know she

BOX 21

was capable of. I think she's made up her mind. I don't think she's planning on leaving that morgue.'

Ewert Grens stood completely still. He didn't do that often. He was afflicted by restlessness, always pacing around a room with his heavy body. Even when he was sitting he was in motion, stretching his arms, unconsciously tapping a foot, or turning his upper body this way and that. Never still.

Now he was.

Hermansson had said what he should have seen already.

A few deep breaths, he started moving again, walking round and round in a circle, around their temporary table.

'Bengt.'

Bengt Nordwall stood in the doorway, both hands on the doorframe.

'Yes?'

'Bengt, I want you to call her again.'

'Now?'

'I think we're in a goddamn hurry.'

Bengt Nordwall left the door, walked quickly over to the telephone. He didn't sit down, not wanting to waste even a second, while simultaneously trying to suppress the intense uneasiness he'd been feeling since the garden, when images of her whipped back had filled his mind.

He knew who she was.

He'd known since he stood outside that apartment on Völunds Street.

The feeling was stronger now, the anxiety, the fear.

Bengt Nordwall glanced at the note on the wall, at the number he was supposed to dial, while waiting for Ewert to get his headphones on.

He dialled. Eight rings. No answer.

He looked at the wall, at the other note, the number to the mobile phone.

He called again. Straight to answerphone. No answer. He shook his head, put down the telephone.

'She's turned them off. Both of them.'

Bengt Nordwall peered at Ewert, who was pacing in circles, whose face turned red while he screamed.

'A fucking hooker!'

Grens was just about to scream again when he glanced at the time, first at the watch on his arm, then the clock on the wall. He lowered his voice.

'A minute and a half left.'

SHE KNEW THEY would obey. She knew they would still be there. But she opened the door to check on them quickly anyway. They sat in the storage room, archival dust swirling in the air. They were silent with their backs pushed firmly against the wall. They turned when the door opened and saw her. She showed them the gun, pointed it at them long enough for them to feel the fear of death again.

Her father had fallen forward. His hands had been tied behind his back. His face struck the floor hard. She should have run over to him then. But she hadn't dared. The gun was pressed against her head, and the man holding it pushed so hard into the thin skin of her temple it hurt.

She closed the door, returned to the middle room.

She checked her watch. They'd had their five minutes.

She turned on the mobile phone, pressing the green button, and then put in the four digits the doctor told her would unlock it.

She waited a few seconds.

It started ringing, just as she guessed it would.

She let it ring a few more times. Then she answered.

'Time's up.'

Bengt Nordwall's voice.

'Lydia, we need—'

She struck the mouthpiece.

'Have you done what I asked for?'

'We need more time. Just a little longer. Then we'll fix the screw-up with the phones.'

186

She broke out into a cold sweat. Every breath was like a stab to her body. It was difficult to collect her thoughts, to push away the pain. Lydia struck the barrel of the gun on the phone's mouthpiece. More blows this time, and harder. But she didn't say anything.

Bengt Nordwall could hear her footsteps disappearing. She knew he was turning to his colleagues again, gathered around him wearing headphones, trying to understand. He grabbed his phone after a while and shouted as loud as he dared.

'Hello!'

He could hear it echoing. His words danced around the room.

'Hello!'

Then he heard exactly what he didn't want to hear. A gunshot drowned out everything else.

She had fired her weapon in an enclosed space, so the sound was a violent force when it hit the phone.

It was hard to say. If only a few seconds had passed.

Or if it was more than that.

'Now I have three living and one dead hostage. You have five more minutes. The phones need to be able to make outgoing calls. If they don't, I'll shoot another one.'

Her voice was steady.

'You should also remove whoever's sitting out in the corridor outside my door. I'll be detonating a few charges there soon.'

––––––––––

Ewert Grens heard the shot. He had waited out her silence. When she spoke, he focused on her voice, trying to sense if she was calm or pretending to be calm. That was all he could do, because he didn't know one damn word of Russian.

John Edvardson stood behind him, leaning forward, translating what she'd just said. Grens listened and swore.

BOX 21

He turned to Sven Sundkvist, *fix those damned phones, Sven, she needs to be able to dial out again as fast as fucking possible*, then back to Edvardson, they agreed to let the task force retreat a sufficient distance from the morgue, *we're not gonna let any of our guys get blown up!*

Then he was silent for a moment, breathing heavily, put his hand on Sven's shoulder, searching Sven's eyes.

'I want you to put on a bulletproof vest, too.'

Ewert's hand made Sven jump, and Ewert realised he'd never touched him before.

'I want you to go down there, Sven. Down to the basement corridor. I need to know. I need to get your impressions. Eyes I can trust.'

———

Sven Sundkvist was positioned about fifty metres from the morgue's door, at the place where the corridor divided into two. He was waiting behind the new corridor's last piece of wall next to three members of the SWAT team. He'd been crouching there less than two minutes when he heard the door they were guarding open. He got down on his knees and shuffled forward to look into the mirror.

The hallway was dark, but a light shone brightly from inside the morgue. A male was moving in the dim light, his body just a dark silhouette. He was bent over and pulling something forward.

It took a moment for Sven Sundkvist to understand what it was. The man was holding an arm and dragging a body.

Sundkvist grabbed the night vision binoculars from the bag of the officer sitting next to him, considered the risks of exposing himself, but held them so that when he leaned forward, he could see around the corner.

It was difficult to make out any details of the man's face, but

Sven saw him suddenly drop the arm, hurry back, and close the door to the morgue behind him.

Sundkvist scooted backwards, protected by the corner.

He was panting, and held the radio close to his mouth when he called.

'Grens, over.'

It crackled, like they always crackle.

'Grens here. Over.'

'A man just walked out of the morgue dragging a body. He's gone now, but the body is there. I saw wires running out of it. We can't approach! It's rigged!'

Ewert Grens started to reply, but his voice was drowned out by the odd sound of a human body exploding.

The radio was silent, or maybe it wasn't, perhaps Sven's scream had been there from the beginning.

'She did it, Ewert! She blew up a human being!'

His voice was weak, almost cracking.

'Do you hear me, Ewert! There's nothing but shit. Nothing but shit left!'

LISA ÖHSTRÖM WAS SCARED. She'd been carrying this pain in her stomach for a long time now, this burning, screaming pain that could stop her mid-step while she fought to keep breathing. She'd seen the man who'd probably beaten up Hilding then watched her brother's wheelchair disappear down the stairs, and she'd known those images would stay with her longer than she could stand.

She hadn't eaten, had tried to force down a sandwich and an apple, but couldn't do it. It was as if she couldn't swallow, as if she no longer had any saliva.

She couldn't make sense of it. He was truly dead now.

But she didn't know if what she felt was mainly relief, to know at last exactly where he was, what he *wasn't* doing, that he wasn't hurting himself or others. Or if it was grief. Or if she was just preparing herself for the task of telling Ylva and her mother.

But mostly she thought of how she was going to explain this to Sanna and Jonathan, her beloved niece and nephew, her stand-in children, the children she never had.

Uncle Hilding is dead.

Uncle Hilding was beaten to death in a staircase.

Lisa Öhrström walked into the break room again, looking for coffee that had been made this morning. She'd pleaded until one of the policemen who'd stayed in the ward finally told her more than he should have. She knew now that the man with the shaved head – the man who had beaten her brother to death, the man she'd pointed to in photo thirty-two – was named Lang, and that he was a hitman who'd beat up anyone for the right price. She also found out he'd been convicted of violent crimes before, but was suspected of doing much more. Witnesses to his crimes had a tendency to change their minds. That's how things work – the threat of violence shuts people up.

Jochum Lang sat in the car outside the hospital entrance and never turned around. Slobodan was out there running around like a little boss, getting a hard-on from the fact that this time he was doing the clean-up, while Jochum was the one leaving witnesses these days. That's just how it is, he thought, sooner or later you drop your guard, sooner or later the little guys get a whiff of weakness and go after you, and you just have to remind them how things work.

He leaned against the driver's seat, turned the ignition key half a turn, and glanced at the clock lit up at the bottom of the dashboard.

Slobodan should have had time to have a little chat with her by now.

Lisa Öhrström stood in the break room, leaning against the sink. The coffee was stronger than it should be, but she drank it anyway, happy to be able to swallow. She wasn't even halfway through the list of patient visits in the pocket of her white coat. It had been a chaotic morning, and it was going to be a long day.

She was just about to put down the cup when the charge nurse walked in through the door. She seemed worried, her cheeks red.

'Shouldn't you be at home?'

'Not alone. I couldn't stand it, Ann Marie. I'm staying here.'

The nurse shook her head slowly.

'There's been a murder. You've seen it. You should at least contact the hospital crisis services.'

BOX 21

'People often die here.'

'This was your brother.'

'My brother has been dead a long time.'

The nurse put a hand gently on her colleague's cheek before taking a deep breath and continuing.

'There's someone here to see you.'

Lisa met her gaze, the cup of coffee still in her hand, and slowly drank the last of it.

'Who?'

'I don't know, but I don't like him.'

'A patient?'

'No.'

The charge nurse sat down at the table, put her hand on the red and white checked plastic tablecloth. Lisa Öhrström caught her eyes.

'What did he want?'

'He wouldn't say. He wanted to speak to you. That was all I could get out of him.'

She sank down at the kitchen table next to the charge nurse.

Then the floor beneath her suddenly started to tremble, the dishes in the kitchen cupboards started to rattle.

It was as if the whole building was shaking.

She knew sections of the hospital had been evacuated but she didn't know why, and when the room started moving she had the impression it might be caused by a bomb exploding. Not that she'd ever been around any exploding bombs, but still that's what occurred to her.

———

Jochum Lang turned the ignition key again, put on the windscreen wipers – he wanted to be able to look out while he waited. It was that kind of day, rain until darkness came.

It happened suddenly.

He heard it clearly, a muffled bang coming from inside the hospital. He tried to see through the rain-soaked glass of entrance doors. Explosives. He was sure of it. It was that kind of sound.

He prepared himself for more, but nothing came, a single bang, and then silence again.

The room was too bright. Ewert Grens had been irritated by those damn lights since he had stepped into this operating room and started moving furniture out of the way. He just heard the blast of a human body exploding, and Sven's frantic call over the radio. These fucking lights, he thought, I can't take them any more, what the hell am I supposed to do with these lights? He almost ran across the room, past the table where Edvardson and Hermansson were sitting. He threw himself at the switch on the wall and turned off the lights.

Just for a moment. No exploding bodies. No hookers who had power over other people's lives. Just for a moment, the lights, the irritation, the darkness, the switches on the wall, just until he could grasp this, just for a moment.

It was still bright enough for them to be able to see each other. Ewert started pacing around the room in the circular motion that calmed him. He forgot the lights, could feel his breath and the colour in his face returning to normal. He stopped in the corner and put his hand on Bengt's shoulder.

'You have to call her again.'

The building stopped shaking as quickly as it started. Lisa Öhrström was still sitting at the kitchen table, and she put her hand on top of the nurse's.

'Ann Marie.'

'Yes?'

BOX 21

'Where is he?'

'Outside your office. He scares me. I don't know why. I guess between the murder and having the police here all morning, it's just too much.'

Lisa Öhrström was quietly staring down at the red and white checked pattern, when there was a knock on the door. A man, dark hair, moustache, slightly overweight. She could see the charge nurse carefully nod her head in confirmation.

'Sorry to interrupt you, ladies.'

He had a smooth voice, almost friendly.

'Were you looking for me?'

'Yes.'

'What's this concerning?'

'It's a private matter. Can we talk somewhere else?'

She could feel her stomach knot up. She looked at him and part of her wanted to scream, to run away. But another part of her felt angry. This fear wasn't hers – it belonged to Hilding and his fucking drugs. When he was alive, her life had been ruled by his addiction, and now he still managed to have all the power.

She shook her head, hesitated. Stomach burning, fear tearing at her.

'I think I'll stay here.'

Ewert Grens had asked him to call her, so Bengt Nordwall reached out and lifted the receiver. Bengt would rather have waited a little longer, would have wanted more time to calm down. The whole building had shifted under his feet, and he didn't like it.

His mouth was dry. He swallowed, but couldn't shake this uneasiness and discomfort. He wondered if he should tell them that he knew who she was.

Not yet.

It wasn't necessary yet.

Instead he did what Ewert wanted, leaned forward to dial the number to the morgue's landline.

He was too late. The phone was ringing already.

He looked at Ewert, who nodded and put on the earphones hanging around his neck. Bengt waited two rings, then replied.

'Yes?'

'Nordwall?'

'Yes.'

'You heard?'

'I heard.'

'Then you know now.'

'We do.'

'Too bad it took a dead hostage for you to get it.'

'What do you want?'

'First, I do not negotiate. Second, you can't get in here without blowing us all to kingdom come.'

'We understand that.'

'The hostages are rigged, the morgue is rigged.'

'Lydia, if you stay calm, I'm sure we can make a deal. But we need to know why you're doing this.'

'I will tell you.'

'When?'

'Later.'

'And now?'

'*You* need to come here.'

He now knew why she'd taken hostages. Somehow he'd known all along. The discomfort he'd felt turned into something else, something he'd never really felt before, mortal dread.

He closed his eyes as he continued.

'What do you mean?'

'It's tough for me to guard the hostages if I have to run around playing telephone games with you. I want you here. You

BOX 21

and I can speak Russian here, and you can stay on the phone with your colleagues.'

Ewert Grens listened to their conversation without understanding. Bengt Nordwall was breathing heavily while quickly conveying her request, and Grens shook his head emphatically.

'Not that. Never that.'

The two policemen were making their way on foot around Söder Hospital when they saw the car in the parking lot outside the main entrance. It was new, expensive, and illegally parked: two wheels up on the narrow pavement. It was difficult to see into with all the rain pouring down, but they could make out a man sitting in the passenger seat. They walked over to the car, stood on either side of it, and knocked on the front windows lightly.

'You can't stay here.'

He was powerfully built, completely bald and had a fake tan. He smiled, but didn't answer.

'This whole area is cordoned off. No cars are allowed here.'

He was still smiling, but nothing more.

The policeman standing by the rolled-down window was starting to lose his patience. He glanced at his colleague, making sure that he was prepared.

'ID, please.'

The man in the passenger seat made no move, as if he hadn't even heard them, or maybe hadn't made up his mind.

'Your ID. Now.'

He sighed loudly.

'Sure.'

He took his wallet from his back pocket, handed over an ID. The police officer held it in his hand, leaning towards the car door while searching for his radio.

'Hans Jochum Lang. 750725-0350. Can you check that?'

A minute passed.

They could all hear it when the answer came.

'Hans Jochum Lang. 750725-0350. Wanted since this morning.'

He laughed as they forced him out of the car. He asked them what witnesses they thought they had, as they pushed him down onto his stomach on the wet asphalt. He laughed even louder when they handcuffed him and put him in the back of the police car and drove away.

―――――

Bengt Nordwall saw Ewert vigorously shaking his head, and knew that it meant a clear no.

He felt suddenly light, his energy returning. It was Ewert's decision. It was Ewert who could say no.

He picked up the phone again.

'I'm sorry. I can't.'

'Can't?'

'If I were to go down to the morgue . . . it's against our hostage negotiation policies.'

'Killing people is against policy. Yet that's what I did. And I'll kill another one if you don't come down here.'

'There must be another solution.'

'You can have the rest of the hostages, the ones that are still alive, if *you* come here. Three hostages for one person.'

He was convinced now. He knew where this was going.

'No. I'm sorry.'

'I want you, Russian speaker. You have thirty minutes. Then I kill another one.'

That overwhelming anxiety. He was so scared.

'Lydia, I—'

'Twenty-nine minutes and fifty seconds.'

―――――

BOX 21

The man standing in the doorway to the break room wanted to speak privately. He turned to the charge nurse.

'It's best that you leave.'

The charge nurse looked at Lisa Öhrström, who nodded. The nursed nodded back and then hurried out into an empty corridor.

Slobodan watched her go, then turned to Lisa Öhrström and smiled. She was just about to smile back, until she watched him walk over to just a metre or so from the table where she was sitting.

'Look. Here's how this works.'

He paused.

'You didn't see a fucking thing today. You don't have a fucking clue who visited Oldéus.'

She closed her eyes. No more. Not now.

The pain in her stomach made her vomit into her lap and onto the table. Her eyes remained closed the whole time. Fucking Hilding.

'Lisa.'

Her eyes closed. Her stomach cramping. She fought the overwhelming nausea.

'Lisa. Look at me! That's all you need to do. Keep your mouth shut. It's that simple. You talk, you die.'

Ewert Grens should have felt more when he got the message that Jochum Lang had been apprehended. He had been waiting so long, and finally he had a credible witness who would testify to first-degree murder.

He felt nothing.

It was as if he'd been anaesthetised by how Grajauskas was playing with people's lives. It had taken all the energy he had. Later. He could enjoy this later, when she was done.

But still he left the command centre to call the prosecutor Ågestam. He needed to explain that they had a witness, a doctor who'd seen Jochum Lang assault Hilding Oldéus. They also had a motive. Lang, according to the report Ewert Grens received from two detectives at the County Criminal Police, was acting on behalf of his former Yugoslavian employers, who didn't like Oldéus mixing their dope with detergent. He wouldn't under any circumstances end his call to Ågestam until the prosecutor understood the situation fully and decided to hold Lang on reasonable suspicion of murder, and then conduct a comprehensive body inspection to search for traces of Oldéus's blood and DNA.

———

Lisa Öhrström couldn't hold it in any longer. She turned her head towards the table and threw up again. She could feel the man threatening her getting closer and closer.

'You don't seem to be doing so well, Lisa. You know, I had to wait for a while. First down by the entrance, so many cops running around. Then up here, outside your office. So I made a few calls. Did you know that, Lisa? A few quick calls to the right people. That's all it takes, when you're a king.'

He pushed his face close to hers.

'You're not answering. Then maybe you should listen instead. Your name is Lisa Öhrström. You're thirty-five years old. You've been a doctor for the last seven. Put in two years here at Söder Hospital.'

Lisa Öhrström sat completely still. If she didn't move, if she didn't say anything.

'You're single. No kids. And yet, on your bulletin board you have these.'

He held two photographs in his hand. One taken during the summer of a six-year-old boy lying next to his older sister on a

BOX 21

jetty. It was sunny, and the children were starting to get a little burnt. The second was in front of a Christmas tree, the children surrounded by ribbons and wrapping, their now pale faces looked expectant.

She closed her eyes.

She saw Sanna, she saw Jonathan. They were all she had. She was proud of them. Like she was their substitute mum. Sometimes, they lived more with her than with Ylva. Soon they'd grow up. In this fucking world. They should never be affected by their uncle's addiction. They should never be haunted by the sick actions it created. They should never ever know anything like the fear she felt right now.

She closed her eyes, wanting to keep them that way until this was over. What you can't see, doesn't exist.

'EWERT?'

'Yes?'

'How's it going?'

'I don't know.'

Ewert Grens had no idea. He still felt nothing. She had given them thirty minutes. Why not twenty? Or ten? Or a single minute, what does it matter when you have no choice?

'Ewert?'

'Yes?'

Bengt Nordwall was gripping onto the edge of a hospital bed. He was having a hard time speaking or even standing up. Why am I asking? Why am I pushing for this? I'm saying things I don't want to say, and I'll end up having to do things I don't want to do. I don't need this. I don't need this fucking shit tearing my chest apart. Nor the hole knocked into the apartment door or the lashes on her back. Nor the *Stena Baltica*. Not that.

'You know I have to, Ewert. We have no choice.'

Ewert Grens knew that was true.

And he knew that it wasn't true.

The minutes were disappearing. There was always a solution, but this time there wasn't. Sometimes you have nothing.

Grens wanted to leave the room, but he had to stay.

He'd just made a phone call once again to negotiate with Ågestam about Lang, and he looked around now, searching for John Edvardson, who must be sitting in another room somewhere reporting to his superiors. He looked around for Sven

BOX 21

Sundkvist, but he was in the basement corridor waiting to see if the front door of the morgue would open again.

He needed them here. Hermansson was clever, but he didn't know her as well as the others, and Bengt, well, this concerned Bengt, so that was the last person he wanted to talk to.

'She wants you in there. She'll trade them all for you.'

Ewert stood in front of his friend and colleague.

'I just don't understand. Do you?'

Bengt Nordwall was sitting with his headphones on. He'd long since hung the phone up, but the conversation was continuing inside him. He could hear what she said and what he said, and it went no further, just the same sentences again and again.

He understood. But he would never admit it.

'No, I don't understand either. But if you want me to go in, I will.'

Ewert turned to the phone that was their way into the morgue. He picked up the receiver and listened to the monotonous dial tone. He screamed into it, something about whores and bodies rigged to explode and the clock on the wall ticking away whatever time they had to think.

His face stayed red, even after he hung up and made a lap or two around the trolley.

'It would be a breach of duty. If I let you go in there. You know that.'

'I know that.'

'And?'

Bengt Nordwall hesitated. I can't, he thought. I can't, I can't, I can't.

'It's your decision, Ewert.'

Grens continued to pacing, round and round in a circle.

'Hermansson?'

'Yes?'

'What do you think?'

She looked at the watch. Three minutes left.

'You can't use the SWAT team. We've evacuated half of the hospital because we knew she had explosives, which she's already used once and threatens to do again. You can't persuade her to do as you please, you've tried. She seems to have made up her mind. And you don't have time to find any other way in.'

She checked the time, again. Then she continued.

'She chose an isolated room. It's the perfect place. As long as she keeps the door closed and her gun pointed at the hostages, we can't get in there. Breach of duty? Yes, it would be a gross breach of duty to send Nordwall down there. But what's the alternative? We have sent in police officers to replace hostages before. And there are three people down there who want to live a little longer.'

Ewert Grens knew that just over two minutes were left, and he started to pace in a circle one last time. Now that he'd heard what Hermansson had to say, he realised he should have asked her much earlier. He would tell her that later. He glanced briefly at Bengt, who was sitting with his headphones still on, a man with children and a beautiful wife, and a garden, which . . .

The radio.

Sven Sundkvist's voice.

'She has just fired her gun. No doubt about it. One gunshot. From inside the morgue.'

Bengt Nordwall listened, but couldn't stand any more right now. He took off his headphones. The feeling that was tearing at his chest tore harder. Ewert took a step forward, grabbed the headphones, and shouted back.

'Jesus Christ, we have almost two minutes left!'

Sundkvist was on the move – the radio crackled.

'Ewert?'

'Over.'

BOX 21

'The door is open. One of the hostages is standing in the hallway, holding onto the arm of a person who is lying on the floor. They are dragging out another one, Ewert. It's hard to make out from here, but I'm sure of it, the person on the ground is . . . lifeless.'

BENGT NORDWALL WAS was standing in one of the dark corridors of the basement, far from the lift and the close to the morgue's front door. He was freezing, even though it was the middle of summer. The floor was chilly against his bare feet, the air conditioning too cold for bare skin. He was stripped to his underpants, a small microphone and an earphone attached to one ear.

He understood what was waiting for him on the other side of the door. He knew who she was, that this was a matter of life and death for her. For him. For others. And he was the target. He was responsible for the fact that several people were in mortal danger. Bengt Nordwall turned around, had already done so twice, making sure that the three police officers from the SWAT team had their weapons raised behind him.

'Ewert, over.'

He spoke in a quiet voice, wanted to stay in contact with the command centre as long as possible.

'I hear you. Over.'

There was nothing to hold on to.

He didn't know if he could stand up much longer.

He thought about Lena. About how she was probably sitting in their home, curled up with her legs under her, a book in her hand. He missed her. He wanted to sit beside her.

'One thing, Ewert.'

'Yes?'

'Lena. I want you to talk to her. If something happens.'

He waited. No answer. He cleared his throat.

BOX 21

'I'm ready now.'

'Good.'

'Ewert, I'll go in whenever you say.'

'Now.'

'Now. Is that correct?'

'Yes. Walk over to the door and wait there. Hands above your head.'

'I'm going.'

'Bengt?'

'Yes?'

'Good luck.'

His steps were silent as the thin skin of his feet met the concrete floor. So cold. It was so cold. He froze as he stood in front of the morgue's door, the SWAT team ten or fifteen metres behind him. It didn't take long. He counted the seconds and hadn't made it to thirty when the door opened and an older man with grey hair exited and passed by without looking at him. Bengt Nordwall glimpsed his name tag, Dr Ejder, and also a thread of explosives hanging across his shoulders and around his neck. The doctor was holding a mirror in his hand, and he angled it so that the person just inside the morgue door, who Nordwall couldn't see but whose breath he could hear, would be able to make sure the visitor was undressed and alone.

'Ejder?'

Bengt Nordwall whispered, but the doctor, who was still staring past him, lowered the mirror and waved it. They were supposed to go in.

He stood still, just a little longer. Closed his eyes.

The air came in through his nose and out through his mouth.

He turned off his fear. His task from now on was to observe. He was responsible for their lives.

Ejder was impatient, wanted to go back in. They both stepped over the man lying on the floor and left the corridor. Bengt

Nordwall carefully lifted his shaking hand and pressed a finger to the small electronic device in his ear, making sure it was still in place.

He was freezing and sweating.

'Ewert.'

'Over.'

'The hostage in the corridor is dead. I don't see any blood, don't know where he was shot. But the smell. It's overpowering, Ewert, and bitter.'

He saw her as soon as he came into the room. It *was* her. He recognised her. The *Stena Baltica*. He'd found it difficult to look at her face the other day, her whipped back, the blanket over her as they carried her away. Now he was sure.

He tried to smile at her but his mouth cramped up.

She stood in the middle of the room, holding a gun to the head of a young man in a white doctor's coat.

She was small, her face swollen and scratched, one arm in a cast, and she was leaning heavily on one leg. She was in pain from either a hip or knee.

She pointed at him, spoke.

'Bengt Nordwall.'

Her voice was just as steady as before.

'Spin around, Bengt Nordwall. Keep your hands above your head.'

He did as she said. He spun around slowly and caught sight of the explosives attached to each doorframe.

He did a whole three-sixty and stood staring at her again.

'Good, Bengt Nordwall. You can tell them to leave now, one by one through the door.'

————

Ewert Grens was sitting on the floor of the temporary command centre, listening to the voices inside the morgue. John

BOX 21

Edvardson was on a stool beside him, interpreting the Russian. Hermansson had a pair of headphones on now and was scribbling down all of the absurd dialogue, mostly to keep calm and give her hands something to do.

Bengt had entered the morgue. He directed the hostages to leave on Grajauskas's orders. He was alone there.

Suddenly he started speaking Swedish again, his voice strained, Ewert knew it well. He could hear Bengt was close to breaking.

'Ewert, it's a fucking con, all of it. She didn't shoot anyone. They were all still here, all four of the hostages. They're alive, and they just walked out. She's rigged three hectograms of Semtex around those doors, but she has no way to trigger it.'

She interrupted heatedly.

'Speak Russian!'

Ewert Grens had heard, but didn't understand. He looked at the others, saw his own surprise reflected on their faces. There must have been more of them in there. From the beginning. More than five. She'd shot one through the kneecaps. One she blew up. Nevertheless, four were alive, four had just walked out.

Bengt Nordwall's voice again, in Swedish, probably still facing her.

'The only thing she has is a gun. A nine-millimetre Pistolet Makarova, a Russian officer's weapon. She's not going to be able to trigger those explosives without a generator or a battery. I can see a battery, but I can't see any cables connected to it.'

'You speak Russian! Or you die!'

Ewert Grens was still sitting down, listening to Edvardson's translation.

She explained that Bengt had to stand still and silent in front of her.

She spat on the floor in front of him, demanded that he take off his underwear, too.

When he hesitated, she pressed the gun to his head until his underwear lay on the floor beside him.

Grens stood up quickly – her deception, Bengt's naked body – and looked at Edvardson, who nodded.

He picked up the radio, signalled the SWAT team to prepare for an attack, gave the snipers permission to fire.

———

'You're naked.'

'You wanted that.'

'How does it feel? To stand naked in a morgue, in front of a woman with a gun in her hand?'

'I've done what you asked me to.'

'You feel humiliated. Right?'

'Yes.'

'Alone?'

'Yes.'

'Scared?'

'Yes.'

'Down on your knees.'

'Why?'

'Down on your knees with your hands behind your head.'

'Isn't this enough?'

'On your knees.'

'Is this OK?'

'See – you *can* do it.'

'And now what?'

'Do you know who I am?'

'No.'

'Do you remember me?'

'What do you mean?'

'I mean what I said. Do you remember me, Bengt Nordwall?'

'No.'

BOX 21

'Really?'

'No.'

'Klaipeda, Lithuania. The twenty-sixth of June, two thousand and two.'

'I don't know what you're talking about.'

'The *Stena Baltica*. The twenty-sixth of June, two thousand and two. At eight twenty-five p.m.'

———

Ewert Grens had only seen Lydia Grajauskas once, less than twenty-four hours ago, lying unconscious on the other side of a broken-down apartment door. He'd just pushed past somebody they called Dimitri Pimp-Fucker, and walked quickly down the hall towards a naked body. She had a broken arm, a swollen face, and was covered in blood. Her back had more lashes on it than he could count. He'd met women like her before. Their names were different, but not their stories. Young women raped, beaten, then patched up well enough to be raped and beaten again. They often disappeared, as suddenly as they arrived, changed apartments and customers. They made a few rounds, and then they disappeared for ever. There was always somebody new to sell, three thousand euros for one of the younger ones, girls who could take even more beatings.

He'd watched her carried off on a stretcher.

He could understand her hatred. It wasn't difficult to imagine that at a certain point when someone has suffered that much, if they managed to survive, they might want to make someone else suffer.

But what he couldn't understand was her strength. How could she keep that destroyed body upright giving orders in that weak voice? And why was she targeting doctors in white coats and a police officer? He couldn't understand *what she truly wanted.* Not even when he interrupted Edvardson's simultaneous translation and started screaming.

'The *Stena Baltica*? It's a fucking boat! This is something personal! Bengt, over. Damn it, Bengt, fall back! Fall back now! SWAT team, you're clear to go in. I repeat, SWAT team is cleared to go in!'

———————

Afterwards their descriptions differed somewhat when it came to the timeline. Time is often the most difficult thing to understand when someone stops breathing. But their observations of the events, what happened and in what order, were virtually identical. In the temporary command centre they'd stood next to each other listening to the same radio, heard two shots in quick succession, another one not long after, then a powerful explosion as the SWAT team penetrated the morgue's outer door and went in.

Now
Part Two

A DEATH KEEPS GOING.

Ewert Grens knew that. He had been a police officer for over thirty years, investigating homicides for most of them. His work often started with the death itself, that's what he worked on, the aftermath, the continuation.

And every time was different, the way people continued to live on, afterwards. Some just disappeared silently, no questions asked, no one to miss them, as if they'd never existed.

Others seemed even more alive in their deaths, the commotion, the hunt, all those words from people who knew them and people who didn't, but who now repeated their stories until they became the truth.

You're breathing, and just a moment later, you're not.

But how your death keeps going is almost entirely dependent on why you stop breathing.

So when the sound of three shots in the morgue rang inside his headphones, he was already sure things had gone to hell. It was that kind of sound, the kind that crawled inside you.

He might have expected the grief, the grief he wouldn't allow himself to feel, but that would eat at him until the day he died. He might have foreseen the loneliness, which would be even more profound than he feared.

But not the rest.

Despite the strange and violent death he'd just listened to, Ewert Grens never could have foreseen *how this death would keep going*, that the days ahead would be the worst days of his life.

———————

He didn't cry. It's hard to know why, he couldn't give any reasonable explanation, but he couldn't cry. He didn't do it later either, not when he stepped over the broken-down door of the morgue, not when he found two people on the floor with holes through their heads, their blood still fresh.

Bengt lay on his back, shot twice.

Once through the left eye. Once through his genitals, and his bloody hands lay in front of them.

She'd shot him there first, and he had instinctively moved his hands down to protect himself.

He was naked, pale bare skin resting against the grey-tile floors of the morgue. Lydia Grajauskas lay next to him, her broken arm twisted beneath her. She had shot herself in the temple. She must have fallen hard, almost bounced, to end up on her stomach like that.

Ewert Grens walked cautiously along the freshly drawn lines dividing the room. He needed an overview if he was going to be effective. This was what he'd always done, worked worked worked to avoid feeling. He didn't need any drugs to turn off his emotions, he just put his head down and moved forward, until the worst was over.

He poked a pale thigh gently with his foot.

You damn idiot.
How can you lie there without looking at me?

From not far away, Sven Sundkvist watched as Ewert pushed his foot into Bengt Nordwall's thigh and then stood there wordlessly, above a dead body encircled by white lines.

BOX 21

'Ewert?'

'Yes?'

'I'll take over.'

'I'm the one who's in charge here.'

'I know that. But I can take it from here, just for a bit, I'll finish the examination. You don't need to be here, not right now.'

'I'm working, Sven.'

'I know it can't be—'

'Sven, how could a whore trick us so completely?'

'Ewert, go now.'

'Do you understand it, Sven? If not, then move over, you might have something else to do.'

You fucking idiot.
Say something.
You're not talking.
You're lying there naked on the floor with your mouth shut.
Get up!

Grens recognised all four forensic technicians kneeling in the rooms of the morgue, looking for the things forensic technicians look for. Two of them were his age, and they'd been meeting like this for many years, at crime scenes where life became death, then had no contact at all while an investigation was under way until a few months passed, and they met at the next death. He gently poked at Bengt's thigh for a second time, then walked over to a technician who was dusting a plastic grocery bag for prints.

'Nils?'

'Ewert, I'm sorry, I mean, Bengt . . .'

'Not now. I'm working. Is that hers?'

'It would seem so. Plenty of ammunition left. Some more

plastic explosives and some blasting caps. A couple of pages torn out of a notebook. And a videotape.'

'How many people's prints are on there?'

'Two. Small hands. Two right, two left. I'm pretty sure that they are both women.'

'Two women?'

'One set probably belongs to her.'

The forensic technician whose name was Nils Krantz nodded at Lydia Grajauskas's motionless body. Ewert looked at her, then at what Krantz was holding in his hand.

'Can I get that later?'

Ewert pointed at the videotape.

'That is, when you're done with it.'

'Just need a few more minutes.'

Ammunition. Plastic explosives. A videotape. Ewert Grens studied her flayed back.

What did you *really* want?

A man started shouting from the corridor, somewhere close to where the door to the morgue used to stand.

'Ewert?'

'I hear you.'

'Come here for a minute.'

Ewert was surprised Errfors had got here so quickly.

'Look here.'

The medical examiner was standing in the middle of what had once been a human body – the body she'd had them drag out and blown up to prove how serious she was. He pointed to a torn-off arm, bent down and picked it up.

'Ewert. Look here. A dead human being.'

'I don't have time for games.'

'I want you to take a look at it.'

'What the hell's the matter with you? I heard the body being blown to smithereens. I know that he or she is dead.'

BOX 21

'It *is* a dead person. And it *was* a dead person at the time it was blown up. This guy's been dead for a week.'

Ewert touched the arm that Errfors was holding. It was colder than he'd expected. He had felt . . . fooled before. Without really knowing why. Now he knew.

'Look around, Ewert. No blood. Just a smell. You recognise it?'

'Yep.'

'What does it smell like?'

'Bitter. Like bitter almonds. Bengt tried to describe that pungent odour. Before he went in.'

'Formaldehyde. You transfuse it into a corpse in order to preserve it.'

'Formaldehyde?'

'She blew up a corpse. She shot another one. Those weren't hostages. Only the first one, Larsen, the medical student, who tried to overpower her. That was the only hostage she shot.'

Errfors was holding an arm that had been dead for a week, and he shook his head, then bent down and put it on the floor in exactly the spot he'd found it. Then Ewert Grens started searching through the corridor, walking from one body part to another.

No blood, but the same odour.

She had blown up a corpse. She'd left the hostages alone. She'd wanted Bengt, and only Bengt.

That was what she really wanted.

He walked back into the morgue and over to Bengt's naked body, next to a woman in too-large hospital clothes.

You're not saying anything.
Bengt.
Say something, damn it!

218

As he tried to get closer to them, he almost stepped into the blood that had flowed from her temple.

So he was the one you wanted.
Fucking whore!
I don't get it.

He didn't hear Nils approaching from behind him, nor did he hear him offering the plastic bag and video. So Nils tapped him on his back and repeated what he'd just said.

'The tape, Ewert. The videotape. You wanted it.'

'Fine. Fine. Thanks. You find anything else?'

'Just like the rest. Two sets of prints. Probably women, Grajauskas and someone else.'

'And it was with the ammunition?'

'In a grocery bag.'

He was already on his way to the next thing. Grens shouted after him.

'You want it back?'

'No, chain of evidence, send it on to County Criminal.'

Grens watched as Nils walked over to a door that seemed to lead to some kind of storage and started to gently examine the strands of doughy material that she had daubed around the doorframe.

'Ewert?'

Sven Sundkvist was waiting next to the landline telephone she'd called them from, which they'd turned off then on again. Grens closed his eyes, trying to see her in front of him, her gun pointed at the hostages, making threats but no demands into the phone. Skinny and bandaged in her hospital clothes, she'd forced them to evacuate a significant portion of one of Sweden's largest hospitals, had attracted every police officer and journalist in driving distance to the scene, for a few hours

BOX 21

this woman was able to terrify as many men as she'd been bought by.

'Ewert?'

'Yes?'

'The widow.'

Ewert Grens heard Bengt's voice, but as if from a distance. It was the last conversation they had. When his closest friend, his only link to his past, was still alive. He'd stood there in his underwear in this fucking corridor and asked Ewert to talk to Lena. *If something happens*, he'd said, *if something happens, I want you to talk to Lena.* As if he'd known. As if he'd sensed what was waiting for him inside.

'What do you mean?'

Sundkvist shrugged.

'You know her. You have to go out there.'

Sven hadn't been able to see it before, but now he did. The pale body seemed so calm, hands resting together on its stomach, almost interlacing, legs straight out, feet pointing outwards. It was as if the fear of a gun to the head had never existed.

So I'm the one who's supposed to talk to Lena.

Say something!

I'm the one who has to go out there.

I'm the one who's alive.

Dead!

You're not alive.

You're dead!

Grens knew he'd already made them wait too long. This was urgent. Lang needed to have his body inspected, and every minute that passed by decreased their chances of finding what they needed: blood and DNA belonging to Hilding Oldéus.

He'd insisted on being there for the examination. He needed to be in control of everything until the man he hated was locked up. He commandeered a patrol car that was leaving Söder Hospital and got them to take him back to the police station, thanked the officers for the ride, entered the building, and took the lift up to the holding area.

The infirmary was at the end of the corridor. Ewert Grens hurried past the rows of thick steel doors that led to narrow jail cells. His limping step and the click of his hard heels echoed down the ugly, dimly lit hall.

He'd been in the infirmary several times before at informal hearings, or for the occasional hasty deliberation. It was a fully equipped hospital room, a hospital bed pushed against the wall, a rolling table with metal instruments, a couple of electronic devices that Grens didn't have a clue about.

He searched the room.

So many people. He counted ten.

With a bright light directed at his body, Lang stood naked and handcuffed. Shaved head, muscular body and cold, staring eyes. He stared at Grens when the door opened.

'You too.'

'Lang?'

'You also want a good look at my cock.'

Ewert Grens smiled at him. Try to provoke me all you want. I don't hear you. Not now. My best friend just died.

Grens nodded towards the others, received nods in return. Four uniformed police officers, three prison guards, two forensic technicians.

He recognised them all.

Then he looked at the hospital bed, at the paper bags lying there with Lang's clothes inside them, one bag for each item. One

BOX 21

of the technicians, a pair of plastic gloves on his hands, was putting a black sock into the last bag. His colleague stood beside him with an arm in the air and his fingers around a tubular lamp.

The forensic technician turned it on and pointed it at Lang's body. A blue light swept slowly from his face to feet.

It didn't need to go far before detecting probable bloodstains. A cotton swab was put to the skin by someone collecting samples for analysis. They methodically searched each part of his body. What they found might mean the difference between an acquittal and a conviction.

'What do you say, Grens?'

Jochum Lang stuck out his tongue, thrust his genitals back and forth.

'What do you say? Every fucking time. The same thing. You all crowd in here. Every fucking faggot in the police force. Try to get a peek.'

Lang was thrusting his genitals faster now, and moaning, wagging his tongue at the two police officers standing closest to him.

'Like these fellas. No fucking ways these guys are cops, Grens. No fucking way. These guys are the Village People, for fuck's sake. Be proud, boys. Be gay. Sing it with me now. *It's fun to stay at the* YMCA.'

Lang kept his stance wide, continuing to sing and thrusting his hips until one of the younger officers couldn't take it any more and moved in close. Just stood there, breathing heavily.

'Step back, officer.'

Ewert Grens shot him an angry stare and didn't relent until the young officer backed off to his original position.

Grens looked at Lang.

'You're going down. Life sentence. Which you should have been handed twenty-five years ago. We have a witness.'

'Life? For bodily harm?'

Lang thrust his genitals forward violently one last time, *be proud, be gay*, and blew a kiss.

'Jesus Christ, Grens. It's called a line-up. Heard of it? They never work out. You know that.'

'Threats.'

'That's something else I've been acquitted of. Six times.'

'Obstruction of justice. That's what we call it around here.'

The two forensic technicians looked at Grens, who nodded for them to continue.

The bluish light, the cotton swabs searching for fragments of DNA in armpit hair.

Ewert Grens had seen what he came to see. One day, maybe two, and they'd get test results back.

He sighed.

This fucking day.

He knew where he had to go. Soon he would have to visit Lena, bearing the news of death. Bengt was still alive for her.

'Hey! Grens!'

Jochum Lang still stood naked in the middle of the room – a technician was digging under his toenails.

'Yes?'

Lang's puckered his mouth and blew Grens a kiss.

'I heard about your colleague. That guy in the morgue. Too bad. Guess he ended up on the floor? It's just so sad. Guess you knew each other? Just like with that chick from the SWAT team? I know it can be . . . tough. Isn't that right, Grens?'

Lang smacked his lips again, blowing kisses.

Ewert Grens took a deep breath, then turned and walked away.

It was about a twenty-five-minute drive to Eriksberg – the suburb Grens had visited just a week earlier. They sat in silence

BOX 21

throughout the trip. Before Sven picked up Ewert, he'd called Anita and Jonas to tell them he was going to be even later. Maybe they could eat cake together tomorrow instead. Errfors was in the back seat. Grens had asked him to bring along a sedative, because you never know how someone will react when death arrives.

Grens's mind was still in the infirmary. A naked Lang had stood there thrusting his hips, but he had no idea that he was just setting himself up for a life sentence, because as long as he continued to act like a fucking gangster, as long as he kept his fucking mouth shut – denying and lying and sitting in silence, the typical interrogation game – as long as Lang refused to admit to at least *assaulting* Oldéus, the more likely he was to be sentenced to murder. The fucker had no idea there was a witness willing to testify, despite the threats. Ewert Grens was struck by the irony that when he finally had a witness, someone to testify and connect Jochum Lang to a violent crime, that he himself was on his way to tell Bengt's wife of his death. A meaningless fucking death in the same building where Lang made the mistake of being seen by the wrong person. Anything. Anything but this, to be on the way to a woman who still didn't know.

They weren't that close.

He'd sat in their garden or living room, drunk their coffee once a week since they moved out there, since she married his closest friend. She had always treated him with warmth and kindness, and he had done the best he could, but they'd never become close, maybe because of the age difference or maybe they were just too different. They shared Bengt and maybe that shared love was enough.

Grens was still in the car staring at the front of their small house. The kitchen and hall lights were on, but the second floor was dark. She was probably down there waiting for her husband to come home. Ewert knew they usually ate late.

I can't do it.

Lena is inside, and she has no idea. He's still alive for her.

As long as she doesn't know, he's still alive. As soon as I've told her, he's truly dead.

He knocked on the door. They had young children, maybe they were asleep? He hoped they were. When do children go to bed? He waited with Sven and Errfors behind him on the gravel path below the steps. She dawdled. He knocked again, a little harder, a little longer. He heard her walking across the floor, caught her hasty glance through the kitchen window. She unlocked the door and opened it. He had done this so many times before, brought this news to relatives, but never to someone he actually cared about.

I shouldn't have to stand here.
If you were alive I wouldn't be here, waiting outside a door
holding your death in my hands.

He never said a word. He just stood in front of her, held her tight on the doorstep with the door still open. He had no idea how long it would take until she stopped crying.

They went into the kitchen. She put on coffee and put out four cups, and he told her what he thought she wanted to know. She said nothing, nothing at all, not until they were all on their second cup. Then she asked him to tell her again exactly how it happened, who this woman was, how Bengt had been murdered, what he looked like afterwards, what *exactly this woman wanted*. He did as she said. He described what had happened in detail until she was satisfied. He knew it was the only thing he could do, tell her again and again, until she slowly started to understand.

She cried a long time at the kitchen table holding on to his

BOX 21

arm, asking him what he thought she should say to the children, Ewert, what do you want me to say to the kids?

———————

Grens's cheek was hot.

He was in the car on his way back, watching streetlights light up over the deserted streets.

She'd hit him hard.

He hadn't been prepared. They were out in the hall just about to go, and she suddenly ran over to him and shouted *you can't say those things* and then slapped him hard across his left cheek. At first, he hadn't understood, but it quickly occurred to him that she probably had the right to do it. Then she screamed it again, *you can't say those things*, and raised her arm. He'd stood where he was. What else could he do? Grab hold of her like he would usually do when he was threatened? She had screamed shrilly, and Sven had stepped forward, taken her arm and pushed her back into the kitchen.

He looked at Sven, who was driving, then touched his own cheek. It was almost numb. She'd struck his cheekbone.

He understood her.

He had come to her bearing death.

———————

It was past ten and still light outside. The rain was finally gone. It had turned out to be a beautiful evening. Sven dropped Grens off at Kronoberg. They'd been just as silent on the way back as they'd been on their way there. They could feel her despair, and it weighed on them. There were no words.

Ewert Grens walked into his office, a pile of yellow and green Post-its lay on his desk, messages from journalists who had called and would keep calling. He threw them all in the bin. He'd arrange some more press conferences far away from here, and he'd ask some PR people to answer the questions he had no desire to hear. He sat down at his desk. The whole building was quiet. He spun around in his chair a few times, stopped, spun again. He wasn't thinking, just trying to go through what had happened over the last few hours: Bengt's death and Grajauskas's death and the hostages she hadn't hurt, and Bengt who wouldn't look up from that fucking floor, and Lena who sat at her kitchen table clutching his arm tightly. He tried to take it one thing at a time. It didn't work. He couldn't. His thoughts weren't his own. He sat there spinning around and couldn't manage to hold on to any of them.

One and a half hours. Alone in that chair without a single thought.

The janitor, a smiling young man who spoke decent Swedish, had knocked and Ewert let him in. At least it was an interruption, someone moving around him for a few minutes with a mop, emptying the rubbish on his way out, better that than the thoughts he couldn't think.

Anni, help me.

Sometimes he missed people. Sometimes loneliness was so incredibly ugly.

He lifted the telephone and dialled a number he knew by heart. It was late, but she was usually awake. When your life was like being asleep, maybe you didn't need to rest as much.

One of the young assistants answered. He knew who she was. A young woman who'd worked part-time in the evenings for the last few years, working extra to supplement her student loans.

'Good evening. This is Ewert Grens.'

'Hello, Ewert.'

'I'd like to speak with her.'

BOX 21

A pause, as if she were glancing at the clock sitting behind her at the reception.

'It's a little late.'

'I know that. But it's important.'

The young nurses' assistant left her place, and he could hear her footsteps disappearing down a corridor. A couple of minutes, and then she was back.

'She was awake. I told her that you wanted to speak to her. There's a staff member in her room holding the phone up for her. I'll connect you.'

He heard deep breaths. She babbled as she usually did when she was on the telephone. He hoped they were wiping the saliva off her chin.

'Hello, Anni. It's me.'

Her way too loud laughter. It made him feel warm, almost calm.

'You have to help me. I don't understand anything any more.'

He spoke to her for just over a quarter of an hour. She was panting, laughing at times, but mostly quiet. He missed her already when he hung up.

He stood up. His big body felt heavy, but not tired. He walked a few doors down the hall. The oversized conference room was always unlocked.

Grens stood for a moment in the dark, searching for the switch, found it higher up than he remembered, and it turned on the lights, TV, VCR, and whirring projector simultaneously. He had never mastered these damn machines and swore out loud until he managed to locate the right channel for the VCR.

He put on a pair of plastic gloves and gently coaxed the videotape out of the grocery bag. He'd been carrying it in his inner jacket pocket since leaving the morgue.

The image was flooded by a strong bluish light. Two women

on a sofa in front of a window, the sun shone in and whoever was holding the camera had no clue how to adjust the white balance and sharpness.

But they were clear enough.

He recognised them both.

Lydia Grajauskas and Alena Sljusareva, in the apartment with electronic locks, where he'd first seen them.

They are waiting silently, probably for a sign from the cameraman who is moving the lens up and down, while he turns on the microphone, as if to test it.

They look nervous, as people do when they're not used to staring into an eye that captures and keeps whatever it sees.

Grajauskas speaks first.

'Это мой повод. Моя история такая.'

Two sentences at a time.

She turns to Sljusareva, who continues in Swedish.

'This is my reason. This is my story.'

Grajauskas again, she looks at her friend, and says two more sentences.

'Надеюсь что когда ты слышишь это того о ком идет речь уже нет. Что он чувствовал мой стыд.'

She nods, looking serious, waiting for Sljusareva to address the camera and translate.

'When you hear this, I hope the man I speak of is dead. That he has felt my shame.'

They speak slowly, careful to make sure that every word in Russian and every word in broken Swedish can be understood.

Ewert Grens sat quietly in front of the television for twenty minutes.

He saw and heard something that didn't exist.

BOX 21

He saw her again as victim rather than perp, as battered woman rather than whore.

He slammed the table in front of him like he always did, clenched his fist until it hurt. He screamed and crashed around, sometimes he couldn't do anything else.

I was just there.
I was the one who had to tell Lena!
Who do you think is going to tell her this?
She doesn't deserve this.
Do you understand!
She should never have to hear this.

He thought the scream had been inside him, had been sure it was, but he felt it in his throat.

He turned to the VCR, looked at the flickering screen. He rewound the tape.

'When you hear this, I hope the man I speak of is dead. That he has felt my shame.'

Grens listened to their first sentences once more, rewound to the beginning. He saw Bengt and Lydia in front of him, lying on the morgue floor next to each other, she on her stomach her arm twisted, Bengt naked, his genitals shot, a hole in his eyes.

Maybe if you had admitted it when she asked you.
Jesus Christ, Bengt!
She did ask you!
If you had said yes.
If you'd told her that you knew who she was.
Maybe you'd still be alive.
Maybe that would have been enough.

If you'd just acknowledged her.
Said you understood.

He hesitated for a few seconds, then pressed the red record button. He was going to erase what he'd just seen. From now on, it would no longer exist.

None of it.

He pressed the same button twice, but nothing happened, the taped moved neither forward nor backward.

He took the black plastic tape out of the VCR, looked at the back, and discovered the security tab had been broken. They had done what they could to protect their story, so that it would be impossible to take it away from them, so that it could never be recorded over.

Ewert Grens knew what he had to do.

He put the tape in his inner pocket and walked out of the room.

It was after midnight, and Lena Nordwall stood at the sink in front of four cups still smelling of coffee.

She washed them in hot water, in cold, warm, cold, she washed them for thirty minutes before she had strength to let them go. She dried them afterwards one by one with a tea towel. They had to be completely dry – one more towel, had to be sure. She put them in a row on the kitchen table, and they shone under the fluorescent lamp in the ceiling.

She lifted them and threw them, one by one, into the hall and at the wall there.

She was still at the sink when her son came downstairs in his pyjamas. The boy pointed to the porcelain mugs lying on the floor and told his mother those cups make a loud sound when they shatter.

Thursday, 6 June

EWERT GRENS's back ached.

The sofa in his office was too small. He needed to have it replaced. It had been hard to sleep. Bengt's lie, Grajauskas and the other woman on the tape, Anni's hand that he could no longer hold, the weeping that left him empty. His clothes were wrinkled and his breath stale. He sat up through the wee hours of the morning, trying to work on the Lang and Oldéus investigation, but Grajauskas and her friend kept intruding. There they sat pale and exhausted. They spoke of his best friend and the shame they hoped he would suffer. He had tried to fall back asleep, tossing and turning until sunrise forced him up again.

He patted the plastic bag and tape that still lay in the inside pocket of his jacket, absently running his fingers over it. He had tried to erase it, but failed. But he'd already made up his mind. Nothing had changed. It had to disappear.

Grens left his office and walked along the empty hallways of the police station. He bought a stale cheese sandwich and a juice from the vending machine. He went to the locker room, undressed, and took a long shower.

I have to go to her soon.
I brought death last time.
Should I bring shame this time?

That fucking morgue, he let it wash off him and run down the drain in the floor. The water beat against the crown of his bald head and his shoulders. At least for a brief moment he felt his irritation cease. He grabbed a towel someone had left there. He dried off, got dressed, walked out to the hallway and the vending machine again. A cup of coffee. Black, as usual. He was starting to slowly wake up again.

'Grens.'

He heard her voice from inside the office he'd just passed. She had papers scattered across the desk, the visitors' sofa, and whatever free space there was on the bookshelf.

'Hermansson. You're here early.'

She was so young and so ambitious. Time usually took care of that.

'These are the witness statements from Söder Hospital. They're quite interesting. I wanted to go through them in peace and quiet.'

'Anything I should know?'

'I think so. I'm waiting for a statement from the guard Grajauskas knocked out. And the boys who watched TV with her. They're printing out right now.'

'And?'

'The connection between Grajauskas and Sljusareva seems very likely.'

Maybe it was her southern accent. Or her calm demeanour. He was listening. Just as he had listened to her – too late – yesterday in the temporary command centre in Casualty. He should tell her that. That she was good. He believed what she said. That didn't happen often.

'I want to know more.'

'Can you give me a few more hours? Then I'll have a clearer picture for you.'

'After lunch.'

He was on his way out. He should say it.

'By the way.'

'Yes?'

BOX 21

She looked at him. He should continue.

'You did well yesterday. Your analysis. What you said was spot on. I'd gladly work with you again.'

She smiled. He hadn't expected that.

'Praise. From Ewert Grens. That doesn't happen every day.'

Grens just stood there. Vulnerable, naked. He didn't recognise this feeling, almost regretted saying anything to her, and so he changed the subject, it didn't matter to what.

'The AV storage room.'

'What?'

'I need a few things. But I've never been there. Do you know where it is?'

Hermansson stood up. She laughed. Ewert Grens didn't know why. She looked at him and laughed, and he felt very uncomfortable.

'Listen, Grens. Just between us, OK?'

'Yes?'

'Have you ever praised a female police officer before?'

She was still laughing as she pointed out where the AV storage was.

'Down there next to the coffee machine.'

She went back into her office, rooting among the papers she'd put on the floor. She had laughed at him. He didn't understand why.

———

Lisa Öhrström had kept her eyes closed for a long time.

She'd heard the dark-haired man who'd threatened her get up and leave. But she remained paralysed, not daring to move, until Ann-Marie left the glass-walled nurses' station and came back into the kitchen. The older woman had spoken to her quietly, cleaned her up, held her, sat down next to her at the table. They had even played the children's game of slapping their hands on top of each other over and over again.

She had gone home after that. She didn't meet her patients, even though she wanted to. Fear had drained her – she'd never felt anything like it before.

It had been a long night.

She had tried to reason away the ache in her chest. Her heart had raced, and she tried to take deep calming breaths to slow its rhythm. Instead the sound of her own breath terrified her. She didn't dare to fall asleep, afraid she might never wake up again – don't fall asleep, don't close your eyes, not any more.

Jonathan and Sanna.

The whole night had been spent thinking about them.

She had kept her breath slow, trying to push the thought of them away. She loved them. More than she'd ever loved anyone. Except maybe Hilding, that is until he forced her to stop. But Jonathan and Sanna were a part of her.

The man had been holding their photos. He knew they existed.

That terrible ache in her chest.

They were her weakness and her strength. They were the only thing she couldn't bear to lose. And yet her love of them made it possible to make it through the panic.

Detective Inspector Sven Sundkvist, who had interrogated her after Hilding disappeared down the stairs, called her early in the morning. She was still in bed. He'd apologised, but explained that they had to move fast. He asked her to come into the police station as soon as she could.

Now she was waiting in a dark room somewhere in the station. She wasn't alone. Sundkvist was standing nearby, and a lawyer who she assumed was representing the suspect had just entered.

BOX 21

The detective asked her to take her time. There was no hurry. It was important that she was sure of her choice.

She walked over to the window.

Sundkvist had assured her that she was hidden from the people on the other side of the glass. They saw only a mirror.

There were ten men there.

All about the same height, same age, all with shaved heads.

They had signs hanging down over their chests. Black numbers on a white background. They stood side by side, shoulder to shoulder, staring at her. Or at least that's how it felt, as if the men on the other side of the glass were watching every move she made.

She looked for a few seconds at each of them, from head to toe. She avoided their eyes.

'No.'

She shook her head.

'None of them.'

Sven Sundkvist moved closer to her.

'Are you sure?'

'He's not there.'

Sundkvist nodded towards the window.

'They're going to walk in a circle now. I want you to look at them again.'

The man standing at the far left with the number one across his chest. He took a few steps forward, slowly making a lap in the rather large space. She followed him with her eyes. He had a swaying gait, a confident way of moving. It was him.

That was Lang.

Stupid fucking Hilding.

She saw him stop in the same place he'd just left, and number two took a lap. She followed each one as they did the same. They'd all looked alike not long ago, but now she could see their differences more clearly.

Sven Sundkvist was silent through it all. Now he turned to her again, waiting for her response.

'Now you've seen them all again. Face, posture, the way they move. Do you recognise any of them?'

She didn't look at him. She couldn't.

'No.'

'None of them?'

'None of them.'

'You're completely sure? None of these men was the one you saw just before he killed your *brother*, Hilding Oldéus?'

He looked at the woman in front of him. Her reaction surprised him. Her brother's death hadn't made her sad. She seemed more angry than sad.

'Haven't you ever heard of sibling love? I loved him. I loved the Hilding I grew up with. But not the man who died yesterday. Not Hilding the junkie. I hated him. I hated who he forced me to become.'

She swallowed. She swallowed everything that was knocking around inside her: anger and hate and fear and panic.

'And as I said before, I don't recognise any of the ten men standing on the other side of the glass.'

'So you've never seen any of them before?'

'No.'

'And you are absolutely sure of that?'

The lawyer, a man in his forties wearing a suit and tie, who'd entered the room last, spoke for the first time. He had a piercing voice, and he was upset.

'It's enough now. The witness has told you she can't identify any of them. And still you keep pressuring her!'

'I'm just trying to see why this doesn't fit an earlier witness statement.'

'You're pressuring her.'

He leaned over towards Sundkvist.

BOX 21

'I want you to release Lang. Now. You've got absolutely nothing.'

Sven Sundkvist took his arm and led him gently towards the exit.

'I know how this works. If you'll excuse me, I'm in the middle of a conversation.'

He escorted the lawyer to the door, made sure that it was closed. Lisa Öhrström stood at the window, staring at it. The room on the other side was now empty.

'I don't understand.'

Sundkvist went over to the window, inserted himself between it and Lisa.

'I don't understand. Don't you remember our conversation yesterday?'

Lisa Öhrström's neck was flushed. Her eyes were pleading.

'Yes.'

'Then you must remember what you said.'

'Yes.'

'You pointed out the man in photo number thirty-two. I told you his name was Jochum Lang. You stated several times that you were sure that he was the one who'd beaten Hilding Oldéus to death. I know it, and you know it. That's why I don't understand why the hell you don't seem to be able to recognise him in the flesh.'

She didn't say anything, just shook her head and lowered her face to the floor.

'Have you been threatened?'

He waited for her answer. It didn't come.

'He usually works like that. Silences with threats. So that he can continue to hurt people.'

Sven Sundkvist tried to catch her eyes again, waiting her out.

'I'm sorry, Mr Sundkvist. I really am sorry. I have a niece and a nephew. Do you understand that? I love them.'

She cleared her throat.

'Do you understand?'

_____

Morning rush hour had dissipated, so it was an easy drive across the city. It took less than half an hour, and he arrived there for the second time in less than twelve hours.

Lena was glad to see him.

Before he even started to go up the short staircase to the front door, she walked out and hugged him. Ewert Grens wasn't used to physical contact. His first instinct was to pull back, but he remained where he was. They both needed this. She grabbed a jacket. It was still chilly out even though the rain had stopped. It was the kind of summer that never really got warm.

They had been walking in silence, lost in thought, for twenty minutes across an open field, headed in the direction of the Norsborg waterworks, when she asked Grens who the woman was.

The girl who shot him.

The one who had ended up on the floor beside Bengt.

Grens asked if it was important, and she nodded. She wanted to know, but she couldn't really explain why. He stopped and looked at her. He told her about the first time he'd seen Grajauskas in an apartment with electronic locks. She'd been unconscious and her back covered by the deep lashes of a whip. She listened, then walked a little further, and asked another question.

'I want to know what she looked like.'

'Now? Dead?'

'Before. I want a picture from before. Of who she was. She took the rest of our life together away, Ewert. I know you understand, if anyone could, what that means. I've looked for her on whatever newscasts I was able to endure. I looked through the morning papers when I woke up this morning. They're not showing any pictures of her. Maybe there aren't any. Maybe it

BOX 21

doesn't matter to anyone else what she looked like. Maybe it's enough for them to know what she did, and how things ended.'

The rest of our life together away.

Ewert Grens had said and thought the same thing.

The wind was blowing gently. He buttoned up his jacket while they continued to walk. I have it here, he thought. In my inner pocket. I have the photograph we got from our Lithuanian colleagues.

And Lena, I have that fucking tape. Which will soon no longer exist. There is so much you'll never know.

'I have a photo.'

'You do?'

'Yes.'

Grens stopped, unbuttoned the jacket he'd just buttoned. He held an envelope in his hand, opened it, showed her a black and white photograph of a girl.

She was smiling in the picture. Long blonde hair put into some kind of bow.

'Lydia Grajauskas. She was twenty years old. From Klaipeda. This picture was taken over three years ago, just before she disappeared from her home.'

Lena Nordwall put her fingers on the face, searching it as if trying to find something she recognised.

'Pretty.'

She wanted to say more. He could see it.

She stared at the picture of the young woman who had shot her husband less than a day ago.

She didn't say anything.

Sven Sundkvist had come home late the day before.

It was almost midnight and Anita was sitting in the kitchen reading. She'd waited up for him, just as she said she would. He hugged her for a long time, then went and got the silver candleholders they both liked so much. He lit white candles, and they just looked at each other while they ate from the half a cake that was left and drank a few glasses of wine.

He had just turned forty-one years old and was already on the way to turning forty-two.

He had gone upstairs and into Jonas's room, kissed him on the forehead, and immediately regretted it, because Jonas woke up looking confused, muttering something unintelligible. Sven stayed with him until he fell asleep again, just a few minutes of gently stroking his cheek. He had sought out Anita in the bathroom and told her how beautiful she was, squeezed her hand as they lay down. Her naked body, they held each other for a long time afterwards.

He woke up early.

The house was quiet when he left.

He realised he'd been too eager. He already had photo identification, but still he'd called Lisa Öhrström for a line-up when he got into his office. Photo identification *and* a line-up, it was unprofessional, and he knew it, but this was urgent, and he wanted to be sure. They needed to make sure that the prosecutor Ågestam wouldn't let Jochum Lang go, not this time.

So he was furious now as he left Öhrström standing by the window that separated her from where the line-up had just taken place. He tried not to show it. He knew it wasn't really her fault. She was a victim, terrified by death threats. But he couldn't help it. He was sarcastic and condescending, and over-whelmed by unreasonable anger. It was hard to handle.

He hurried away from there.

BOX 21

Heading to the interrogation room at the Kronoberg police station. Lang wasn't getting out.

———

Construction work somewhere between Skärholmen and Fruängen made Ewert start beating the dashboard and screaming out loud. He was in a hurry. He had to run an errand at the police station, and then head on foot to St Erik's Street for lunch with Sven.

He knew he wasn't any good at this. He'd stood with his arm around Lena and tried to say what he thought he should say. But the only thing he felt now was how miserably he'd failed. He couldn't comfort people, couldn't hold them, and never could. She had stood in that open field, wind blowing, staring quietly at the photo of Lydia Grajauskas in her hand, clutching it hard, until he gently prised it from her fingers.

What had been the point of that visit anyway? Intruding on her grief. Because he missed Bengt? Because she didn't have anyone else? Because he didn't have anyone else?

Traffic crawled forward, three lanes had narrowed to one, and the minutes dripped from his forehead. He was going to be late. But he had no choice.

He needed to go to the storage room before lunch. Sven would have to wait.

———

The interrogation room was as bare as usual.

Sven Sundkvist was out of breath by the time he got there. Anger had followed him through the halls of the police station, and he'd hurried over even more quickly than was necessary. Lang was sitting by the table smoking, and he didn't even look up as Sven entered the room.

INTERVIEW LEADER SVEN SUNDKVIST (IL): You visited Hilding Oldéus at Söder Hospital just before he was found beaten to death.

JOCHUM LANG (JL): According to you.

IL: We have a witness.

JL: That's great, Sundkvist. Then you can bring them in here and arrange a line-up.

IL: The witness who pointed out where Oldéus's bed was.

JL: I mean, aren't they supposed to come and look at me and nine other guys through a window? You should do that, Sundkvist. That usually works out real well.

Sundkvist was boiling inside. Lang was trying to throw him off balance and succeeding. Have to stay calm, have to ask my questions, and no matter what he says, ask them again until I'm satisfied.

He looked at Jochum Lang, who smiled, who'd already heard from his lawyer about the failed line-up. Lawyers were quick to communicate that kind of thing.

But the man making threats wasn't going to be released. Not yet.

He was going to answer the questions again, and he'd say more than he intended, and that would be enough to persuade Ågestam to continue the investigation, with the culprit already locked up.

IL: We picked you up in an illegally parked BMW at the entrance to Söder Hospital.

JL: Really, Sundkvist. You investigate parking tickets, too?

IL: Why were you sitting inside a car in a cordoned-off area?

JL: I can sit wherever the hell I want to.

IL: We're not letting you go this time.

JL: Sundkvist, you better take me up to my cell now. Otherwise, I might do something that you *can* prosecute me for.

BOX 21

Ten past twelve.

Grens parked in front of the police station. Sven was most likely already at the restaurant, waiting impatiently. But he still went into the building, and into the corridor that led to his office. He stopped at the coffee machine, not for coffee, but to go into the storage room that stood next to it, the one Hermansson had pointed out, his destination.

The videotapes lay on a shelf at the back of the stuffy room in brown cardboard boxes with twenty tapes in each. He grabbed one, tore off the plastic, and took a cassette out of its sleeve. He checked it. It looked like the other one. Like they all looked the same.

Grens closed the storeroom and went to his office. Her things lay in a box on his desk. He picked up the grocery store bag and put the new videotape into it.

Lena's shame or hers?

Lena was alive. She was dead.

Grajauskas's story had disappeared. It lay in the waters of Lake Mälaren. He'd stopped by the shore on his way back from Eriksberg. Shame is a lot heavier when you're alive.

Ewert Grens yawned, slowly tossed the grocery bag with the new videotape back and forth a few times across the desk, then put it back in the box with her other belongings.

EWERT GRENS SAT down in one of the restaurant's furthest, darkest corners. A seat that would be difficult to spot if you were to just step inside and quickly glance around. This place is a real dive, he thought, and also not that close to the police station.

But he had no choice.

Journalists had been hunting for him all over Kungsholmen. They knew where he usually ate lunch, and he'd even seen a few on his way there standing on the street chewing the fat.

They weren't getting any answers. They weren't going to get a damn thing. Not from him. Now that the police had a PR division, it was their job to say as little as possible at those screaming press conferences.

So he'd turned the opposite direction, called Sven, and gone to this restaurant a couple of blocks away. He'd eaten here before when somebody's murder was filling up newspaper columns and had been served shitty food in peace and quiet.

He grabbed a newspaper from the next table over and read for a few minutes, six pages on the hostage crisis in Söder Hospital's morgue.

'I'd just got my food.'

Sven Sundkvist clapped him on the back and sat down.

'Sixty-five kronor, and I didn't even get to touch it. And for what? To come here?'

Sundkvist looked around and shook his head.

'Really classy place you chose.'

'Nobody will hound us with questions here.'

'I don't doubt it.'

BOX 21

They both ordered Skånsk beef stew with beetroot.

'How's she doing?'

'Lena?'

'Yes.'

'She's grieving.'

'She needs you there.'

Ewert Grens sighed loudly, put the magazine aside. He was worried, rocking back and forth in his chair.

'Sven, I have no idea what to do. I'm not good at that. I think I might have done the wrong thing. She wanted to see what Grajauskas looked like. I showed her the photograph.'

'Well, if that's what she wanted.'

'I don't know. It felt odd. It was as if she didn't understand. As if for a second she recognised her. She stared at the picture, touched it, she tried to speak, but said nothing.'

'She's still in shock.'

'She doesn't need to know what the woman who killed her husband looked like. I felt like I was rubbing it in her face.'

The food was mostly sauce with a piece of meat here or there. They ate because they had to.

'Ewert?'

'Yes?'

'It did not go well just now.'

Grens was chasing a beetroot across his plate. He gave up when it disappeared into the sea of instant gravy.

'Do I even want to know?'

'No.'

'Tell me anyway.'

Sven Sundkvist relived his morning for Grens.

Lisa Öhrström's fear and reluctance, which he'd felt as soon as she arrived. How she'd refused to point out any of the ten men, how he'd asked her to look again, but the whole time her reluctance and unwillingness to participate were obvious. His anger when he realised she'd been threatened. How she spoke about her love of her niece and nephew. Her denial and her shame and the lawyer who demanded Lang should be released.

Sven had anticipated his boss's reaction.

Ewert Grens put down his cutlery. His face turned red, his eyes narrowed, and the vein in his temple started to pulse. He was about to slam the table when Sven grabbed his arm to stop him.

'Not here, Ewert. We don't want to attract any attention.'

Grens was breathing heavily. His voice could barely contain his fury.

'Jesus Christ, Sven, listen to yourself.'

Ewert Grens stood up, walked around the table, kicking each table leg as he passed.

'Ewert, I'm as mad as you are. But you need to control yourself. Please. We're not in the office.'

'He threatened the doctor! He threatened the children!'

Sven Sundkvist hesitated before continuing, then took a small tape recorder out of his jacket pocket, and placed it on the table between their only half-eaten plates of food.

'I interrogated Lang afterwards. Listen.'

Two voices.

One trying to have a conversation.

One who was trying to avoid it.

Ewert Grens stopped pacing around the table, every muscle of his face tensed as Jochum Lang started to speak. He didn't say anything until the tape stopped, and Sven Sundkvist reached out to take back the tape recorder.

'One more time. Just the end.'

The sound of chairs scraping against the floor. The agitated breathing.

Lang's voice.

'Sundkvist, you better take me up to my cell now. Otherwise, I might do something that you can prosecute me for.'

BOX 21

Grens screamed loudly, and the few remaining customers turned towards the corner where a large, older man stood next to a table punching the air with his fists.

'Sit down, Ewert.'

'This, Sven, I don't buy it. No way I'll allow Lang to be in charge any more! He's going down this time. And I don't give a fuck what it takes.'

Ewert Grens pointed to Sundkvist.

'Lisa Öhrström's phone number.'

'Why?'

'Do you have it or not? Give me her number! We're going to do some actual police work, you and me, from this very restaurant.'

The young waitress cautiously approached their table. She took a deep breath, avoided Grens and looked at Sven Sundkvist, pleading for silence, and for some respect for the other guests. She explained that otherwise she'd be forced to call the police. Sundkvist apologised, promised they wouldn't make any more trouble, and asked for the bill.

'Here.'

Sundkvist handed Ewert Grens his diary. Lisa's number was printed neatly inside. Grens smiled at his younger colleague, the names and telephone numbers were listed in alphabetical order. That's how Sven did things.

Grens took out his phone and dialled the number. He reached her at the hospital. She had gone straight there after the line-up this morning.

'Öhrström? Detective Superintendent Ewert Grens here. In an hour I'm going to send some photos over to you. I want you to take a look at them.'

She hesitated, as if trying to understand what he said.

'What's this about?'

'Murder, robbery, assault and battery.'

'I don't understand.'

'What's your fax number?'

She was silent for a moment. It was obvious she didn't want to continue.

'Why do I need these pictures?'

'You'll understand when you see them. You'll be hearing from me in an hour.'

Ewert Grens waited impatiently while Sven Sundkvist emptied a glass of low-alcohol beer and searched for the money he was sure he had with him. Grens waved his hand at Sundkvist and paid for them both, leaving a bigger tip than the food called for.

They were on their way out of the door and into the chaos of St Eriks Street, when Grens spotted a few journalists. He asked Sundkvist to stop and waited with the door half open until he was sure they'd gone by.

They exited the aroma of Skånsk beef stew, walked quickly side by side for a few minutes down Fleming Street, headed for the police station, where they parted ways. Grens went to his office, left a few minutes later with two black and white photographs in his hand, headed for the fax machine in the corridor.

'Grens?'

He turned around. She had laughed at him when they met early this morning.

'Hermansson. You promised me a report. After lunch. It's after lunch.'

He wondered if he sounded angry. He wasn't.

'I'm ready.'

'And?'

'I've gathered all the witness statements. I've gone through them. They're very interesting.'

Ewert Grens was holding two pictures in his hand. She pointed to them, *are you faxing something, I can wait,* but he put them to the side and asked her to give him the report.

'The guard's statement in particular. He remembers a woman

BOX 21

visiting the disabled toilet just before Grajauskas. From his description, I'm almost sure it's her friend, Alena Sljusareva.'

Ewert Grens listened. He thought of this morning. He had praised her and then almost felt uncomfortable, vulnerable, and he didn't know why, not then and not now. He wasn't used to that.

'Also, the two young boys who were sitting with Grajauskas in the TV room. One of them remembers the same woman walk by. His description is almost identical to the guard's. Both accurate descriptions of Alena Sljusareva.'

Hermansson was carrying a folder filled with papers. They were part of the investigation, which would soon be twenty-four hours old, of a murder-suicide in a morgue. She held it up and tried to give it to him.

'It had to be her, Grens. She had to be the one who provided Lydia Grajauskas with weapons and explosives. I'm sure of it. Alena Sljusareva is an accessory to aggravated kidnapping and murder. We'll find her soon, she has nowhere to go.'

Ewert Grens took the folder. He looked at the young police officer who was just about to leave and cleared his throat.

'By the way.'

She stopped, turned around.

'You were wrong. You're the second female police officer I've praised. And I should do it again.'

She shook her head.

'Thank you. But that's enough for now.'

Hermansson was about to leave again, but he asked her to wait for one more question.

'What you said this morning.'

'Yes?'

'Did that mean you think I have a problem with female police officers?'

'Yes, that's what I meant.'

She hadn't hesitated. She had been calm and dispassionate, and he stood there feeling just as vulnerable.

But he understood. He thought of Anni.

Grens cleared his throat loudly. The coffee machine was next door, and he needed black coffee in a plastic cup. That's what he needed – the simple things that calmed him. He drained his cup, pressed the button for one more. He knew she was right, of course. And he knew why he had a problem with female police officers. With all women. Twenty-five years. It had been twenty-five years since he'd been with a woman. He could barely remember how it felt, but he missed it, even if he couldn't remember.

One more cup.

He drank the last one slowly. He never took more than three, and he liked to savour the peace the last one gave him. He was still drinking unhurriedly with one hand, when he realised he had two photographs in the other.

He knew they would work. Lisa Öhrström answered after five rings.

'One hour. You're very punctual.'

'I want you to go to your fax machine.'

Ewert Grens heard her footsteps in the corridor of her department in the hospital. He knew exactly where she was.

'Did you get them?'

'Yes.'

'And?'

'I don't know what you want.'

'What do you see?'

She sighed. He waited for her to speak again.

'What's this about?'

'You're a doctor. Look at the pictures. What do you see?'

Lisa Öhrström was quiet. He could hear her breathing, but she didn't say anything.

BOX 21

'For the last time. What do you see?'

'A left hand. Three of the fingers have fractures.'

'The thumb. Correct?'

'Correct.'

'Five thousand kronor.'

'I don't know what you're getting at.'

'Index finger. One thousand kronor. The little finger. One thousand kronor.'

'I still don't understand.'

'Jochum Lang. Those are his rates. And his signature. These photos are from a discontinued investigation. This guy owed seven thousand kronor. One of Lang's victims. That's the kind of professional you're protecting. And as long as you protect him, he'll keep working.'

Ewert Grens was silent for a moment, and then hung up. She'd sit there with three broken fingers in black and white in front of her. She'd do it until he contacted her again.

A door opened just down the corridor, and Grens turned towards it.

Sven Sundkvist seemed to be in a hurry – striding quickly in Grens's direction.

'Ewert, I just got a call.'

Grens sat down on the fax machine, his leg ached as it sometimes did, and he didn't seem to notice the plastic cover creaking under his weight. Sven Sundkvist heard but didn't have time. He looked at his boss.

'Down in the harbour. There's a Russian interpreter on the way.'

'Yes?'

'She was about to board a boat to Lithuania.'

Grens threw his arms wide impatiently.

'Get to the point.'

'Alena Sljusareva has just been picked up.'

THEY HAD TALKED about it so many times.

He'd sat with Bengt in various interrogation rooms or bars or in Bengt's garden, and they'd often end up talking about it – the truth. About how simple it was, there is the truth and there is a lie, and the truth is the only thing a person can really bear to live with in the long run.

Everything else was just bullshit.

A lie leads to a lie leads to a lie, and eventually you're so fucking turned around you wouldn't even recognise the truth if it was the only thing you had.

They had built their friendship on truth. You have to tell the truth no matter the consequences. Now and then when one of them thought the other one was being evasive, keeping his mouth shut out of politeness, they'd close the door and have a screaming match until everything had been said, the truth.

Ewert Grens shuddered. It was all a fucking lie.

Had he really thought he and Bengt shared the naked truth and nothing else?

He was sitting at his desk thinking about the tape, which he had carried around for a day and then thrown to the bottom of Lake Mälaren.

I'm lying now.
For Lena's sake.
Our worthless truth.
I'm lying to protect your lie.

BOX 21

Ewert Grens pulled the cardboard box that stood on the edge of his desk towards him. He leaned forward and lifted the cover off. He looked down at all the worldly belongings of Alena Sljusareva, confiscated when two policemen arrested her in the harbour a few hours ago. He grabbed the cardboard box and turned it upside down. Her life on his desk. It wasn't much, about what a person on the run could carry. He lifted up her things, and touched them one by one.

A money clip with a few thousand in it, her wages for being forced to service twelve johns a day for three years.

A diary, he broke the lock and flipped through it absently, the Cyrillic alphabet and long words he couldn't read.

A pair of cheap plastic sunglasses, the kind you buy in a hurry.

A fairly new mobile phone with more features than you could ever use.

A one-way ferry ticket departing today, 6 June, from Stockholm to Klaipeda. He looked at the time. The ticket had just ceased to be valid.

He surveyed her life again, and started to put it back in the cardboard box. He read the chain of evidence, signed it, and put it with her belongings.

Ewert Grens knew more than he wanted to know. Now he had to interrogate her.

And she would say exactly what he didn't want to hear. So he'd listen, forget what she said, then ask her to pack her bags and go home.

For Lena's sake. Not yours. For her.

Grens got up and walked to the lift that took him to the holding cells. He was expected. A prison guard led him to the cell where Alena Sljusareva had spent the last hour and a half.

The guard did what he always did, peeked in through the small hole on the door. She was sitting on the narrow bunk, leaning forward, her head pressed against her knees, dark hair hanging down towards the floor.

The guard unlocked the door, and Grens went into the tired room. She looked up. She'd been crying. He nodded to her.

'You speak Swedish?'

'A bit.'

'Good. I need to ask you some questions. We'll sit down here on the bunk in your cell with this tape recorder between us. Do you understand?'

'Why?'

Alena Sljusareva made herself smaller. Like she did sometimes, when someone was too rough, when they hurt her down there, when she hoped that no one could see her.

INTERVIEWER EWERT GRENS (EG): Do you remember me?

ALENA SLJUSAREVA (AS): The apartment. You were the policeman who hit Dimitri Pimp-Fucker. He fell down.

EG: You saw that. Then why did you run away?

AS: I saw Bengt Nordwall, too. I panicked. I wanted to escape.

He sat next to a young Baltic woman on a narrow bed in a jail cell. His back ached from too few hours of sleep on the sofa in his office, his leg ached too. Grens took a slow breath. He was tired. He didn't want to destroy the only thing he had left – his pride, his identity. He hated the lie he carried and would continue to carry.

AS: I know it now. Lydia is dead.

EG: She is.

AS: I know it now.

BOX 21

EG: First she killed an innocent police officer. Then she took her own life with the same gun, a shot to the head from a nine-millimetre Pistolet Makarova. I'd like to know how she got hold of that weapon.

AS: She's dead. She's dead! I know it now.

She had hoped – as you always hope – when you don't know for sure that the worst had happened.

Now she was crying.

Her hand shook as she made the sign of the cross in the air and she sobbed, like a person who lost someone she loved.

Ewert Grens waited for her to finish crying. He watched the tape recorder spin around and remained silent until he could repeat his question.

EG: A nine-millimetre Makarova Pistol.

AS: (inaudible)

EG: And plastic explosives.

AS: It was me.

EG: Who?

AS: Who brought it to her.

EG: Where'd you get it?

AS: At the same place.

EG: Where's that?

AS: Völunds Street. In the basement.

Grens slammed his hand hard onto the tape recorder, almost hitting her as well. How the hell could a scared, broken girl on the run have been able to get by the guard outside the building, get down to the cellar, and then get out with enough explosives to blow up a good portion of a city hospital?

His outburst frightened her, reminding her of other violent

256

men she'd known, and she tried to make herself as small as possible.

He apologised. He promised not to hit anything else.

EG: You knew what it was going to be used for.
AS: No.
EG: You handed over a loaded weapon without asking why?
AS: I didn't know. I didn't ask either.
EG: And she didn't say anything?
AS: She knew if she had, I would have demanded to be there.

Ewert Grens turned off the tape recorder, took out the cassette. The lie. This interrogation would never be written down. He would make sure this tape disappeared, just like he did yesterday, when he destroyed their shared story.

He looked at her. She avoided his eyes, didn't want to be here.

'You're going home.'

'Now?'

'Now.'

Alena Sljusareva stood up quickly and combed her hair with her hand, pulled down her shirt a few times in an attempt to stretch it, and put on her prison slippers.

They had promised they would go home together. They couldn't do that any more. Lydia was dead.

She had to go on alone.

Grens ordered a taxi. It was better this way. The fewer people involved, the easier it would be. He walked beside her out onto Bergs Street. An old man with his young woman. An old man with his daughter. They could have been either. Not many could have guessed this was a detective in the homicide division sending a prostitute home.

BOX 21

She crouched in the back seat as the car made its way through inner-city traffic towards the harbour. She would never come to this city again. She would never, ever leave Lithuania again. She knew it. She had made her trip.

Grens paid the taxi, and they walked into the ferry terminal. The next boat was leaving Stockholm in less than two hours. He bought a ticket and gave it to her. She held on to to it tightly, wouldn't let go of it until she got off in the port city of Klaipeda, the home she'd left behind. It was difficult to imagine the place she'd left as a seventeen-year-old. She hadn't hesitated for long when the two men offered her a good paying job just a ferry ride away. What she was leaving behind was poverty, and little hope for anything else. She was supposed to be gone for just a few months. She was supposed to come back. She didn't even explain to Janoz. She couldn't remember why.

She'd been a different person back then.

Just three years ago, but it was another life, another time. Now, she'd lived longer than most people her age.

Had he been looking for her? Had he wondered where she was? She could see Janoz just as she'd left him. She had that image inside her. They had never been able to take it away. They raped her and spat on her, but they couldn't reach her there. Was Janoz still there? Still alive? What did he look like?

Ewert Grens asked her to go to the terminal cafeteria with him. He bought her a coffee and a sandwich. She thanked him and started eating. He bought two newspapers, and they sat at the table reading them, waiting for her departure.

Not even a day had passed.

Lena Nordwall was seated at the kitchen table, staring at something. You are always staring at something.

How long would it take? Two days? Three? A week? Two weeks? A year? Never?

She didn't understand. She didn't need to. Not yet. Right?

Someone was standing behind her. She noticed it now. In the hallway, on the stairs leading to the second floor. She turned around and saw her daughter watching her quietly.

'How long have you been standing there?'

'Don't know.'

'Why aren't you outside?'

'Mum, it's raining.'

Their daughter was five years old. Her daughter was five years old. That's how she had to start thinking. *Her* daughter. She was the only adult in the house now. She was alone. With the responsibility. With their futures.

'How long, Mum?'

'How long what?'

'How long is Dad going to be dead for?'

Her daughter's name was Elin. She had her boots on. Wet and muddy. Lena didn't notice. Elin walked from the stairs in the hallway to the kitchen table, leaving muddy footprints behind her.

'When is he coming home?'

Elin sat down on the chair next to her mother. Lena noticed that but nothing else, she didn't hear her daughter's endless stream of questions.

'Isn't he coming home?'

Her daughter reached out her hand as far as she could, and caressed her mother's face.

'Where is he?'

'Daddy is sleeping.'

'When is he going to wake up?'

'He won't.'

'Why?'

BOX 21

Her daughter threw questions at her, and they slammed into Lena's body, pulled at her skin and then crept inside. She stood up. She didn't want any more questions. She screamed at the little girl who was just trying to understand.

'Stop it! Stop asking questions now!'

'Why did he become dead?'

'I can't take this! Can't you see that? I can't take any more of this!'

She was about to strike her child. Her arm was suddenly up in the air, the questions still hammering through her mind. She held up her arm, but she didn't strike. She never had before. She started to weep now, sat down and held her daughter in her arms — *her* daughter.

———

Sven Sundkvist had laughed aloud to himself as he left the crappy lunch restaurant and walked back alone to the Kronoberg police station. Not about the food, even though that pathetic meat and instant gravy deserved to be laughed at. He was laughing at Ewert. The sight of him walking around the table, kicking each leg as he passed, cursing at the tape with Lang's voice on it, until their waitress had to ask him to settle down or she'd have to call the police.

He laughed without thinking how it might appear, and two ladies he passed by both looked at him pityingly, mumbling about alcoholism and mental health. He had taken a deep breath, trying to calm down. Ewert Grens was a lot to handle. But he was never dull.

Ewert had left to interrogate Alena Sljusareva. Sven Sundkvist had been sure she would have at least some information to help them figure this out. So he lengthened his stride as he headed towards his office. He was going to put Lang aside for a moment and start investigating the hostage situation again. The morgue had left him with a sense of dread, and it wasn't just because of his discomfort with death.

There was something else there he couldn't quite put his finger on.

Her remarkable tenacity and brutality, the doctors she held hostage at gunpoint, the blown-up corpses, Bengt Nordwall traded for all the others, and his shooting and her suicide. And all of it without her ever saying *what she wanted*.

He broke down the day of the fifth of June minute by minute, each element had taken up a precise amount of time. From twelve p.m., when Lydia Grajauskas sat watching the news on a sofa in the common room, to four ten p.m., when those wearing headphones heard two gunshots followed by a pause and then another one, and then a loud bang as the SWAT team broke down the morgue's door. He read the statements of the hostages, Dr Ejder and his four medical students all painted a similar picture of Grajauskas: calm, always in control of the situation, and she'd never harmed anyone, other than Larsen, who attacked her.

Their impressions painted a clear picture. They told him everything except what he needed to know the most. Why did she do it?

Finally, he checked the chain of evidence sheet that the forensic technicians compiled in the morgue sometime after four p.m. and before seven a.m. It gave him just as little as he feared it would. Nothing was unexpected. Nothing he couldn't foresee.

Except for one thing.

He read those two lines again and again.

A videotape in a plastic grocery bag. No case. But with Cyrillic letters on the adhesive label on its side.

BOX 21

They had exchanged newspapers. He bought more coffee and a piece of apple pie for both of them. She ate it with as much gusto as she had the sandwich.

Ewert Grens studied the woman in front of him.

She was beautiful. Not that it mattered, but she was.

She should have stayed at home. What a fucking waste. So young, so much life ahead of her, and then this, forced to spread her legs for horny johns tired of mowing lawns and whiny kids and a woman who was growing older.

Grens shook his head. Such a fucking waste.

He waited until she finished eating and put the spoon on her plate.

He had it in a folder, and he took it out now and laid it on the table.

'Do you recognise this?'

She looked at the blue notebook and shrugged her shoulders.

'No.'

Grens opened it to the first page, and pushed it across the table to her.

'Do you understand this?'

Alena Sljusareva looked over what was written there. She read a few lines, then met his gaze.

'Where did you get this?'

'We found this next to her bed at the hospital. It was the only thing she left behind. It is hers, right?'

'That's Lydia's handwriting.'

He explained that he had tried to get the text translated while she was still holding hostages in the morgue, while she was still alive, but he had taken too long to find someone who knew Lithuanian.

While Bengt was still alive, he thought. While the lie he was carrying still didn't exist.

Alena Sljusareva flipped slowly through the notebook, read the five pages Lydia had written. Then she translated it.

Everything.

Everything that had happened barely a day earlier stood there. In detail.

Grajauskas had planned what she was going to do down to the most minuscule detail. The delivery of the weapon, explosives, twine and videotape in a waste bin in a disabled toilet. Knocking out the guard, walking down to the morgue, taking the hostages, blowing up the corpses, the request for an interpreter named Bengt Nordwall.

Ewert Grens listened. He listened and swallowed. It was all there. Everything. If only I had known. If I only he'd got this translated. I never would have sent him down there. He would still be alive.

You would be alive!
If you hadn't gone down there you'd be alive.
You must have known that!
Why didn't you say anything?
To me? To her?
If only you'd admitted you recognised her. If only you'd let her have that.
You would be alive.
She didn't want to shoot.
She wanted confirmation that it wasn't her fault, wasn't her choice to sit in an apartment waiting to take her clothes off for men.

Alena asked if she could keep it. Grens shook his head, reached for the blue notebook and put it back into his briefcase. He waited until there were just twenty minutes left. Then he asked her to get up, and they walked together to departures.

BOX 21

Alena Sljusareva held her ticket in her hand, showed it to the woman sitting behind a glass wall wearing the shipping company's uniform. She turned around, thanked Grens, and he wished her a pleasant journey.

He left her there in line to board and walked across the terminal to get a good view of all the travellers departing and arriving on the ferry. He leaned against a pillar, trying to think about the other investigation, about Lang sitting in jail, about Lisa Öhrström receiving those faxes and about to receive more, but he couldn't keep his mind on that. He couldn't shake the thought of those women from Klaipeda, and in the meantime he rather absently watched the newly arriving travellers still walking on their sea legs. He liked watching people from a distance. They were all heading somewhere. Some with red cheeks carrying big plastic bags of tax-free alcohol, who had drunk and danced and flirted until they fell asleep alone in a cabin on the lower deck. Others dressed in their finest, who had scrimped and saved for several years to be able to afford a week in Sweden. One or two arriving with no baggage, their clothes crumpled – they'd left in a hurry. He studied them all and forgot the rest for a moment. Soon she would be gone. Ewert Grens was just about to turn around when he noticed what might have been the last group of passengers embark.

He recognised him immediately.

It hadn't been much more than a day since Grens had watched that man be escorted to a flight at Arlanda.

Dimitri Pimp-Fucker.

That same suit he'd worn when he was escorted to the airport and standing in the doorway of the apartment where he'd just mercilessly beaten Lydia Grajauskas unconscious.

Dimitri Pimp-Fucker was not alone. He stopped once he passed passport control and waited for two young women, or rather girls, maybe sixteen or seventeen years old. He stretched out his hand, and they both gave him something. Ewert Grens knew what it was even though he couldn't see it.

Their passports.

Their debt.

A woman in a tracksuit walked over quickly to meet them. She had her hood up and her back to Grens. Even though he couldn't see her face, he could tell she was saying hello to all three in the Baltic way, light kisses on both cheeks.

She pointed towards the nearest exit, and they all followed her outside. None of them had any luggage.

Ewert Grens felt sick.

Lydia Grajauskas had just shot herself in the temple. Alena Sljusareva had escaped and was just a ferry ride from getting home again. They had been used by strange men in apartments with electronic locks for three years. They had been threatened, beaten, forced to pretend to be horny while inside they were broken. It took one day, one whole day for them to be replaced! Replaced by two new young women with no idea what awaited them, who would soon be trained to smile while a man spat at them, just so the people who owned her could get their one hundred and fifty thousand kronor a month out of her vagina.

Grens stood there a couple more minutes waiting for the ferry to leave the dock. He watched them disappear: the Baltic woman with a hood over her head, Dimitri Pimp-Fucker next to her, and finally the two girls who had just given away their passports, so young they barely had breasts.

There was nothing he could do. Not now. Grajauskas and Sljusareva had dared to question, hit back, but that was rare, or rather, he'd never heard about it. Those two, still so young, they would never dare to testify. They would be too terrified to say anything against him, and the pimp would just deny it.

BOX 21

Thus there was no crime.

But he knew that he or a colleague would eventually meet both of them. He didn't know where or when, but sooner or later it all went to hell.

As soon as Sven Sundkvist saw the note in the chain of evidence list – one videotape in a plastic grocery bag with both Grajauskas's and Sljusarevas's fingerprints on it – he put everything else aside.

First, he sought it out in the place where it should be, the forensic technicians' department.

It wasn't there.

He checked with the officers on night duty, then with the linguists who might be looking at the Cyrillic letters on the videotape's label.

It wasn't there.

He even checked with lost and found, just in case it could have ended up there.

He felt his uneasiness in his stomach.

It was an uneasiness that was intensifying, turning into irritation then anger. It was a strange feeling, and he hated it.

He sought out the forensic guy who got to the morgue first, Nils Krantz, who'd shown up at every crime scene for as long as Sven had been a detective, and long before that. He reached him in a home on Regerings Street where someone had been assaulted. Krantz was in a hurry, but he gave Sven the time he needed, describing briefly how the videotape had been found and what had been on it, confirming what Sven read on the list of evidence.

'Good. Good, Krantz. And the contents?'

'What do you mean?'

'I mean, what was on the tape?'

'I don't know.'

'You don't know?'

'That's your job.'

'That's why I'm trying to track it down.'

He heard Nils Krantz turn away from the phone, he was speaking to someone else, but it was hard to make out. In less than a minute, he was back.

'Did you need anything else?'

'Yes. Do you know where it is now? The tape?'

Krantz chuckled resignedly.

'Why don't you guys ever talk to each other over there?'

'What do you mean?'

'Talk to Grens.'

'Ewert?'

'He asked for it. I gave it to him as soon as we were done with it, in the morgue.'

Sven Sundkvist took a deep breath. The pain in his stomach, irritation, anger.

He left his desk, passed by four doors, and knocked on Ewert Grens's door.

He knew Ewert was interrogating Alena Sljusareva right now. He tried the door. It wasn't locked.

He entered and glanced around. It was an odd feeling. He was just there to pick something up, but for a moment he felt like an intruder – uninvited and unwelcome. He had probably never been in Ewert's office alone, maybe no one had. It took him just a few seconds to find what he was looking for. It was on the shelf behind Ewert's desk, next to the old tape recorder that delivered Siw Malmkvist to this room. There was a label on the back – Cyrillic letters he couldn't read.

He put on plastic gloves, picked up the videotape, weighed it in his hand, and randomly fiddled with it. She had meticulously planned everything. She'd never hesitated. There was a purpose

BOX 21

in every step she took towards her own death. Sven Sundkvist turned over the tape, felt its smooth surface. This was no coincidence. She had a reason for this too. She wanted to show them something.

He closed the door carefully behind him, went out into the corridor and walked to the meeting room. There was a VCR in there at the bottom of the end table.

He put in the tape.

He sat down on the same chair Ewert Grens sat on late last night.

But what he saw was something else.

Jonas, his son, used to call that kind of image the war of the ants. The tape made a loud buzzing sound, but there was no picture, except for grey flickers.

A videotape that shouldn't exist, that wasn't in the chain of protocol, which wasn't registered anywhere. A videotape with nothing recorded on it. That feeling in his stomach that had turned from uneasiness to anger suddenly became a fury so intense it made him nauseous.

Ewert, what the hell are you up to?

———

Alena Sljusareva had boarded and the ferry was now making its way through Stockholm's archipelago in search of open sea, headed for Lithuania and Klaipeda. Once Alena arrived she'd never look back again. Ewert Grens was waiting for a taxi that never came. He swore and called again and demanded that the switchboard operator tell him why. She apologised, and said she couldn't find any record of his call – no Grens whose destination was the police station on Bergs Street – but she could send one his way if he wanted her to. Grens swore again and shouted about their organisation being a bunch of clowns, asked for her name, and made a scene he later regretted until a taxi finally showed up.

He looked out over the water, caught a glimpse of a building on the other side of the bay.

It was pouring from her head.

I held her in my arms, and the blood never ever stopped pouring from her ears, nose, mouth.

He missed her.

He longed for her, more than he had for many years. He couldn't wait until next Monday morning. He wanted to go straight over to Lidingö, past Millesgården, into the parking lot, and then run inside the nursing home to be with her, just be there, together.

But she didn't exist.

The woman he missed and longed for hadn't existed for over twenty-five years.

You took her from me, Lang.

The taxi got stuck a few times in the afternoon rush hour, half an hour to get back to the police station. He'd had plenty of time to calm down by the time he paid and climbed out of the car. Despite the chill of yesterday's endless rain, it was starting to get warmer again. He could feel the sun, and the wind had died down. He would never understand the weather.

Grens walked into the building and headed for his office. He turned on his stereo and heard Siw Malmkvist over those tinny mono speakers. They sang it together: 'Lyckans ost', 1968, original, 'Hello, Mary Lou'. He opened the folder lying on his desk – the investigation against Jochum Lang.

He knew that they were in there.

He studied the pictures of a dead man on the floor, one at a time. Clumsily taken: coarse, badly lit, and almost blurry.

BOX 21

Krantz and his forensic technicians were good at what they did, but they couldn't take a decent photo. He sighed, picked out three photos that were fairly good and put them in an envelope.

Two phone calls, then he'd be ready.

He called Lisa Öhrström first. She answered sounding stressed. He informed her that he and Sven Sundkvist would soon be heading over to the hospital to show her some more pictures. She protested, said she was busy, and she wasn't interested in seeing any more grisly black and white pictures. Ewert Grens said it would be nice to see her again soon and hung up.

The second call was to the prosecutor Ågestam. Grens briefly explained that a doctor named Lisa Öhrström had chosen to testify against Jochum Lang, that she definitely pointed him out as the one who was guilty of the murder of one of her patients. Ågestam was unprepared and wanted to know more, but Grens interrupted him. He'd learn more about this and about the Grajauskas investigation when they met tomorrow.

Siw was still singing. He joined her, started moving lightly across the room, 'Mamma är lik sin mamma', 1968, original 'Sadie the Cleaning Lady'.

There weren't many who noticed the car arriving at 3 Völunds Street. It wasn't particularly big, or new, or fast. The man in the driver's seat opened his door. There were two pretty girls, maybe sixteen or seventeen years old, sitting in the back seat. The girls were looking around curiously.

Maybe it was a father and his two daughters.

He then opened their door. The girls got out and looked up at the row of identical windows. It didn't seem like they lived there. They were looking at the house as if for the first time.

Maybe they were there to visit someone they knew.

The man and the two girls walked towards the front door. Just as he grabbed hold of the door handle and opened the door, he turned around, and said something that made one of the girls scream and cry. The other girl held her. She seemed stronger, caressed her cheek, and tried to help her to keep walking.

He kept talking as they entered the building, and the girl continued to cry. Even if someone had happened upon them there, they probably would not have understood what he was saying. He was speaking a language few in Sweden knew. So if what he said was that these girls were now in his debt, and he'd start getting his money back by fucking their little cunts until they were bleeding, then few in this country would have understood him.

Sven Sundkvist walked out of the conference room with the blank videotape in his hand. He stopped at the coffee vending machine, pressed the button for a coffee with extra milk. He needed energy but had to careful. His stomach was cramping in anger.

The videotape was blank. He was sure that hadn't been Grajauskas's intention. She had meticulously planned every moment of the last hours of her life. He knew that videotape must have had a purpose.

He went into his office again. He called Nils Krantz a second time. Krantz answered immediately, sounding busy and annoyed, still at the apartment on Regerings Street.

'That damn tape. Again?'

'I want to know if it was new.'

'New?'

'Had it been used?'

BOX 21

'It had been.'

'How do we know that?'

'*I* know it because there was dust on it when I opened it. *I* know because the security tab on the back was broken. Which you'd only do if you wanted to protect a recording.'

Sundkvist held the videotape in his hand. He moved his desk lamp so that the light fell directly on the tape. It was so new it gleamed. Not a speck of dust on it. The security tab was still intact. He picked up the phone again.

'I'm coming to meet you.'

'Later. I don't have time right now.'

'I want you to look at the videotape again. It's important. Something isn't right.'

Lars Ågestam didn't know if he should laugh or cry. He'd just had a phone call from Ewert Grens, who told him that he would be providing information about the circumstances of three deaths connected only by time and place – Lydia Grajauskas and Bengt Nordwall and Hilding Oldéus – and also about the other two people who were involved in these catastrophes – Alena Sljusareva and Jochum Lang. A year had passed since he'd worked with Ewert Grens on the unusual trial of a father who shot dead his daughter's killer. He had been the youngest and most ambitious prosecutor in the office, and something big landed in his lap. He'd been in charge of the investigation and formally Ewert Grens's superior, a man he'd heard of and admired from afar, and then suddenly they were working together.

And their partnership couldn't have gone any worse.

It was as if Grens made up his mind from the very beginning that he and the prosecutor wouldn't agree on anything, and not even for the sake of the investigation would he pretend to be nice.

So now, Lars Ågestam had decided to laugh. It was just easier that way. If he was going to be assigned to work with Grens again, a year later, on *two* investigations, then he was going to spend his time laughing rather than crying. Somebody seemed to think their partnership had turned out well last time, so here he was stuck with Grens again.

Partnership, my arse.

Ågestam laughed so hard his slender body shook. He took off his jacket and put his shiny black shoes up on the desk, ruffled his close-cropped hair, and kept laughing until the tears streamed down his face. Partnership, my arse.

Sven Sundkvist stood on Regerings Street staring up at the sky, which should be a clear summer blue, but stared back at him grey and ugly and tired. The rain was on its way back again. He'd been there for a while. He should go back to the police station. But he was unsure if he could. If he went back to the station he'd have to continue down the path he'd started on. It made him furious, made him feel like he was disintegrating from the inside. Nils Krantz, stressed out and irritated, had been in the middle of another crime scene in an expensive apartment and looked at the videotape. It took him just a few seconds to confirm that the tape wasn't the one he'd analysed. Sven had already known, but still he'd hoped he was wrong, as you do when you are faced with the unthinkable.

Now he knew. Or rather, he didn't know a goddamn thing.

The Ewert Grens he knew and admired didn't switch video-tapes during an investigation.

The Ewert Grens he knew was an arsehole, but a straightforward and honest arsehole.

This, this was something else.

The sky was still staring down at him obstinately when the

BOX 21

phone rang. Ewert. Sven took a deep breath. He didn't know if he was ready. He wasn't. Not yet. So he listened. They were going back to Söder Hospital. They were going to meet Lisa Öhrström again. Ewert wanted to show her a few more pictures. He would stand here for a few more minutes, then Ewert would pick him up.

It was hard to even look at Ewert. Sven Sundkvist avoided meeting his boss's gaze. He would later, when the time was right, but not now. Now he was sitting next to him in the car, grateful that he could look out the front window at the anonymous car ahead of them, as they slowly made their way south in rush-hour traffic towards the hospital. Sven thought of the woman they would soon be meeting. He was still upset about that fiasco of a line-up, when Lisa Öhrström reversed her story. She had been threatened, and he could understand her fears. But it had been more than that. She had been more than just afraid. She also felt shame – the kind of shame he had tried to describe to Ewert. It had been obvious to him when he questioned her that she not only mourned Hilding Oldéus, but also felt anger and hate towards her little brother, who was at least indirectly responsible for his own death.

She hadn't been able to prevent it. And that was her shame, and that – together with the threats directed at her – had given her a reason to refuse to recognise Lang behind that window.

Sven was sure she was the type to always feel inadequate, the type who would always be there to help, but never felt she'd done enough. And Hilding was probably the reason why she became a doctor, because she thought she had to save, help, rescue, help.

Now he was dead, despite all her help. Now her shame would be everlasting.

Now she would never be free from it.

She was already waiting for them in the nurses' station when they got to her ward. Her face was pale and her eyes tired. Grief and fear and hate drain you of energy, and eventually they drain you of life. She didn't even say hello when they opened the door and walked in. She just gazed at them with an expression that resembled disgust.

Ewert pretended not to notice her attitude, or maybe didn't notice. He briefly reminded her of their last conversation and the pictures of three broken fingers worth seven thousand kronor. She looked away, maybe to prove a point or maybe because it was just too much for her, and Ewert told her forcefully to turn around. She was going to have to look at even more pictures.

It took a while until she moved her eyes from the wall, until she looked at the black and white photo on the table in front of her.

'What do you see?'

'I still don't know why you want to play this game.'

'I'm just curious. What do you see?'

Lisa Öhrström stared at Grens for a moment, then shook her head slightly. She picked up the photo and touched it – it had been developed on rough paper.

'A fracture. A left arm.'

'Thirty thousand kronor.'

'Excuse me?'

'The pictures I faxed to you. You remember them? Three broken fingers. A thumb for five thousand and the other two for a couple of thousand. I told you that was Lang. That's his price and his signature. That poor guy with the broken fingers owed seven thousand. I lied. It was thirty-seven thousand. An arm, that's worth thirty.'

Sven Sundkvist was sitting a bit behind Grens. He was

BOX 21

ashamed. You're bullying her, Ewert, he thought. I know what you want, and I know we need her testimony, but you're taking this too far.

'I have another one here. What do you have to say about this one?'

A new black and white photograph. A person lying naked on a trolley. The picture had been taken from above and from the side, the lighting was clumsy, but it wasn't hard to imagine what it depicted.

'You're not saying anything. Here, I'll help you. This is a corpse. The arm you were just looking at belongs to this corpse. Do you see? And the fingers sitting there are on the corpse's arm. You see, I lied again. That corpse didn't owe thirty-seven thousand kronor. He owed one hundred and thirty-seven thousand kronor. Lang's price for a corpse is precisely one hundred thousand kronor. So this guy, he's debt free. He has paid it off. One hundred and thirty-seven thousand kronor.'

Lisa Öhrström clenched her jaw. She didn't say anything. She didn't move. She pressed her lips tight to keep a scream inside. Sven looked at her. You're going to succeed, Ewert. You're close now. But you've gone too far. You've hurt her, Ewert, and soon you'll hurt her even more. But I can take it. I can be ashamed for you, of you, because what I see is the most capable police officer I ever met. You need her testimony, and you're going to get it. But the other one! The other investigation! I guess I should be taking part in this extortion, be happy you'll soon have her where you want her, but Ewert, Ewert! What are you up to in the investigation against Grajauskas? I can't concentrate on this because I have just been with Krantz. That's why I don't even want to look at you. That's why I'd like to lie down on the table between us and scream until you listen. Krantz told me what I already knew. It's another tape. Another tape, Ewert!

Ewert Grens stretched himself. He waited for Öhrström to break down. He could wait a little longer.

'By the way, I have another set of photos for you.'

Lisa Öhrström whispered. That voice, she couldn't take any more.

'I get your point.'

'Good. Good. Because I think you're going to find these new pictures even more interesting.'

'I don't want to look at them. And I don't really understand. If this really is Lang's work, then why isn't he locked up?'

'Why? You ought to know that, Lisa. You've been threatened. Right? Then you know how he works.'

That man had stood in this very kitchen. He'd been holding pictures of Sanna and Jonathan. She could feel it again, how her chest ached, how her body couldn't stop shaking.

Grens put an envelope on the table. He opened it, and placed the top photo in front of her. A new hand. Five new fractures. You didn't need to be a doctor to see that all five fingers were crushed.

She sat in silence. He took out the next picture, put it in front of her. A shattered kneecap, just as clear.

'It's like a puzzle, right? That hand there and this knee here. Obviously they belong together. But this time it wasn't about money. This time it was about respect.'

Ewert Grens pushed the two pictures up to her face.

'This was a message. Never mix Yugoslavian amphetamines with dishwashing detergent.'

He took out the last picture out of the envelope, and pushed it even closer.

A picture taken by someone who was standing a few steps above the scene, and through the lens appeared a man who had just died, a wheelchair beside him, and his blood was pooling around his head.

BOX 21

She looked at it, then turned her face away abruptly. She started to weep.

'That's what this guy did. His name was Hilding Oldéus.'

———

Sven Sundkvist made a decision in the car on the way back from Söder Hospital. He was going to wait, keep his mouth shut until they got to the police station, then lock himself in his office and not leave again until he found it.

He looked at the stack of printed statements, lifted them from the floor.

He knew that he'd seen it somewhere.

He read through them again slowly. It had to be there, and he didn't have time to miss it.

It only took him fifteen minutes.

He started with the female medical student. A very brief statement, because she'd still been weak. It would take a while for her to understand. Then he flipped forward to the statement of Dr Gustaf Ejder. It was considerably longer, more like a conversation – Ejder handled his fear with logic, used his intellect and reason to avoid emotion. Sundkvist had seen that strategy for avoiding panic before. Everyone has their own way. It also made Ejder an ideal witness. He recounted his experiences in such great detail, it was if you were there with him, bound and powerless on the morgue floor.

Sven found what he was looking for about halfway through Ejder's statement.

The questions in that section revolved around her grocery bag, because that's where she kept her weapon, and Ejder suddenly started to describe the videotape.

Sven Sundkvist moved his finger slowly underneath each word, making sure not to miss anything.

Ejder had seen the black videotape when Lydia Grajauskas

278

pressed down the edges of the plastic bag to take out the explosives. This was early in the hostage crisis, when he was still trying to build a relationship with her, gain her confidence, in order to keep the other calm. She had refused to answer him, but he kept asking, so finally she had tried to explain in her broken English.

She had said that the tape was *truth*. He asked her what she meant by that, and she repeated the word three times. *Truth. Truth. Truth.* She was silent for a moment, looking down as she shaped the plastic explosives, then she turned towards him and spoke again.

Two cassettes.
In box station train.
Twenty-one.

She indicated the number with her hands as well, flashing all her fingers twice, and then holding up a single finger.

Twenty-one.

Gustaf Ejder said in his statement that he remembered every word. He was sure that was what she had said verbatim. She'd said so little, and it seemed to cost her a lot to say it, so it wasn't hard to remember.

The truth. Two cassettes. In box station train. Twenty-one. Sven Sundkvist flipped back and reread the passage.

He was convinced now. There was another tape. Box number twenty-one at the Central Station. With the security tab removed and contents that were more than just a grey flicker.

He put the stack of witness statements to the side and stood up – it wouldn't take him long to get there.

———

BOX 21

He had pushed those photos into her face.

Lisa Öhrström had thought she was incapable of hate. She'd never hated anyone or truly loved anyone either, maybe because she'd considered love and hate two sides of the same emotion, and if she couldn't feel one, she couldn't feel the other either. But this police officer, she actually hated him. The last twenty-four hours had been so strange. Her grief for Hilding that wasn't really grief, her fear of a vague threat made against her niece and nephew, which wasn't really fear. It was as if at the age of thirty-five all her emotions had been plucked out of her for a few hours, and now she had to push all of them back inside, and hide them behind her shame, and never truly learn to know herself. She didn't even recognise them! She had never felt this kind of emotion – so strong, so naked, so impossible to hide from.

And then some limping cop rubs it in her face, literally.

She knew immediately it was Hilding, and now she stood up, grabbed the pictures, and tore them to tiny pieces, throwing the scraps against the glass wall of the nurses' station.

She knew where she had to go. She ran through the corridor towards the exit. She had several hours left on her shift, but for the first time in her life she didn't care. She ran out of the hospital and turned towards Tanto Park, crossed the railway track, and wasn't even fazed by the dogs that started barking wildly at her frantic running. She continued to run past the apartment buildings at Zinkensdamm, over Horns Street, and didn't stop until she reached the shadow of Högalid Church.

She wasn't even tired, didn't feel the sweat running down her face. She just stood there for a minute, until she felt ready, then walked across the lawn and down the hill towards the home she visited as often as her own.

The door to the sixth-floor apartment on Völund Street had been replaced. The hole that had been there just a few days earlier was gone. There was no sign that the police had broken it down to try to stop the brutal beating of a naked young woman, who ended up with thirty-five bullwhip lashes on her back.

The two girls who were sixteen and seventeen years old stood behind a man who looked like their father waiting for him to unlock the door. When they went into the hall of the apartment, they saw the electronic locks, but had no idea what they were. The man closed the door and then showed them their passports. He explained for a second time that passports cost money, that they were now in his debt, and they'd have to work it off. They could expect their first customers in two hours.

The girl who broke down by the front door was still crying. She tried to protest until the man, who until recently had been known as Dimitri Pimp-Fucker by two other young women, put a gun to her head. For a moment, she thought he was going to press the trigger.

He told them to undress. He wanted a test fuck. It was important they learned how to please a man.

———————

Lisa Öhrström felt overheated from her long run from the hospital to Ylva's house on Högalid Street.

She'd been wrong before. Of course she could love. Maybe not a man, but she loved her niece and nephew more than her life itself. She'd put off coming here, even though she usually visited them every day, because she hadn't had the strength to tell them their uncle was dead, that he fell down a stairwell yesterday.

They had worshipped their uncle. To them he wasn't a junkie, they'd only known the other Hilding, the newly released Hilding with a round face, whose calm only lasted a few days. Then

BOX 21

the world around him got to be too much, and he went in search of something to turn it off. They'd never seen the ravages of his drug use, never seen how it changed him. He always spent just a few days with them and was gone by the time he turned into somebody else.

Now she had to tell them. Nobody would ever push black and white photos into their faces.

She was holding Ylva's hand. They silently hugged each other in the hallway, now they were both sitting on the sofa in the small living room. They both felt the same thing, not quite grief, more like relief, to finally know exactly where he was. They weren't sure if they were allowed to feel like that, but it was easier to feel what you weren't supposed to feel if somebody else felt it too.

Jonathan and Sanna sat in front of them in two armchairs. They sensed that something wasn't right.

She hadn't even started yet, but they knew on some level as soon as she opened the door. From the way she pushed down on the handle, the way she said hello, the way she walked through the hall, it was obvious to them this was no ordinary visit.

She didn't know how to start. She didn't have to.

'What is it?'

Sanna was twelve, in that land between girlhood and her teens. She looked at the two adults she trusted the most, and repeated her question.

'What is it? I can tell something's wrong.'

Lisa leaned forward and put one hand on Sanna's knee, and the other one on Jonathan's knee – he was still so tiny that her fingers reached around his whole leg.

'You're right. There is something. It's about Uncle Hilding.'

'He's dead.'

Sanna hadn't hesitated. As if she'd been waiting to say it.

Lisa held on tighter, nodded.

'He died yesterday. At the hospital. In my ward.'

Jonathan, who had only six years in his little body, watched his mother and his aunt Lisa cry, and he didn't understand, not yet.

'Uncle Hilding wasn't old. Was he? Was he so old he died?'

'You're so dumb. You don't get anything. He died from drugs.'

Sanna looked at her little brother, projecting onto him all the thoughts she didn't want anything to do with any more.

Lisa raised her hand and stroked her niece's cheek.

'Don't say that.'

'It's true.'

'That's not what happened. It was an accident. He died in a stairwell. He lost control of his wheelchair. Don't say any more of those things.'

'It doesn't matter what you say. I know he did drugs. I know that's why he's dead now. I know, no matter what you pretend.'

Jonathan heard what she said, but he didn't agree. He stood up in his chair and started to cry. His uncle wasn't dead, he couldn't be. Jonathan leaned over and screamed.

'This is your fault!'

He ran out of the room, out of the front door and barefoot across the concrete slabs of the courtyard, and he screamed the whole way.

'This is your fault! You're just stupid! If you say it, it's your fault!'

The afternoon slowly started to turn to evening, and Lars Ågestam looked up in surprise when Ewert Grens opened his office door without knocking. Ågestam noticed that he looked like he always did, the huge body, the thin grey hair, the leg he kept straight while he limped.

BOX 21

'You were coming by tomorrow.'

'I'm here now. I have some facts.'

'Really?'

'About the murders. About the investigations at Söder Hospital. Both of them.'

He didn't wait for Ågestam to ask him to sit down. He grabbed a chair by the door, covered with papers. He moved them carelessly onto the floor, pulled the chair over and sat down opposite one of the many young prosecutors that he considered a prig.

'First Alena Sljusareva. The other Baltic woman. She's on a boat home now. She's crossing the Baltic Sea. I talked to her. She didn't have anything for us. She didn't know who Bengt Nordwall was. She didn't know how Grajauskas got hold of that weapon and the explosives. She didn't know anything at all about any kidnapping plans. So I helped her get home. To Klaipeda, Lithuania. She needs it. And we don't need her.'

'You sent her home?'

'Do you have a problem with that?'

'You should have informed me first. Then we could have discussed it. And if we came to the conclusion that it was the right thing to do, I would have made the decision to send her home.'

Ewert Grens looked at the young prig with disgust. He felt like screaming. But he refrained.

He had lobbed a lie onto the prosecutor's desk.

For once, he chose to swallow his anger.

'Are you done?'

'You also sent home a person who could be guilty of accessory to aggravated theft, endangering the public, and aiding and abetting in aggravated kidnapping.'

Lars Ågestam shrugged.

'But sure. If you say so. If she's on board, she's on board.'

Grens suppressed the contempt he felt towards the young

man on the other side of the desk. He wasn't even sure why, but he couldn't stand people who got their experience from books, who hadn't learned things the hard way.

'Jochum Lang, however.'

'Yes?'

'It's time to lock him up for good.'

Ågestam pointed to the documents that Ewert Grens had put on the floor.

'There, Grens. Interrogation after interrogation. And nothing. I can't hold him much longer.'

'Yes, you can.'

'No, I really can't.'

'You can hold him on suspicion of the murder of Hilding Oldéus. We have a witness.'

'Who?'

Lars Ågestam was slim and wore small round glasses and his hair brushed to the side. He'd just turned thirty, but sitting there in his oversized leather chair he looked more like a little boy than ever.

'Lisa Öhrström. The doctor in the ward where Oldéus had a bed. She's also Oldéus's sister.'

Ågestam was quiet. He pushed his chair back, stood up, and looked at Grens.

'According to the report I received from your colleague Sundkvist, the line-up she was involved with did not go well. His lawyer has also been by here. He's obviously asked me to drop the charges immediately because *no one* identified him.'

'Did you hear what I said? You *have* a witness. I'll bring her in tomorrow morning.'

Lars Ågestam sat down again, pulled himself back to his desk with his feet. He raised his arms up in the air, like in the movies when someone's being threatened.

'I give up, Grens. Explain. Explain what you're up to.'

BOX 21

'You'll get your witness identification tomorrow. There's nothing more to explain.'

Ågestam sat there trying to understand what it was he'd just heard.

He was technically in charge of two investigations that Ewert Grens was working on, both concerning deaths that had taken place around the same time in the same building.

But the answers he was getting seemed too simple. This conversation, Sljusareva already on her way home, a positive identification on Lang – he should feel calm, the detective in charge of both investigations had just said he had everything under control. But Ågestam didn't feel calm, something didn't add up, didn't add up at all.

'The reporters are pushing us for answers.'

'Fuck 'em.'

'They want to know why Grajauskas did this. What motive a prostitute would have for killing a police officer and herself in a morgue. I don't have any answers. I want one.'

'We don't have any yet. We're investigating that.'

'Here we go again, Grens. I don't understand it. If you don't have a motive – why send Alena Sljusareva home? Probably the only person who could really tell us anything?'

Ewert Grens felt the rage he always felt when he faced one of these young prigs. He wanted to raise his voice, but Bengt's fucking lie prevented him, turning him into someone he wasn't. He had to watch what he said for once. He lowered his voice instead, almost to a hiss.

'Listen, Ågestam, stop acting like this is an interrogation.'

'I've gone through all the transcripts of your communications during the hostage crisis.'

Ågestam had pretended he hadn't heard the threat in Grens's voice and avoided looking at the huge detective while he searched for a few pages from the pile on his desk. He found what he was searching for in the middle, put his finger under a line of text, and read out loud.

'You're the one who says it, Grens, you even shout it, and I quote: *This is something personal! Bengt, over. Damn it, Bengt, fall back! Fall back now!* SWAT *team, you're clear to go in. I repeat,* SWAT *team is cleared to go in!*'

Ågestam threw his skinny arms in the air.

'End of quote.'

The phone on the desk rang suddenly. They both looked at it. It rang seven times, then fell silent, leaving space for their conversation to continue.

'You can quote whatever the fuck you want to. You weren't there. Right? Yes, I got that feeling for a moment. That it was something personal. I still believe that may be the case. But I don't know how.'

Lars Ågestam tried to look Grens in the eye, but after just a moment he turned and looked out the window instead, at the view of a city that never gave him any peace. It was too big for them to ever be able to catch up.

He hesitated.

This strange feeling, these unwelcome thoughts. He knew he was saying something that might be construed as an accusation against the man who possessed the most informal power in this whole building, but he couldn't not say it. He had no choice.

'So you have . . . nothing? I don't know exactly what's going on. I can't put my finger on it, Ewert – I don't think I've ever called you Ewert before. But, Ewert, do you really know what you're doing here? I mean, you're investigating your best friend. Your best friend's death. I understand that would be difficult. And I'm also wondering if it's appropriate. I'm just thinking about the grief you must be feeling, being so close to this.'

Ågestam took a deep breath and continued.

BOX 21

'What I mean is . . . would you like this case to be reassigned?'

Ewert Grens got up quickly, getting ready to leave the room.

'You sit behind that desk reading papers! But you know what, you little climber, I was investigating crimes, real crimes, back when your mother first lifted her skirts for your father. And I still am.'

Grens pointed to the door.

'Now I'm headed back. To the hitman and the hooker. Did you need anything else?'

Lars Ågestam shook his head, watched him go, and sighed.

He knew Grens was a detective who seldom failed. A detective who didn't make clumsy mistakes. That's how it was, no matter what you thought of his methods or his complete inability to communicate.

He trusted Ewert Grens.

He decided to continue trusting him for now.

––––––––

The evening had patiently carried away all the commuters who spent so many hours of their lives moving between a home in the suburbs and a job in the city. Stockholm Central Station was quietening down, gathering its strength for the next morning, for the new streams of commuters that would hurry back and forth from one platform to another.

Sven Sundkvist was sitting on a bench staring blankly at an electronic arrivals and departures timetable. Thirty minutes earlier, he'd left the station's large hall and entered the storage room and found number twenty-one at the bottom in the middle of a long row of locked doors. He knew these lockers well: though intended for temporary visitors, they were often used as long-term storage for the homeless or a place for criminals to stash drugs, stolen property and weapons. He stood in front of it for a while, running his hand along it, while he considered how to proceed. Maybe he should just forget the fact that he'd read through those statements again.

No one else would read them.

He could just go home to Anita and Jonas.

No one else would ever think about it. Home, it would be so easy to just forget this shit.

But he continued standing there. He felt that anger again, the pain in his stomach which had become more than a feeling. He thought of his conversation earlier with Krantz, how sure the old forensic technician had been.

The tape had been used. The security tab had been broken. Now it wasn't on any of the reports.

You're risking thirty-one years of service. I don't understand it. That's why I'm here. In front of a locker door in Stockholm's Central Station. I have no clue what I'm going to find here, what Lydia Grajauskas wanted to tell us, but I'm already sure it's knowledge I'd rather not have.

It had taken fifteen minutes to convince the woman working in the hole in the wall called luggage storage that he really was a police officer from the Homicide Division, and he really did need her help to break into a locker that didn't belong to him.

She shook her head repeatedly, and only after he started to yell at her about her responsibility as a public servant and a citizen to follow the orders given to her by a police officer did she reluctantly call somebody at the security company that kept the extra sets of keys.

Sven Sundkvist saw the man in a green uniform as soon as he came through the main entrance doors. Sven stood up from the bench, walked straight towards the guard, flashed his badge and said hello. They continued side by side into the room of numbered boxes.

A heavy key ring.

BOX 21

Number 21 looked just like all the others.

The guard stepped aside after he turned the key. The lock had opened easily. Sven Sundkvist stood in front of two shelves attached to metal walls. The space inside was quite dark, and he took a step closer to get a better look.

There wasn't much there.

A plastic bag with two dresses in it. A photo album of black and white pictures of a family, taken in a studio, everyone dressed in their finest with nervous smiles on their faces. A cigar box filled with cash, which he counted quickly – one hundred and five hundred bills, he counted quickly, about forty thousand kronor altogether.

Lydia Grajauskas's property.

He held the metal door open, and it hit him that box 21 contained her life. What little she had left of the past. Whatever future she might be able to imagine. This had been her hope, her escape, the feeling that she existed beyond the prison of that apartment.

Sven Sundkvist opened his briefcase and put the dresses, the photo album and the cigar box inside.

He then stretched his arm into the upper shelf and found a videotape labelled with Cyrillic letters.

She'd run after him into the courtyard, through the front gate, and out onto the pavement of Högalid Street. He stood there barefoot with tears flowing down his cheeks. She loved him. She hugged him, lifted him up, and carried him in her arms, saying his name over and over again. His name was Jonathan and he was her nephew, but she couldn't have loved a child of her own more.

Lisa Öhrström stroked his hair. She should be going soon. It was late and getting dark, or as dark as it gets this close to midsummer, the day slowly transitioning to night. She kissed his cheek – Sanna had already gone to bed – and then looked at Ylva, her sister, and closed the front door behind her as she left. There weren't many of them left now. Dad gone, Hilding gone. She'd been expecting it for a long time and now here it was, an ever-expanding loneliness.

She decided to walk. She crossed Väster Bridge, and made her way along the water on Norr Mälarstrand, then she turned onto the side streets. It didn't take long, only half an hour in the Stockholm twilight. She'd been to the police building a few times before.

She knew he'd be working late. Both because he told her, but also because he was the type. He probably didn't have much else in his life. He'd be sitting there trying to wrap up this investigation, last week it was some other investigation, and next week there'd be one more – there would always be a reason to not go home.

She called ahead to warn him. He answered immediately. He wasn't surprised. He was waiting for her.

He met her at the entrance and led her through the dark corridors of the police station. The air was stuffy, and his limping step echoed against the walls. It seemed like a sad place to choose to live. She stared at his wide back. He was overweight, balding, lame, his body slightly bent. He shouldn't seem so strong, but that was the impression he gave off in those dusty corridors – the kind of strength that makes you feel safe, the kind of strength that comes from a conscious decision.

Ewert Grens opened the door to his office, asked her to sit down, pointing to a visitor's chair in front of the desk. She looked around the room. Dreary. The only sign of individuality among the standard issue office furniture was the tape recorder that stood behind his back, a monster that looked about a hundred years old, and the sofa behind her, which was ugly and run down. She felt sure he usually slept there.

BOX 21

'Coffee?'

He didn't mean it. But that's the sort of thing you're supposed to say.

'No, thanks. I didn't come here to drink coffee.'

'I guessed as much. But still.'

He lifted a plastic cup, half filled with what looked to be black coffee, and drained it.

'So?'

'You don't seem surprised to see me here.'

'Not surprised. But happy.'

It occurred to Lisa Öhrström that what she felt, what was dragging her down, was fatigue. She'd been so tense. She relaxed now, as much as she dared, and the last few days drained her.

'I don't want to see any more of your pictures. I don't want anyone else who I don't know and don't want to know pushed into my face. I've had enough. I'll testify. I'll identify Lang as the person who visited my brother yesterday.'

Lisa Öhrström leaned forward, her elbows on the desk, her chin on her hands. She was so tired. She would soon go home.

'But you should know one thing. It wasn't just the threats that silenced me. I decided some time ago to never let Hilding and his addiction control my life. And I've been living that way for the last year. I wasn't enabling him any more. But it doesn't seem to matter. I'll never be free of him! He's dead now. And even dead, he's costing me more energy than ever! So I might as well be a witness.'

Ewert Grens tried not to smile. He knew it was over.

Anni, it's over.

'Nobody blames you.'

'I don't want your sympathy.'

'That's your choice. But it's true. No one blames you for not knowing what to do.'

Grens stood up, searching through his cassettes. He found what he was looking for and turned on the tape player. Siw Malmkvist. She was sure of it.

'Now I want to know something. Who threatened you?'

Siw Malmkvist. She'd just made one of the most difficult decisions of her life, and he was playing Siw Malmkvist.

'It doesn't matter. I'll testify. But on one condition.'

Lisa Öhrström sat still with her hands under her chin.

'My sister's children. I want them to have protection.'

'They already have protection.'

'I don't understand.'

'They've had protection since the line-up. I know, for example, that you were there today, that one of the kids ran out barefoot onto the pavement. The protection will continue, of course.'

Fatigue paralysed her. She yawned, didn't even bother to try to stifle it.

'I'm going home now.'

'I'll ask someone to drive you. In a civilian car.'

'To Högalids Street. To Jonathan and Sanna. They're sleeping now.'

'I'll make sure you get even more protection. We also put a man inside the apartment. If you agree?'

It truly was night.

The darkness, the silence, as if the whole of this huge building was empty.

She contemplated the policeman standing by his tape player, singing along to that cheerful melody and its meaningless lyrics, and she pitied him.

Friday, 7 June

HE HAD NEVER liked the dark.

He'd grown up in the far northern city of Kiruna and lived through the never-ending Arctic darkness. After he moved to Stockholm to go the police academy, he worked plenty of night shifts, but he'd never really accepted it, didn't want to get used to it. In his world the darkness could never be beautiful.

He looked out of the living room window. A June night dominated the woods outside. It was as dark as a summer evening could get in those densely growing trees. He got home just after ten with the videotape and her other possessions in his briefcase. Jonas was already asleep, and Sven Sundkvist did what he usually did, kissed his forehead and then lingered for a moment listening to his regular breathing. Anita was in the kitchen with a crossword puzzle, and he squeezed in close to her on her chair. An hour or two, she had three empty boxes in three different corners, missing a couple of letters here and there as always.

They made love after that. She'd undressed him and then herself, wanted him to remain there on the kitchen chair and sat naked in his lap – their bodies in need of closeness.

He waited until she fell asleep. And just after midnight, he climbed out of bed and threw on a T-shirt and some sweatpants. His briefcase was still in the kitchen.

He grabbed it and went into the living room.

He wanted to be alone when he took out the videotape. Alone with this intense uneasiness in his stomach.

What Anita and Jonas didn't know couldn't hurt them.

The darkness outside. He could make out the contours of the trees, but no more.

Ten past one. He'd been sitting there staring into space for an hour.

He couldn't put it off much longer. She had told Ejder that there were two tapes.

She'd made a copy. In case what happened did happen. In case someone tried to tape over the one she had with her, or if someone simply made it disappear by switching it for a blank tape.

Sven Sundkvist didn't know if what he was seeing and hearing now was identical to what had been on the other tape.

But he assumed it was.

They look nervous, as people do when they're not used to staring into an eye that captures and keeps whatever it sees.

Grajauskas speaks first.

'Это мой повод. Моя история такая.'

Two sentences at a time.

She turns to Sljusareva, who continues in Swedish.

'This is my reason. This is my story.'

Grajauskas again, she glances at her friend, and says two more sentences.

'Надеюсь что когда ты слышишь это того о ком идет речь уже нет. Что он чувствовал мой стыд.'

She nods, her face serious, waiting for Sljusareva to address the camera and translate.

'When you hear this, I hope the man I speak of is dead. That he has felt my shame.'

BOX 21

They speak slowly, careful to make sure that every word in Russian and every word in broken Swedish can be understood.

He leaned forward, and stopped the tape.

He didn't want to continue.

What he felt was no longer uneasiness, nor fear, it was anger welling up in him, a feeling he seldom had much use for. There was no doubt any more. He hoped, like you always hope. But he knew now, he knew Ewert had suppressed evidence, and that he had a motive for doing so.

Sven Sundkvist went into the kitchen, measured out some coffee grounds, and put on the coffee maker. He needed to think – it was going to be a long night.

The crossword was still on the table. He moved it, picked up some of Jonas's tracing paper, which lay in a heap on the window sill behind him, and stared at the blank paper. He grabbed one of Jonas's purple markers, and pushed it aimlessly over the white.

A man. An older man. Barrel-chested, not much hair, intense eyes.

Ewert.

He smiled to himself when he saw he'd somehow managed to draw Ewert in purple ink.

He knew why. The long night ahead was there on the table in front of him.

He'd known Ewert Grens for almost ten years. He'd been just like all the others. Grens had shouted at him, until somehow something like a friendship started to develop between them. Sven became one of the few that Ewert talked to, invited in, as much as he could let anyone in. Over the years he'd got to know Ewert Grens quite well, but also not at all. He'd never been to his home. It was hard to say you knew a man well when you'd never been to his house. Ewert had been in Sven's home, sat at this kitchen table with Anita on one side and Jonas on the other. He'd had coffee here, eaten dinner here.

Sven had invited Ewert into his home, where Sven was most himself. But Ewert had never reciprocated.

He looked at the drawing, gave the purple man purple shoes and a purple jacket. He didn't know anything about the private life of Ewert Grens. He knew the policeman Grens, who was the first one at work at dawn, blasting Siw Malmkvist, and the last one to leave in the evening, often even spending a night on his office sofa in order to continue an investigation when the next day dawned.

He knew that Grens was the best police officer he'd met. He knew he was the kind of detective that didn't make stupid mistakes. He knew that a good detective always followed the truth no matter the consequences, the truth and nothing but the truth mattered, there wasn't room for anything else.

Now he didn't know anything.

Sven Sundkvist emptied the cup in front of him, then grabbed the coffee pot. He needed more coffee.

Another marker, a hysterical green.

He started writing on the empty space next to the purple man.

Gustaf Ejder sees a videotape in Lydia Grajauskas's plastic bag.

Nils Krantz finds it during the crime scene investigation, states that it has been recorded on and finds the fingerprints of two different women on it, one of which is Lydia Grajauskas. Nils Krantz gives it to Ewert Grens in the morgue.

Ewert Grens takes it, but doesn't report it anywhere. Doesn't enter it into the evidence list, doesn't give it to the forensic team.

Sven Sundkvist finds it on the shelf in Ewert Grens's office and discovers that it's blank.

BOX 21

Gustaf Ejder reports that Lydia Grajauskas said there was another videotape, a copy, in a storage locker at Stockholm Central Station.

Sven Sundkvist opens this locker, takes this copy home with him, gets up in the middle of the night and finds out this tape is far from empty.

He stopped writing. He could have added *but was too much of a coward to watch it further.* Instead, Sven studied purple Ewert. What have you done? I know you destroyed evidence, and I know why. He crumpled up the paper and threw it at the sink. He pulled the crossword over to him, looked at the three empty boxes, tried letter after letter without solving the puzzle and gave up. He left the kitchen and went into the living room again.

That troubling videotape.

He could have just not gone to get it. He could have left it where it was.

He had no choice. He had to watch it.

Lydia Grajauskas again. The picture is a blur for a few seconds, then she gets the go-ahead from the cameraman and continues talking.

'Когда Бенгт Нордвалл встретил меня в Клайпейде сказал он что это была хорошая высокооплачивая работа.'

She's still looking at her friend, waiting for her to translate.

Sljusareva pats her friend's cheek, then turns towards the camera.

'When Bengt Nordwall met me in Klaipeda, he told me it was a good job with a high salary.'

Sven Sundkvist stopped the tape again and walked out of the living room, escaping for a second time into the kitchen. He opened the refrigerator and drank straight out of the milk carton, closed the door gently, not wanting to wake Anita.

He hadn't been able to articulate it. But this was precisely what he feared.

Another version of the truth.

With another version of the truth comes the possibility of a lie. And as long as no one unmasks the lie it will continue to exist.

He returned to the living room and sat down quietly on the sofa.

Now he was acquainted with Bengt Nordwall's lie.

He was sure Ewert was too. He was sure that the videotape Ewert was given contained the same information as this one. Ewert had watched it, erased it, and decided to protect his friend.

Now he was stuck with Bengt Nordwall's lie, which was also Ewert's lie. And if he chose not to reveal this it would become his lie, too. He would be doing exactly what Ewert did, looking away from what he'd seen in order to protect a friend.

He started the tape then fast-forwarded it. There was another twenty minutes of recorded material. He looked at the time. Two thirty. If he rewound he'd have time to hear the whole of Lydia Grajauskas's story before three o'clock. Then he could creep up to his bedroom and leave a note on his pillow for Anita, telling her he was needed on the night shift, get dressed, go out to his car, and be in the city in twenty minutes.

IT WAS A QUARTER TO FOUR when he opened the door to his office.

Morning was already here. The light was streaming in from over the sea as he drove down the deserted highway that connected Gustavsberg and the inner city of Stockholm.

He got himself another cup of coffee. Not so much to stay awake, his thoughts were too confusing to let him sleep, but more so he could focus before those chaotic thoughts led him to the wrong conclusions, which sometimes happens late at night.

He cleared off his desk, put the piles of paper and photos and folders on the floor. For the first time since moving into this office five or six years ago, the wooden surface of his desk was completely empty.

He took a wad of paper out of his pocket, which he'd fished out of the sink before leaving home. He unfolded it, and put it in the middle of the empty desk.

He knew now that the man he'd drawn in purple marker had crossed the line by tampering with evidence in an ongoing investigation in order to protect his own interests, in order to cover up someone else's lie.

Sven Sundkvist absently traced the purple lines with his finger. He was filled with fury, and yet he had absolutely no idea how to proceed now that he had this knowledge.

Lars Ågestam did what he always did when he couldn't sleep. He put on his suit and his black shoes, emptied his briefcase so it would be as light as possible, left his house in Åkeshov and started walking at dawn. It took him three hours to get from Stockholm's western suburbs to the offices of the Swedish Prosecution Authority.

It had been an unusual conversation. He'd found it difficult to follow, and he didn't usually have that problem. Ewert Grens, whom he both admired and felt sorry for, sat down in front of him and *on the one hand* explained why they still had no motive for Lydia Grajauskas knocking out her guard, taking hostages, and executing a police officer and then shot herself, and then *on the other hand* explained why her friend Sljusareva didn't have any information for them, and therefore was on a ferry headed for a city on the other side of the Baltic Sea.

He hadn't been able to sleep.

At the time, he'd decided to place his trust in Grens.

Now he was walking in the dawn light, and he had already called the guard at Söder Hospital to say he was on his way. Ågestam was going to visit the morgue one more time.

He didn't knock. That was just his way. That was how Ewert Grens always did it.

Sven Sundkvist jumped a little and looked at the door.

'Ewert?'

'Jesus, Sven, you're here early.'

Sven's face reddened. He knew it must be visible, and he looked down at his desktop in embarrassment, as if he'd been exposed. There sat the little purple drawing of Ewert.

'It just turned out that way.'

'It's not even half past five yet. I usually have the place to myself at this time.'

Grens stood in the doorway, about to come in. Sven Sundkvist

BOX 21

glanced down at the paper with the purple man on it, and put his hand over it.

'What are you up to, kiddo?'

Sven was not a good liar. Not to the people he really valued. 'I don't know. It's just too much right now.'

He felt like he was suffocating. He was surely very red by now.

'Ewert, you know how it is. Söder Hospital. Reporters hounding us. You wanted to avoid it. But we have to come up with something. The press demands it.'

He looked down at his desk. 'I can't take it.'

Ewert Grens took a step towards him, stopped, hesitated a moment, then turned around. He spoke loudly, his back to the open door, as he left the room.

'Good, Sven. I'm sure you know what you're doing. I'm glad you're taking care of all that press stuff.'

———

Söder Hospital was huge, hulking and ugly, but in the morning sun it almost looked beautiful with bright red gleaming from the windows and metal roof. Lars Ågestam walked through the empty entrance hall. It wasn't even six o'clock yet, but soon this building would start to wake up.

He took the lift down to the basement and walked the same path that Grajauskas had in her oversized hospital clothes concealing a plastic bag, a beaten-up woman that no would ever abuse again.

Blue and white police tape cut across the last part of the corridor where Sundkvist had been stationed, thirty metres away from the morgue, but still close enough to see the place where the door had been. He ducked under the tape and zigzagged around remnants of the blown-up wall, until he reached the entrance to the morgue. It was sealed off by several metres of tape snaking back and forth, attached to what was left of the doorframe. He tore it down and stepped inside.

First, the elongated hall-like entrance area, then the room where they died. The white chalk still kept them next to each other on the cold tile floor. Her body next to his. Their blood mingling. He died with her. She died with him. Ågestam was sure there had to be a reason why they met their end here together.

It was quiet. He stood in the middle of the room and looked around. He usually felt panic in the face of death. He didn't even wear a watch any more, because it reminded him of the passage of time. Now he was in a morgue, alone, trying to understand.

He put the tape player in the middle of the floor. He wanted to hear their conversation.

He wanted to participate, like he always did, after the fact.

'*Ewert.*'

'*Over.*'

'*The hostage in the corridor is dead. I don't see any blood, don't know where he was shot. But the smell. It's overpowering, Ewert, and bitter.*'

Bengt Nordwall's voice was steady. Or at least it sounded steady. Lars Ågestam had never met him, never heard him speak before.

He was trying to get to know a dead man.

'*Ewert, it's a fucking con, all of it. She didn't shoot anyone. They were all still here, all four of the hostages. They're alive, and they just walked out. She's rigged three hecto-grams of Semtex around those doors, but she has no way to trigger it.*'

BOX 21

He heard the fear then. Nordwall had continued observing, describing, but the voice was different – he'd realised something that the people listening didn't know yet, something Ågestam still didn't know.

'How does it feel? To stand naked in a morgue, in front of a woman with a gun in her hand?'

'I've done what you asked me to.'

'You feel humiliated. Right?'

'Yes.'

'Alone?'

'Yes.'

'Scared?'

'Yes.'

'Down on your knees.'

Not two days had passed. The voices on the tape still seemed alive, as did the Russian interpreter's version. Every word rang out clear in that closed room. She had made up her mind. Lars Ågestam was sure of it. She'd had her mind made up from the very beginning. She was going to die here. He was going to die here. She was going to humiliate him, then they would both stop breathing.

They'd end up next to each other on the floor of a morgue, together for an eternity.

Ågestam stood where Nordwall stood and wondered if Nordwall had known he had only a few seconds left, a few moments, then nothing.

———

Ewert Grens was having a hard time concentrating.

He hadn't slept at all, he should have lain down on the sofa for a while, but he had too much on his mind, too much to agonise over for him to sleep at home. It was just impossible.

He had promised to have lunch with Lena. She wanted to talk more about Bengt. At first he told her no, he had no desire to do that. He missed him, yes, he did, but he'd also realised that the man he missed was a different person to the one he was learning about now.

If only I had known.
Did you think about her? Even once? Did you go home to her after that and love her? After that?
I'm doing this for Lena.
You're no longer alive.

So he told her yes when she asked him a second time. She hadn't eaten anything. She just poked at her food, and drank two bottles of mineral water. She had cried, mostly because of the kids, that's what she said. The kids don't understand, and if I don't understand either, Ewert, how can I explain it to them?

Afterwards he was glad he'd gone. She needed him. She needed to say the same thing over and over again until she slowly understood.

He wasn't any good at grieving.

But it felt good to see someone else brave enough to do it.

———

Lars Ågestam had played the tape over and over again. He stood still in the middle of that huge room listening. He sat on the floor with his back to the wall like the hostages, he lay where Bengt Nordwall had, surrounded by the white chalk marks on the floor. He was smaller than Nordwall, so there was plenty of space. He even held his hands in front of his crotch like

BOX 21

Nordwall, stared at the ceiling like Nordwall. He had listened to the entire conversation with Ewert Grens, and he was sure now that by the time Bengt Nordwall ended up at the very spot where Ågestam was lying now, he'd known exactly who Lydia Grajauskas was. They had some kind of connection, and Grens had guessed it, and for some reason he was willing to throw away his entire career to protect the truth.

Ågestam stayed in the morgue for exactly two hours. By the time he was ready to leave, he was hungry for a breakfast in a café surrounded by lots of people chewing and living. He needed to get out of here. His fear of death suddenly returned.

'I had this cordoned off.'

Ågestam hadn't heard him come in. Nils Krantz, the forensic technician. They'd met, but didn't know each other.

'I apologise. I had to. I'm looking for answers.'

'You're tramping around on a crime scene.'

'I'm the prosecutor in charge of the investigation.'

'I know, and I don't give a fuck who you are. You have to walk inside the chalked lines like everyone else. I'm the one who's responsible for the evidence in here.'

Ågestam sighed loud enough for Krantz to hear it. The prosecutor had no desire to argue. He turned around, picked up his tape recorder, grabbed his notes and put them into his briefcase, on his way to that breakfast again.

'You seem to be in a hurry.'

'It felt as though that's what you wanted.'

Nils Krantz shrugged, walked slowly into the room while studying the doorframe to the storage room where the hostages were kept near the end. There were still remnants of plastic explosives around the mouldings. He spoke loudly with his back to Ågestam.

'By the way, we got the test results back. Thought you might be interested.'

'What tests?'

'The other investigation. Lang. We inspected his body.'

'Yes?'

'Nothing.'

'Nothing?'

'There wasn't a trace of Oldéus on his body.'

Lars Ågestam was about to go, until Krantz raised his voice. Now he stood there empty and unable to move.

'There you go.'

He gazed at Krantz, who continued searching along the doorframe with plastic gloved hands. Ågestam stared listlessly at him for a while, then picked up his briefcase again, took a few steps towards what had once been a door. He was about to walk out when Nils Krantz raised his voice again.

'But.'

'Yes?'

'Lang's clothes. We went through those too. On the shoes. We found it. Both blood and DNA. From Oldéus.'

Ewert Grens left Lena at the restaurant. She explained that she felt like staying there for a while, ordered a third bottle of mineral water, and hugged him tightly before he left. He started walking back to the Homicide Division, but then changed his mind, took a short detour by the jail.

He just couldn't let it be.

It hadn't been enough that a respected doctor identified the murderer with one hundred per cent certainty out of a stack of photos. When that murderer managed to intimidate and threaten the doctor into refusing to point him out in a line-up, he was going to be set free, free to kill again, according to the law.

Not this time. This time was it.

BOX 21

Grens rode the lift up to the second floor of the jail. He noti-
fied the guard he wanted to meet Jochum Lang in one of the
interrogation rooms.

They walked down the corridor, the guard a few steps ahead,
past silent jail cells. Number eight was closed, like the others.
He nodded to the guard, who opened the little hatch on the
door.

He was lying on the bunk, on his back with his eyes closed.
He was sleeping. What else was there to do for twenty-three
hours a day in a few shitty square metres with no newspapers,
radio, or television.

Ewert Grens shouted through the hatch.

'Lang. You can wake up now.'

He heard. But he didn't move.

'Now. We're gonna have a little talk. You and me.'

Lang turned on his side with his back to Grens, who slammed
the hatch shut and nodded to the guard that he wanted the door
opened. Grens entered and stood just inside the door, asked to
be left alone.

The guard hesitated. Jochum Lang was classified as dangerous. He was supposed to stay there. Ewert Grens explained, as
patiently as he could, that he would take full responsibility if
things went to hell.

The guard shrugged his uniformed shoulders, walked out,
and closed the door behind him.

Grens took another step into the cell, just a little to the left of
the bunk.

'I know you can hear me. Get up.'

'Fuck off, Grens.'

He took a final step, close enough now to touch the body
that refused to get up, but instead Grens grabbed the edge of
the bunk and started shaking it violently until Lang was
standing.

They were facing each other, the same height, staring straight into each other's eyes.

'To the interrogation room, Lang. Now.'

'Go fuck yourself.'

'We have blood type. We have DNA. We have a witness. You're going down. For murder.'

Just a few centimetres between their faces.

'Listen, arsehole. I don't know what the fuck you're up to. But maybe you should think twice. Cops have been known to fall out of cars and hurt themselves.'

Ewert Grens smiled.

'You can threaten me however the fuck you want to. I've got nothing you can take from me that isn't worth seeing you spend the rest of your days jerking off behind bars.'

It was hard to say who hated whom more.

They stared into each other's eyes, searching for something there. Lang's warm breath hit Ewert's face as he lowered his voice.

'I'm not going to participate in any more interrogations. That's just how it is. If you or anyone else comes in here again and says I have to go down to interrogation again, I will do my very best to hurt that person very badly. I'm warning you just this once. Go to hell. And close the door behind you.'

Sven Sundkvist called home and tried to explain why he'd disappeared in the middle of the night, why he'd left a note on his pillow without waking her up. Anita was upset. She didn't like it when he didn't talk to her. They said they would never just take off without telling each other why. It ended with an argument. Sven called hoping to make things better, but he'd only made them worse. So he was on his way home, driving fast out of irritation, not much traffic except by Slussen, and he'd just

BOX 21

driven past the huge Viking Line ferries when Lars Ågestam called and started talking to him in a quiet voice.

He asked Sven to come to the Swedish Prosecution Authority. He wanted to meet, just the two of them. Long after business hours, when everyone else had gone home.

Sven Sundkvist had stopped the car, called Anita again and made everything even worse. Now he was still in the city, alone, unsure what to do with all this time, really just a couple of hours to wait but it felt like an eternity.

It was probably a beautiful evening, mild June evenings sometimes are. He walked slowly away from the Kronoberg police station, circling around Kungsholmen. He could hear the music and smell the cuisine at pavement cafés as he passed. Life was being lived around him, and it should make him smile, but he barely noticed it.

It had been a long night and an even longer day.

He had no more energy for that videotape or for the bitter truth he was carrying.

Was that what Ågestam wanted to discuss?

Was he going to try to shake Sven's loyalty?

He was too tired for decisions right now.

They met at Kungs Bridge a few minutes after eight o'clock. Lars Ågestam was waiting for him outside the entrance, looking like he always did, hair to the side, suit, and shiny shoes. He shook Sven's hand and opened the door with his key card. They didn't say much, just stood side by side in the lift – they'd talk soon enough.

They exited on the ninth floor. Lars Ågestam showed him into his office, Sven caught a glimpse of the city through Ågestam's window, summer darkness slowly pushing away the day.

He sat down in one of the two visitors' chairs at the short end of the desk. Ågestam excused himself, walked back out into the corridor for a minute, and came back carrying two cups of coffee and a tray with a braided sweet pastry sliced up on it. He put them down on a sideboard next to a couple of thick investigations.

'Sugar?'

'Milk, please.'

Ågestam was doing what he could to make the situation less dramatic and stressful for the two of them. It wasn't working particularly well. They knew they weren't here to eat sweet pastry. It was late, everyone had long since gone home, and they were here to talk about the sort of things you take in confidence, things not meant for other ears, things that should go no further.

'I had trouble sleeping last night.'

Ågestam stretched his arms high above his head, as if to emphasise how tired he was.

Me too, thought Sven. I didn't sleep at all. The fucking videotape and Ewert, of course, is that what we're here to talk about. I'm still not sure.

'I was lying there thinking about your friend. Your colleague. Ewert Grens.'

Not now. Not yet.

'I need to talk to you, Sven. Something isn't right.'

Ågestam cleared his throat, almost seemed like he was going to stand up, but stayed put.

'You know we don't exactly like each other.'

'You're not the only one.'

'I know. But still. I want to emphasise that this has nothing to do with what I think about Ewert Grens as a person. This is an official matter. His role as the investigating police officer in an investigation that I'm leading.'

This time he did stand up. He looked at Sven, then paced restlessly about the room.

'Yesterday. Yesterday I had a very strange meeting with Mr

BOX 21

Grens. He'd just put Alena Sljusareva on a ferry back to Klai-peda, Lithuania without clearing it with me first.'

He was waiting for a reaction.

He didn't get one.

'I went to the morgue early this morning. I was trying to understand. I've spoken with many of your colleagues about that day. According to Sergeant Hermansson, a very good cop that I've never talked to before, we have two witnesses who describe a person matching the description of Alena Sljusareva visiting the disabled toilet just before Lydia Grajauskas also vis-ited it and exited in possession of a gun and plastic explosives. It's not difficult to imagine that she was the one who supplied Grajauskas with those weapons. So why was Grens in such a rush to send her home?'

Sven Sundkvist sat quietly.

The videotape. He'd been afraid this meeting was going to be about a police officer switching a videotape. A videotape that he was now aware of. The videotape that would soon force him to decide whether to speak or hide behind a lie.

'Sven, I'm asking you directly. Do you know something that I should know?'

Sundkvist remained silent, because he had no clue what he should say.

Lars Ågestam repeated his question.

'Is there anything?'

He had to answer him. He answered.

'No. I don't know what you're talking about.'

Ågestam continued pacing and breathing nervously. He was just getting going.

'He's one of the force's most respected officers. I should just sit back and relax, right?'

A few more deep breaths.

'But it just doesn't make sense. Do you understand? That's

why I can't sleep. That's why I walked to work in the middle of the night and lay down in the chalk outlines of a dead man on the floor of the hospital's morgue.'

Sven met his gaze, but stayed silent. What he should say would never be enough.

'I called Vilnius. I asked our Lithuanian colleagues to locate Alena Sljusareva. They found her. She's staying with her parents in Klaipeda.'

The prosecutor sat on the edge of the desk, picked up the huge stack of papers behind him, the investigation he was discussing.

'There are no notes here from Grens about his interview with Sljusareva. He decided himself that she should leave the country. All we know is what he's told us.'

His voice cracked. He knew what he was about to say was the last thing you should ever say, not to a cop, not about a colleague.

'Ewert Grens's story doesn't hold up.'

A pause, then he continued.

'I don't know why, but I think he's manipulating the investigation.'

Ågestam pressed play on the tape recorder on the desktop. They listened, and both heard the end of the conversation.

'The Stena Baltica? *It's a fucking boat! This is something personal! Bengt, over. Damn it, Bengt, fall back! Fall back now!'*

No words. No decisions about loyalty or the truth. Not yet.

'Sven?'

'Yes?'

'I want you to go to Klaipeda. I want you to question Alena Sljusareva, and report back to me. I want to know what she really said.'

Saturday, 8 June

PALANGA AIRPORT had a peculiar smell. As soon as he left the gate and headed for the baggage claim, he was struck by the scent of disinfectant coming from the still wet floor, the smell of a foreign country, chemicals that were probably long since outlawed in Sweden.

One hour and twenty minutes, he thought. One lousy hour and even the disinfectant's different.

It was his second time in Lithuania, in fact in any of the Baltic States. He didn't recall much from his first visit. He'd been new to the force back then, didn't even remember where they landed. He was part of a special transport of a prisoner to a prison in Vilnius. It had been such a big deal at the time to be travelling outside Sweden with an infamous criminal, and the only thing he remembered now was the prison. It was like travelling back in time. The barking dogs, damp corridors, the quiet, shaved, pale prisoners packed into tiny cells. The air had been difficult to breathe, and there were signs everywhere warning about TB. It was such a strange experience that he'd never spoken about it to anyone, not even to Anita.

He exited the terminal and hailed one in a row of yellow taxis. Twenty-six kilometres south. To Klaipeda. To Alena Sljusareva. To what he didn't want to know.

He'd called home from Arlanda, said good morning to Jonas and promised to buy him something. A surprise. Some sweets. That was the only thing he'd have time to buy. He wasn't in Lithuania for long. He would head back early tomorrow morning, and he knew what he had to accomplish before that.

The taxi slowly drove down the highway from Palanga to Klaipeda. Sven Sundkvist was about to ask the driver to go a little faster, but decided not to and leaned back. It wasn't worth trying to explain for the few minutes he might gain. The countryside looked beautiful, he thought, the sun high in the sky. Poor, that much he knew, with eight out of ten living close to the poverty line, but also there was a kind of dignity to the land that he admired, the opposite of the prison. On the news they only showed clichés, so he expected grey people, grey clothes, grey seasons, but right now it was summer – real people, real lives, real colours.

He asked to go directly to the hotel. He was early. Check-in wasn't until after lunch, but the Hotel Aribò was far from full, and they let him into one of the clean, empty rooms.

He rested for a few minutes in the narrowest hotel bed he'd ever seen. He tried to picture Alena, the woman he'd soon meet, what she looked like and how she spoke. It had been so chaotic in the apartment. She'd been upset, screaming about her friend, who was lying unconscious on the floor, and about the man she called Dimitri Pimp-Fucker, who was standing just a couple of metres away in a shiny suit in front of a hole in the front door. Sven Sundkvist didn't have time to get a good look at her, could never guess that a week later he'd see her again on a videotape and then meet her on the other side of the Baltic Sea. She'd been in the other room, as naked as the young woman lying unconscious on the floor.

Then she disappeared while they were busy taking care of the brutally beaten woman and the pimp running around with his Lithuanian passport and claiming the apartment as Lithuanian land.

And she'd been gone since then.

Until she was arrested at the harbour, shortly before boarding a ferry.

BOX 21

Ewert had interrogated her, and a few hours later he decided, despite everything, to send her home again.

Sven Sundkvist showered and changed into lighter clothes. He hadn't realised it would be so warm – those grey clichés. He stared into his briefcase for a moment at the little tape recorder that lay there. He was going to take down her statement. But he was going to do it with pen and paper, he wasn't sure why. Maybe he was afraid of what she'd say, of hearing her voice again if she said things he didn't want to hear.

He walked through the city. The houses were beautiful and seemed to exude another time. He kept seeing Lydia Grajauskas in the faces of the people he passed by.

She had asked him to go to the Curonian Lagoon, and take a small ferry to Smiltynò. The heat from Palanga had followed him to Klaipeda and was even worse now on the deck. He could feel the sun burning his neck. He should have put on sunscreen – he'd be bright red by evening. He was supposed to turn right when he stepped ashore, walk along the beach, exactly as she described. The large aquarium was located inside an old fort, one hundred species of Baltic fish and a dolphin show. He saw posters for it as soon as he left the boat. She wanted to be surrounded by people, said there'd be a lot of visitors here at lunchtime, tourists, school classes, and they could walk around looking at the fish and have a long chat without attracting any attention.

He stood outside the entrance, which was where he thought he was supposed to stand. He was almost twenty minutes early. It had been difficult to calculate how long it would take to get from the city centre to this Baltic-Sea-themed aquarium on something called Smiltynò.

He sat down on a bench just a few metres away from where they were supposed to meet. The sun beat down into his face, and he squinted at people arriving. He did what he usually did when he watched strangers – he searched for himself. He was somewhere in this stream of strangers, or at least someone like him. A man his age with a woman he loved by his side, their child walking in front of them. Maybe a police officer or something else that required dedication and long evenings. The kind of man who would always rather be at home, but spent most of his time away from it. There was someone like that in the crowd, without Ewert's aggressiveness, without Lang's obstinacy, without whatever gave Grajauskas the strength to rise up after countless times of being violated and exact her revenge, someone without any of the characteristics that made a person anything other than predictable, boring, and normal.

He saw himself. Different versions. The people he might have been, if he'd happened to be born here. He was smiling at one of them, a man in short sleeves wearing thin trousers, when she tapped him on the shoulder.

He hadn't even seen or heard her. She was wearing sunglasses, a sweater and slightly too big jeans. Otherwise, she looked about how he'd pictured her. Dark long hair, a beautiful face, not very tall. She'd spent three years as someone else's property, being raped many times a day. But you couldn't see it, not on the outside. She looked like women do when they're twenty years old, as if their life has just begun. But inside. He could never understand. She had to be old inside. That was where her wounds were. This was a woman who would probably never truly be whole again.

'Sundkvist?'

'Sundkvist.'

He nodded as he stood up from the bench. They understood each other well enough. He used his rusty schoolboy English, and she used a richer language, an English that certainly had its foundation in school, but that had been formed over three years in foreign lands. She preferred it to speaking Swedish.

BOX 21

'You knew who I was?'

'I recognised you from the apartment.'

'It was pretty chaotic in there.'

'I would have known it was you anyway. I've learned what Swedish men look like.'

She pointed towards the entrance, and they went inside together. He paid for both of them. He couldn't decide when it would be appropriate to start asking questions. She helped him.

'I don't know what you don't know. But I'll answer you if I can. I'd be grateful if we could start now. I trust you. I saw how you worked when you came into the apartment, but I would like to get it over with. I want to go home. I want to forget. Do you understand?'

She stood in front of the glass wall with water and fish behind it. She looked at him pleadingly. He tried to appear calm, calmer than he was. What she might say frightened him. He wasn't completely sure why.

'I don't know how long this will take. It depends where our conversation takes us. But I understand what you mean. I'll do my best to be quick.'

He didn't understand the point of aquariums. He didn't understand the point of zoos either. Trapped animals didn't appeal to him. So the crowds around him and the fish on display were something he had no problem ignoring. He could give his full attention to Alena Sljusareva and her story.

The story he feared.

The story he wished had never happened.

They talked – it was more a conversation than an interrogation – for almost three hours. She told him about the days she spent wandering Stockholm after fleeing the apartment, the feeling of freedom coursing through her body mixed with the fear of being arrested, plus her worry for Lydia, who she'd left unconscious with her back flayed. They swore never to leave each other until they were both free, but at the time, when she ran down the stairs and out of the door, she'd been sure she was more help to Lydia away from the apartment that she was in it.

He interrupted her when there was any uncertainty, and she clarified things for him. She was never inconsistent, at least not as far as he could tell.

They walked slowly, passing by more people staring at more fish through the aquarium windows, and she told him about the call she received from Lydia one day after escaping the apartment. She'd been at the docks, contemplating going home, when Lydia contacted her from her hospital bed and asked Alena to fetch all the things she would later use in the morgue.

Alena asked him to believe her, in a quiet voice, when she said she had no idea how Lydia would use it.

He stopped, looked at her, and explained that the purpose of this conversation was *not* to determine if she was guilty of accessory to kidnapping and murder.

She met his eyes and asked what this was about, in that case.

'Nothing. And everything. That's all.'

Simple chairs and a small round table and big blue fish on the tablecloth – he bought them each a cup of coffee, and they sat down in the middle of the cafeteria surrounded by families.

She told him about the box at the Central Station and the burglary in the storage room and the grocery bag she put in the bin in the disabled toilet. He stopped her, to make sure she was telling the truth.

'What was the number?'

'Number?'

'On the box.'

'Twenty-one.'

'What was in it?'

BOX 21

'Mostly my things. She almost only took money for doing extra.'

'Extra?'

'Hitting. Spitting. Filming. Use your imagination.'

Sven Sundkvist swallowed, and he could see her discomfort.

'And what did *she* keep there?'

'Money. In a box. And two videotapes.'

'What kind of tapes?'

'The truth. That's what she called them. *My truth.*'

'What does that mean?'

'She told everything. I helped her by translating. About how we came to Sweden. About the people who treated us like we were property that they owned. And why she hated the policeman she shot in the morgue.'

'Nordwall?'

'Bengt Nordwall.'

Sven Sundkvist didn't tell her that he'd been to box 21, or that he'd watched their video while sitting at home on his sofa. He didn't tell her that no one could see the tape Lydia Grajauskas had brought down to the morgue, because it had disappeared. A policeman had destroyed their story to protect another policeman. He didn't tell her that he felt ashamed of the fact that he hadn't even decided yet if their suffering was more important than informing on a colleague and friend. He had no idea if he'd ever tell what he knew, that there was a copy of that tape, and that it contained another truth.

'I saw him.'

'Who?'

'I saw him there in the apartment. Bengt Nordwall.'

'You saw him?'

'And he saw me. I know he recognised me. I know he recognised Lydia.'

He found it difficult to listen to her after that.

She continued to tell her story, and he asked her clarifying questions, but he was somewhere else.

He was filled with pure rage. He had never been so filled with rage. He needed to scream.

But he didn't.

He was one of those boring, normal people.

He choked on it, could feel it was pressing into his chest.

He continued to pretend he was calm, unafraid of what she said. He didn't want to scare her. He understood how much it took for her to tell this, how brave she was.

He screamed.

He screamed, and then begged her forgiveness. He was in pain, he explained, and it wasn't her he was yelling at. He was in pain, here, in his chest.

———

By the time they were on the Smiltynò ferry heading back to the centre of Klaipeda, he knew all the details of what happened to her from the time she escaped the apartment on Völund Street until she was arrested in the harbour. Rage still churned in his stomach and chest, but it felt as if their conversation wasn't over yet. He wanted to know more. He wanted to know about those three years, about how sex trafficking worked, how a woman's body could sold again and again so that someone else could get a fancier car or more money in a bank account.

He asked her if he could buy her dinner. She smiled.

'I'm not up for any more of that. Home. I haven't been home in three years.'

'You will never again be bothered by a Swedish police officer in this matter. I promise you.'

'I don't understand, you want to know more?'

BOX 21

'I spoke with the Lithuanian ambassador in Sweden a few days ago. He came to the airport to make sure the man you call Dimitri Pimp-Fucker would be sent home. He was extremely unhappy. He gave me an idea of how massive the world you just escaped from really is. I want you to tell me about it. I want to learn.'

'I'm so tired.'

'One evening. One conversation. Then never again.'

He blushed suddenly, because he realised he was demanding her attention, just like all the Swedish men she had come to hate.

'I apologise. That was not an invitation. Please don't misunderstand. I really want to know. And I have kids. I'm married.'

'They always are.'

———————

He walked past the old beer factory, hurrying back to the Hotel Aribò. He needed another shower to wash off the heat. He changed clothes for the second time since checking in eight hours earlier.

She'd asked two elderly women as they were getting off the boat, and they suggested a Chinese restaurant – Taravos Aniko, big portions, and you could watch them cooking if you got one of the tables at the back.

She was already there when he arrived. The same clothes she wore at the aquarium. She smiled, he smiled, they ordered mineral water and the fixed-price menu – starter, main course and dessert.

It took her a long time to find the words, and he didn't hurry her.

She started somewhere in the middle, and slowly filled in from there. She introduced him to a world he thought he knew something about, but he'd been wrong. She cried and whispered, and eventually she spoke non-stop. It was the first time she'd described what had been the whole of her adult life to another person. The first time she'd heard her own words, and he listened and was amazed by her strength, by the fact that she was so whole despite everything.

He waited until she was finished. Until she couldn't go on. Until she sat staring blankly ahead.

It was done now, she was done, and she would never tell her story again to someone who demanded it.

Sven stooped over. His briefcase was at his feet. He picked it up, and put it on the table beside an empty plate.

'I have something that isn't mine.'

He opened his briefcase, took out a small brown box and two neatly folded dresses.

'I think this was Lydia's.'

She looked at the box, the dresses, she knew where they came from, and she glanced questioningly at Sven, who nodded. Yes, she was right.

'The box is empty now. Rented to someone else. I'm giving this to you. I would guess those were her dresses. And her box. There's forty thousand in it.'

Alena didn't move, stayed silent.

'You can do whatever you want with it. Keep it for yourself or give it to her family if she still has one.'

She leaned forward, ran her hand over the black, glossy fabric.

The only thing she had left of her friend.

'I was there yesterday. I went looking for her mother. Lydia spoke about her often.'

She looked down at the table.

'She's dead. She died two months ago.'

Sven hesitated, then pushed the box and the dresses over the table to Alena. He closed his briefcase and put it on the floor.

BOX 21

'I would like to know more about her. Who she was. All I've seen is a person who had thirty-five lashes on her back and who took hostages. That's all.'

Alena shook her head.

'No more.'

'On some level I understand what she did.'

'Not now, not ever.'

———

They sat there saying very little, until the waiter kindly asked them to leave because the restaurant was closing. They stood up and were just about to go when a man in his twenties came in through the front door and walked over to the table. Sven studied him quickly: tall, blond and tanned. He seemed calm, not the type to look for conflict. Alena went over to him, kissed his cheek, and put her arm in his.

'Janoz. I went away from him. He was still here. I'm so incredibly grateful for that.'

She kissed his cheek again, pulled him close. She told Sven briefly about how Janoz had searched for her for the first seven months, spending time and money, but finally he gave up.

She laughed. For the first time all day she laughed. Sven smiled, he congratulated them, and for a moment he felt something besides despair.

'Lydia? Did she have somebody?'

'He was named Vladi.'

'And?'

'He earned his money from her.'

She didn't say any more, and he didn't ask. They parted outside, and Sven Sundkvist promised again that she would never have to speak to another Swedish police officer.

She started to go, but after only a few steps, she turned around.

'One more thing.'

'Of course.'

'Out there at the aquarium. The interrogation. I don't really understand that. Why did we do it?'

'For a criminal case. The police, we take witness statements when something has happened.'

'Yes, I understand that. But you already had mine.'

'What do you mean?'

'I already told everything to the other policeman.'

'Who?'

'The older one. He was with you in the apartment.'

'A man named Grens.'

'Yes.'

'The same questions?'

'Everything I told you at the aquarium, I told him too. The same questions, same answers.'

'Everything?'

'Everything.'

'About your conversation with Lydia? About how you picked up the videotape from the box? About getting the weapon and explosives? About leaving the plastic bag in the handicap toilet?'

'Everything.'

—————

It was two o'clock by the time he lay down in his narrow bed. He hadn't bought anything for Jonas. He was going to sleep a few hours, go to St John's Lutheran Church to light a candle in the place where Lydia Grajauskas's mother was buried, then go to the airport to take the morning flight to Stockholm. He could buy sweets in the duty-free shop. He'd have time to pick up some chocolates or jellybeans in shiny paper.

BOX 21

He lay in the dark with the window open. Klaipeda was silent.

He knew he didn't have much time left.

He had to make a decision. He possessed the truth. Now he had to decide what to do with it.

Sunday, 9 June

THE TWO NEW girls weren't much fun when he test-fucked them.

Virgins, except for that little bit in the cabin on the ferry.

But they were getting better. This was their third day in the apartment on Völund Street. They'd soon be up to twelve johns a day, just like that lunatic Grajauskas and her dirty little friend were doing until they lost their minds and ran off.

But these new girls were missing something. They needed to put on more of a show. Act horny. That was important. The johns needed to feel wanted, beautiful. Like they were part of a couple for a while, otherwise they might as well jerk off into a sink.

He knocked them around a little, needed to break them in. Just a few more days, and they'd stop crying so fucking much. He couldn't stand that about new girls, all the fucking snivelling.

He missed Grajauskas's and Sljusareva's professionalism. They took off their clothes, and they did it well. But it was nice not have to put up with their sneers. He'd seen it on their faces more and more, and also pleasant not to have to hear *Dimitri Pimp-Fucker* as soon as he hit somebody.

The first john would be here soon. Just after eight.

They usually came straight from home, from some fat wife. They wanted a little fun before they went to work.

He was going to observe the girls today. This was their exam. Then he'd know if they were ready to start fucking or if they needed more lessons.

First, the one who'd moved into Grajauskas's room. He'd put her there on purpose. They looked alike, so it would be easier for her to take over Grajauskas's clients.

She fixed herself up, just like she should, put on the underwear the client wanted. It looked good on her.

There was a knock on the door. She checked the mirror, then walked over to the electronic locks, which were turned off while she was being supervised, and opened the door. She smiled at the customer, who wore a shiny grey suit, light blue shirt and black tie.

That smile. She kept smiling even when he spat. More like he dropped it at her feet, near her black high heels.

He pointed.

His finger straight down.

She bent down, still smiling at him like she was supposed to. She sank down to the ground, her nose almost touching, put her tongue against the cold floor, and took the spit into her mouth, swallowed it.

Then she stood up again, her eyes closed.

He slapped her. She kept smiling the whole time just like she'd been taught.

Dimitri liked what he saw. He gave a thumbs up to the man in the grey suit, and got a thumbs up back.

She was approved.

He'd be able to book her up now.

Lydia Grajauskas no longer existed, not even here.

———

He always felt a little afraid when an aeroplane was landing. The bang as the wheels came out, the ground getting closer outside the tiny window, the first contact with the asphalt. It got worse every time he flew. Especially in a plane like this one, a thirty-five-seater so small it was hard to stand up straight. He

BOX 21

always regretted flying, until the bouncing stopped and the plane started rolling smoothly down the runway.

Sven Sundkvist was able to breathe again. He deplaned, exited Arlanda airport. It would be just over half an hour's drive back to Stockholm, if the traffic in the northern suburbs wasn't too bad.

His thoughts were a jumble. He was sixteen years old again, touching Anita for the first time, he was in the stairwell with Jochum Lang who was beating up Hilding Oldéus, he was on the floor with Lydia Grajauskas next to the corpse of the man she hated, he was with a one-year-old Jonas when they picked him up in Phnom Phenh, with him a week later when he said Daddy the first time, and with Alena Sljusareva, who wore an oversized red sweater in a Chinese restaurant in Klaipeda and told the story of three long years of complete abasement and . . .

Anything to avoid thinking about Ewert.

There were roadworks as he passed Sollentuna, two lanes merged into one.

He crept forward, stopped, crept again, stopped. He looked at the people around him who were doing the same thing, sitting in their cars waiting for time to pass. They all stared straight ahead. They must have their own troubles, their own Ewerts to think about.

He shuddered with uneasiness.

He decided to drive a bit further, to circumvent the city by way of Eriksberg, the suburb where Lena Nordwall lived.

He needed more time.

———

The wooden bench was hard. He'd spent hours sitting there through the meaningless denials of hooligans. Now it was quiet in the crummy courtroom. They were alone, at the back, waiting. Ewert Grens was actually fond of this old courtroom in the town hall, despite hard benches and chattering lawyers, because when he came here it felt like a kind of reward, closure. It meant that his investigative work had led to something.

Five more minutes. Then the guards would open the door, escort Lang in, tell him to sit down for a detention hearing that would be just the beginning of a long prison sentence.

Grens turned towards Hermansson, who sat next to him.

'Feels good, right?'

He had asked her to accompany him here. He couldn't get hold of Sven, Bengt was dead, and he'd never be able to comfort Lena enough. But it was nice to sit here with someone, and that someone was Hermansson. He admitted to himself reluctantly that he liked her. It should have made him furious when she insinuated he had problems with female officers, with women in general, but she'd been so calm when she said it, so matter of fact, maybe because she was right. He should ask her to consider staying in Stockholm when her temporary position was over. He hoped he could work with her again, maybe talk to her some more. She was so young, so it could have been creepy, but this wasn't because he was an old guy trying to grope young women. He was just surprised there were still people he'd like to get to know better.

'Yes, feels good. I know what we have, and it's enough. Lang and the hostage situation were definitely worth coming to Stockholm for.'

A courtroom felt naked without judges, jurors, prosecutors, defendants, plaintiffs and a curious public. They were there to express the drama of the crime in terms of both the assault and the victim, every word illustrating and measuring the harm that has been done.

Without that it wouldn't come alive.

Grens looked around, at the gloomy wooden panels on the wall, the big dirty windows, the incongruously beautiful chandelier. The smell of old law books.

BOX 21

'It's strange, Hermansson. Professional criminals like Lang. I've worked with them all my life, but I don't understand them any more now than when I started. They have a certain attitude towards law enforcement. They won't talk. Whatever we say, whatever we ask, they keep their mouths shut. *Don't know. Don't recall that.* They deny everything. And I guess that's a good strategy. It's up to us to prove they did what we claim.'

Ewert Grens pointed at the wall opposite them, at a door of dark, heavy wood similar to the walls.

'In a few minutes Lang will enter from there. He's gonna play the same damn game. He'll keep quiet, deny, mumble *I don't know*, and because of that, Hermansson, he's gonna lose this time. This time, that game will be the biggest mistake of his life. Because here's the thing. I think he's innocent, at least of murder.'

She looked at him in surprise, but before he could explain further the wooden door opened and four prison guards stepped in with two armed police officers, Jochum between them in handcuffs wearing an ill-fitting prison jumpsuit. Lang saw them immediately, and Ewert Grens waved and smiled. He turned to Hermansson and lowered his voice.

'I read the technical report and Errfors's autopsy, and I no longer believe it was a murder. I think Lang broke five fingers and a kneecap. That was his assignment, and the death was neither ordered nor paid for. It was Hilding Oldéus himself who took those stairs straight into a wall.'

Ewert pointed for emphasis in the direction of Lang.

'Look at Lang, such an idiot. This time his silence will cost him life in prison for murder, when he could have talked and ended up with a couple of years for assault instead.'

Grens waved again in the direction of the man he hated. Lang's gaze had the same force as yesterday, when they'd sized each other up in the cell. Behind his shaved skull, people continued to enter the courtroom. Ågestam came last and nodded at Grens, who nodded back. For a moment Ewert Grens wondered what the young prosecutor was thinking after that meeting they had, after the lie he'd fed him. He pushed that away. He had to. He leaned over and continued whispering to Hermansson.

'I know it, Hermansson. It wasn't a fucking murder. But believe me, I wouldn't lift a finger to tell anyone. No question about it, that bastard is headed to prison!'

Dimitri was satisfied. The new girls were soft and smooth and fucked pretty well. He'd bought them on an instalment plan, and if they hadn't worked out he was going to quit paying.

But they did. So he would.

The cop was gone now. But the woman he worked with did just as good a job without him. She'd delivered two new whores, as agreed. She was waiting for him now. She wanted the second payment. They cost three thousand euros each. She would get a third of it now.

He opened the door to Eden. A naked woman was gyrating on the stage, groaning and whimpering and pressing her chest to an inflatable sex doll. Every single man had his hand down his pants.

The only woman in the audience was sitting in her usual spot, the far back corner by the emergency exit.

He walked over to her, and they nodded to each other.

Always the same sweat suit. Always the same hood pulled over her head.

She wanted him to call her Ilona. He did, though it annoyed him. That wasn't her name.

They didn't say much to each other. They never did. A few pleasantries in Russian, no more.

BOX 21

He gave her the envelope of money. She didn't count it, just stuffed it in her bag.

In one month.

One month and he'd give her the last instalment. Then they'd both belong to him.

———

Ewert Grens stood up, gestured to Hermansson to do the same, and they walked out of the courtroom just before the detention order was handed down. He hurried three storeys down stone stairs to the basement level, through the passageway that led to the underground garage. Hermansson asked where they were going, and he replied, you'll know soon enough. He was panting from the exertion, but didn't stop until surrounded by the stale dust of the garage. He'd been searching for something and found it – walked over to the metal door to the lift that took you all the way up to the jail.

He knew they'd have to pass by here. Jochum Lang would have to go through that door to go back to the jail.

Grens only had to wait a few minutes.

Lang, the four prison guards and the two policemen entered the garage and headed for the metal door.

Ewert took a few steps forward to meet them, asked them if he could just have a minute alone with Lang and got what he wanted. The prison guard in charge wasn't happy about it, but he'd met Grens before and knew there was no use arguing.

Lang and Grens stared at each other, almost out of habit. Grens was waiting for Lang to react, but Lang just stood there, handcuffed, his large body swaying, as if he hadn't decided if he should beat someone up or let it be.

'You stupid son of a bitch.'

They were so close to each other, Grens only had to whisper for Lang to be able to hear.

'You kept your mouth shut. Like you always do. But you were arrested anyway. And you're going to be convicted, too. I know you didn't kill Oldéus. But what the hell are people going to think? As long as you act like a criminal, denying everything, it's going to cost you life in prison. Congratulations.'

Ewert Grens waved to the prison guards to come back.

'That's all, Lang.'

Jochum Lang never said a word and never turned around.

That is until the guards were opening the metal door, and Grens ordered him to. Lang spat while the detective superintendent shouted, remember the body inspection, remember how you scoffed at my dead colleague. Grens screamed, *Do you remember*, and then he pursed his lips and made a loud smacking noise, returning the air kisses, while Lang was led into the lift and back to jail.

Sven Sundkvist parked on a small residential street filled with children playing hockey between two home-made goals. They'd seen the car approaching, but didn't seem to care. He'd waited until two nine-year-olds sighed and moved the goals aside for the old guy that wanted to get through.

He knew now. Lydia Grajauskas had been determined to kill Bengt. To kill herself. And when she wanted to show them why, wanted to describe her shame, Ewert had prevented her.

Who gave Ewert that right?

Lena Nordwall was sitting in her garden. Her eyes were closed, a radio was playing on the table. He hadn't seen her since the night they'd brought the news of Bengt's death.

Ewert wanted to protect his friend's wife and children.

But it deprived a dead woman of her right to speak.

'Hello.'

It was hot, he was sweating, but she sat in the sun in dark

BOX 21

trousers, wearing a jean jacket over a sweater. She hadn't heard him, he walked over to her, and it startled her.

'You scared me.'

'I'm sorry.'

She held out her arm and invited him to sit down. He moved the chair she was pointing at, turning it so that he sat in front of her with the scorching sun on his back.

They looked at each other. He'd called and asked to come here, so he had to speak first.

It was difficult. He didn't really know her. They had met, but always in the company of Bengt and Ewert, a few birthdays, that kind of thing. She was one of those women who made him feel stupid and ugly. It embarrassed him, left him searching for the right words. He didn't know why. She was beautiful, of course, but he had no problem talking to beautiful women. She just radiated something that made him feel insecure and small, as some people do.

'I'm sorry if I'm disturbing you.'

'You're here now.'

He looked around. He'd been in this garden once before, five or six years ago. Ewert was turning fifty and Bengt and Lena arranged a birthday dinner. The only party of that kind Ewert had ever allowed. Sven and Anita sat on either side of him. Jonas had been small then, running around on the grass with the Nordwall kids. No one else had been there. Ewert was quiet all evening. He'd been glad to have the company, Sven had known it, but he'd been uncomfortable being celebrated.

She rubbed her hands up and down the sleeves of her jean jacket.

'I'm so cold.'

'Now?'

'I've been cold since you came here four days ago.'

He sighed.

'I'm sorry. I should have understood.'

'I'm sitting fully clothed in the sun. It's almost thirty degrees, and I'm freezing. Do you understand that?'

'Yes. I can understand that.'

'I don't want to be cold.'

She suddenly stood up.

'Do you want some coffee?'

'You don't need to go to any trouble.'

'No. But do you want some?'

'Thank you, yes.'

She disappeared through the patio door. He heard her turn on the water and take out the cups. The kids playing hockey were screaming on the street. Maybe someone scored a goal or maybe another old fart wanted to break up their match and drive through their arena.

Large glasses, milk foam on top, like you'd get in one of those fancy cafés he never had time to go to. He took a sip, then put the glass on the table.

'How well do you know Ewert?'

She scrutinised him with a look that made him feel insecure.

'Is that why we're sitting here? To talk about Ewert?'

'Yes.'

'Is this some kind of interrogation?'

'Absolutely not.'

'What is it then?'

'I don't know.'

'You don't know?'

'No.'

She rubbed her hands on her arms again, as if she were still freezing.

'I don't understand what you're talking about.'

'I wish I could be clearer. But I can't. You can consider this

BOX 21

as just my private speculations. As far from police work as you can get.'

She drank more coffee, waited until she'd emptied her cup completely.

'He was my husband's oldest friend.'

'I know that. But how well do you know him?'

'He's not that easy to get to know.'

She wanted him to leave. She didn't like him. He knew that.

'Just a little longer. Try.'

'Does Ewert know you're here?'

'No.'

'Why not?'

'If he did, I wouldn't need you to answer my questions.'

The sun beat down. His back was soaked with sweat. He would have preferred to sit somewhere else, but he stayed where he was. Things were tense enough as it was.

'Has Ewert talked to you about the morgue? About what happened to Bengt?'

She didn't hear him. Sven could tell. She pointed at him, holding her hand in the air until he felt uneasy.

'He was sitting there.'

'What?'

'Bengt. When you called him in. To the morgue.'

He shouldn't have come here. She should have been left alone with her grief. But he was searching for another picture of Ewert, a better one. She should be able to give him that. He repeated his question.

'Has Ewert told you anything? About what happened to Bengt?'

'I've asked him. He hasn't told me anything that you couldn't read in the newspaper.'

'Nothing at all?'

'I don't like this conversation.'

'You haven't asked him why Bengt was the one shot by that woman?'

She stayed silent for a long time.

He had delayed asking this question. It was the one he'd come to ask, and now he had.

'What are you trying to say?'

'Have you and Ewert talked about why she murdered Bengt?'

'Do you know something?'

'I'm asking you.'

She looked at him, her eyes boring into his.

'No.'

'And you never wondered?'

Suddenly she started to weep. She curled up into a tight ball on the chair, shaking with sadness.

'I have wondered. And I've asked him. But he hasn't said anything. Nothing at all. It was bad luck. That's what he said. It could have been anyone. But it ended up being Bengt.'

There was someone approaching from behind him. Sven Sundkvist turned around. The little girl wasn't very old, younger than Jonas, maybe five or six years old. She'd come from inside the house. She had on a white short-sleeved shirt and a pair of pink shorts. She stopped in front of her mother, understood she was upset.

'What is it, Mummy?'

Lena Nordwall leaned over and held her.

'Nothing, sweetie.'

'You're crying. Is it because of him? Was he mean?'

'No. He's not mean. We're just talking.'

The girl in the white shirt and pink shorts turned around. Her big eyes stared at Sven.

'Mummy is sad. Daddy is dead.'

He swallowed, smiled, trying to look serious and kind at the same time.

BOX 21

'I knew your daddy.'

Sven Sundkvist gazed silently at the woman who'd been left to raise her children alone four days ago. He sensed the pain she felt. He understood why Ewert had chosen to protect her. Why he felt she didn't need to know the truth.

Ewert Grens couldn't wait until tomorrow. He missed her too much.

Sunday traffic was sparse, and it didn't take long to drive through the city. He was listening to Siw on the car's tape deck, singing along to the chorus loudly as he passed over Lidingö Bridge, didn't even notice the rain starting to fall.

The usually empty parking lot was full. He was confused for a moment, almost thought he was at the wrong place, then remembered that he'd never been here on a Sunday. This was the busiest day for visitors.

The receptionist at the front desk looked surprised to see him. Tomorrow was his usual day. He smiled at her and enjoyed her surprise, kept walking in the same direction as usual. She called after him, telling him to stop.

'She's not there.'

He didn't hear what she said at first.

'She's not in her room.'

He stood completely still. In the time it took her to continue speaking, he felt what he'd felt once before, like dying, again.

'She's on the patio. It's Sunday. Afternoon tea. We try to sit outside during the summer. There are big umbrellas out there.'

He wasn't listening. The young receptionist kept talking, but he wasn't listening.

'You can go out there, of course. She'll be happy to see you.'

'Why isn't she in her room?'

'Excuse me?'

'Why isn't she there?'

He was dizzy. He sank down on the chair just inside the front door, took off his jacket and put it in his lap.

'Are you OK?'

The receptionist squatted down in front of him.

'Is she outside?'

'Yes, Mr Grens.'

Four large umbrellas with ice cream ads on them shaded a good portion of the patio. Ewert knew a couple of the staff members and everyone who was waiting in a wheelchair or next to a walker.

She was sitting almost in the middle. A coffee cup in front of her, half a cinnamon bun in her hand. She was laughing like a child. He could hear it despite the patter of rain on the umbrellas and the folk song a few of the others were singing together. He waited until they'd finished. He walked over to them, rain falling on his shoulders and back.

'Hello.'

He was addressing one of the people in white coats, a woman his own age with a kind smile.

'Welcome. And on a Sunday!'

She turned to Anni, who stared at him without recognition.

'Anni. You have a visitor.'

Ewert walked over to her and put a hand on her cheek like he always did.

'Can I take her away for a bit? We have something to talk about. Good news.'

The assistant pulled back the lever that put the brakes on the wheels of Anni's wheelchair.

'Of course. We've already been out here for a while. And if you have a gentleman visitor why would you want to hang out with us old ladies?'

She had another dress on today, a red one he'd bought for her

BOX 21

long ago. It was still raining, but not heavily. She hardly got wet in the short distance from the umbrella to the protection of the overhang of the roof. He walked behind her, rolling the wheel-chair through the front door, down the long hall and into her room.

They sat like they usually did.

She was in the middle of the room, and he was on the chair next to her.

He caressed her cheek again, kissed her forehead. He took her hand and squeezed it, and almost thought she squeezed back.

'Anni.'

He looked at her, wanted to make sure she was looking at him before he continued.

'It's over now.'

It was one o'clock, and Dimitri had promised her an hour's break. She'd had johns non-stop since this morning, since that first man came and spat on the floor, and she had to smile and lick it up.

She wept.

Seven men had penetrated her after him. She had four left. Twelve each day. The last one would come at six thirty.

An hour's rest.

She lay on the bed in the room that she supposed was hers now. It was a nice apartment on the sixth floor of a normal resi-dential building. A couple of the men had called her Lydia. She'd told them that wasn't her name, but they told her as far as they were concerned it was.

She knew now that Lydia was the woman who'd lived in this room before her. That these men had been her customers. And now she had inherited them.

Dimitri wasn't hitting her as much any more.

He'd said that she was starting to learn. She needed to make more sounds, that's what was missing. She needed to moan when they put their penis inside her, maybe whine a little. The customers liked it when you made sounds. It was like they weren't paying for it then.

She only cried when she was alone. He hit her if he saw her crying.

She had an hour to rest. She had closed the door, and she could cry until her break was over. Then she'd make herself look pretty and put her hands over her crotch just like the guy coming at two had asked her to.

Ewert Grens had only been in his office for an hour or so. Still, he felt restless and found it hard to concentrate. He went to the toilet. Then got coffee from the vending machine in the hallway. He'd been to the front desk twice to ask if his pizza had been delivered. Now he was alone with the door closed.

It was as if he was waiting for something.

He danced to Siw Malmkvist on the floor between his desk and the sofa and heard nothing but her soft voice.

He had no idea where Sven was. He hadn't heard a thing from Ågestam.

He raised the volume. It was soon evening again. His office was warm from the sun beating on the window all day. He was sweating while he swayed to the sound of the sixties.

I miss you, Bengt.
You betrayed us.
Do you understand that?
Lena doesn't know. She doesn't know anything.
You had her. You had the kids. You had something!

BOX 21

He walked up to the tape player, turned it off, took out the tape.

He looked around.

Not tonight. Not here.

He left his office, walked down the deserted corridor, opened the front door, and stepped into fresh air. He went to the parking lot and the car was unlocked as usual. He sat in the driver's seat, hands on the wheel without starting the engine.

He'd just drive for a while. It had been a long time since he just drove.

It was half past six, and she'd just serviced her last and twelfth john of the day.

It had been quick. He didn't hit her, didn't spit, just penetrated her anus and asked her to whisper that she was horny. It didn't hurt that much.

She showered a long time, even though she had done so several times since this morning. It was here, with the water flowing over her, that she cried the hardest.

Dimitri told her she was supposed to be fully clothed and looking happy on her bed by seven. The woman who claimed her name was Ilona, who'd met them at the boat, was coming here. She was going to make sure things were going well for them. Dimitri explained that the woman still owned a third of them, so what she thought was still important for another month.

She arrived on time. According to the clock in the kitchen it would be exactly seven in thirty seconds. She looked the same as at the harbour, a hoodie pulled up over her neck and head. She didn't even take it down when she passed by the electronic locks and into the apartment.

Dimitri greeted her, asked her if she wanted something to

drink, and she shook her head. She was in a hurry, she said. She just wanted to check on her property.

She tried to look happy for the woman just like Dimitri told her to do. The woman asked her how many men she'd serviced today, and she answered twelve.

The woman looked pleased, said that was good for such a young piece of Baltic cunt.

Afterwards, she lay on her bed and cried. She knew that Dimitri didn't allow it, that he'd soon come and knock, but she couldn't help it. She thought about the woman in the hoodie, the men who'd penetrated her, and about how Dimitri said they'd have to pack their bags again, go to another apartment, in Copenhagen. She felt like dying.

———————

He'd been driving aimlessly through the city for almost two hours. First he took the busiest streets in the centre of the city, traffic lights, people running down the middle of the street, and idiots constantly honking. Then he drove over Slussen, down Horns Street, took the ring road, Göt Street, the part of Söder-malm that was supposed to be so bohemian, but was just like any other small city. Then headed to Östermalm, past the life-less façades, drove down to the TV building near Gärdet, down to Värta Harbour, to the big boats that brought whores from the Baltic. He yawned. Took Valhalla Road to Roslagstull and the roundabouts in the shape of eternity.

So many people.

So many lives headed somewhere.

Ewert Grens envied them. He had no idea where he was going.

He was tired. Just a little bit longer.

He drove towards St Erik's Square. The traffic had subsided. Evening was always calmer. A few side streets, back and forth.

BOX 21

He turned left onto Atlas Street. Drove down the hill, parked in front of the gate. Could it only be a week since he'd been here the first time?

He switched off the car engine.

It was quiet, the kind of quiet that falls over a city when the day has run its course.

All those windows, apartments with fluffy curtains and big potted plants. People lived here.

He sat in the car outside the front door. A few minutes past. Maybe ten. Maybe sixty.

Her back had been raw from the lashes of a whip. She was lying naked on the floor, unconscious. Alena Sljusareva was in the room next door, screaming at the man in the suit, who she called Dimitri Pimp-Fucker.

Bengt had stood outside the door and waited for almost an hour. Grens could see the whole thing it in front of him again.

Bengt had been standing outside.

You must have known already.

Ewert Grens stayed in the car. Not yet. A few more minutes. He wanted to wait until he'd calmed down. Then he would drive away from here. To the place he still called his home, the apartment he rarely visited. A few more minutes.

Suddenly the front door opened.

Four people on their way out. He recognised them.

A few days ago, when he'd been dropping Alena Sljusareva off at the ferry that took her across the Baltic Sea to Klaipeda.

They'd just left that same ferry, just arrived in Sweden. The man was still wearing the same suit. Dimitri Pimp-Fucker. After he passed through customs, he'd turned around and waited for two young women, who were no more than sixteen or seventeen years old. He had stretched out a hand and demanded their passports, their debt. A woman in a tracksuit, with her hood pulled up over her neck and head, had also met them there, greeted them like Baltics do, with a light kiss on either cheek.

Now they walked out of the door in front of him, Dimitri first, his two new girls behind him with their bags in their hands, and last came the woman hidden by her hoodie.

Grens watched them walk away along the pavement.

He then called someone at the Foreign Ministry and asked a few questions about Dimitri Simait.

He had enough to do right now.

But he wanted to know if the pimp still had diplomatic immunity and told them to find out who the woman he worked with was.

He'd take care of them later. Both of them.

When this was over. When Lang was in prison. When Bengt had been buried.

When he was sure that Lena would be able to go on, without the lie.

THE DAY HAD ENDED without him noticing.

He'd woken up this morning in a narrow hotel bed in Klaipeda, drove a car from Arlanda to the home of Lena Nordwall, who wore a jacket even in the sun, then to his office at the police station, then gone to meet the prosecutor Ågestam, who'd made him wait longer than he really had the patience for.

Sven Sundkvist wanted to go home.

He was tired, but this day had saved its longest hours for the end.

Lena Nordwall chased after him there in her front yard in Eriksberg, after their empty conversation, when he was on his way back to his parked car and the kids playing hockey in the street. She was out of breath by the time she grabbed his arm and asked if he knew about Anni. Sven had never heard the name before. He'd known Ewert ten years, worked closely with him, considered him a friend, but he'd never heard her name. Lena Nordwall told him about what happened when Ewert was in command of a SWAT team bus, about Anni and Bengt and Ewert, and an arrest that had gone as badly as any arrest ever could.

Sven Sundkvist tried to stand still, but could feel his body start to tremble.

There was so much in this life he didn't understand.

He had no idea where Ewert lived. He had never, not once, visited his home. It was somewhere in central Stockholm, that was all he knew.

He laughed briefly, but his face wasn't smiling.

It was strange how one-sided their friendship had been.

How Sven did the inviting, how Ewert was invited.

He believed in sharing thoughts, warmth, energy, and Ewert hid behind his right to privacy.

Sven Sundkvist found the address in the police personnel records. Now he stood in front of the entrance to a rather beautiful apartment building on the busiest stretch of Svea Road.

He'd been waiting for almost two hours. He'd passed the time by peering at the row of windows on the fourth floor where the apartment should be, but it was difficult to make out anything. They all looked alike from a distance, as if the same person lived in the entire building.

Ewert arrived shortly after eight. Swaying and lumbering along on his stiff leg. He opened the front door without turning around and disappeared inside.

Sven Sundkvist waited another ten minutes. He took a deep breath. He was nervous. It had been a long time since he'd felt this alone.

He pressed the intercom. Waited. No answer. He pressed again, longer this time.

The speaker in the wall crackled as clumsy fingers lifted a telephone on the fourth floor.

'Yes?'

The voice sounded irritated.

'Ewert?'

'Who is it?'

'It's me. Sven.'

He could hear the silence.

'Ewert, it's me.'

'What are you doing here?'

'I'd like to come up for a bit.'

'Here?'

'Yes.'

BOX 21

'Now?'

'Now.'

'Why do you want to do that?'

'We need to talk.'

'We can talk tomorrow. In my office.'

'That's too late. We need to talk tonight. Open the door.'

Silence again. He stared at the speaker, which was still on. It took a long time. Or at least it felt that way.

The lock on the door finally clicked. He pressed down on the handle: it was open.

Ewert's voice was low, hard to hear.

'Fourth floor. Grens on the door.'

The pain in his stomach – which he'd been carrying and that he would soon hand over – was as intense as when he first watched that videotape.

He didn't ring the doorbell, he didn't need to, the door was open.

He looked down a long hallway.

'Hello?'

'You can come in.'

He couldn't see him, but it was Ewert's voice, coming from a room further inside.

He stepped in, stood on the hall carpet.

'To the left. Down the hallway, the second door.'

Sven Sundkvist wasn't sure what he'd expected.

But whatever it was, it wasn't this.

The largest apartment he'd ever been inside.

He looked around as he walked down a hallway that never seemed to end.

Six, maybe seven rooms. High ceilings, tile fireplaces in almost every corner, rugs on perfect hardwood floors.

But more than anything, it was empty.

Sven barely breathed.

As if he were intruding. Even though no one was there. He'd never seen anything so abandoned, so big, so clean, so unspeakably alone.

Ewert sat in what could be called the library. It was one of the smaller rooms, with bookshelves on two of the walls, filled from floor to ceiling, an ancient black leather armchair and a floor lamp beside it.

Sven barely noticed. There was something else. On the wall by the door. A framed needlepoint canvas, red cloth with yellow letters, the words MERRY CHRISTMAS. Beside it, two black-and-white photos, portraits of a man and a woman in police uniforms, both in their twenties.

A large apartment with no end. But this much was clear. Those two photos and that Christmas needlepoint were the centre.

Ewert looked at him, sighed. Gestured with one arm, asking Sven to step inside. He pushed the footstool he had his feet on towards Sven, who took it and sat down.

He'd been reading a book when Sven rang. Sven tried to see what it was, looking for a way to start this conversation, but it was on a small side table with its title facing down. He stood up again instead, pointed in the direction he'd just come from.

'Ewert, what is this?'

'What do you mean?'

'Have you always lived like this?'

'Yes.'

'I've never seen anything like it.'

'I spend less and less time here.'

'Your hallway is the size of our house.'

Ewert Grens nodded to him, wanted him to sit down. He shut his book, leaned forward, his face turning red. He had no patience for meaningless chatter.

BOX 21

'It's a Sunday evening. Right?'

Sven didn't respond.

'It's past eight. Right?'

He didn't want an answer.

'It's my goddamn right to be alone. Right?'

Silence. Nothing else.

'So why did you come here and push your way inside?'

Sven Sundkvist tried to control his breathing. He'd seen the anger before. But not the fear. He was sure that's what it was. Ewert had never shown it to him. But here, in his leather arm-chair, Sven saw fear hidden behind the aggression.

He scrutinised his older colleague.

'The truth, Ewert. Do you know how difficult that can be?'

He didn't care that Ewert wanted him to sit down. He stood up. He stared out of the window, watching the cars hurry from one traffic light to the next. He walked a bit further away, lean-ing against one of the bookshelves.

'You are the person I spend the most time with. More than my wife, more than my son. I'm not here for the fun of it. I'm here because I have no choice.'

Ewert Grens remained seated, leaning back, staring at him.

'A lie. Ewert, a big fucking lie!'

He didn't move, only staring.

'You lied. And I want to know why.'

Ewert Grens snorted.

'So Mr Interrogator has come to visit me?'

'I want you to answer my questions. You can snort and call me whatever you want. I'm used to it.'

Sven walked back to the window. To the cars that were becoming fewer and fewer, driving slower and slower. He longed to be out there, to be done with this.

'I called in sick the last two days.'

'And yet you seem healthy enough to stand here playing the interrogator.'

'I wasn't sick. I was in Lithuania, in Klaipeda. Ågestam asked me to go.'

Sven Sundkvist had expected it. He knew that Ewert would stand up and start screaming.

'That little prosecutor prick! Did you go to Lithuania behind my back on his orders?'

Sven waited until he was done screaming.

'Sit down, Ewert.'

'Fuck that!'

'Sit down.'

Ewert Grens hesitated, eyeing Sven, then sat down, put his feet on the stool again.

'I met Alena Sljusareva. In an aquarium, a tourist trap in Klaipeda. Heard her story, found the answers we needed, about how Lydia Grajauskas got hold of that weapon and those explosives in Söder Hospital.'

Sven waited. No reaction.

'I learned they communicated several times before the hostage crisis. By mobile phone.'

He looked at the man in the armchair.

Say something!

React!

Don't just sit there staring at me!

'Before we parted late in the evening outside a Chinese restaurant something peculiar happened. She asked me why I had asked her all those questions. She'd already answered all of them. In an interview with another Swedish police officer.'

Silence.

'Don't stay silent, Ewert.'

Again.

BOX 21

'Say something!'

Ewert Grens started to laugh and kept on until he was crying.

'You want me to talk? And what should I talk about? Two fucking brats who don't know shit about anything?'

He laughed even louder, wiping tears away with his sleeve.

'Ågestam, I know what he is. But you, Sven, like a little brat!'

He looked at his uninvited guest, who rang his doorbell at eight o'clock on a Sunday evening, when he had every right to be left alone.

He continued to laugh, more quietly now, shaking his head.

'The perpetrator, Grajauskas, is dead. The plaintiff, Nordwall, is dead. And who the hell cares about how and why? Not the people, not the ones who pay your salary, Sven, don't you believe otherwise.'

Sven Sundkvist stood at the window. He wanted to scream, wanted to drown him out, but he knew this aggression was only hiding fear.

'Ewert, is that your reality?'

'It's your reality, Sven.'

'Never. You see, we kept talking. In a restaurant in the centre of Klaipeda. Alena Sljusareva told me, I asked her to tell me, about the three years she and Grajauskas were moved around Scandinavia like chattels. Forced to service twelve johns a day. Imprisonment, slavery, humiliation. I thought I knew, but I didn't have a clue. The Rohypnol you take to bear it, the vodka you drink to turn yourself off, to live with the shame, so it would never catch up with you.'

Ewert stood up, walked towards the door. He waved to Sven, wanting him to come along.

Sven nodded but lingered, looking at the two photographs again, young people filled with hope. And the man's eyes, Sven couldn't stop looking at them. He'd never seen those eyes before. They didn't seem to belong to this apartment. They had a lustre, filled with life.

Here there was only emptiness, as if everything had stopped.

He left those eyes and that room, walked down the long hallway, past two more rooms and into a third, the kitchen. The kind Anita liked to talk about. Large enough to cook in, large enough to socialise in.

'Hungry?'

'No.'

'Coffee?'

'No.'

'Then I'll drink alone.'

Water in a pot on the stove, the burner glowing red.

'I don't care about coffee, Ewert.'

'You're no better than anybody else, Sven.'

Sven Sundkvist waited, searching for the energy to continue, needing it to get through this.

'She also talked about how they got here. About a long boat ride. The man who took them here. And I know, Ewert, I know you know who it was.'

The water was boiling, Ewert Grens turned off the stove, filled an empty cup. A couple of teaspoons of instant coffee, which he stirred.

'What are you saying?'

'Am I right?'

Grens took the cup in his hand, walked into the dining area of the kitchen, six chairs around a circular table. His face was red, and Sven wondered if it was from anger or fear.

'Don't you see, Ewert? It wasn't enough! Rohypnol and vodka weren't enough to turn it off! So they found new ways. Lydia Grajauskas had no body. She didn't feel it. When they penetrated her, it wasn't her body.'

BOX 21

Ewert Grens contemplated his coffee cup, drank half, said nothing.

'And Alena Sljusareva. She did the opposite. She felt her body, felt how they used it. But she didn't see their faces. They had none.'

Sven took a step forward and grabbed Ewert's cup, pulled it away, forcing him to look up.

'But you know that already. Ewert? Because they told you that, on the videotape.'

Grens stared at his cup, at Sven's hand, but remained silent.

'I went through the investigation. I knew something didn't add up. She had a videotape in that plastic bag. I saw pictures of it on the crime scene photos, lying on the floor. I contacted Nils Krantz, and he confirmed he had given it to you.'

Ewert Grens stretched out his hand for the cup. He grabbed it, drank his coffee. He asked once more if Sven wanted any, and Sven said no again. They stood in the kitchen, on either side of a large kitchen island with knives and ladles and cutting boards.

'Where's your TV?'

'Why?'

Sven went out into the hallway, headed for the front door. He picked up the bag he'd left there and went back.

'Where is it?'

'In there.'

Ewert pointed to the room across the hall. Sven went inside and asked Ewert to follow him.

'We're going to watch a videotape.'

'I don't have a VCR.'

'I guessed as much. So I brought one with me.'

He unpacked it, attached the cords to the back of Ewert's TV.

'We're going to watch this. Together.'

They sat at either end of a sofa.

Sven, remote control in hand, started the tape he'd just inserted. A black picture with white noise. The war of the ants. Sven looked at Ewert.

'But this is blank.'

Grens didn't respond.

'And that's how it should be. Because this isn't the tape you got from Nils Krantz. Right?'

The noise, an annoying sound, grinding on and on.

'I know, because Nils Krantz has confirmed that the tape he gave you was used, dusty and bearing the fingerprints of two women. This tape probably only has our fingerprints on it.'

Ewert Grens turned away now, couldn't even look at the colleague he outranked.

'I'm curious. Ewert, what was on the original tape?'

Remote control pointed at the TV, he turned off the offending sound.

'OK. Very well. A little more clearly now. What was on the original tape that could have been worth risking thirty-one years of exemplary service for?'

Sven Sundkvist leaned over to his bag again, took out another tape. Replaced the tape in the VCR with this one.

Two women. A blur. The cameraman moves the camera back and forth while adjusting the lens.

The women seem nervous, waiting for the signal to start.

One of them, blonde with terrified eyes, speaks only Russian, two sentences at a time. She then turns to the other one, dark-haired, who translates into Swedish.

They are serious, their voices strained. They have never done this before.

They speak for about twenty minutes. Their three-year-long story.

BOX 21

Sven stared straight ahead stubbornly. He was waiting for Ewert's reaction.

It didn't happen immediately, but it did come after the two women had finished speaking.

He wept.

He held his face in his hands and let go of thirty years of tears – which he had feared, hadn't dared to release.

Sven couldn't bear to look at him. Not like this. Discomfort and anger rushed through his body. He stood up, walked over to the VCR, took out the tape and put it on the table in front of them.

'You only switched one copy.'

Sven pushed it in the direction of Ewert.

'I went through the interrogations from the morgue. Gustaf Ejder mentioned two tapes. And a storage box at the Central Station.'

Ewert sighed deeply, looked at Sven but said nothing, while still crying.

'I found this inside it.'

He poked at the tape again, all the way across the table past a vase filled with flowers, until it was in front of Ewert. Anger that had to come out.

'Who the hell are you to take that right away from them, their right to tell their own story? Just to protect your best friend from the truth!'

Ewert looked at the tape in front of him, picked it up, but stayed silent.

'And not only that. You broke the law! You withheld and destroyed evidence, you protected a criminal by sending her home, afraid of her words. How far were you willing to go? How much are those lies worth, Ewert?'

Grens fingered the plastic case.

'For this?'

'Yes.'

'Do you think I did it for my *own* sake?'

'Yes.'

'Really?'

'For your own sake.'

'So it's not enough that she's a widow? Should she have to deal with this too? *His* fucking lies!'

He threw the tape back on the table.

'She's been left with nothing but emptiness! Lena doesn't need this shit! She'll never need to know!'

Sven Sundkvist didn't want to hear more.

He had confronted his friend. He had seen him weep. He knew now about the grief that had filled his life for so long. He just wanted to get away from here, from this day.

'Alena Sljusareva.'

He turned towards Grens.

'You see, Ewert, she spoke of *her shame*. Which she tried to rinse off twelve times a day. But this. This!'

Sven struck the television screen, aiming at what had just been there.

'This, this was because *you* couldn't take it. Because, Ewert, you can't handle the guilt you feel for what you've done to other people. The shame you feel when you face what you've done to yourself. The guilt alone you can endure. But the shame is unbearable.'

Ewert sat quietly, looking at the man speaking in front of him.

'You felt guilty because it was your decision to send Bengt into the morgue, into his death. That's understandable. Guilt is always possible to understand.'

Sven raised his voice, as you do sometimes when you don't want to show you've run out of steam.

'But the shame, Ewert. The shame is incomprehensible! You

BOX 21

were ashamed that you let Bengt fool you. And ashamed that you had to tell Lena who Bengt really was.'

He continued, even more loudly now.

'Ewert, you aren't trying to protect Lena. You're just trying to escape. *Your own shame.*'

It was strangely cold outside.

The month of June should be much warmer than this. He waited at the red light outside Ewert Grens's apartment building. It took a long time to change.

He had finally unburdened himself of the lie he'd been carrying.

The story of two young people erased to protect a third person from the truth.

Bengt Nordwall was a pig, a man Sven Sundkvist could hate. Even in death he was a pig, even in the morgue. Even there, naked with a Russian gun to his head, he denied her shame. And Ewert continued in his stead. He exchanged her shame for black and white noise, the war of the ants.

The light turned green. He crossed Svea Road, heading north, had to get away somewhere. Through the summer traffic, past Vanadis Park, headed to Haga Park.

Lydia Grajauskas was dead. Bengt Nordwall was dead.

Ewert had known that.

No plaintiff. No perpetrator.

He liked Haga Park, so quiet despite being close to the asphalt. There was a dog owner shouting desperately for a loose German shepherd and a couple holding each other tightly in the grass, but otherwise the park was that peculiar kind of empty that happens during these precious summer holiday weeks.

No one spoke for the dead. Not then, not now. He sighed heavily – if he reported the best police officer he ever met, what would that change, really? And if he demanded answers from the others, the ones who were still alive? Was it to be Ewert Grens working in the police building as he'd always done or Ewert Grens exiled to the emptiness of his home?

He had arrived at the edge of the water, at the reflection of the evening sun.

Sven Sundkvist was still holding the bag in his hand. A portable VCR, some paper, and two videotapes. He opened it, took out the tape that once lay in box 21 in the Central Station with a note in Cyrillic letters on its back. He dropped it to the ground, stomped on it until the plastic case broke, picked it up again and fished out the brown magnetic strip inside. He pulled it out like ribbon for a birthday present.

The water was almost completely still, a tranquillity that sometimes just appears.

He took a few steps forward, gathered together the elegant ribbon around the tape.

Then he raised his arm and threw it as far out as he could.

———

He felt both heavy and light. Perhaps he even cried, maybe they were Lydia's tears. He saw himself as if from a distance doing the same thing he had just condemned. He had taken away her right to speak.

Ågestam would never know what Sljusareva really said.

He felt ashamed.

Three Years Earlier

IT'S A SMALL APARTMENT. Two rooms and a kitchen.

Five people live there – herself, her mother, brother, sister, grandmother. She hasn't thought much about it before. That's just how it's always been.

She's seventeen years old.

Her name is Lydia Grajauskas. And she dreams of going somewhere else.

She wants to have her own room, her own life. This, this is just too crowded. She's a woman now. Or soon will be. She's grown. She needs space.

She misses him.

She thinks about him all the time. Dad always got it. In fact, he had always been there for her.

She's asked, she has, but still she can't understand why he had to die.

What she misses most are their walks. Wandering far and wide, hand in hand, planning the day they would finally leave Klaipeda. They used to go all the way to the city limits, just like she did with Vladi now. They'd stop there and look at the city, really look at it. Her father usually sang to her then, songs he learned when he was little, which she never heard anyone else sing. They used to dream of something else. That's what they did, dreamed together.

This apartment. It's so crowded! There is always someone here. Always.

She thinks about last night. About the men who came into the café.

She'd never seen them before. They were friendly. They greeted Vladi, her Vladi who had always been hers, who lay there beside her on the sofa when military police broke down the door and screamed *zatknis* while pushing her father to the floor.

Both the men smiled when they ordered coffees and sandwiches. They spoke Russian, but one, who was a little older, didn't look Russian. He looked like he might be from Sweden or Denmark.

They stayed for a long time. She refilled their cups twice. Then Vladi left, and the men talked a bit with her, first just *hello* and the like, then, when she wasn't as busy, they asked for her name, how long she'd worked there, what she made waitressing in a café. They were nice, not like so many others, not sleazy, not trying to flirt, none of that. She sat down at their table for a while. She wasn't supposed to do that, but there weren't many customers and not much to do anyway.

They talked about all sorts of things. That's really how it was. She couldn't believe it, two men who were so nice, for real. She laughed a lot, more than she had in a long time. They didn't laugh much at home.

THEY CAME BACK.

Today, when she was getting ready to close, the two men stopped by again. She knows now that their names are Dimitri and Bengt. Dimitri lives in Vilnius, and Bengt lives in Sweden. Bengt is a police officer working on an investigation in Klaipeda.

They seem to know each other well. They've been meeting for many years. She's not sure, but she guesses that Dimitri is somehow connected to the Lithuanian police.

They're still just as nice. And they were shocked when they heard how little she earned at the café. They compared it to what she would make in Sweden. Twenty times as much. Every month! She couldn't believe it. Twenty times as much!

She told them about her dreams. About the crowded two-room apartment, about her long walks with Vladi, about how Klaipeda just wasn't enough.

They ordered more sandwiches, asked her to sit down at the table.

They laughed together again. It was nice, the laughter was cleansing.

THIRD DAY IN A ROW.

She was almost waiting for them. Served them their coffee and sandwiches before they even had time to order.

They'd asked her yesterday if she wanted their help, they could arrange what needed to be arranged, if she wanted them to – a job in Sweden, twenty times the pay.

She laughed and asked if they were crazy.

Today she asks *them* how they would do it.

She needs a passport. One that would say she was a little older. They can get that, but it's expensive. They'll pay for it, for now. She can work off the debt, repay them from her salary in Sweden.

They've done that for other Lithuanian girls. No one Lydia knows – she asks and they mention several names. They know a woman in Sweden, who's good at helping girls get settled.

They stay at the table for a long time. She treats them to coffee.

They tell her she doesn't have to decide until she's sure – it's important she takes time to think. But if she wants to, if she really wants to get far away, they can get her a passport in time for the ferry departing for Stockholm in two days. That's when they're leaving, too.

IT'S WARM WHEN she arrives at the port. Vladi is holding her hand, and he seems happy, for her sake. The rain that was pouring down is gone. It's sunny, almost no wind. She packed a bag, mostly just clothes, a few photos, a diary, as many toiletries as she dared to take.

She didn't say anything.

Mum wouldn't understand – she didn't dream of leaving.

She'll call later, once she arrives. She'll call from work, tell her she's sending money. Every month. Mum will surely understand then. What this is about. Another life.

They were going meet at the terminal, near the entrance.

She sees them from a distance. Dimitri is dark-haired, in a grey suit. Bengt's blond, a little shorter, his eyes kind. He hands Vladi an envelope. It makes Vladi happy, but afterwards he won't meet her eyes. He embraces her, then leaves. Meanwhile, a young woman has arrived. About the same age as her. Dark hair, she looks nice.

They introduce themselves – her name is Alena. She, too, has a bag and a false passport.

It's a nice boat. The biggest one she's been on. There are a lot of Swedes, some Lithuanians, and some who are hard to place. She smiles as she boards, leaving behind her old life.

———

She and Alena share a cabin.

They get to know each other quickly. Alena is the open type, curious about people, a good listener. She laughs often, and it's easy to laugh with her. That's how it is – you feel it in your body, when you're headed somewhere.

They're going to eat soon.

But first they have to go up one deck to Dimitri and Bengt's cabin, pick them up so they can all go together.

THEY KNOCK ON the cabin door.

It takes a while.

Bengt opens, smiles, and gestures for them to enter. They look at each other, feeling a little shy. It feels strange to step into a man's cabin.

———

Then everything falls apart.

A single breath.

That's all it takes.

———

The two men raise their hands and hit them hard across their faces.

They beat them until they fall to the floor.

They tear off their nice dresses, rip them to shreds, push the fabric into their mouths.

They force their thighs apart, and push their way inside.

———

Lydia will always remember the sound of his breath on her face.

SHE DOESN'T SLEEP that night. She lies on the bed in her cabin holding a pillow in her arms.

They screamed at her. They hit her. They held the cold metal of a gun to her head and explained she had two choices – silence or death.

She doesn't understand it. She just wants to go home.

Alena is lying in the bed beneath her. She doesn't cry as much. She says nothing. She doesn't make any sound at all.

Lydia looks at her bag standing there on the floor, by the sink. She packed it without telling anyone. She left home less than a day ago.

_____

She can hear the water lapping against the prow of the ship. She can hear it through an open window, too small to climb out.

_____

The trip is over in the morning.

She's still lying there.

She doesn't dare to move.

She tries to ignore the banging on the door, someone shouting that they have to leave the cabin and go ashore.

DIMITRI IS A FEW steps in front of her, Bengt behind her. She has to walk towards the exit, through passport control.

She wants to scream. But she doesn't dare to.

She remembers the blows to her face. The pain as they forced their way inside her, even though she begged them to stop.

It is a large terminal, bigger than the one in Klaipeda. People are hugging each other. They've missed each other.

She feels nothing.

Only shame.

She doesn't know why.

She shows her passport to a man in uniform inside a glass box. *Silence.* The man flips through it, glances at her, nods. *Or death.* She passes by. Alena hands hers over.

When Lydia is in front of the gate Dimitri turns around and tells her he wants her passport. She's in debt, and from now on she'll have to start repaying it.

She doesn't hear what he says.

The people around her disappear, the large terminal hall slowly emptying. They wait a little way from the passport control by one of the kiosks selling newspapers.

Finally she arrives. The woman they've been waiting for. The woman who Dimitri and Bengt work with.

She's wearing a jogging suit. A grey hood pulled up over her neck and head. She's quite young, smiles at Dimitri, kisses him on the cheek, smiles at Bengt, kisses him on the mouth, as if they belong to each other.

She turns to Lydia and Alena, still smiling, says something they don't understand, probably in Swedish.

'So these are our new little Baltic whores.'

She walks over to them, kisses Lydia on the cheek, kisses Alena on the cheek, smiles and they try to smile back.

They don't hear when Bengt Nordwall leans over to her, gently lifts the edge of her hood, whispers.

'I've missed you, Lena.'

Instead they hear *her* words. She's still smiling at them, speaking in Russian.

'Welcome to Sweden. I hope you like it here.'

from the authors

Box 21 describes a reality that exists around all of us, women as products, investments meant to generate returns – a reality that will continue to exist in the apartment next door for as long as there are men willing to pay.

It also describes shame, the driving force, the expressed and unexpressed urge, what so many fight against, try to escape, or at least to understand.

We do not like collective shame, and yet, for those who test-fuck girls, those who threaten, and those who get it up for a woman who was forced to undress, for them, as men, we feel ashamed.

Other things are not entirely true.

The morgue is in the wrong place, hospital floors have been rearranged, offices at the City Police station have been invented.

That happens in a novel, where a story is more important than a map.

We are grateful to

Damila and *Irena*, who shared their hellish days as prostitutes in Vilnius with us, we hope you are still alive; *Mia, Sally, Nilla* and *Viv*, working as prostitutes in ordinary flats in Swedish cities, who explained what it feels like to be purchased; *Lasse Lagergren* and *Håkan Sandler* for their knowledge of both living and dead bodies; detective *Jan Ståhamre* for details about police work; detectives on the national task force to stop human trafficking, *Kajsa Wahlberg* and *Karin Svedlund*, for their knowledge of the business of trading in people; *Anders Göransson* for speaking better Russian than us; *Rolle Eriksson* for his description of how a prison cell smells; *Fia Svensson*, our first reader, who continues to read and care; *Astrid Sivander* for always seeing what we don't see; and our agent *Niclas Salomonsson* for being one of the people who gives us strength.

And to

Mikael Nyman, Ewa Eiman, Vanja Svensson, Anna Nyman and *Jan Guillou* for your careful close readings.

Anders Roslund & Börge Hellström